Dean's Darlin'

Dean's Darlin'

An opposites attract, instalove, suspenseful, sports romance book.

Galactic Wrestling Association
Book 2

Leah Mae Wright

Copyright

Copyright © 2023 Leah Mae Wright
All Rights Reserved.
Updated June 2025.

No part of this book may be reproduced, scanned, or distributed in any printed or electronic format without the prior written consent of the author.

eBook ISBN: 978-1-968513-12-2
6x9 Paperback ISBN: 978-1-968513-13-9
Imprint: Leah Mae Wright

5x8 Paperback ISBN: 9798392230983
Imprint: Independently published.
Only on Amazon

This is a work of fiction. Names, places, characters, and incidents are the product of the author's imagination and are fictional. Any references to actual persons, living or deceased, events, organizations, or locations are used fictitiously.

Cover photo licensed through iStockPhoto.com.
Credit: Viktoriia Hnatiuk
Stock Photo ID: 1176237669

www.leahmaewright.com

Contents

Dedication

To those of us who didn't quite make it to living out our childhood dreams. Even if there are obstacles in your way to prevent you from physically achieving them, it's still not too late for you to live them out. You just might have to do like I did in this book and live them out by writing them as the backstory for a cameo character. Don't argue that you can't do that because you're not an author. If you don't feel comfortable writing yourself, send me an email (leah@leahmaewright.com) with a brief description and I'll gladly add you and your dream life to a future book.

Introduction

Dean Hunter enjoyed his life, living like a rock star while traveling the world, as one of the top stars of the Galactic Wrestling Association, after growing up with wealth and privilege in Heart's Destiny, Texas. He didn't have relationships with women because he was literally in a different city at least three-hundred days a year. But after his best friend lifted the ban on dating his sister, Dean was starting to wonder if he should act on the crush he'd had on her in high school.

He contemplated how to make a long-distance relationship with his best friend's sister work, until a week after the ban had been lifted. Then, when he saw the newest addition to the women's division of the GWA roster for the first time, Dean felt like he'd been struck by lightning. For the first time in his life, he understood what everyone in his hometown was talking about when they discussed instalove, and knew he didn't feel it for his high school crush because he fell instantly for the newest woman to join the GWA roster.

Allissa Walters grew up in a trailer park about an hour outside of Las Vegas. Raised by a single mom and surrounded by the other women who worked in the brothel across the road, she learned young not to trust men. With limited resources, she had to use her physical attributes to earn a living. But instead of stripping, or becoming a prostitute, like many of the women she knew growing up, Allissa took every modeling or acting gig she could find. She got lucky when one of her first gigs turned out to be as a ring girl for a mixed martial arts fight, and she caught the eye of a local fight promoter, who was looking for women to work in his independent wrestling promotion.

It took almost a year to save up the money from her modeling gigs to pay him to train her to become a professional wrestler. But from the first moment she stepped inside a squared circle, Allissa was hooked on the adrenaline of performing. She soaked up every lesson in the ring like a sponge, dreaming of the day she'd be good enough to work on bigger shows with a worldwide promotion.

She finally achieved her dream when she got a try-out match with the Galactic Wrestling Association. She signed a contract with them that night and took off traveling with the GWA the next day.

Unfortunately, dreams sometimes come true with a side dish of nightmares. She could handle the flirty, male wrestlers hitting on her. If she ignored them, they eventually backed off. She could even handle the booker who tried to get a little handsy. She was a trained fighter, after all, so spraining his wrist, as she got away from his hands, was simple. And more than enough to teach him to keep his hands to himself. But she wasn't sure what to do when she found herself the target of a stalker.

Dean was confused by what he'd done wrong to cause the woman of his dreams to hate him. But months after Allissa had come to work with the GWA, she was still doing everything she could to avoid him. None of his typical flirting techniques had worked. Neither had enlisting the help of the matchmaking women, who had recently paired off with his twin brother and best friend and now worked with Allissa closely enough to become her best friends. Even contriving situations to spend time with her had backfired.

But when Dean found out Allissa was in danger from a stalker, he was determined to protect her, whether she liked it or not. He just hoped there really was a fine line between love and hate, so maybe he could convince Allissa to cross it with him.

DISCLAIMER: This opposites attract, instalove, suspenseful, sports romance book contains threats from a stalker, gun violence during a kidnapping attempt, profanity, and graphic sex scenes. It is intended for adult readers (18+) who are not easily offended.

Glossary of Professional Wrestling Terms

Aerial Wrestler: A wrestler, usually of smaller stature, who uses the ring's posts and ropes to demonstrate their acrobatic abilities with flashy, high-flying moves.

Agent: The individuals employed by a wrestling promotion to assist the wrestlers in planning out their matches to fit the angles written by the bookers. Often former wrestlers who no longer perform due to injury or age.

Angle: Storyline or feud between wrestlers.

Armbar: When a wrestler grabs their opponent's arm at the wrist and twists. Multiple variations exist depending on the position of the two wrestlers' bodies.

Babyface (or Faces): Wrestlers in the good guy role.

Backflip Splash: When a wrestler climbs to the top turnbuckle, facing out at the crowd, and does a backflip before landing belly to belly in a perpendicular position to their supine opponent. Typically, the opponent is laying on the mat, but they can catch the wrestler performing the backflip splash while standing and fall to the mat.

Bear Hug: When a wrestler in a standing position wraps their arms around their opponent's chest, midsection, or thighs and locks their hands to hold their opponent tightly to their chest. Sometimes lifting their opponent completely off the ground. Their opponent's arms can be trapped in the bear hug, or they can be free to fight the tight grip around them.

Beatdown: When a wrestler or other performer is the recipient of a beating, usually by a group of wrestlers.

Body Slam: When a wrestler in a standing position lifts their opponent above their head with one hand on the shoulder and one hand on the crotch before throwing them to land on their back on the mat.

Booker: The individuals employed by a wrestling promotion to write the angles and plan the shows.

Botched Move (Botching a move): When a wrestler makes a mistake and the move they're attempting doesn't go as planned. Often leading to injuries to either themselves or their opponents.

Breather: When a wrestler takes a rest break, usually outside the ring, in the middle of a match. Can be due to needing to catch their breath after a cardiovascularly intense sequence of moves or having the breath knocked out of them by a hard impact. Can also be a work to sell the intensity of their opponent's attack.

Card: The order or series of matches on a given show.

Chop: A strike to the opponent's chest, shoulders, or neck with the edge of the hand.

Collar & Elbow Tie-Up (Lock-Up): When two wrestlers are standing facing one another and grab each other with their left hand at the collar, back of the neck, or on the trapezius muscle while gripping their opponent's left elbow with their right hand.

Dark Match: A match on the live card that's not televised when the rest of the show is broadcast. Often used as a tryout for local talent on TV days.

Dirty Finish: When a match ends because of cheating, outside interference, or disqualification.

Leah Mae Wright

Diving Stomp: When a wrestler jumps down from a raised position, usually one of the turnbuckles or ropes, to land on the feet with at least one foot making contact with their opponent.

Double Leg Takedown: When two wrestlers are standing facing one another and one of them ducks down and grabs both of their opponent's calves to pull their legs out from under them.

Double Turn: The rare occurrence when both the heel and face switch roles during an angle or match.

Faction (Stable): A group of wrestlers within a promotion who have a common element that puts them together as a unit of three or more.

Figure 4 Leglock: When the wrestler performing the move is standing over their opponent, who is laying on their back on the mat, grips both feet of their opponent, performs a spinning toe hold to bend their opponent's left leg at the knee, and drops down to sit on the mat with their legs straddling their opponents straight right leg and looped over their opponents bent left leg at the ankle and calf. Invented by Buddy Rogers and made famous by Ric Flair.

Finish: The planned end of a match or card.

Finisher: The primary wrestling move a wrestler uses to finish a match. Usually, their favorite or best move, thought to be most effective for incapacitating an opponent to win a match. Professional wrestlers often try to add drama to their matches by naming the move and over-exaggerating its usage.

Future Endeavoring: When a promotion fires someone, they often send a letter or issue a public statement wishing them well on their "future endeavors," thus leading to the term future endeavoring meaning firing.

Gimmick: Anything made up about a wrestler or the props used in a wrestler's performance, from their ring name to their costuming to the origin story of the character they portray. *Example: The Dangerous Twins have a biker gimmick.* Can also be used as a verb to describe a prop that has been prepared to be used in a match without causing actual harm to an opponent. *Example: The table was gimmicked before the Dangerous Twins slammed their opponents through it, so it would break where they wanted it to without splintering.*

Go-Home Show: The final televised show before a pay-per-view.

Go Over: To win a wrestling match.

Gorilla Position: The staging area just behind the curtain where wrestlers come out to the ring. Named after Gorilla Monsoon.

Ground and Pound: A wrestling style where a wrestler likes to get their opponent on the mat, so they have a dominant position over them, from which they deliver punches, elbows, and other strikes.

Headscissors: When a wrestler grips their opponent's head between their legs. Called a neckscissors when the grip is around the neck to perform a chokehold.

Heat: A loud negative reaction from the audience. Considered a good thing when the fans boo the heels. Can also mean friction between performers.

Heel (or Heels): Wrestlers in the bad guy role.

Hook (Left or Right): A boxing punch where the person throwing the punch bends their elbow at a 90-degree angle to strike their opponent in the side of their head or body with the punch arcing through the air from off to the side of the body toward the midline of the body. Punches of any kind are not legal moves in the sport of wrestling, but they are often used by heels in professional wrestling as a way to cheat when the referee isn't watching.

Hot Streak: A period of time when a wrestler wins so many matches they appear to be unable to lose.

House Shows: Shows performed live but not televised.

Jab (Left or Right): A boxing punch where the person throwing the punch extends their arm straight out in front of them to strike their opponent's head or body. Punches of any kind are not legal moves in the sport of wrestling, but they are often used by heels in professional wrestling as a way to cheat when the referee isn't watching.

Jerking the Curtain: Wrestling in the first match on the card.

Job (Jobbing): To lose a wrestling match.

Jobber: Wrestlers who primarily lose their matches.

Kayfabe: Presenting professional wrestling as being a legitimate sport, entirely real and unscripted. Breaking Kayfabe is when the wrestlers drop the act to let the fans know the scripted show isn't real.

Kip-Up (Kipped-up): When a wrestler laying in a supine position lifts both legs toward their chest, rolls up on their shoulders while placing their hands beside their ears to push off the surface they're lying on, then rapidly extends their legs while pushing off with their hands to flip up and land in a standing position.

Local Competitor (Local Talent): An unsigned wrestler who works a show either as a tryout or as a jobber to keep the main talent roster from having to job.

Main Eventer: A wrestler who is seen as the highest talent level in a promotion. Typically headlines shows. Usually, the current or former champion, or other performers who often wrestle for the title of a promotion.

Mid-Carder: Most of the wrestlers who work for a promotion are classified as mid-carders because they perform in the middle of the card, not the first match or the main event, a majority of the time.

Old-School Grappler: A wrestler who uses more joint locks and submission holds in their matches. This style of wrestling is reminiscent of the catch wrestling matches performed back when pro wrestlers traveled with carnies.

Pinfall: When a wrestler holds their opponent's shoulders to the mat for a three count to win a fall or match.

Plancha: An aerial wrestling maneuver where one wrestler flies out of the ring or off the top turnbuckle into an opponent on the floor outside the ring in which they land chest-to-chest in a crossbody position.

Pop: A loud, cheering reaction from the audience.

Put Over: When a wrestler boosts the credibility of another wrestler, usually by losing a match to them or selling their moves as painful.

Ring Name: The gimmick name used by a wrestler whenever they perform on a professional wrestling show. May or may not include part or all of the person's real name.

Ring Psychology: Using wrestling skill to draw an emotional reaction from the fans watching.

Ring Rats: Groupies. Fans who follow the wrestlers with the hope of having sex with them.

Ring Rust: When a wrestler's in-ring skill declines after not working in the ring for a while. Can be from just a few months off after an injury, or after several years off after retirement.

Roundhouse (Roundhouse Kick): When a wrestler who is standing with one foot in front of the other spins their body to strike their opponent with the shin or top of the foot on their back leg, not stopping the spin of their body until their leg has completely passed their opponent's body.

Run-in: When a wrestler (or wrestlers) not involved in a match in progress "runs in" to interfere with the performance. Usually, this is done by a heel to beatdown a face they are feuding with, but it can be done by a face to defend another face who is being excessively punished by the heel in the match.

Sell (Selling): Acting as if something is real when it is choreographed or faked for the show. Pretending a move or hold is more painful or effective than it really is. Overselling is when the wrestler has too much of a reaction to their opponent's moves and takes the pretense too far, usually trying to be funny or because of a botched move.

Showing Light: When a wrestler visually shows they aren't making contact with their opponent. Comes from being able to see the stage lights between the wrestler's hand or other body part supposedly making contact with their opponent and their opponent's body, where they were supposedly just hit, kicked, etc.

Side Headlock: When a wrestler wraps their arm around the head of their opponent, squeezing their opponent's face into the side of their chest.

Spinning Toe Hold: When the wrestler performing the move is standing over an opponent laying on their back on the mat with their legs in the air, the wrestler performing the move grasps their opponent's foot and spins around 360 degrees to make it look like they've twisted the toe, foot, leg, or ankle of their opponent.

Splash: When a wrestler jumps from a position raised above their opponent who is laying on the mat and lands stomach first perpendicularly across their opponent's body. Usually performed from the top turnbuckle, but can be launched from any of the ropes around the ring.

Suplex: When a wrestler in a standing position lifts their opponent off their feet and uses their own body weight to propel them both toward the mat with both wrestlers landing on their backs. There are different variations of the move depending on the body position of the wrestlers before the lift and how the offensive wrestler grabs their opponent for the lift portion of the move.

Swerve (Swerve the fans): Confusing the fans by doing the opposite of what they expect or doing something off the wall that nobody would ever expect.

Tapping (Tapping Out): When a wrestler slaps their hand on the mat, their opponent's body, or on anything they can reach to signal they are forfeiting the match or to get an opponent to release a hold. Usually three slaps of the hand, but can be more or less depending on the rules of the promotion.

Try-Out Match: A match performed between wrestlers already on the promotion's roster and local talent trying to earn a spot on the promotion's roster. The practical testing phase of an interview for a job with a wrestling promotion.

Turnbuckle: The metal component of the wrestling ring that connects the ropes to the corner posts. Usually covered with padding. One of the top turnbuckles is usually used as the platform wrestlers jump off of for aerial moves.

Tweener: A morally ambiguous wrestler, who is neither a face nor a heel.

Uppercut (Left or Right): A boxing punch where the person throwing the punch bends their elbow at a 90-degree angle to strike their opponent under the chin or in the torso with the punch coming from their waist upward. Punches of any kind are not legal moves in the sport of wrestling, but they are often used by heels in professional wrestling as a way to cheat when the referee isn't watching.

Work: Fake but presented as real to the audience. Can refer to a wrestler's overall performance, specifically appearing to target a body part to cause an injury, or an injury if it is scripted as part of the angle and the wrestler isn't really hurt. Can be used as a noun or a verb. *Examples: (Noun) His broken arm is a work. (Verb) They worked the crowd. James really worked Dion's left knee in their last match.*

Worker: Another term for a professional wrestler. Often used in the context of describing in-ring skill level.

Workrate: The in-ring performance level a wrestler puts into their matches. Judged by a combination of skill and effort. A wrestler considered talented in the ring has a high workrate.

Wrestling Clinic: When wrestlers perform so well in the ring that their match could be used to teach the other wrestlers how it should be done. Considered the epitome of performance standards, regardless of whether they are in the main event.

Prologue

Friday, October 5, 2018, Las Vegas, Nevada

With both his twin and their best friend meeting their soulmates the previous weekend, Dean Hunter spent the last few days examining his life and contemplating what he wanted for his own future. He wasn't sure he was truly ready for a relationship that could last forever the way James and Anthony obviously were after meeting Randi and Kay, but he was also getting tired of sharing hotel beds with random ring rats without any feelings coming into play.

In addition to feeling like his brother and best friend were both moving into the next stage of life without him by reaching that point where they wanted to settle down with *The One*, he was facing a future where Anthony's sister, Becky, was now a valid prospect for dating. Dean'd had a huge crush on Becky back when they were all in high school and would have jumped at the chance to date her back then. If only Anthony hadn't blatantly told all their friends that she was off-limits.

Since the girl he'd wanted was unattainable, Dean spent his high school years honing his sexual expertise with more than his fair share of the buckle bunnies, who came to town for the rodeo, and a few of the cheerleaders, who wanted to rebel against the old-fashioned values of their parents and the small Texas town where he grew up. Once he went to college in Austin, he expanded his repertoire with the more experienced sorority girls, who chased him for his status as an athlete.

When he and James graduated and started traveling with the GWA, they traded the mat rats of college life for the ring rats, who just wanted to say they'd fucked a professional wrestler. While that meant he had plenty of variety to be able to indulge his sexual appetite for women in all shapes, sizes, and ethnicities, none of those sexual experiences were as satisfying as the relationships he'd grown up seeing all around his hometown of Heart's Destiny.

While the Burlesons had the honor of saying it was their ancestor who named their town after moving there to be with the woman he fell in love with at first sight, they were not the only family in town with a family tree filled with similar stories of feeling like they'd been struck by lightning when they met *The One*. Dean's parents, grandparents, and great-grandparents, who all shared the Hunter last name, had all told him similar stories of meeting one another over the course of his life. So had his grandparents, aunts, and uncles on the Myers side of the family, as well as the Walkers, Martins, Whitmans, Deeres, Thompsons, Taylors, Reillys, Miltons, and Bensons from all around town.

Growing up hearing all those stories about falling in love at first sight really set the bar high for what a man expected to feel for the women he dated. And even as much as he'd crushed on Becky Burleson for a little over a decade, he couldn't say he'd ever had that love-at-first-sight feeling for her. That made it really hard for him to decide if he wanted to pursue a relationship with her, now that Anthony had lifted the ban on dating his sister. So, as he was getting changed into his workout clothes for sparring and in-ring rehearsal for the show that night in Las Vegas, Dean was still trying to decide what he felt for Becky almost a week after Anthony had given him the green light to ask her out.

Hell, since I was a newborn at the time, I can't even remember the first time I met her. So, there's no way I can say I fell in love with her the first time I saw her. But even if I wanted to say that about the first time I noticed she was a girl in eighth grade, I don't think it was love. More like puberty making my dick stand up and take notice whenever she was around.

*But fuck, at fourteen, the smell of a girl's perfume got my dick hard, and Becky wasn't the only girl he wanted to come out and meet. So that doesn't track with how everyone always says, "You won't want anyone else after you meet **The One**," and neither does the fact that I'm still attracted to other women and have no problems performing in the bedroom with anyone I choose for a night.*

*Fuck! That means Becky's not **The One** for me. And I can't even have the fun of one night with her because she'll want forever.*

It wouldn't be fair to either one of us to shackle us together when there's still a chance we'll each meet our soulmates. Maybe, if we're both still single at forty, I'll reconsider asking her out then.

And tonight, I'll go out and enjoy the ladies of Vegas. Who knows? My Ms. Right could be a showgirl.

While he tried not to dwell on the fact that he'd just ruled out dating the woman he'd had a crush on since he was a young teenager, Dean wasn't overly optimistic that he would meet the woman of his dreams at whatever seedy Vegas club the guys decided to party at after the wrestling event that night. But he plastered a smile on his face as he laced up his wrestling shoes to walk out to the ring with his brother.

Can't let James see how fucking jealous I am that he gets to talk to his girl every night, when I can't seem to meet a woman I want to have more with than a night of hot sex.

When he got to the ring, the owner and promoter of the GWA, Rick Robertson, was introducing the local talent there for try-out matches that night to the wrestlers on the roster that they would be working with for those early matches on the card. It wasn't uncommon for there to be several guys trying out for a spot on the roster whenever they were in a larger city with a fight school of some sort or a history of promoting fighting sports such as Vegas.

Dean and his brother, James, had actually earned their spot on the roster by going for a try-out match with the GWA when they were in Austin in the fall of 2015. They'd had to wait about six months, until after they finished the spring semester of college to graduate with their degrees, before accepting the traveling positions, but it was the try-out match they'd had that earned their jobs.

It wasn't the men there to try out that night that caught Dean's attention, though. It was the lone woman among the rookies that drew his focus. She was spectacular, even though she was dressed for the rehearsal in yoga pants and a tank top like the women already on the roster.

Fuck! As smokin' hot as she is in workout clothes, I bet she'll look even better in wrestling gear. Or, fuck, one of those business casual outfits we all have to wear to travel. I'm gonna have all kinds of sexy librarian fantasies about her after seeing her in a dress or one of those business suits some of the ladies wear. Or even better, her working as my sexy secretary when I start my investment firm after retiring from the ring.

Rick introduced her as Allissa Walters, who worked as a heel under the ring name of Victoria Vicious. Once Rick paired her with the women's division champion, Holly the Hottie, for her try-out match, Dean quit listening to what his boss was saying about the other people there to try out that night.

*Fuck! So this is what Dad and PopPop meant when they said it feels like being struck by lightning the first time you lay eyes on **The One**. And what James and Anthony both described when they first saw Randi and Kay.* Dean couldn't take his eyes off the petite beauty as everyone started separating off into small groups or pairs to choreograph their matches for the night. *Damn, I could spend hours just playing with her hair, running my hands through the long strands to see just how many blonde highlights she has in those soft, coppery-brown waves.*

While she was probably average height for a woman, somewhere around five-and-a-half feet tall, she was model thin, which had Dean worried about whether or not she was strong enough to lift her opponents for some of the maneuvers required to be a professional wrestler. He wasn't sure what was going on in his head, giving him unusual feelings about wanting to be the only person to work with her in the ring, as if that would protect her from possibly being injured while wrestling. So, he tried to shake it off as an anomaly, having never felt that protective of anyone before.

Fuck, she looks too dainty and delicate to work in the ring. But even if she needs time to bulk up to be able to handle wrestling, maybe I can convince Rick to hire her as a manager, so I can date her while on tour. Hell, maybe training her will be a good way for me to gain her interest.

"Dean, dude, are you even paying attention?" James punched Dean in the shoulder, drawing him into the conversation being held around him.

"Sorry, lost in space," Dean chuckled, trying to cover for his momentary lapse.

"More like lost in checking out the new girl," Brandon Braddock, the wrestler who used the ring name Blade, taunted Dean as he walked by with Surfer Josh Parker, whom he was wrestling that night.

"Good luck getting anywhere with Allissa," one of the two local workers standing by Dean and his brother chuckled. Dean assumed they were standing together because the Dangerous Twins would be working their try-out match that night. "She hasn't given any of us so much as the time of day for the entire time she's been with VPW. We'd originally thought it was just because she was in training that she blew us off. But even the last couple of years since she earned a spot on the roster, she won't even go out with us as a group after a show."

VPW was Vegas Pro Wrestling, the local independent promotion that trained talent for the local wrestling circuit in Nevada. The owner also ran Vegas Pro Boxing and Vegas Pro MMA to cover all the major fighting sports in the area. It was one of the many fight schools, promotions, and gyms that Rick worked with around the country, so the wrestlers on his roster could always find a place to train while traveling.

Damn. Maybe I should have checked out the VPW gym last time we were in Vegas, so I could have met Allissa before now.

Realizing he was being watched closely by the rookies, Dean straightened his features to cover his thoughts.

Fuck, I don't want to let any of these guys know I'm interested in her yet. Well, except maybe James, who'll probably figure it out through our weird twin thing. So I'd better think of something else to say to change the subject.

Dean decided to turn the focus of the conversation to the two newcomers to take the heat off his attraction to Allissa. "Sorry, I didn't catch ya'll's names or wrestling histories. How long have you been training with VPW?"

"I'm Cruz Bennington, and this is my younger brother, Dane." The one who'd commented about Allissa seemed to be the spokesperson for the Bennington brothers. He gave Dean a brief overview of their history of attempting MMA careers before switching to professional wrestling a few years ago. "We've just been wrestling singles matches using only our first names as ring names, so trying out as a tag team is gonna be a little outta the norm for us."

"Ah, it's not that much different." Dean shook his head and grinned, hoping to ease the rookie's nerves. "Just gives you a better chance of being signed because you get a couple of breaks in the middle of the match while your partner is in the ring, and you both get to work with more than one of us, so Rick can see how you work different styles."

"With you guys being twins, though, you probably wrestle with a similar style?" Dane gestured between James and Dean. "Where I'm more of an aerial wrestler while Cruz is more ground and pound."

"Yeah, I guess we are both more old-school grapplers," Dean agreed, nodding. "At least, when it comes to moves we'd pick for a real fight. But I'm more theatrical than James, so I'll sell your high flyer moves more than he will once the cameras are rolling."

"It's not that I won't sell them," James protested, shaking his head at Dean. "I just won't oversell them and put something over that I don't even feel."

When the Benningtons both gave James a nervous look, he clarified, "I want to make everything look more realistic. So, if you want me to sell a hit as painful, you have to make contact. It doesn't have to be hard contact, but I'm not going to sell something that's showing light. Whereas, Dean here, will act a fool and go down like it was a knockout because he thinks it's funny."

"Gotcha," the Benningtons nodded in unison, looking more like brothers than they had before.

Dean somehow managed to keep his focus on planning out their match for the night, only keeping Allissa in his peripheral vision the rest of the time they were rehearsing for the show. He tried to limit his longing looks in her direction as they all met up backstage for dinner in catering and while waiting for their turns in the ring during the show. But James obviously noticed, especially when he couldn't take his eyes off the monitor while she was wrestling her try-out match.

Damn, she's phenomenal in the ring. Way better than I expected, for as little as she is. She's out there showing Vegas just how true that old saying about dynamite coming in small packages really is.

"Guess you won't be asking Becky out, huh, Bro?" James nodded at the monitor, where Allissa and Holly were putting on a match that could easily be a main event sometime in the near future.

"Nope, definitely not asking Becky out," Dean agreed without taking his eyes off of the woman he intended to pursue as soon as she signed on with the GWA.

~~~

Allissa Walters couldn't believe how much bigger the crowd was for the GWA show than the shows she'd worked for VPW. The roar of such a large crowd as she worked her try-out match with Holly the Hottie truly fed her soul. She just thought she'd been exhilarated the first time she'd stepped into a ring to learn to wrestle four years earlier. Even the natural high she'd gotten from working the local independent shows for the last two years seemed mild compared to how she felt after performing in the ring in front of the massive GWA crowd. She felt like she was floating outside her body as she made her way backstage after the match.

I don't care what Mom and her friends say about orgasms. Their romance novel descriptions of them are just fiction. They can't feel as good as this.

Not that she would know. After being raised in a trailer park across the street from the brothel, where her mother worked, and being picked on in school for her mother's profession, Allissa didn't want to bother with finding out.

She'd always been embarrassed whenever anyone found out what her mother did for a living, even after she transitioned to managing the bar in the brothel when she aged out of the job she'd performed for most of Allissa's childhood. People always made assumptions about her based on her mother's chosen profession. Assumptions about her promiscuity that Allissa had spent her whole life trying to prove inaccurate.

She may have used her looks to earn a living as a model since she turned eighteen, and picked her wrestling attire to accentuate her body to keep the interest of the fans, but she'd avoided men as much as possible all her life. She didn't follow the typical stripper-to-prostitute career path as the other women in the trailer park where she grew up. She also refused any modeling jobs she was offered that required her to appear nude or show more skin than her bathing suit. Even lingerie
~~~

shoots were a no-go for her, since she couldn't be sure the material wouldn't be see-through.

On top of refusing to wear less than a bikini for her career, she refused to hang out with guys, even when the other wrestlers at VPW invited her to hang out with the entire group after a show. Since the other women who trained there were just as catty as the girls she'd known in high school, she never felt like she'd be safe going to a club with the group as a whole because she didn't have anyone there she trusted to watch her back.

She never had a boyfriend in school, never went on a date, or even attended a school dance. At almost twenty-three years old, she'd never even been kissed, much less had any experience with sex. Not that she'd ever even wanted to experiment with anything of a sexual nature, after the way her mom had told her how painful it was during *the talk* when she was a kid.

From the time she'd first started developing boobs, her mother, and the other women in the trailer park where she'd been raised, had all taught her that boys were only after one thing. And while they were all open to one day finding the men of their dreams, who would sweep them off their feet with all the romantic gestures they read about, Allissa believed what she saw in real life over the fairy tales.

None of the women she knew ever had a successful relationship, and some had actually had a few disastrous ones, so Allissa hadn't seen the point in even trying to date. And she certainly wasn't holding out any hope for one day finding her Prince Charming.

Once the early childhood fairy tales morphed into the horror stories of how painful sex could be during her teen years, she decided orgasms weren't worth the risk. And after a painful pelvic exam, when her mom insisted she went on the pill when she was sixteen, just in case she ever decided to have sex, she hadn't even wanted to try to orgasm on her own by using a toy.

Even after her mom completely changed her tune when Allissa made it to twenty-one without ever dating, Allissa still believed the first stories she'd heard about the pain, instead of the orgasmic bliss her mom tried to show her through sharing her romance novels. Between those stories and the bruises she'd seen on her mom and her mom's friends over the years when they'd been out with a guy, or dumb enough to live with one, Allissa learned to believe what she saw and not what she read.

The closest she'd ever even felt to attraction to a man was earlier in the day, when she'd watched the Dangerous Twins rehearsing with the Bennington brothers. After working with the Benningtons for years, she knew the flutters in her belly when the four men were in the ring weren't because of the two of them.

It was most definitely one of the Dangerous Twins who awakened a sexual side she didn't know she possessed. She felt an instant attraction to them when they walked down to the ring just before Rick introduced her and the Benningtons to the GWA wrestlers. It was like nothing she'd ever felt before.

Those flutters just got worse when they took their turn in the ring rehearsing with the other two wrestlers from VPW there with Allissa for a tryout with the GWA that night. When they took off their shirts, her whole body started fluttering internally, the way her mom and her mom's friends had mentioned over the years.

At that point in time, she didn't even know which of the twins was which, but the one with the fewest tattoos seemed to draw her eyes to him without even acknowledging her. With his long hair and beard, he reminded her of the actor who played the lead character in the *Aquaman* movie that every woman she knew was drooling over and anxiously waiting to see when the movie was due to come out in theaters in a couple of months.

Oh, gawd, that body, she'd thought as she watched the Dangerous Twin, who could have easily been Jason Momoa's stunt double in the film. *Why do I suddenly want to know what it would feel like to run my hands all over him? Why do I suddenly want to know what it would feel like to have him touch me all over?*

Mom taught me to stay away from guys like him, who would only hurt me with their perfect bodies and bad boy ways. She knows from first-hand experience how bad boys like that can hurt a woman both physically and emotionally. So, why do I want to take a chance with him to try to prove her wrong?

Seeing him and his brother standing in the gorilla position as she came back through the curtain brought her earlier thoughts back to the forefront of her mind. She quickly stepped around him without acknowledging his remarks about her match or the sexy smile he gave her.

Crap! Being attracted to one of the Dangerous Twins means I've inherited my mom's bad taste in men. Good thing I'm smart enough to learn from her mistakes and shut that shit down right now. Nothing good can come from being attracted to long-haired, tattooed, bad boys.

"Excellent job, ladies!" Rick Robertson, the owner of the GWA, applauded when Holly joined her in the backstage area and gave her a quick hug.

"Great job, Victoria," Holly whispered in her ear as Allissa briefly returned the hug. "I look forward to working with you often in the coming months."

"Thanks. I couldn't have asked for a better performer to work with tonight." Allissa stopped short of saying what she thought as she released the embrace — that she wouldn't have looked as good in the ring if it hadn't have been for working with the GWA women's division champion. She didn't want the owner of the company to realize she wasn't as confident in her ability in the ring as she'd stated in her earlier interview, so she didn't risk tanking her chance at signing a contract with the GWA to work in her dream job.

"Allissa, I'd like to talk to you in my office as soon as I'm finished watching the next try-out match," Rick informed her as Holly walked off toward the dressing room. "You've got about thirty minutes to grab a shower and think about when you'll be available to join our roster."

"I'm available now, sir," Allissa blurted, mentally squealing like a little girl, excited to hear she'd made the cut when she'd just doubted herself. "Before we were sent over here for the tryouts, we were all informed that we could be signed tonight and fly out with the GWA tomorrow morning. So I packed everything I might need before even coming to Vegas for the night."

The VPW trainer had given them all a rundown of how the GWA worked with regard to hiring new performers when he offered them the opportunities for the tryouts. He'd not only told them to expect to sign that night and fly out of Vegas the next morning, but he'd also run through the dress code and professionalism rules the GWA expected their performers to adhere to from day one, so none of them would embarrass him by showing up unprepared. Allissa had soaked up every word, and made a mental list of what clothing she needed and what she already had that would meet the requirements, planning to pack well in advance of the show she'd be trying out on that night.

Her mother might have told her she was being foolish for packing most of her belongings and getting a motel room for the night, but Allissa didn't want to have to rush home to the trailer an hour outside of Vegas to spend the night packing. It might have been overly optimistic of her, but she didn't want to take a chance on oversleeping and missing the flight out of town with the GWA, if she managed to earn her spot on the roster.

"Excellent. Then we'll go over your contract in about thirty minutes." Rick smiled before turning to focus on the monitor, where the Benningtons were making their ring entrance.

Allissa barely made it to the women's locker room, where she thought she was alone since she saw Holly leave as she entered, before letting out the squeal of delight that she'd been holding back in front of her new boss. "AAAAAWWWWW!"

"Holy shit!"

"What the fuck!"

Allissa wasn't sure who was hollering back from the bathroom stalls, but she instantly felt bad for startling them. "Sorry!" Allissa apologized as she made her way over to the locker she'd used earlier for her gear bag. "Didn't mean to scare anyone. Just couldn't contain my excitement about joining the GWA roster."

"No worries," one of the women laughed before flushing.

"Amethyst did the same thing when we were first signed," the other woman added, before also flushing.

As they stepped out of the stalls and over to the sinks to wash their hands, Allissa recognized them as Amethyst and Emerald Stone. At least, those were the ring names they used. Allissa hadn't been formally introduced to them to know their real names.

"You're Victoria, right?" Emerald tossed the paper towel she used to dry her hands as she turned to look at Allissa. "I'm Teagan, but everyone calls me by my ring name of Emerald."

"Nice to meet you, Teagan. I use the ring name of Victoria Vicious, but my real name is Allissa. You can call me either, and I'll answer." Allissa smiled at the strikingly beautiful African American woman as she finished putting in the combination on her lock and grabbed her bag to head for the shower.

"I'm Aiken," Amethyst introduced herself as she, too, finished washing her hands. "But like everyone else in the GWA, I tend to go by my ring name more often."

"Nice to meet you, Aiken." Allissa smiled at the gorgeous Asian American woman before holding up her bag and nodding her head in the direction of the showers. "I'd love to spend some time getting to know both of you, but I have to rush through a shower to be on time to meet with Rick to sign my contract."

"Oh, yeah, definitely don't let us hold you up." Aiken waved Allissa toward the showers.

"But you have to go out with us after the show, so we can all get to know one another," Teagan added with a grin.

Allissa wasn't sure where they were planning to go, or if it was someplace she'd feel comfortable, but she wanted to get to know her new coworkers and possibly make some new friends, especially since all the women she'd met in the GWA were much more welcoming than the women she'd worked with at VPW. So she smiled and agreed before heading to the showers.

It'll be nice to have some girlfriends who don't know about my life before now. And these girls seem a whole lot friendlier than the women I worked with in VPW, so maybe I can make some friends, instead of feeling like I have to keep my distance to avoid being stabbed in the back.

Several hours later, after signing a contract with the Galactic Wrestling Association to be the newest female performer on the roster, Allissa still felt like she needed to pinch herself to make sure it wasn't a dream. But since her new coworkers dragged her into one of the local clubs to celebrate and get to know one another, she refrained, assuming someone there would pinch her before the night was over based on the looks of the crowd.

She couldn't believe she was going to be flying out of Vegas the next morning to start working for the largest wrestling promotion in the world. She really couldn't believe how much money she would be making for wrestling while traveling around the world with all expenses paid. She knew the top stars in the sports entertainment business made millions of dollars each year, but she hadn't expected to earn a starting salary in the mid-six-figure range.

Mom's never going to believe how much I'm making on this job. But maybe, once I show her my bank statement on our first holiday break, she'll finally quit her job and let me take care of her for a change.

She loved her mom, even though she hated the things her mom had to do to provide for her over the years, and wanted nothing more than to get her mom out of that life. She wanted to give her mom the life they both deserved — a nice, safe house to live in, and no more worries about money, or men messing things up.

Though since she'd spent her most recent check from a modeling job on the motel and new ring attire she'd bought for tonight, she couldn't start saving for that new house or sending her mom enough to pay the bills, so she could quit her job, until she got her first direct deposit from the GWA in the middle of the month. So, the fact that she only ordered a bottle of water at the bar was more about the lack of discretionary funds in her wallet than her aversion to alcohol.

She didn't really have a true aversion to alcohol. She didn't drink often, and never more than a single glass of wine when she did. But her avoidance was all because of the excessive cost of cocktails and maintaining a training diet to stay in shape for her jobs. She wasn't the child of an alcoholic, or anything like that.

Well, that she knew of anyway. She had no idea who her father was, having never met him, so he could possibly have a problem with alcohol that she knew nothing about. But since he was a random client at the brothel where her mother worked, Allissa had no desire to look him up to find out.

As she sat down at a table with her new coworkers, Allissa put all of her family drama out of her mind. She focused instead on getting to know Emerald and Amethyst, while trying to avoid the advances of the men in the club, both the normal Vegas crowd of locals and out-of-towners looking to party, and her new male coworkers, who joined them by pulling a few tables together to make one big grouping for all of them.

Thankfully, the ring rats who kept coming up to hit on the guys made avoiding most of them fairly easy. But even seeing how much of a player the Dangerous Twin in attendance was with all the women he flirted with and posed for pictures with at the opposite end of the space the GWA crew had commandeered, Allissa couldn't stop herself from stealing glances at him all night.

I wonder how many of those women actually recognize him from the GWA? And how many just think he's hot because he looks like Aquaman?

When he caught her looking and smiled at her, she felt her nipples hardening from what she thought was arousal for the first time in her life. *Oh, this is bad. Very, very bad. And as hot as it is in here, I can't even blame it on being cold if anyone notices.*

Allissa crossed her arms over her chest, hoping to hide the evidence, so none of her new coworkers would notice. *Yeah, maybe I should invest in some padded bras with my first big paycheck from the GWA.*

"Oh, we need to go dance to this song," Emerald squealed, grabbing both Allissa's and Amethyst's hands to drag them out onto the dance floor.

"Oh, yeah, I love this song," Amethyst agreed, starting to dance before they made it a foot away from the table.

Since Allissa loved to dance, and thought it would be a good distraction from getting hot and bothered over the Dangerous Twin at her table, she gladly joined in on the dancing. "This is one of my favorites, too."

The three women all grinned at each other as they took over a section of the dance floor. After hearing the song a few times on the radio on her many drives back and forth between her hometown of Dead End, Nevada, and Las Vegas for work, she couldn't resist singing along with the chorus every time she heard it. And while dancing in the club, the urge to sing along was no different than when she was driving.

"I love it when you call me puppy!" Allissa sang along with her new friends.

"Did you just say *puppy*?" Amethyst laughed.

"Yeah, isn't that the line?" Allissa questioned, knowing it was very possible she'd inherited her mother's tendency to mishear lyrics and sing the wrong ones.

"No, it's not," Amethyst laughed, shaking her head. "It's *Papi*, not *puppy*."

"I think I like it better as *puppy*," Emerald giggled without stopping the gyrations of her body to the music. "'Cause I'm damn sure not gonna call a man Papi when we're hookin' up, but I might call him Puppy."

The ladies all laughed in agreement and continued to sing their own version of the song.

Yeah, I probably shouldn't tell them I wouldn't call a man either, because I have no intention of ever hooking up with one.

They danced to a few more songs, intentionally coming up with their own humorous lyrics to sing instead of the original words, before going back to their table to grab a drink and cool down some. Allissa ignored the ring rats, who had to be shooed out of their seats when the ladies got back to the table.

No point in being irritated by them trying to hook up with the guys, just because I have no desire to do the same, she lied to herself. *Being aroused tonight for the first time in my life doesn't mean a thing. I'll get over it by morning.*

"Why is it only the female ring rats are brave enough to approach our group?" Amethyst looked around the room, shaking her head. "What's a girl gotta do to get a little attention from the men in Vegas?"

"Sorry, I didn't realize we were looking to hook up tonight," Emerald shrugged, leaning her head toward the wrestler Allissa only knew as Red beside her. "If I had, I'd have gotten a table to ourselves instead of letting the guys join us. But I thought we'd all want to get to know the newbs at once, instead of making them repeat themselves a billion times over the next few days."

"You realize we're not really newbs, right?" Dane Bennington arched an eyebrow at Emerald as he waved a hand between himself, his brother, Cruz, and Allissa. "We've all been wrestling for years and wouldn't have gotten signed tonight if we were newbs."

"I just meant that you're new to the GWA," Emerald clarified, smiling flirtatiously at Dane. "And because you're new to our crew, we're all curious about you. But we don't want to make you feel like you're having to spout your résumé more than once or twice tonight."

Allissa was distracted from Dane and Emerald flirting with one another by a server walking up to deliver a drink. She was confused by the woman putting the cocktail in front of her. "Um, I didn't order this," Allissa pointed out.

"The gentleman at the end of the table ordered it for you," the server explained, motioning toward the only Dangerous Twin at the club. Allissa wasn't sure if it was James or Dean, but she wasn't about to embarrass herself by asking one of her new coworkers to find out.

"Oh, Dean's markin' his territory," Red snickered, answering her question without her even having to ask.

"Well, I don't want it, so since he ordered it, he can drink it." Allissa handed the drink back to the server, who did as she instructed and took the bright red, frozen, fruity, whipped cream-topped concoction down to the other end of the group and placed it on the table in front of Dean.

Allissa couldn't hear what Dean said to the server, but his smile from earlier disappeared as he pulled out his wallet and handed her a wad of cash that was obviously way more than the cost of the drink and a typical tip. *What's that all about?*

As the server walked away with a huge smile on her face, a few of the guys teased Dean about the exchange. With so much noise in the crowded club, Allissa couldn't make out what all was said, but she got the general gist that it had something to do with him getting lucky with the waitress since Allissa had turned him down.

Yeah, he's definitely not the type of guy I should be attracted to, so I'm gonna have to ignore the way he makes me tingle like no man ever has. Even if he's the world's greatest lover and could make sex enjoyable for me, he's too much of a player to make it worth the risk of messing up my new job by getting involved with him.

She tuned back into the conversation going on around her, fighting not to roll her eyes at how Amethyst and Emerald flirted with the Benningtons. After sitting there for the better part of an hour without really contributing much to the conversation, Allissa was trying to figure out how to politely excuse herself to head back to the motel without offending her new coworkers, when Dean appeared beside her.

"Hey, Darlin', come dance with me." Dean held out his hand as if reaching for hers to pull her up from the table.

"No, thanks." Allissa had more than enough of the party scene for the night, and Dean's derogatorily calling her *Darlin'* was the final straw that pushed her over the edge to fully irritated. "I'm ready to call it a night and head back to my hotel."

She said her "goodnights" to Amethyst and Emerald, along with a general "see ya in the morning" to the rest of the GWA crew before pushing back from the table and standing.

"Yeah, it's been a long night," Dean nodded and smiled. "Let me walk ya out, Darlin'."

"I don't need an escort to the door," Allissa objected, jumping away when she felt his hand moving toward the small of her back. "And don't call me *Darlin'*! I'm not one of your ring rats!"

Chapter One

Thank fuck, James is finally on board with helping me win over Allissa, Dean thought as he stood at the bar and watched the crowd arriving for James and Randi's joint bachelor and bachelorette party. *Surely, being paired together for all the wedding events this week will let her see that I'm not really the player she thinks I am, so she'll quit rebuffing me every time I flirt with her.*

Dean had been trying everything he could think of to get Allissa's attention, since the first night she worked a GWA show back in October. He'd given her his panty-melting smile at the club they all went to after that first show, but it hadn't had the same effect on her that it did on most women. He'd also tried sending her a drink, which she refused. After seeing how much she liked to dance, while he enjoyed the show of her dancing with the Precious Stones, he'd tried asking her to dance with him, which she'd also refused. He'd never had to work so hard for a woman's attention in all his twenty-six years. At least, not until he'd met Allissa.

When he overheard the Precious Stones talking about planning something for Allissa's birthday a couple of weeks after she joined the GWA roster, he'd tried to assist by planning a party at one of the local clubs after the show in Columbus, Ohio, on her birthday. But not only had Allissa vetoed his party plans, she'd also convinced Emerald and Amethyst to do a spa day for just the girls before the show, and wouldn't even let them give him any ideas for what to buy her as a birthday present.

Since that dreary October night, he'd tried everything else he could think of to get to know the little spitfire. From helping out with

Randi's wrestling training anytime Allissa was also in the ring, to orchestrating times when they had to spend time together outside of the arenas where they performed, he'd tried to stick close to her. He tried everything he could think of to let her get to know him as a fellow performer, with the hopes of them one day being more to one another.

He'd learned a lot about her over the last few months. Not just that she was born on October twenty-third and was two-and-a-half years younger than him. But also, that she listened to mostly the current popular dance music, shared his soon-to-be sister-in-law's taste in romance novels, even if she didn't want anyone to know she read them, and had a passion for performing in the ring that he'd never seen in a woman before. But almost eight months after they first met, she still considered him a player and not worthy of her time.

Damn, doesn't she realize that after almost eight months of celibacy, I've relinquished my former player status? Although, I suppose for her to realize that, I'll have to tell her I've only fucked my hand since the first time I laid eyes on her. And I'm not about to tell her that 'cause I know she won't believe me.

"Whatcha scowling at?" Anthony joined him at the bar and turned to follow Dean's line of sight to Allissa. "You're never gonna win her over if you keep glaring at her like that."

"Didn't realize I was scowling," Dean admitted, faking a smile at his friend. "Just lost in thought."

"Uh-huh, sure." Anthony shook his head, obviously skeptical of Dean's admission. "I'll let you get away with that avoidance for now, but only 'cause we have other things we need to do and can't talk about it right now."

"Thanks." Dean nodded at the man who'd been one of his best friends since before he could even remember, knowing Anthony would hold him to talking about his feelings for Allissa later.

"So, how 'bout we set up the tabs for everyone's drinks tonight and get this party started?" Anthony nodded toward the other end of the bar, where Leo Walker was starting to take orders from the partygoers. "Figured we'd split it like you and James did for my party, if that's okay with you."

"Sounds good," Dean agreed, raising a hand to flag down Leo. "Yo, Leo, don't charge them for their drinks. Put the guys' drinks on my tab and the girls' on Anthony's. And we're ready for the first few pitchers of beer for the guys."

"Everyone? Or just the people here for the party?" Leo arched an eyebrow at Dean as he started filling pitchers of beer.

"Dude, everybody here is here for the party," Dean laughed and shook his head at Leo. "And even if someone who didn't know about the party first shows up, ya know James'll just invite 'em to join us."

"You realize you just set us up to pay for every cowboy, buckle bunny, and barfly who stops by for a drink tonight, right?" Anthony gave Dean a bemused look.

"Naw," Dean disagreed with a grin. "There's not a rodeo in town this weekend, so the only people who might stop by are either friends with us or one of your siblings or cousins. Even the old timers who regularly hold down a barstool here on a Saturday night will vacate the premises as soon as the girls pull out the Pin-the-Dick-on-the-Dude game. And if Ol' Man Thompson stops in to see his daughter play that game, then I'll gladly buy him a drink."

"Good point," Anthony chuckled as they each grabbed a tray with the first round of beer for the guys before heading to the back room to leave the front half of the bar for the ladies and their bachelorette games.

Dean tried to put Allissa out of his mind while he enjoyed hanging out with his friends, both old and relatively new. But even with his hometown crowd blending with the GWA crew throughout the bar for the party, none of them could keep his focus off of the brunette beauty sitting next to his future sister-in-law in the next room.

She was dressed in a red blouse and black slacks, one of his favorites of the business casual outfits she wore while traveling with the GWA. The conservative outfit didn't show off her curves nearly as well as her ring attire, but it still led to lots of dirty office fantasies whenever Dean saw her on the plane or at one of their hotels. Tonight was no different. He still felt drawn to watching her, even in the crowd of people in his hometown's only bar.

Even through several rounds of pool and various toasts to his brother, Dean's gaze kept gravitating toward the doorway between the two rooms. When the girls got up from their tables to play the games they had for the night, Dean moved around the back room to keep Allissa in his line of sight.

"You should go ask her to dance as soon as the ladies finish this round of shots." James slapped a hand on Dean's shoulder and nodded toward the other room.

"She'll just turn me down," Dean sighed, shaking his head at his twin.

"Tell her ya'll need to practice before the wedding party dance at the reception next week," James suggested with a slight grin. "She can't really refuse to practice before having to dance with you in front of our families."

"Dude, there's no such thing as a wedding party dance," Dean objected, resisting the urge to roll his eyes at his brother. "There's the first dance of the bride and groom, the father-daughter dance, and the mother-son dance, but not one for the random people in the wedding party to hafta dance together. Hell, even if you spring that dancin' our way into the reception thing on us like at Anthony's wedding, we'll just wing it like I did with Deanna then."

"So?" James shrugged. "We'll be the first to make one up, then. Or tell her that ya'll have to choreograph your entrance dance."

"No way," Dean refused, shaking his head. "She's too smart to buy that."

"Oh, she might not want to believe it at first, but I'll back you up if she questions it," James reassured him. "Besides, we're gonna do the same thing for the entrance to the reception that we did at Anthony and Kay's wedding, so ya'll will have to dance together then. She won't be able to refuse to dance with you then, even if we don't make another special wedding party dance later. And since she's not a country girl, she won't know how to two-step her way into the reception, so ya gotta teach her this week."

Dean still looked at his brother skeptically.

"And if Randi and I can't convince her that she needs to spend some time practicing to dance with you, I'll cover your half of the tab for tonight," James smirked.

"Are you trying to place a bet on whether or not she'll go along with your made-up dance?" Dean couldn't believe his reserved brother was the one suggesting such a thing. Normally, it was the other GWA wrestlers that placed bets on random events and new couplings amongst their group of coworkers.

"No, no bets." James held his hands up as he shook his head. "I know better than to bet on anything a woman will do. I'm just trying to offer you a consolation prize if we can't get your dream girl to dance with you tonight."

"What aren't we betting on?" Liam Connery, the wrestler known by the ring name of Red, walked up from where he'd been playing a game of pool with one of Anthony's cousins.

James filled Liam in on his suggestion for Dean. "Oh, yeah, you should definitely go ask her to dance," Liam agreed with James, nodding his head. "We've all seen her starting to steal glances at you when she thinks nobody's watching, so I think you're starting to wear her down. Now you need to make the most of being paired with her in the wedding to make your move. And what better way than to start with a dance tonight?"

"Fine." Dean acquiesced, holding up his hands in surrender before Liam called over a few more of the guys to give their opinions. He didn't give either of them a chance to say anything else as he walked away from the guys to go into the other room.

He took a deep breath and smiled with his usual confident swagger as he made his way through the tables to stand directly behind Allissa. "Pardon me, girls," he started, but didn't get to finish his sentence.

"We're not girls," Randi corrected him. "We're women, and we find it very patronizing to be addressed as if we were still children."

"Sorry," Dean apologized, raising his hands in surrender once more, and hoping it would placate his future sister-in-law. "I didn't mean to sound disrespectful."

"Good." Randi nodded and grinned. "Now, what can we do for you?"

"I just found out that Allissa and I are going to have to dance together at your wedding reception," Dean explained, smiling at Randi before turning to look at Allissa. "So, I thought we might wanna get in a little practice while we have music and a dance floor, so we don't stomp on each other's feet next weekend in front of the whole town."

"Oh, yes, you should definitely do that," Randi agreed with a huge grin. "Like right now. James and I should probably practice, too."

Randi downed the shot in front of her and leaned over to whisper something to Allissa before she got up and headed into the back room to find James.

"Well, Darlin', whaddya say?" Dean held his hand out to Allissa, ready to pull her up into his arms if she agreed.

"I'm not giving you a blow job, Aquaman." Allissa shook her head before downing the whipped cream-covered shot in front of her.

Aquaman? Not my favorite superhero, but I guess I do look a little like him. Dean grinned at her until the rest of her sentence finally sunk into his brain.

"I wasn't askin' for a blow job, Darlin'," Dean sputtered, shocked at her reply.

"Damn, Vic, you're hilarious when you're drunk," Teagan Shields chuckled. "And I think that's the last blow job shot for you tonight. Can't have you too drunk to practice dancing for the wedding reception."

"Oh," Dean chuckled, realizing Allissa was talking about giving him the shot she had just drank. "No, I don't want a shot. I've already switched to water, so I'm sober enough to drive home tonight. I just want to practice dancing with you, so we don't look foolish at the wedding reception."

Dean wasn't about to mention that he wasn't really worried about looking foolish. Or that he loved to dance and didn't really need to practice. And he wasn't about to start feeling guilty for taking advantage of her not knowing how to do the country dances favored by his family and friends to get her in his arms for a few minutes on the dance floor.

"Oh, okay." Allissa nodded, pushing back her chair before wobbling as she stood up. "I do need to learn how to do that two-something before the wedding."

"Damn, we really shouldn't have forgotten what a lightweight you are before giving you so many rounds of shots." Teagan steadied Allissa from the other side as Dean took her hand closest to him to keep her from falling over as she stood. "She's talking about a two-step. Hopefully, she's not too drunk for you to teach her tonight."

"Yeah, hopefully," Dean agreed, holding Allissa up and worrying about the possibility of alcohol poisoning. "Maybe we should get you some coffee before we dance."

"There was coffee in the blow jobs," Allissa slurred, leaning on him as she wobbled.

"That was coffee-flavored liqueur, not actual coffee," Aiken Pearson giggled.

"Oh." Allissa's red lips formed a perfect O as she breathlessly mouthed the word.

Even in her obviously inebriated state, the sight of her red lips in the same position he'd imagined them in around his cock had him hard as a rock in less than a second. He absolutely loved it when she wore red and matched her lipstick to her outfit. And with James and Randi picking red as their primary wedding color, Dean imagined he'd be seeing Allissa in red a lot this week.

"Yeah, let's step over to the bar and get you some real coffee first," Dean insisted, resisting the urge to scoop her up into his arms to carry her across the room as she staggered along beside him.

He helped her onto a barstool and waved Leo over to order Allissa a cup of coffee, hoping his friend knew to make it strong. He had to help her doctor it up, so it was sweet enough she could drink it without wanting to spit it back out at him. But she eventually started sipping the dark brew.

As they sat there making small talk about the wedding while she tried to sober up, Dean couldn't stop himself from trying to imagine what she would look like in the red bridesmaid's dress she'd be wearing at the wedding. But without having seen which of the dresses Randi had finally picked, he was having a hard time picturing her in anything but his favorite of her red wrestling outfits that he'd seen her in since she started work with the GWA.

It was a red velvet bra top, short skirt, and hooded cape that were all trimmed in white faux fur. Unlike the one-piece leotard style tops she usually wore with skirt-short combos to wrestle, it actually revealed her flat stomach and a generous amount of her cleavage, which was probably why it was Dean's favorite.

She'd paired the outfit with a black belt and boots at the **Christmas Chaos** pay-per-view for a naughty Mrs. Claus look that had him stretching the limits of his wrestling tights' ability to conceal his erection. He'd teased her then about how she should have worn it at the company Halloween party and gone as Little Red Riding Hood with him dressed up as the Big Bad Wolf.

She'd worn the outfit again, only with a white belt and boots, at their house show in Kansas City, Missouri, on Valentine's Day. He'd loved it just as much the second time he saw her wearing the hot outfit. Unfortunately, he'd pissed her off that night by commenting that he liked it better than the pink number she'd worn for the **Saint Valentine's Day Massacre** pay-per-view.

Fuck! That wasn't the only way I pissed her off on Valentine's Day.

Dean had helped orchestrate a room swap between the single performers and the couples with kids for the night, so the couples could have a romantic night alone while the rest of the crew watched their kids. He'd hoped to spend the whole night with Allissa helping to take care of a couple of kids, thinking he'd maybe get to make his move on her once the kiddos went to bed.

He'd gotten his wish to spend the night in the same suite as Allissa, but only because Tank and Tina's twins were more than one person could handle alone. He and Allissa hadn't gotten any time alone that night, though. Or any sleep. Just as soon as they thought they had both of the twins down for the night, one of them would wake back up and wouldn't stop crying until they were being held, even when they had full bellies and clean diapers.

I seriously thought babies slept through the night by the time they were a year old. But Travis and Trent sure proved me wrong that night.

Dean shook off the memory as Allissa asked him about the dance she needed to learn before the wedding. With the way her words still slurred, he knew they wouldn't be trying it that night.

"I'll have to try to teach ya to two-step later this week, Darlin'," Dean drawled with a shake of his head. "I don't think you'll remember it tomorrow if we started tryin' to practice now."

"Ohb-dee, kay-dee," Allissa slurred, bobbing her head for a second before laying it on the bar.

He couldn't understand what else she said, but he thought he heard something about a nap. "Yeah, you take a nap, Darlin'. I'll make sure you get safely back to your room tonight."

And hopefully, you won't be creeped out by me watching over you while you sleep it off.

"Damn, Dean, maybe you should say no next time someone asks you to be a groomsman," Leo chuckled from behind the bar. "Seems like every time you're in a wedding, you're cursed to be stuck helping a drunk bridesmaid home for the night without even gettin' a kiss outta the deal beforehand."

Dean just shrugged, not wanting to tell one of his childhood friends that he didn't really mind so much this time. "Yeah, well, hopefully, when it's my turn to get hitched, I can leave the drunk bridesmaids with my groomsmen."

Though if I can one day get Allissa to walk down the aisle with me for real, I won't mind helping my drunk bride-to-be home from our bachelor and bachelorette party.

~~~

Sunday, May 26, 2019, Heart's Destiny, Texas

Allissa wasn't sure how she got roped into being a bridesmaid in Randi's wedding, or how she was supposed to get through the wedding shower with a hangover from hell. But she was pretty sure every wedding event this week was just one small piece in a much larger ploy to set her up with Dean. It was bad enough that she had to fight his constant flirting and her newly awakened libido to continue resisting him. But having her friends teaming up with the group they called the Matchmaking Mommas in his hometown of Heart's Destiny, Texas, to keep forcing them together all week was obviously going to make her battle to keep from falling for one of his lines even harder.

She blamed her heavy drinking the night before on her friends, thinking the rounds of shots they kept ordering were their misguided attempt at getting her to let down her guard and give him a chance the next time he hit on her. Though she was pretty sure their plan backfired because she got too drunk to even let him teach her the dance she needed to learn before the wedding. Not that she could remember for sure, since she didn't even remember how she got back to the bed and breakfast the night before.

And I'm sure him carrying me to bed was just a dream, she decided. *Since he wasn't still there when I woke up this morning, there's no way him watching over me while I slept to make sure I didn't have a bad reaction to the alcohol was anything more than a dream.*
~~~

Although, his family does own the hotel, so he would have the easiest access to the room keys to be able to take me to my room without asking me for my key. But why would someone raised in the lap of luxury like Dean waste his time taking care of someone like me? We can't have anything in common, since I was living paycheck to paycheck until I got this job with the GWA, and he's obviously from a wealthy family.

No, it was probably Emerald or Amethyst, who helped me to bed and left a bottle of water and over-the-counter painkillers on my bedside table. I just don't remember giving them my room key, much like I don't remember them helping me to my room. If it had been Dean, he'd have taken me up on the offer when I asked him to kiss me goodnight.

She did remember really wanting to kiss him the night before. She'd only resisted leaning over to find out what his lips would feel like on hers while they sat at the bar because the alcohol she'd consumed with the ladies made her more belligerent than normal. And in her belligerent state, she was more determined than ever to push away anyone who resembled the rich pricks who frequented the brothel where her mother worked.

She'd had no idea how her body would respond to more than one alcoholic drink before starting her job with the GWA. But it was only because her fellow female performers had gotten her sloshed once before in one of their hotel rooms while on tour that she'd trusted herself not to give in and kiss him after several rounds of shots. She knew the alcohol would only exacerbate her distrust of men, especially wealthy men who thought they were entitled to whatever and whoever they wanted for a night.

Adding in the coffee starting to sober her up also helped her maintain some self-control as she sat at the bar talking to him about their fittings at the bridal shop on Tuesday and the other events going on that week. Granted, she still didn't get sober enough to learn how to two-step, which she apparently needed to learn before Saturday night, but she decided that was a good thing.

Probably not a good idea to let him wrap his arms around me to dance in the middle of a dimly lit bar. Even with the alcohol helping to make me distrust him, it didn't do a damn thing to stop my body from responding to him. I'll be better off learning in broad daylight with some of the older people in town watching us to keep our physical contact to a minimum, so I can keep those reactions hidden.

Not that he actually had to touch her to get her body to take notice of his presence, or that she could do more than conceal the reactions, since she couldn't stop them. Even after knowing him for seven-and-a-half months, she couldn't prevent her nipples from getting hard every time he smiled at her.

To make matters worse, she'd noticed her panties getting damp whenever he called her *Darlin'* in that sexy drawl of his, and her whole body seemed to tingle whenever he walked into a room. She didn't even have to see him to get the tingles and know he was there. It was like her internal receptors recognized his essence and turned on whenever their energy fields were in the same space.

She didn't understand why those things only happened in response to Dean Hunter. It never happened with anyone else she knew. Not with her mom, any of her acquaintances from back home, any of the other wrestlers in the GWA, or any of the people she met the night before, when she felt like she met half the town of Heart's Destiny, Texas.

If it was some kind of biochemical reaction, she would have thought his twin would elicit the same response in her. But, nope, James didn't give her tingles of any kind. Not that she wanted to feel tingles for James, especially since he was marrying one of her best friends. But she'd like to be able to fool herself into believing the tingles didn't mean anything by feeling them for someone other than Dean.

Unfortunately, if all the stories she kept hearing at the wedding shower were to be believed, those tingles meant more than she wanted to feel for any man, especially a player like Dean Hunter.

It's crazy how everyone in this town seems to believe in love at first sight, to the exclusion of finding a life partner in any other way.

She'd already heard about how Randi and James fell for one another the night they met from hanging out with them while traveling with the GWA. Allissa had also witnessed part of Kay and Anthony's whirlwind romance, with Kay joining the flight crew less than a week after she'd started working with the company. But while seated at the table with the rest of the bridal party for the wedding shower, she got a recap of Amy and Justin's love-at-first-sight story, along with a few generations of the Burleson and Hunter families' love stories.

"So, what's ya'll's story?" Justin waved a finger between Dean and Allissa.

"We don't have a story." Allissa mimicked Justin's finger wag between her and Dean. "I'm just here as Randi's friend to stand up with her and got paired with Dean because he doesn't have a partner."

"Don't let her fool you," Dean disagreed, wrapping an arm around her shoulders that she surprisingly didn't want to push away. "I knew Allissa was *The One* the first time I saw her standing at ringside on the day she tried out to join the GWA roster. She's just making me work for it."

"Whatever," Allissa rolled her eyes and pushed his arm off of her, no matter how much her body protested the act. "I didn't even notice you then. And I think I made it very clear that I wasn't interested that night, when you kept trying to hit on me at the club."

"Don't lie, Darlin'," Dean drawled. "You couldn't keep your eyes off me any more than I could keep my eyes off you that night."

"Oh, please. I didn't even know who you were until Red called you by name. I might have looked before then, but only because of hearing from Emerald and Amethyst what a nice guy James is earlier in the evening. And I was hoping you were him," Allissa blatantly lied. "Then when I found out he was already taken, I quickly lost interest."

Shit! I hope my acting skills are good enough to keep everyone from reading the truth all over my face. I don't need anyone to realize I'm attracted to Dean and not James. They'll just keep pushing us together, and eventually, he'll wear down all my defenses. And I definitely can't let that happen!

"Keep it up, Darlin'," Dean smirked as the guys at the table teased him for being shot down again. "I'm keepin' a count of all these lies and I'm gonna enjoy punishing you for each and every one of 'em once you finally admit how much you want me."

Holy shit! Punishment? Like in those BDSM romance novels Kay recommended we all read a few months ago? Allissa sat there speechless, unable to even imagine the dirty things Dean might do to punish her. *Yeah, I'm gonna keep that in mind whenever I feel like I might waver in my resolve to resist him. Even if I'm ready to try kissing, there's no way I'm ready for the advanced course in sex education he seems like he's able to give me.*

Luckily, she didn't have to say anything in response, since one of the women announced it was time to set up for the Newlywed Game. As everyone stood from their tables to rearrange the room to set up for the game, Allissa's phone rang in her purse. Recognizing her mother's ringtone, she excused herself to take the call out in the main entryway of the church, instead of staying in the room where they'd all met for the party and lunch.

"Hi, Mom," she greeted her mother in a cheerful tone, surprised to hear from her, since she'd told her on Friday night where she was for her week off.

"Please tell me you're surrounded by security and safe while you're at your friend's wedding this week!" Windy Walters demanded of her daughter through the phone.

"We only have a security team at the shows, Mom," Allissa sighed, confused by her mother's sudden outburst. "But I'm sure being in a church for a wedding shower is the safest place I've ever been in my life."

"Oh, thank God! Say an extra prayer for my safety while you're there."

"Mom, what's going on? Why are you suddenly so worried about our safety?" Since Windy Walters never seemed to be afraid of anything, her mother's worried tone of voice was starting to frighten Allissa.

"Oh, Lissie, I don't know how to tell you this," Windy wailed. "But I think you have a crazy stalker, and he knows where we live."

"What? Why would you think something like that?" Since she started this job back in October, Allissa had started getting some fan mail through the GWA office, and the occasional fan would drop off a gift at one of their shows or the front desk at the hotel, but she never thought any of them were from a stalker. They were usually sweet things, like flowers or teddy bears, and never anything she thought was truly bad. She even laughed off the lingerie she'd started getting the last couple of months, thinking they were just from someone with a crush on her.

"Well, I didn't open the first two packages you got since your break started on Friday, but today you got flowers, so I didn't have to open them to know the meaning."

"Okay…" Allissa trailed off, trying to think of any flowers she wouldn't appreciate receiving, and not coming up with any negative meanings for any of the flowers she knew about. "So, do like I do with the flowers I get on the road and go donate them to a hospital or nursing home."

"Lissie, they're black roses," her mother screeched, causing another new tingle in Allissa's spine. But unlike the tingle of excitement she got whenever Dean was near her, this was a tingle of fear.

Black roses? Like people might use to decorate at Halloween because they're a symbol of death?

"I almost threw them away, but Kandi told me to keep them long enough to call the police first, so they can document them as a death threat. But you know the cops here. They wouldn't even come out to take a statement about you possibly having a stalker who wants to kill you."

Kandi King was her mom's best friend, who had an obsession with shows like *CSI* and *Criminal Minds*. Allissa didn't usually trust Kandi's hunches when she thought she spotted nefarious behavior, but she had to wonder if she might be right about the black roses.

"So, I figured I'd better tell you about them, so you can talk to your boss about what we should do with them. Maybe his security company can refer us to the right people to call with, like, the FBI or whatever."

"I doubt we need to call in the FBI," Allissa groaned, rolling her eyes at how overdramatic her mother could be, as she felt Dean's presence behind her, replacing the momentary tingle of fear she'd just experienced. His presence almost gave her a sense of peace, like he'd be there to protect her if these flowers really were a death threat. *Yeah, I don't even want to think about what that means right now.* "But I'll talk to Rick about getting some extra security, and what we can do to keep you safe at home, since whoever sent them knows where we live."

"Okay, call me back as soon as you talk to him. I'm gonna go stay at Kandi's until we figure out what we need to do about your crazy stalker."

Leah Mae Wright

"I will," Allissa sighed, thinking being next door at Kandi's trailer wouldn't be any safer for her mother than staying at home. *But if I try to tell her to go out of town for a little bit without it coming from someone with security experience, she won't listen.* "And I'll go talk to him right now. I love you, Mom."

"Love you, too, Lissie."

Before she could even swipe the end call button on her phone, Dean's deep baritone rang out behind her. "Why does your mom think you need to call the FBI?"

"It's nothing." Allissa waved off his concern as she turned to face him. "She's just freaked out about some gifts from a fan arriving at the house this weekend."

"How the fuck did a fan get your home address?" Dean's expression mirrored the anger she heard in his voice.

"I have no idea." She shook her head. *It's not like I want anyone to know where I grew up.* "The only time I've semi-recently given out my home address was when I filled out my human resources forms for Rick back in October. And since that's all computerized, I don't think he even saw it then."

"He wouldn't give it out, even if he had." Dean shook his head before turning and ushering her back into the party. "But I'm sure he can hook you up with a security company to put in an alarm system at your mom's house to keep her safe, just in case it's not one of our normal fans sending gifts."

Yeah, I doubt an alarm is going to do much with the paper-thin windows and doors on the trailer. Even beefing up the locks won't do much to stop someone from breaking down one of the doors, when they're so weak that we can't even lean on them without risking falling through.

She wasn't about to mention any of that to Dean, however, so she just nodded and followed his lead to go find Rick. They found him sitting off to the side of the room with his fiancée and future in-laws.

Yet another love-at-first-sight story from someone in this weird little town. Allissa pushed the thought out of her head, needing to focus on the potential stalker situation, and not her fear of being bitten by the Heart's Destiny Love Bug while she was in town for James and Randi's wedding.

"Hey, Rick, can we pull you away for a minute?" Dean got Rick's attention while Allissa was momentarily distracted by her thoughts. "Allissa's got a potential stalker fan we need to figure out how to deal with."

"You don't need to be here for this." Allissa glared at Dean momentarily before turning to direct her next comment to Rick and Fiona. "Sorry for interrupting your conversation, but I promised my mom I'd ask your opinion about what to do with the gift she feels threatened by that arrived at her house today."

"Don't apologize for interrupting for something like this." Rick shook his head as he stood. "I always want to know immediately anytime there's a security issue with any of our GWA family. But maybe we should take this conversation somewhere private, so we don't disturb the party."

"You can use my office." The preacher, who would soon be Rick's father-in-law, gave them directions to his office in the back of the church.

"Thanks," Rick nodded to his future father-in-law before turning to kiss the top of Fiona's head. "Fifi, will you get Bobby Burleson to join us? With Cage not being here this week, he'll be the best person here to help me assess the risk and take the appropriate precautions."

"Of course," Fiona agreed, nodding as she turned to survey the room.

Allissa followed Rick to the pastor's office, not all that surprised that Dean followed them, even though she'd already told him he didn't need to be involved. "You really don't need to be here, ya know. You should go back to the party and be supportive of your brother while he's playing the Newlywed Game."

When they entered the room, Rick took the seat behind the desk while Allissa took one of the seats in front of it.

"Sorry, Darlin'," Dean disagreed, shaking his head as he took the seat beside her. "Considering our mother runs the bed and breakfast where you're currently staying, and she's also playing the game, I figured I was the only one in my family available to make sure we know what precautions we need to take at the B and B, if one of these deliveries shows up this week."

Crap! That actually seems like a plausible reason for him to be involved in this talk.

"It's up to you if he stays or not." Rick dipped his chin at Allissa, his lips turning up slightly at the corners. "But it can't hurt to have an extra set of eyes watching out for you, if you've picked up a stalker."

"Fine," Allissa capitulated with a huff.

"So, tell me about this delivery that frightened your mother," Rick directed her, just as Bobby Burleson stepped into the room.

Allissa waited for Bobby to take a seat off to the side of the desk before she started explaining. "Apparently, I've gotten gifts delivered to my mom's place for the last three days. Mom said she didn't open the first two, but the one today was flowers, so she didn't have to open it to know it was a threat."

"Why would she think flowers are a threat?" Rick arched an eyebrow, obviously as skeptical as she'd been before her mother mentioned the color of the flowers.

"Because they're black roses."

"The kiss of death," Bobby mumbled, shaking his head. When everyone turned to look at him, he shrugged and explained, "I did some research on the meanings of different flowers and different colors of flowers when Brie and I first got together, so I could show her my feelings since I'm not all that great with words. Anyway, I learned there are actually roses you don't send to your sweetheart. Specifically, black roses, because they symbolize the kiss of death. Your mom's right in thinking they're a threat."

"Really? I just thought she was letting her best friend influence her to be overly paranoid." Allissa shuddered at realizing there really was a threat implied with the roses.

"I mean, if you got 'em around Halloween, you could possibly say it was someone celebrating the holiday, but not in May," Bobby disagreed. "And with ya'll being in the public eye, I'd definitely classify this as a threat from a celebrity stalker."

"Well, it's too bad you aren't the police chief in Dead End, Nevada," Allissa huffed, feeling way more nervous about the meaning behind the gifts she received after hearing Bobby's opinion than she had before. "They apparently didn't agree that the roses are a threat, which is why Mom wanted me to get Rick's opinion on whether or not we need to get the FBI to investigate who they're from, and what she needs to do if the guy shows up instead of just sending stuff."

"Yeah, I don't think the FBI would get involved with something like this." Rick shook his head.

"No, stalking falls under the local police jurisdiction," Bobby clarified. "And if the local LEOs aren't taking it seriously, then I'd suggest getting a security company involved. They can protect both you and your mom while investigating to find the stalker."

"Anthony said ya'll's cousins have a security company," Dean addressed Bobby with his comment. "Do you think they'd take the case?"

"Yeah, I'm sure they would," Bobby assured them, taking his phone out of his pocket, and dialing a number. He placed his phone on speaker mode before setting it on the desk in the middle of everyone in the room.

"Hey, Bobby, what's up?" The voice on the phone sounded jovial, which helped Allissa relax a little.

"Hey, Byron," Bobby greeted the man she assumed was his cousin. "I have you on speaker with some friends who are in need of some security services."

"Oh?"

"Yeah, you know Anthony works with the Galactic Wrestling Association, along with a couple of our friends from here in town, right?"

"Yeah, but we don't really handle security for the venues where they have their shows." Byron sounded skeptical of being the right fit for what they needed. "Unless a performer hires a bodyguard for whatever reason, the venues provide security."

"Yeah, well, one of the female wrestlers has picked up a stalker, and needs protection for both her and her mom, along with a team to investigate. So, I figured while I have her and the company owner here this week, you might be able to help them out."

"Oh, well, yeah, we can definitely do that." Byron's jovial tone returned. "Fill me in on the details of the case so far, so I can plan for how many of the boys to send out there."

"Since she's sitting right here, I'll let Allissa do that." Bobby smiled as he turned to look at Allissa. "Sorry, I'd introduce you to my cousin, Byron Avington, but I didn't catch your last name last night when we met."

"Walters," Allissa blurted, feeling too flustered to think before she spoke. She shook off the uncomfortable feeling before properly introducing herself. "Sorry, I'm Allissa Walters. It's nice to meet you, Mr. Avington. I really hope you can help me keep my mom safe."

"Nice to meet you, too, Allissa," Byron Avington replied. "Though I'm sorry it's under such stressful circumstances. Now, tell me what's going on."

"Well, I'm not really sure what's going on, since I wasn't at home when it started happening. My mom called me this afternoon, hysterical because I've started getting packages from a fan at her house in Dead End, Nevada. She didn't think anything of it at first, because like me, she just assumed it was more of the fan mail I get through the GWA office, or like the gifts some of the fans bring to the arena, or drop off at the front desk of our hotels. But today it was a delivery of black roses, which apparently are a coded death threat."

"You get packages at our hotels?" Rick looked concerned. "Before or after our shows?"

"Yeah, all the time," Allissa shrugged, not sure why he looked so worried. "Sometimes it's when we first check-in, and sometimes it's when we get back from the arena. It's mostly just teddy bears and trinkets of appreciation from fans. Nothing creepy like today's roses. Well, except maybe the lingerie."

"You shouldn't be getting anything from fans at the hotels." Rick shook his head before directing his next comment to the phone on the desk. "Byron, I'm Rick Robertson, owner of the GWA. When I took ownership of the company, I put precautions in place to protect the families that travel with us. With those precautions, the fans shouldn't be able to track us down at the hotel, unless they follow one of us from the arena."

"And you really shouldn't be getting lingerie from fans." Dean fumed beside her as Byron and Rick discussed the various precautions that needed to be taken at the hotels.

"Shouldn't you be paying attention to the hotel precautions they're discussing?" Allissa rolled her eyes at Dean's unnecessary jealous act.

"Don't worry, Darlin'," Dean drawled, dipping his chin toward the phone. "I heard all that and know we're already following all those precautions at the B and B."

"How are the packages addressed? And do you still have any of them that my team can examine?" Byron's questions cut off her ability to think about how to reply to Dean. "Also, has there been any electronic communication? Email? Texts?"

"No, no unusual emails or texts. You'd have to ask the team Rick has running my social media if there are messages there, but I haven't gotten anything on my private accounts. I'd have to ask my mom about the packages she's gotten the last few days," Allissa admitted, wishing she'd thought to ask some of these questions while she was on the phone with her mother earlier.

"But I don't have any of the ones I've gotten at the arenas or hotels the past couple of months. I can't carry around all that extra stuff while traveling so much, so I usually try to find a place to donate it, if I can, before we leave to go to the next city. And I'd say most of the fan mail and stuff is addressed to Victoria Vicious, in care of the GWA offices. When fans give me stuff at the arenas, it's not really addressed."

"What about when it's dropped off for you at the hotels? Are they using your stage name or your real name?"

Byron's questions triggered her to think back to the things that had started showing up at the hotels before the GWA arrived in town in the last couple of months. That tingle of fear creeping down her spine was back as realization dawned. "They have my real name on them. But the fans shouldn't know my real name."

"It sounds to me like this might be someone who knows you," Byron confirmed her worst fear. "And with them knowing what hotels the company uses, I have to wonder if it's a fellow employee, or possibly a former employee of the GWA. With no electronic communication, I'd suspect the perp is older or technologically challenged for some reason. Do you have any ideas for who might want to do you harm? Someone you don't get along with at work? Or maybe someone who might come on too strong with their romantic advances?"

"I'm the only one who comes on too strong with my romantic advances," Dean quipped. "And I'm not the one sending her creepy death roses."

Dean's words, along with the introduction he made to Byron and the responses of the security expert to Dean's joking statements, went in one ear and out the other as Allissa flashed back to the issues she'd had with the former booker that Rick had to fire back in February. Ron Langston had taken a special interest in her not long after she signed on with the GWA.

She hadn't thought anything of the extra interest he'd shown in wanting to help choreograph her matches when she first started with the company. She was happy to take the direction of one of the bookers to make sure her in-ring performance meshed well with the style the GWA wanted for the shows overall.

But over time, he became more and more hands-on with his choreography assistance. It got to the point where she felt uncomfortable with the way he would touch her in the ring, culminating with her having to physically remove his hand from her breast in January. She momentarily flashed back to how she'd escaped his hold and feigned botching a move to twist his wrist to the point that she knew she'd injured him to get him to stop touching her inappropriately.

Unfortunately, when he backed off from working with her in the ring while his sprained wrist healed, he retaliated by booking her to job a majority of her matches over the next few weeks. Thankfully, Rick had finally seen the sexist behavior Ron had been hiding from their boss and fired him the weekend of the *Saint Valentine's Day Massacre* pay-per-view.

"Ron," Allissa barely breathed out the word to answer Byron's question, interrupting the discussion Dean and Rick were having with Byron, which Allissa had missed while lost in thought about Ron Langston. When all the eyes in the room turned to her, she dipped her chin to Rick to let him take over explaining the situation with his former employee to the security expert on the phone.

"Ron Langston was a booker my father hired a few years back. I had to fire him back in February after we found out he was sexually harassing some of our female performers."

"Motherfucker," Dean cursed, drawing her attention away from Rick and Byron's discussion about Ron.

Allissa wasn't sure if she should be afraid of the murderous expression on Dean's face or not, since the expression was clearly directed at Ron and not her.

I don't even want to think about the flutters in my belly that just started at seeing how he wants to protect me. Or what they mean.

"Okay, it sounds like I need to send two teams, one to protect Allissa, and one to protect her mom." Byron's booming voice brought Allissa back to the moment. "Since the packages are currently going to her mom's house, I'm assuming that Ron, or whoever this might be, doesn't know where Allissa is on your week off. So, I'm gonna scramble the first team available to Nevada, which I can get out there today. But it'll take me a couple of days to get another team available to send to Texas. Bobby, do you have the resources to keep her safe until I can get a couple of guys there?"

"Even if he doesn't, we've got enough wrestlers here to watch her back this week," Dean interjected. "Hell, we'll all still watch her back, even after you send a security team to protect her."

"Between the GWA crew and our security when we leave here, I'm not sure I need an extra security team," Allissa protested. "I'd prefer you send them to protect my mom."

"How about I get my security chief, Cage Dalton, to give you a call, Byron?" Rick suggested. "The two of you can work out what needs to be done to keep Allissa safe on the road, with your team in Nevada heading up the investigation."

"And since we're already paired up in the wedding this week, I'll personally keep an eye on Allissa to make sure she doesn't go anywhere without protection, until ya'll find her stalker," Dean added.

Great! Yet another reason I have to be paired up with Dean this week. And unfortunately, his protective side just makes him more appealing. This is going to be a hard week to get through without giving in to his advances.

Chapter Two

Monday, May 27, 2019, Heart's Destiny, Texas

Dean hated that Allissa was dealing with the stress of a stalker. While he wouldn't wish the experience on any of his friends or coworkers, he was even more worked up about the situation than he would be if the stalker was after anyone else in the company because Allissa was the one suffering through it. Regardless of whether she ever allowed him to be more to her than a friend and coworker, Dean was determined to keep her safe from the aggressive advances of the asshole targeting her.

The day before, when Allissa had requested a moment to talk to Byron Avington alone to fill him in on her mother's personal information, Dean had talked to both Rick and Bobby about his plan to be the point person when it came to protecting Allissa. They had both balked, claiming he didn't have the proper training to act as her bodyguard. Dean had to point out that he'd not only been the state wrestling champion every year all through high school and college, but he'd also won several youth shooting competitions through the 4H programs at the youth center in town as a kid.

While he wasn't planning to extend his concealed carry permit to be armed to defend Allissa when they left the state of Texas to go back on tour, they both had to concede that he was more than capable of disarming someone and keeping her safe until the authorities could get there to arrest the perpetrator. Bobby had still insisted on giving Dean a crash course in personal security procedures that night, and Rick had insisted on Dean meeting with Cage as soon as they got on the plane the following Monday morning to review his procedures for providing security to the rest of the company, but they'd both finally relented.

Now he just had to figure out how to get Allissa to agree to let him shadow her twenty-four-seven. *Fuck! She's gonna be a lot harder to sell on this idea than Bobby and Rick were yesterday,* Dean realized as he walked into the dining room at the B and B building they'd recently renamed the Heritage House for breakfast with the rest of the GWA crew in town for the week.

Damn, I wish James had planned more wedding events during the week. It was a lot easier to stay glued to her side yesterday at the wedding shower than it's gonna be between now and Friday when we have the rehearsal without specific wedding party duties to push us together.

Although, I guess we have a couple of things we can do tomorrow to at least be in the same place at the same time. I'll just need to check with Anthony to see if the baby shower tomorrow is co-ed or not. And if it's not, then I'll have to get with his mom to suggest it being co-ed as a great way for her to do a little more matchmaking.

Oh, speaking of matchmaking, I bet Ma will be happy to help me with ideas to win Allissa over this week. She might even be a better person to talk to than Hazel to suggest the baby shower tomorrow would be better if it was co-ed.

Dean had to chuckle at how he was planning to use the Matchmaking Mommas to his advantage, while all his friends were trying to avoid the schemes and plots of the middle-aged women in town. *Maybe those guys aren't as smart as they claim to be.*

With a plan to keep an eye on Allissa at more than just the formalwear fittings the next day, Dean detoured to the kitchen to find out where to find his mother. Once he was told she was in her office in the original building of the B and B, Dean skipped the breakfast line for the moment to go find her.

He walked into her office without bothering to knock. "Hey, Ma, got a minute?"

"For you, always." Mandi Hunter smiled up at her son from her place behind her desk as he plopped down in the chair across from her. "What's got you lookin' so worried first thing on a Monday morning?"

"I need your help comin' up with ideas for how to get Allissa to spend time with me this week, when we're not already obligated to be together for the wedding events," Dean admitted, knowing his mother would be thrilled at hearing he was interested in a woman. "And the ideas can't be too date-like, 'cause she'll just turn me down."

Mandi's brow furrowed in confusion about Dean's request.

"I guess you want me to start at the beginning and explain, huh?" Dean sighed as his mother nodded at him. "I've known since I first saw her in October when she did her tryout with the GWA that she's *The One*. But everything I've tried to get her attention has bombed. Now she has a stalker and needs someone to watch her back until the security company Rick's hiring to protect her catches the psycho. And even if she never agrees to go out with me or wants to be more than friends with me, I still want to be the one to protect her this week, while we're waiting for the bodyguards to get here. I just have no idea how to get her to let me, when there's not something wedding related going on when we'll already be paired up together."

"And that's where you want me to come in with ideas," his mother guessed.

"Yeah," Dean nodded his agreement. "I already thought you might be able to convince Mrs. Hazel to make the baby shower tomorrow co-ed, so I can go, even if I still have to watch over her from across the room the whole time. But I have no ideas for things we can do as a group the rest of the week."

"Yeah, I can definitely talk to Hazel about the baby shower tomorrow." His mom grinned at him from her seat across the desk.

"Thanks, Ma." Dean smiled back at his mother, grateful for her help. "Now I just have to figure out things we can all do today, Wednesday, Thursday, and Friday before the rehearsal."

"Okay, so group outings with everyone from the GWA, so it doesn't seem like you're asking her on a date." Mandi nodded, her eyes lighting up as she came up with a few ideas. "Well, there's the Memorial Day picnic in town today. That's being held at the park. Then you could suggest our trail rides on Wednesday, and maybe bowling on Thursday. I'll have to think of something for Friday."

"Oh, um, maybe figure out when we can spend some time with me teaching her how to two-step, too." Dean shrugged when his mother gave him a quizzical look. "James and Randi told her we have to two-step together at the reception, so now I have to teach her, and we need some time to practice since she's never two-stepped before."

"Okay, well, you know the ballroom is available every morning for you to practice," his mother offered. "And by Friday we'll have it set up in the basic configuration for the rehearsal dinner and wedding, so you'll know the exact space of the dance floor, if that helps her feel more comfortable before everyone else is there Friday and Saturday night."

"Thanks, Ma," Dean grinned at his mother, thinking he could fill in the times he didn't have something else to do with her with dance lessons and practice. "I knew you'd be the perfect person to come up with some ideas for me."

"You're welcome, Son." His mom smiled at him before her smile turned pensive. "I think it's great that you want to help protect her, but maybe you should back off on trying to ask her out while she's dealing with this stalker thing."

His mother raised a point that he hadn't wanted to think about. He suddenly feared his caveman instinct to claim her as his woman might come across as similar to her stalker's obsession with her. *Fuck! Even if it kills me to keep from claiming her as mine, I can't take the chance on doing anything that might make her think I'm anything like him.*

"Don't worry, Ma," Dean smiled reassuringly at his mother, resolving to keep his possessive feelings for Allissa to himself as much as possible. "I can't completely stop flirting with her because that's just not me, but I'm not a predator. You raised me to know better than to take advantage of her fear of a stalker to get her to go out with me. But I can't completely walk away when she needs me either, so I'm just gonna be a good friend she can depend on to keep her safe."

"Good, now let's go get you set up with a picnic basket for this afternoon, in case she wants to eat something a little healthier than the burgers and hotdogs being grilled in the park."

Having watched Allissa diligently over the last few months, Dean knew she always seemed to gravitate toward the lighter fare when they ate in catering at the shows. So he agreed with his mother and followed her back to the kitchen at the Heritage House. Once the basket full of fresh fruit and veggies, turkey breast sandwiches, bottled water, and sports drinks was requested to be ready for him to pick up by noon, Dean went through the breakfast line and joined his coworkers in the dining room.

Allissa was sitting with the Precious Stones and Protection Detail, so Dean pulled over a chair from the next table to sit at the end between Allissa and the female third of Protection Detail, Chastity. "Morning ya'll," Dean grinned at the six people taking up the two sides of the table. "Whatcha got goin' on before the picnic this afternoon?"

"What picnic?" Harrison Thorne, the wrestler who used the ring name of Magnum because of his legitimate six-foot-seven, three-hundred-pound stature, arched an eyebrow at Dean.

"The Memorial Day picnic in town," Dean explained, arching an eyebrow back at Magnum, when he didn't seem to understand it was a holiday. "The unofficial kick-off to summer, and the holiday honoring our fallen war heroes."

"You do remember we're Canadian, right?" Cameron Wentworth, Magnum's tag-team partner, who used the ring name Trojan, chuckled. "We had our unofficial kick-off to summer last Monday for Victoria Day."

"Dang, you guys should have told me sooner about the day your whole country celebrates my gimmick," Allissa teased the Canadian tag team. "I'd have carried a Canadian flag to the ring to play it up as the narcissistic heel."

While Dean was glad to see Allissa in a better mood than she'd been in the day before after learning about her stalker, he still felt jealous of the way she easily bantered with the other men at the table, while practically ignoring him. He might feel like he needed to back off and try just being friends with her while she was in a vulnerable state with a psycho after her, but he didn't want anyone else slipping in to make a move on her to take advantage of the situation, either. *But fuck, how am I supposed to get these assholes to back off on flirting with her if I don't stake my claim?*

"We'll have to remind you next year," Cameron joked back with Allissa. "But I doubt it'll get you over, unless we're actually in Canada that day."

"So, we'll just have to ask Rick about booking us in Canada on Victoria Day next year," Harrison added with a flirtatious grin at Allissa.

"Anyway," Dean interjected, hoping to redirect the conversation back to his original plan to get Allissa to spend more time with him, without letting his inner caveman out to deal with the newest additions to the roster. "I thought we might do our first two-step lesson this morning after breakfast, then get a group together to go to the picnic this afternoon. I checked with my mom on my way in here this morning and the ballroom is free every morning this week, so we have plenty of time to practice before dancing at the rehearsal dinner and reception."

"Oh, um, okay," Allissa sputtered, turning to look at the Precious Stones on her other side. "You guys want to learn it with me?"

"Sure," Amethyst shrugged. "Might be nice to know, so we can dance with the locals at the wedding without looking stupid."

After getting nodding agreements from the rest of the table, they quickly scarfed down breakfast before gathering a few more of their coworkers to all head to the ballroom. Since Dion and Liam had spent some time learning to two-step when they were in town for Anthony's wedding and the New Year's party over their winter break, Dean recruited them to help him teach the other wrestlers who didn't already know how to do the country dance.

Since they had several more single male performers than single female performers on the roster, the same could be said of the mix of people who joined them in the ballroom to learn to two-step. So, Dean called Meemaw and his mom to invite over a few of the single ladies in town, who already knew how to two-step, to help him teach the guys.

Unfortunately, the women they most wanted to match up with the other GWA wrestlers all had other plans for the holiday, so it ended up being Meemaw, Mandi, and Dean's cousin, Ashley Myers, who worked as the head chef at the B and B, that came to help him out. Since they still had more men than women, Dean wasn't sure it would all work out so that he could stay paired with Allissa the whole time. But his eighty-year-old Meemaw surprised him with her solution to the mismatched numbers.

"Don't worry, Dean," Meemaw reassured him, patting his arm as she walked by him as they were pairing up couples to start trying to teach the dance. "I called Joan, and she's on her way. And since these boys are less than half our ages, we're each gonna take two, so when they're added up, they're old enough to dance with us."

Leah Mae Wright

The Joan she was referring to was Dean's other grandmother, who was seventy-five years old.

"Do PopPop and Grandpa Don know you and Grandma Joan are gonna be dancin' and probably flirtin' with guys young enough to be your grandsons?" Dean joked with Meemaw, who only grinned and shrugged as she walked away to pick out her two victims from his unsuspecting coworkers.

"Ah, now I see where your flirtatiousness comes from," Allissa giggled as she watched Meemaw walk over to Protection Detail and motion for Magnum to go first as her partner.

"Probably," Dean chuckled as he stepped closer to Allissa and started getting into position to start the dance just as his mother got the music started. "But hopefully, I'm not as outrageous as Meemaw."

"Only half the time," Allissa quipped as he directed her to put one hand on his shoulder while holding his hand with her other.

He put his free hand on her waist, making sure to maintain plenty of distance between their bodies as he instructed her on the steps of the dance. As much as he wanted to pull her close and really hold her in his arms, he knew she wasn't ready for him to make his move on her just yet. Not to mention how she'd probably feel offended, if they were close enough she could feel how his body responded to just the minimum physical contact between them for the dance he was teaching her.

Thank fuck, I started wearing compression shorts all the time to hide the boners I get whenever she's around.

After seeing her in the ring and freestyle dancing with the other women on the rare occasions when she went out with the rest of the crew after a show for the last several months, Dean was surprised at how she didn't seem to get the two-to-one rhythm of the dance and kept trying to alternate her steps, instead of taking two with the one foot before taking the third with the other foot.

It doesn't make sense that she's not getting it. She can't wrestle the way she does without better body awareness than what she's showing right now. Although, it's probably a good thing she's not getting it as easily as I expected. Now we have an even better excuse to spend all our free time this week practicing.

As they continued to practice, Dean got even more confused by her lack of finesse with the relatively simple dance. Especially when he looked around and saw all their friends were picking it up easily, even the guys who were having to shadow dance along with his grandmothers.

Fuck! I hope that's because she's as distracted by being this close to me as I am by being this close to her. I know I can't act on our attraction until after her stalker is caught, but damn, it'd be nice to know she feels it, too.

~ ~ ~

Allissa was still trying to get her libido in check after the morning dance lesson as she rode with the Precious Stones and Dean to the Memorial Day picnic being put on by the town. When he'd said the day before that he was going to stick close to her to watch for any threats from her stalker this week, she hadn't realized he intended to include touching her during daily dance lessons as part of his protection plan.

Though after talking to her mom a couple of times since the day before, she'd decided having Dean and the other wrestlers she worked with watching her back was a way better idea than being shadowed by the Avington Security bodyguards twenty-four-seven. She'd been embarrassed enough having to tell Byron Avington about her mom's job that she refused to quit and the trailer she refused to move out of, but there was no way she could handle looking into the eyes of anyone on the Avington team now that they'd seen how she was raised.

Byron had assured her that none of his team would disclose any of her mother's personal business to anyone in the GWA, or even their Burleson cousins, most of whom she'd just met that week. But she knew if she allowed him to send a team to protect her, they'd look at her just like most of the people in Dead End, Nevada, always had. Either with pity for having grown up as the daughter of a prostitute, or with the assumption that her body was also for sale.

It was because of not wanting that scrutiny that she'd adamantly refused when he offered to send a team to protect her. She'd explained that she didn't think the stalker knew where she was this week, and that Cage would be more than adequate to keep her safe while traveling with the GWA to put him off from sending a team of bodyguards to protect her. Knowing the team he sent would keep her mother safe and investigate to locate the stalker was more than enough for her.

And her mom was thrilled with the three men sent to be her bodyguards and investigate the case. She'd gushed about how all the girls were jealous when she'd gone to work the night before with a hunky stud who spent the whole night watching over her.

Allissa had heard all about how attractive Brady, Miller, and Knight were on Sunday when they'd first arrived to start the investigation. Then this morning, when her mom had called to report about her night with Miller tailing her at work, Allissa had found out that they were taking shifts protecting her mother with Knight on days and Miller on nights.

The third man Byron had sent was his son, Brady Avington, who was there to handle the investigation and cover when either Miller or Knight needed a break from their bodyguard duties. Allissa just hoped her mother didn't drive the two bodyguards insane enough to need Brady to cover too often to effectively investigate her stalker.

Yeah, even having to resist my attraction to Dean while doing dance lessons all week is better than having to endure the judging looks from a team of bodyguards all the time.

Having the Precious Stones and Dean dominating the conversation on the way to the picnic helped her out with dealing with the forced proximity to Dean. While she was still the only one in the front seat with him, at least now she wasn't feeling the heat between them where he touched her during their dance lessons.

How on earth did him touching my hand and my waist feel like he was stimulating my nipples and pussy? And what was up with me feeling like a cat in heat, wanting to rub them on him? Like those thoughts were even semi-appropriate with his mom and two grandmas in the room.

She turned in her seat to at least appear to be participating in the conversation about the history of this weird little town and the Hunter family's part in founding it. In reality, she wasn't really looking at her two friends in the back seat so much as sneaking covert glances at the man behind the wheel, relaying the stories.

She hoped if she could figure out what she found so attractive about Dean Hunter, she'd also be able to find a flaw that would negate that attraction. Unfortunately, as she studied the man beside her in the truck, she couldn't find a flaw in his appearance.

With being almost a foot taller than her five-foot-six, and in prime physical condition for wrestling, he had a body that could be used for demonstrating the ideal male anatomy. Add in his rugged good looks, tan complexion, dark brown hair, and eyes that seemed to change color depending on what he was wearing, and he became exceptionally hard to resist. He was the epitome of the phrase "tall, dark, and handsome" that most women found appealing.

Even his long hair and beard that she'd wanted to count against him when they first met weren't the flaws she'd tried to make them out to be. Yeah, they made him look like Aquaman, but that wasn't necessarily a bad thing. *At least I haven't told Mom I finally understand her attraction to Jason Momoa, so she hasn't asked about Dean since the first time she saw him and James on television and mentioned their resemblance.*

Unlike the unruly beards she found unattractive on men, Dean's was always neatly trimmed. He also pulled his long dark hair back into a low ponytail most of the time, especially as the weather warmed up. So the only time it looked disheveled was when he wore it down and it got messed up in the ring. Since she had the same issue with her hair when she wrestled, she couldn't exactly hold that against him.

Damn it! Why can't this man have some physical flaws to help me get my libido turned back off?

Even the cocky, egotistical attitude he showed on every GWA show, and while out with the crew after work, seemed to be absent now that they were in his hometown. Instead, he almost seemed humble when he talked about his family history, and how he hoped he could find a way to give back to the community the way his ancestors had in the past.

No, I'm not going to let myself fall for this act. Not when I know he'll be back to the asshole player he normally is when we go back on tour next week.

It didn't take long to get from the bed and breakfast to the park across the street from the church, where they'd gone to the wedding shower the day before. As soon as they parked and started getting out of his extended cab pickup, Allissa could smell the food being prepared for the day. Her mouth watered in anticipation of the greasy cheeseburgers being sold at the tent set up just inside the park. *Hell, I hope I can keep myself from scarfing down two or three of those things. I probably should have asked Dean to take me to the grocery store, so I could bring some fresh fruits to fill up on while we're here. As delicious as those burgers smell, I might not be able to resist the temptation, regardless of who's around to see me eat enough of them to feed the whole GWA roster.*

She wasn't sure how she was going to handle the food at the picnic because she'd avoided eating anything considered unhealthy in front of others since she was a teenager. On top of picking on her about her mother's profession, the kids she went to high school with had also teased her about having an eating disorder because of being so thin. She didn't actually have an eating disorder before high school, just a really fast metabolism.

In fact, she had a voracious appetite and could put away two or three plates of food at a single meal. Unfortunately, doing so in the cafeteria in high school led her classmates to accuse her of being anorexic or bulimic. They claimed that she couldn't eat that much all the time without puking it back up or she wouldn't be toothpick thin.

She wasn't sure if the way she'd changed her eating habits because of the teenage taunting could be classified as her having an eating disorder now or not. If she did, it wasn't one she'd ever heard of before. She didn't starve herself or even limit her food intake when she was at home or eating in private. And she certainly never puked up good food. She just stuck with healthy options and small portions whenever she ate in the presence of others, and indulged her insatiable appetite when she ate alone or at home with her mom.

Since starting to work with the GWA, her eating habits had changed slightly. With eating in catering at the arenas most of the time, she filled up on all the fresh fruits and vegetables she could, while picking small portions of the leanest protein options on the buffet. Then the next time she was alone in her hotel room, she'd indulge in the less healthy options available through room service.

She wasn't sure what she'd do at this picnic, almost freezing up as the rest of the crew joined them in the walk toward the food tents. *I guess I'll just pick the smallest burger option available and hope my stomach doesn't growl too loud before I can sneak off to grab more food later.*

"Hey, Allissa, Darlin', wait up," Dean hollered, jogging to catch up to the group.

Allissa stopped, letting the others move around her, so she could find out what Dean wanted. When the crowd cleared, she was surprised to see he was carrying a large picnic basket in one hand with a blanket draped over his other arm.

"I know you don't normally eat much of this unhealthy stuff." Dean nodded in the direction of the food tent their coworkers were lining up for in front of them. "So, I had the kitchen staff pack up all the stuff that would normally be on a veggie tray for an event, the fresh fruits from the breakfast bar, and a few turkey breast sandwiches on whole grain bread to make sure you'd be able to find something you like to eat today."

Allissa was speechless at his thoughtful gesture. She didn't know how to respond to Dean not only noticing her eating habits, but also respecting what seemed to be her dietary choices based on what she ate in public.

After years of people picking on her for whatever she chose to eat in public, she couldn't believe he was the only person who didn't expect her to conform to their dietary opinions. Not that anyone in the GWA had picked on her the way the kids had back in high school, but even her friends had made comments about her having amazing willpower to be able to stick to a diet while traveling for the job. While those comments were always phrased to seem like they were jealous of her willpower, they still made her feel awkward because they were too close to the comments other models had made when she'd tried eating off a veggie tray while on a long modeling shoot.

Part of her wanted to confide in him about her eating issues and the teasing she'd endured in her past, but she was afraid that trusting him with even a little of her history could lead to the slippery slope of falling for him. She stood there floundering for words for a moment before finally uttering, "Thank you."

"No problem," Dean grinned at her before nodding his head in the direction of a stage set up on the opposite side of the park. "Let's go grab a spot to listen to the bands that'll be playin' all afternoon."

Unfortunately, all the picnic tables in the park appeared to be occupied. So, they found a wide-open grassy area to lay out the twin-sized blanket Dean brought to have a place to sit without actually sitting on the grass.

"Are you sure it's okay to lay this out on the grass?" Allissa looked at the obviously handwoven blanket and hated the thought of it ending up grass stained because she sat on it. She pointed to the hay bales being used to section off a makeshift dance floor near the stage where a band was setting up. "We could go sit on those hay bales to keep from getting grass stains on the blanket."

"Oh, no, Darlin'," Dean chuckled, shaking his head. "Sittin' on hay bales is a surefire way to get eat up with chiggers. And these horse blankets have been used for layin' out on the grass since before I was born, so even if they get stained, Meemaw will be able to tell me what to use to get the stains out."

"Oh, um, okay." Allissa conceded, sitting down on the blanket on the other side of the picnic basket from Dean. As much as she appreciated the food he'd thought to bring, she was even more grateful for that large basket to act as a buffer between them to keep her from thanking him with a kiss.

As they started pulling out containers of food, a few of the other GWA wrestlers walked up carrying plates of burgers, hotdogs, and various sides.

"Hey, where are the rest of us supposed to sit?" Amethyst huffed, glaring at Dean.

"Ya'll shoulda waited for me to open up the back of the truck before takin' off for the food tent," Dean chuckled as he reached into his pocket to pull out his keys. "But since I'm a nice guy, I brought enough horse blankets for all of us. Now, ya'll just hafta go back to the truck to get 'em."

"Here, hold my plate and I'll go get them," Emerald suggested, handing off her food to Amethyst, so Dean could toss her his keys.

"I'll help." Dane handed his plate to his brother before following Emerald back to Dean's truck.

Allissa was surprised it didn't take them very long before they were back, carrying several blankets each to pass out to the rest of the crew. With as much as Emerald and Dane flirted with one another, she thought for sure they'd take a few extra minutes to make out in the back of the truck while nobody else was over there.

I don't care how much Emerald denies they're more than friends. They touch each other way too much for me to believe they've never even kissed.

Her thoughts about her friends were derailed when Dean placed a bundle of bananas on the blanket beside the containers of cut-up fruit and vegetables. *Geez, can this picnic quit making all my eating issues so freaking obvious? Please?*

Bananas were the one fresh fruit she'd given up eating in her teen years. Well, at least whenever anyone but her mother was around to witness it. It wasn't that she disliked them. They were actually one of her favorite fruits, and she still ate them if they were peeled and cut up on a buffet bar or used as an ingredient in other dishes. She just didn't peel and eat the whole fruit because of the inappropriate way she learned to eat them as a child.

As a young mother, Windy Walters hadn't realized her daughter would imitate the way she ate. So, she didn't think to change her habit of using bananas to practice giving blow jobs every time she ate one with Allissa watching her. Since Allissa couldn't even remember learning to suck on a banana instead of biting and chewing it because of being so young when she started eating them, she'd been unsuccessful in breaking the habit, when the kids in school pointed out how her blow jobs would be worth the money when she ate one at lunch one day. After that mentally scarring experience, she'd decided it was easier to quit eating them than to eat them like a normal person.

"You okay, Darlin'?" Dean gave her a quizzical look as he passed her a plate to start putting her choices on to eat.

"Yeah, I'm fine." Allissa shook off the old memories, faking a smile as she took the plate from Dean.

"You sure?" Dean looked around before looking back at her. "You looked like you saw a ghost there for a minute. Did you see someone you thought might be your stalker?"

"No, nothing like that," Allissa denied, shaking her head. "Like I told Byron yesterday, I don't think Ron, or whoever it is, knows I'm here this week. So, I'm not afraid I'm in any imminent danger. I think the stress of it all, and maybe the lack of sleep last night, is just finally catching up with me. So I just kinda zoned out, ready for a nap. But I'll be fine once I eat and get up moving around to participate in some of the games and stuff going on here today."

"Alright, Darlin'," Dean smiled tentatively. "But we don't have to stay 'til this is over tonight. So you just let me know if you feel like you need to get to bed early to catch up on some of that missed sleep."

"Thanks." Allissa was speechless once again at another thoughtful gesture from Dean. She filled her plate with a sandwich, carrots, broccoli, apple slices, strawberries, and a spoonful of mixed fruit as she tried to wrap her mind around the recent change in Dean's behavior.

He was still as flirtatious as he always was, but he was also acting more like a friend than normal. It was almost like finding out she had a stalker the day before flipped a switch in him somehow. She wasn't sure how to handle the guy who seemed like he wanted to be her buddy more than he wanted to get in her panties.

Yeah, I'm sure it's just a new tactic from the player to get me to let my guard down. And I'm not gonna fall for it. It's gonna take a lot more than twenty-four hours of acting like a friend for him to get me to break my rules about men.

This isn't going to turn into one of those friends-to-lovers, romance novel stories. No matter how much I love reading them, I know they're nothing but fiction. And Dean Hunter is definitely not book-boyfriend material.

Chapter Three

Tuesday, May 28, 2019, Heart's Destiny, Texas

Allissa was looking forward to going to Kay's baby shower at the church. She loved babies and little kids, even if she didn't expect to ever have any of her own. She had long ago decided to adopt one day, when she had a stable job or enough money to retire comfortably, and a home of her own somewhere other than her hometown. Her job with the GWA had her well on her way to achieving that dream at some point in her thirties. Even though she wasn't in a rush to join her friends in parenting, she still felt drawn to celebrating her friends, who were already living the dream by adding to their families.

Besides celebrating the impending birth of Kay and Anthony's new little one, Allissa was also looking forward to the reprieve from having Dean around for a few hours. His insistence on being her protector all week was already getting on her nerves, and it had only been a couple of days. After the wedding shower, she'd had to escape to her room at the bed and breakfast to give herself a breather from being too close to his intoxicating leather, sandalwood, and musk scent.

Who knew a cologne could be so potent in awakening my previously dormant libido?

Then when she thought she had a day off from wedding events that she had to be paired up with him on Monday, he'd not only started her two-step dance lessons for the wedding reception, but he'd also insisted on taking her to the Memorial Day picnic in town. She'd thought she'd gotten out of having to be too close to him by inviting the rest of the GWA crew to go with them. But even when she'd moved to sit with her girlfriends after they finished eating, he hadn't let her out of his line of sight.

Her friends had tried to convince her to enjoy the extra attention he was giving her, which she'd tried at first. But then, when she'd seen all the local girls flirting with him, and him flirting back, she'd realized it was a stupid move to believe she'd ever be special to a player like Dean. She knew he was only flirting with her because she wasn't giving in like most women. And if he knew about her background, he'd run away from any attraction they had in a heartbeat because they were so mismatched.

That was why she'd insisted on riding with Randi to the bridal shop to pick up their dresses that morning, and ignored him when the guys all came over from the menswear shop attached to the bridal shop to get Randi's approval of their tuxedos. She may have felt like a third wheel in the car with the lovebirds that morning, but it was worth it to avoid Dean.

Thankfully, it's just Randi and I in the car now heading to the baby shower.

James was apparently riding home from the final fittings with Dean, so Randi could make a side trip over to her sister's house to stash her wedding dress where James wouldn't see it before the wedding. Since the ladies were going to the baby shower right after the fitting, it seemed like perfect timing for Allissa to also ditch Dean for the day by continuing to ride with Randi for the quick errand.

Needless to say, Allissa was surprised to arrive at the church for the baby shower to see the fellowship hall, where Kay's mother-in-law was hosting it, already filling up with a mixed crowd for what was apparently a co-ed baby shower. Allissa turned to look at the woman she'd considered her best friend since they started working together on Randi's wrestling training and hissed under her breath, "What are the guys doing here?"

"Normally, I'd say they were being supportive of the father-to-be," Randi chuckled. "But with this group, I'm gonna say making the toilet-paper-diaper game way more hilarious."

"Do I even want to know what the toilet-paper-diaper game is?" Allissa arched an eyebrow at Randi as they walked over to put their gifts on the table with all the others.

"It's not anything bad," Randi assured her, grabbing her arm, and pulling her over to the table set up with the first of a couple of guessing games set up. "Just a game where we pair off with one person standing still while the other person makes them a diaper out of toilet paper."

Allissa didn't know if she wanted to be the person trying to make the diaper or the person standing still while being diapered, but either way, it didn't sound like a fun game to her. *Although, it would be fun to watch the guys make fools of themselves as both the diaperers and the diaperees.*

"Oh, I'm pretty sure I know this one," Randi giggled mischievously.

Allissa looked at the sign on the table telling everyone to guess Baby Sam's birthday and birthtime. There was a stack of small slips of paper with lines for the person's name placing the guess, and the day and time they thought Kay would have her baby.

"After Tia came a couple of weeks early, Kay didn't want to schedule a C-section with Maria, even though she knew she'd probably have to have another C-section to have her," Randi explained as she filled out one of the slips of paper to put in the jar on the table. "Then Maria decided she was too comfortable to come out on time and wouldn't budge for two weeks after her due date. So, Kay told me the other day that she's planning to schedule a C-section for Sam's due date."

"Well, since you're picking her actual due date of the eighth, I'm gonna guess before then," Allissa decided, grabbing a pen, and filling out one of the slips of paper. "I'm thinking the morning of the fourth of July, so he's here in time for the fireworks that night."

"You should probably put nine p.m. instead of between two and three a.m." Randi pointed at the slip of paper, where Allissa had just filled in the early morning time. "If he's born on the fourth, then he'll probably keep them from being able to watch the fireworks."

"No, we're talking about Kay and Anthony's kid," Allissa disagreed. "With those two for parents, he'll be too considerate to make them miss the fireworks. But since we're talking about a baby, and they're known for waking their parents up at two a.m., I think they can count on an early morning wake-up call from day one."

"Good point," Randi laughed as they moved over to the next table, where there was a bulletin board set up with two dozen childhood photos of Kay and Anthony. The directions at this table instructed everyone to take one of the sheets of paper with numbers one through twenty-four listed down the side, and write down which of the two they thought was in each photo and how old they were at the time. "Oh, good, another easy game."

"I think your idea of easy is drastically different than mine," Fiona chuckled as she stood there examining the photos of the expectant couple when they were no older than three. "I can't even tell which of these are pictures of Anthony and which are of Kay, much less be able to guess how many months old they are in the pics."

"It's only easy for me because I've seen all of Kay's baby pictures before," Randi grinned as she started jotting down her answers. "And Mom labeled them in our photo albums."

"Ah, so the secret to this game is to cheat off of you and Anthony's sisters," James chuckled as he walked up and wrapped Randi in his arms from behind.

"Oh, no!" Randi giggled, pressing her paper to her chest to keep James from reading it over her shoulder. "No cheating!"

"Come on, Bro," Dean walked up and slugged James on the shoulder. "We don't need to cheat to know which of these pictures is of Anthony. They were all taken here in town, in places we'll recognize. Like this little buckaroo is obviously Anthony because of the cows in the background."

"Oh, ya think so, do ya?" Randi snickered, finally escaping from James's clutches to move around Allissa, effectively using her as a shield to keep the Hunters from reading her answers. "We have cows in Oklahoma too, ya know. And our mom and Kay lived on our grandparents' farm before Mom married Dad. So that could be Anthony. Or it could be Kay. And none of us who actually know are gonna let you cheat to find out."

Allissa was torn between rescuing her friend from the playful antics of her fiancé and his brother, or teaming with the twins to try and cheat at the game with them. In the end, she opted to save herself from having to interact with Dean in either capacity. She grabbed one of the sheets and backed away from the table. "I'm gonna let you guys fight this one out amongst yourselves, and I'll come back later to look over the pictures to place my guesses."

She walked over to the table set up with finger sandwiches and veggie trays to fill up a plate and talk with some of the other women there she knew from the GWA. She wasn't as close to the married women as she was to the single ladies. But having wrestled against Holland Everett and Shauna Grady so many times over her stint in the GWA, she felt more comfortable with them and the wives of the male wrestlers that traveled with the company than she did the local ladies she'd just met that week. They made small talk as they mingled and ate, with a few of the ladies commenting about how they hadn't known the party was co-ed and had childcare set up until they got there.

"So, are your husbands coming now that you know?" Allissa looked over at the food table and wondered if the family members who set up the party were adequately prepared for the rest of the GWA men to join them. She'd seen the amount of food the guys could put away every night in catering and didn't think a few trays of veggies and finger sandwiches were going to be enough.

"Oh, yeah, they're coming," Holly laughed. "And I can't wait to see Tanner announce his water broke."

"What?" Allissa couldn't fathom why Tanner Everett, who used the ring name of Everest as part of the Mountain Men tag team, would announce that his water broke in the middle of a baby shower.

"It's another game thing," Sarina Kirby, the wife of Tanner's tag-team partner, Donovan, aka Olympus, explained, pointing to the table of drinks set up beside the food table. "They're going to put ice cubes with plastic babies frozen in them in our drinks, and whenever the ice cube melts, we're supposed to announce, 'my water broke.' Only, when Fiona found out the guys could come, she convinced Anthony's mom not to start it until they got here because it'll be funnier coming from the guys."

"And when Rick found out he had to come to a baby shower, he put the word out with the rest of the guys that they had to come too," Jana Evans continued for her with a huge grin. "I don't know who decided at the last minute that this should be a co-ed party, but I have to admit, I wish I'd thought of it for one of mine."

Since she always thought she'd adopt instead of actually giving birth, Allissa hadn't ever thought about having a baby shower, so she stood there quietly listening to the ladies around her as they compared their own baby shower experiences. Wishing Amethyst and Emerald had come to the party, she thought about texting them to grab some of the single guys and come over. But she knew it would be rude to pull out her cell phone in the middle of the party.

Leah Mae Wright

Maybe they'll show up after Rick's directive to the other guys?

As the ladies around her started talking about the other games, she looked around the room and tried to figure out whom she would feel comfortable teaming up with for the toilet paper diaper game that Randi had told her about earlier. Noticing that the few single wrestlers who had already arrived for the party were already talking to the local girls, Allissa wondered if the co-ed aspect of the party was another of the matchmaking plots she'd heard about in town. *I just hope, since it's not a wedding event, they won't pair me up with Dean for the games here, too.*

~~~

Dean was having way more fun at the baby shower than he expected. He'd thought it would just be a few of the guys sitting there, while the ladies all talked about their birth experiences or complained about pregnancy symptoms he didn't want to know about. But it was just another way for both his GWA friends and hometown crowd to hang out together and have fun. With the silly games, it almost seemed like another bachelor and bachelorette party, only without the alcohol since it was being held in the church.

Damn, I should probably have compared it to the wedding shower, since it's more like that than the party at the bar. I guess I just didn't think about it, since I missed a lot of the fun stuff at the wedding shower with finding out about Allissa's stalker.

Not wanting to bring down his mood just as they were getting ready to get started with the more active games, Dean pushed thoughts of Allissa's stalker from the forefront of his mind. He was still sticking close enough to protect her, of course, but he wanted to keep her mind off the situation and make sure she had fun as well. Though he wasn't sure how he could make her laugh any more than hearing all the guys in the room being the only ones to announce, "my water broke," since the ladies had somehow rigged the game to only give the guys the ice cubes that actually melted.

Since pretty much everyone from the GWA ended up showing up after it was switched to a co-ed party, Dean also wasn't sure if he would be able to work his way through the crowd to be paired up with
~~~

Allissa, if any of the games were set up for teams of two. But when they were instructed to find a seat in the circle of chairs set up around the room, he upped his chances by watching where she sat before rushing over to take the seat beside her.

He soon realized that he hadn't had to worry about not being paired with her, when Anthony's mom, Hazel, and Aunt Susan started walking around the room rearranging the group into couples. Hazel gave him a knowing smile as she walked past him and Allissa, without asking either of them to move from their seats.

"Why does it matter how we're seated?" Emerald leaned forward in her seat to look around Dane, who had been moved between her and Allissa.

"No clue," Allissa shrugged.

"Okay, now that we've got an even number of men and women set up to play the first game," Hazel started explaining as she stood between two tables that were set up with dolls and various baby supplies in the middle of the circle. "We're gonna get started with the diaper-change-relay race. We're going to start with Anthony and Kay and move clockwise around the room. When it's your turn, you have to come up and remove the diaper from your baby, mime using a wet wipe to clean the baby up and applying diaper cream or powder, then fold a clean cloth diaper and put it on your baby. Ladies, you'll be using the table on my right, and gentlemen, you'll be using the table on my left."

"Hey! How's it fair to be men versus women, when none of us guys know how to change a diaper?" Liam pointed out the flaw in the game that Dean had also wondered about, but knew better than to specifically mention.

"You really think I know how to fold and change a diaper?" Anthony's cousin, Jen, turned in her seat to glare at Liam beside her. "We were playing with baby cows and baby horses when I was a kid, not baby dolls."

"Don't worry, Liam," Hazel reassured him with a smile. "We made sure there are just as many fathers as mothers in the group playing, so you should have just as many experienced diaper changers on your team as the ladies."

"Yeah, I'm gonna suck so bad at this that I'll probably skew the odds of winning this game to the fathers," Allissa chortled, looking around as if she was trying to find someone to take her place.

"You won't suck any worse than I will, Darlin'," Dean chuckled along with her, remembering back to how it had taken the both of them to change Travis and Trent on Valentine's Day. And they were wearing disposable diapers, not cloth diapers that had to be folded a certain way. "At least the dolls aren't gonna try to pee on us the way Travis and Trent did."

"True," Allissa laughed, obviously remembering the same things he did from that night. "Though I wish they had a stack of disposable diapers up there instead of the cloth ones. It was hard enough using those with both of us working together. I bet this is going to be a lot harder, even without the baby trying to shoot us in the eyes."

"Yeah, I have no idea how to fold a cloth diaper to make it fit on a baby," Dean admitted, shaking his head as he looked at the stack of white pieces of cloth that looked a lot like the shop rags he kept in his garage.

"It's kinda like makin' a paper airplane," Anthony advised as he walked up to the table to take his place as the first guy to compete. "Then put the baby's butt in the middle and fold the nose up between the baby's legs and wings around the waist to pin it in place."

"Except we're not using pins," Kay added, shaking her head at Anthony's paper airplane description, and holding up what looked like a blue piece of rubber in the shape of the letter Y. "We have these clips to hold it together, so we don't poke the baby."

Dean had to laugh at Anthony's plan for folding the diapers. *Guess he has to work his love of planes into everything he does, including covering his baby's ass.*

"Please tell me nobody's filming this," Dane groaned from his seat on Allissa's other side, as Hazel signaled Anthony and Kay to start the game. "We'll lose all our credibility as badass wrestlers, if it's leaked, and our fans see it."

"Oh, pul-ease!" Emerald slapped Dane's chest with a chop. "You work face, so you'll just get more ring rats trying to have your babies. Those of us who work heel are the only ones who'll lose our street cred for rockin' this game."

"You say that like you might actually have a chance at not looking like an idiot when it's your turn," Amethyst snort-laughed at her tag-team partner. "We both know you're more likely to body slam the baby than get a diaper to stay on."

"No body-slamming the baby," Rick commanded, pointing to the wrestlers around the room from his seat. "If video of that made it online, our ratings would tank."

As the crowd around them chuckled, Anthony and Kay finished with their diapering demo to start the relay race. James and Randi took their place, and the first thing James did when he removed the diaper Anthony had put on was unfold it. *Fuck, I hope the rest of the guys noticed that and do the same thing, so we'll all know which paper airplane design to model the diaper after,* Dean thought, watching his brother's hands so he could recreate the correct fold if the guys between them didn't think to do the same thing.

"You don't have to unfold the dirty diaper," Hazel informed James.

"I do if I want to know what kind of paper airplane I'm folding the next one into," James shrugged as he mimed wiping the doll's ass and sprinkling on powder with the closed bottle on the table.

"Seriously? The second person up and the guys are already cheating to win?" Lexi Wilder, one of the local girls who was a couple of years older than Dean, complained from the other side of the room.

"If ya'll didn't want any cheating in this game, ya shouldn't have allowed any of the heels to participate," Dean quipped, backing up his brother.

"Wait," Allissa turned on Dean and glared. "Randi's a heel too, and she didn't unfold the diaper Kay put on to know how to fold it."

"Don't worry, Vic," Randi grinned as she finished using the strange clip thing to secure the doll's diaper. "I didn't have to waste time unfolding Kay's because I already know how to fold a cloth diaper from helping with the laundry when my nieces were babies."

"And I don't know how to fold a diaper, so I'm gonna unfold Randi's to be able to fold the next one correctly," Anthony's sister, Becky, assured Allissa as she stood to take Randi's place at the changing table.

"Now that we all know how we're going to figure out how to fold the diapers, can someone please tell me how to use the hair-tie-looking thing to hold it closed?" Surfer Josh Parker implored the group to help him out as he walked up to the table on the guys' side.

"It's not a hair tie," James chuckled. "It's like those clips Doc uses on ace wraps."

"Okay, yeah, I can work with that," Josh grinned as he started removing the diaper and unfolding it.

"Hopefully, they hold better than those clips," Allissa giggled.

"For real," Dean chuckled along with her, thinking about how he always had to cover them with athletic tape to keep an ace wrap on when he had to wear one. He then nodded over at Anthony and Kay, directing his next comment to them. "But maybe ya'll shoulda added a case of athletic tape to your baby registry, just in case."

"Not necessary, Dean." Kay shook her head at him. "The diaper covers we'll use on Sam will keep everything in place."

"And we're only using cloth diapers at home," Anthony added. "We'll be using disposables when we're working."

His comment led to a discussion about how long it would be before Anthony and Kay were back at work after the baby was born, and the various baby paraphernalia they would need to keep on the company plane to save the hassle of carrying it back and forth every time they rotated through their shifts. While he half-listened to the conversation, Dean focused on watching each of the guys as they unfolded and then folded the diapers, so he could try to help his team catch up with the ladies.

When it was finally his turn, he got to the table just as Allissa was starting to fold her diaper. He couldn't stop himself from watching her as she folded the diaper a different way than the guys had been folding theirs. While he would normally blame that on his obsession with watching her anytime he was in the same place as her, he blamed this instance of him watching her on the fact that the folding technique she was using for the diaper was much simpler than the one all the guys had been using.

"Dude, why are we doing such a complicated airplane fold, while the girls are folding theirs in like half the steps?" Dean glared at Anthony as he removed the diaper from the doll in front of him.

"We have to make sure it's thickest in the front, 'cause we're havin' a boy," Anthony explained with a shrug. "So, that's the way Kay taught me to fold 'em."

"And we've been using the simpler triangle fold because it's faster and the dolls aren't going to actually use them," Kay added with a giggle.

"And ya'll accused us of cheating." Dean skipped unfolding the complicated airplane fold and focused on the task at hand, shaking his head at the laughing ladies around the room as he mimed the wiping and powdering steps.

He then folded the diaper the same way he'd watched Allissa do it and put it on the doll with the clip, just as Emerald started removing the one Allissa had put on. He might not have caught the guys back up enough to sit back down at the same time Allissa had, but he'd shaved off several seconds of the ladies' lead by adjusting the folding technique.

Meemaw came over and stuck her head between Dean and Allissa as soon as he sat down, laying an arm over each of their shoulders. "Don't worry, Dean. When ya'll have kids, I'll get you pre-folded diapers and teach you how to twist them in the middle for a bikini fold. So you won't have to worry about any of those complicated folds with flats."

"Thanks, Meemaw." Dean had to laugh at the absurdity of his eighty-year-old grandmother talking about a bikini fold for his future children's diapers. "But I think I'll stick to disposable if I ever have kids, even though they aren't environmentally friendly."

Meemaw nodded and kissed his cheek before moving back over to the group of older women she'd been sitting with, who weren't participating in the game.

The conversation around them switched to the different folding techniques and which were better based on the sex of the baby. Dean mostly tuned them out, focusing instead on catching covert glances at Allissa and trying to imagine what their future children would look like.

While he had plans to wrestle for at least ten years before he started having children, he had to admit, if only to himself, that he wanted them to be with Allissa. *Damn, I can't wait to start practicing making them.*

Just the thought had his cock starting to thicken in his shorts. He had to look across the room at the table full of grandmothers, from his family and several others around town, to get it under control.

As soon as the ladies eked out a victory in the diaper-changing-relay race, Hazel announced that the toilet paper diaper game was the next game they'd be playing. "Since we already have you sitting as couples, all you have to do is stand up and face your partner to be ready for the next game. We've already put a roll of toilet paper under each of your chairs for you to make a diaper for your partner."

"If we each have a roll of toilet paper, how do we decide which of us is wearing it and which of us is putting it on our partner?" Allissa looked concerned as she got the roll out from under her seat.

"Ladies, you'll make a diaper for the gentlemen first, which they have to keep on while they make a diaper for you," Hazel clarified, even though Dean didn't think she'd heard Allissa's question. "The first team finished wins one of the prizes, but don't stop when you think someone else has won. There's also a prize for the team that keeps their diapers on the longest as we finish out the party with gifts and cake."

Dean bent down and got his roll of toilet paper out from under his seat, thinking the only way he'd be able to keep a toilet paper diaper on would be to stand as still as possible for the rest of the party. *Fuck! This is gonna be tough. If I don't rip through it from getting hard while she's putting it on me, I'll definitely rip through it from getting hard while trying to wrap toilet paper between her legs.*

"Well, this is awkward," Allissa muttered when Hazel gave the signal for the teams to begin, and she realized she was teamed with him. "How are we supposed to make a diaper out of toilet paper?"

"Wrap it around the waist, hips, and both legs like an ace wrap?" Dean shrugged, as clueless about what the diaper had to look like at the end as she was.

"Yeah, okay."

As a few of the teams around them were reprimanded for the guys trying to hold the end of the toilet paper for the ladies, Allissa stuck her tongue out in the cutest way, showing how deep in thought she was about how to get the diaper started. Eventually, she tucked the end square of the toilet paper roll in the pocket of his shorts to hold it in place and started moving around him to circle his waist and hips. After moving low enough, she alternated from side to side to wrap the toilet paper around and between his legs.

Dean tried to think of anything and everything he could to keep from getting an erection, finally resorting to looking at Meemaw and Grandma Joan across the room, instead of watching what Allissa was doing. But even the sight of his grandmothers watching them wasn't enough to keep his cock from thickening once more when Allissa grazed his balls with her hand as she wrapped the toilet paper between his legs.

It wasn't Allissa touching me. It was the toilet paper. Not her hand. He repeated the words over and over in his head, trying to coax the blood quickly filling his cock to head back to his brain. *But fuck, I wish it was her hand stroking my cock.*

Thankfully, she hadn't wrapped the toilet paper too tight and didn't seem to notice that he was causing it to feel tighter than she intended. As she approached the end of the roll, she stood back up to her full height from the slightly hunched-over position she'd been in while wrapping the toilet paper between his legs. She tucked the end under the other layers at his hip, not getting anywhere close to touching his dick.

Fuck! How am I gonna do this without groping her, or tearing this toilet paper? Our height difference is definitely gonna be a problem.

"Now I know why this was ladies first," Dean grumbled as he gingerly lowered himself to his knees in front of Allissa.

"You mean it's not just one of those southern gentlemanly things?" Allissa smirked and arched an eyebrow at him.

"Yeah, that's what I thought at first," Dean admitted as he tucked the end of the toilet paper in her pocket the same way she'd started wrapping him. "But now I know it's because all of us guys are taller than our partners, and Anthony's mom thinks it's funny to watch us try to get up and down while wearing toilet paper diapers."

"At least you aren't having to sit completely down on the floor like Anthony, Magnum, and a few of the other really tall guys," Allissa giggled.

"Damn, Darlin'," Dean groaned, glad he had long arms so he could wrap the toilet paper around her without having to crawl around her like some of the other guys were having to do with their partners. "Only you would make me feel like my six-foot-four is short."

"That's not what I meant." Allissa rolled her eyes at him, but he barely caught the gesture in his peripheral vision as he focused on watching where he was putting the toilet paper, while fighting not to look at her long bare legs sticking out of the bottom of her denim shorts. "But that you got lucky that I'm one of the taller women in the room, so you don't have to bend so far down."

"Oh, I definitely got lucky being partnered up with you, Darlin'," Dean grinned and wagged his eyebrows at her, causing her to roll her eyes at him once more. He snuck a look down her body as he went back to wrapping the toilet paper around her. *Damn, those jean shorts aren't even cut-offs and they're still sexy as fuck paired with that red t-shirt.*

"That's the only way you're gonna get lucky with me," Allissa mumbled, closing her eyes as he moved down with the toilet paper to start wrapping it between her legs.

Dean ignored her comment, resisting the urge to tease her about getting lucky in the future. "Spread your legs a little wider, Darlin'," Dean commanded, needing to make sure he had plenty of room to keep from touching her inappropriately in the middle of a baby shower in the church fellowship hall.

She lightly moaned as she followed his instructions, causing Dean to wonder if she'd make similar sounds when he was balls-deep inside her. He also caught a distinct whiff of her arousal mixed with her lightly floral scent, and any hope he had for keeping his cock under control went flying out the window.

Fuck! She likes being told to spread her legs. I wonder what other commands she'd enjoy me giving her in the bedroom?

The more he thought about the sexual things they could explore, the faster his breathing got from how aroused he was getting. He tried to cover it up by moving his hands even faster, continuing to pass the roll of toilet paper back and forth between his hands with each pass around her body, so he didn't have to move his lower body.

While it didn't do much to decrease his body's response to his desire for her, the increased speed did help him finish making her toilet paper diaper much faster than anyone else in the room. He tucked the end under the other layers at her waist before gingerly standing once again.

"And we have our first winners," Hazel announced, walking over to hand them a gift card for a restaurant on the RiverWalk in San

Antonio. "I hope ya'll can find time this week to use that before you go back to work."

"Oh, yeah," Dean grinned, glad for another opportunity to make time with Allissa. "We can definitely work that in sometime in the next couple of days."

This'll make a nice first date for the two of us. If I can convince her to go off to San Antonio alone with me, that is. And hopefully, she won't be too upset if she realizes it's a date.

<div align="center">~~~</div>

Wednesday, May 29, 2019, Heart's Destiny, Texas

Allissa wasn't sure how she was going to get out of going to the steakhouse they'd won a gift card for at the baby shower the day before, but she had to come up with something that Dean would accept as a valid excuse. It wasn't her eating in public issues that caused her trepidation at the plans he wanted them to make for that evening. It was the fact that she'd be alone at dinner with Dean, which seemed way too much like a date, that made her want to skip it. *No matter how good the food is, I can't spend an evening alone with him. Even if he wasn't a player, way out of my league, and someone I should avoid dating, I don't want my first date ever to be because of winning a gift card at a baby shower.*

She hadn't been able to decline the card when they won it, or suggest they give it to Anthony and Kay to use for a night out without their kids, because she'd been caught up in a fog of lust from the game.

Why did we have to be paired up for that game? Allissa groaned as she laid in bed, remembering the strange feelings she'd gotten while wrapping Dean's groin and having her groin wrapped by Dean. *It wasn't a wedding event, so we should have been able to pick different partners. While that wouldn't have done anything to kill my attraction to him, at least I wouldn't have had to rush back to my room to change my panties right after the baby shower.*

Her desire for him hadn't caused any obvious physical responses while she was the one making the toilet paper diaper. At least, not until she accidentally felt the bulge between his legs with the back of her hand while bringing the toilet paper up from behind him and around his leg. Her nipples had instantly hardened in her padded bra from the feel of what he was packing. And the visual evidence of his reaction to her accidental touch didn't do a thing to help her shut down her attraction.

Thank God I thought to keep it loose as I wrapped the toilet paper around him, so he could have room to move while wrapping me, or he'd have surely ripped it from that massive erection. Although, maybe that would have been a good thing, since we couldn't have won the gift card if he'd torn his diaper before even getting to put mine on.

And what was up with how my panties flooded when he told me to spread my legs? I mean, they've gotten damp from being around him before, but that was next-level wetness, and not something even Dean has caused in the past. Is that normal? Or was it just because his commanding tone reminded me of the alpha hero in the book I read last night? Maybe I should ask Mom or one of the girls what it means.

Just as she was trying to decide if she was ready to be brave and talk to her friends about her lack of experience, or if she should just call her mother, who would have no problems whatsoever with answering any of her questions about sexual arousal, her phone rang on her nightstand. She quickly rolled over to see who it was, swiping to answer the call as soon as she saw it was Avington Security.

"Hello," she croaked out, her voice hoarse from sleep.

"Good morning, Allissa. It's Byron Avington. I wanted to call and update you on what I've found so far on your case."

"Oh, yes, good morning." Allissa sat up in bed, nervous about her mother's safety more than anything else.

"My team in Nevada caught the person dropping the packages at your mother's house. He's a local teenager that was paid to make the deliveries. He didn't know the person who hired him, but his description of the guy didn't match Ron Langston."

"Since you declined a team of bodyguards, I sent the team I planned to assign to you to locate Langston. From what we can tell, he's been in Los Angeles since leaving the GWA. That's not to say he didn't hire a middleman to set up these deliveries for him while staying in LA to maintain his alibi, though. At this point, we can't completely rule him out as a suspect, but we have no evidence against him, either."

Allissa wasn't sure what that meant for her mother's safety, or her own. "Okay, so does that mean we're safe for now? What else do we need to do?"

"Yes, you and your mother are both safe for now. The man who set up the deliveries for this week left them all with the kid, so we have all of them to check for prints and other evidence to keep trying to track down whoever is actually sending them. And according to the kid, he wasn't from Dead End or planning to stick around. My guess is he's already on his way to wherever he plans to send you something next. And he'll probably contract that out to another local kid, or maybe a delivery service, so he doesn't get close enough for you to recognize him."

"At this point, you just keep going about your life. I wouldn't recommend going anywhere by yourself, but the wrestlers you work with should be enough protection while you're in Heart's Destiny. So, just stick with your group of friends and keep an eye on your surroundings. Let me know if you or anyone in the GWA notices anyone suspicious hanging around."

"Bobby and the HDPD are keeping watch while you're in Heart's Destiny, and the only strangers who've been noticed in town are the people with the GWA there for the wedding this weekend. And I've also talked to Cage Dalton, who will be keeping watch once you go back on tour. Stick close to him and follow his directions. And make sure you go with a group of your friends when you go to the airport in San Antonio to fly out."

"Oh, okay," Allissa agreed, thinking Byron's recommendation to stick with a group of her friends to go into San Antonio would be the perfect way to get out of going to dinner with Dean that night. "I can do that."

"I'm gonna keep the teams I have in place with your mom and surveilling Langston, for now. And I have my cyber team getting ahead of the game by reaching out to the hotels and arenas where you're booked for the next month to make them aware to watch for any deliveries for you to, hopefully, catch him before he makes another move. I'll keep you in the loop on what the teams find, and we'll adjust accordingly so you don't have to worry."

"Thanks, Byron. I really appreciate all your help." Allissa felt a little choked up and still worried, no matter how much Byron Avington kept telling her not to worry.

"You're more than welcome." Byron's words sounded almost fatherly, making her wonder what it would have been like to grow up with a father like him. "You stay safe, and I'll call you again in a couple of days with the next update."

They said their "goodbyes" and Allissa decided it was time to get up for the day.

"I'll make sure Dean's downstairs for breakfast when I give Rick this update, and let him and the rest of the guys know I'm not supposed to leave Heart's Destiny unless I'm in a large group, per Byron's instructions. Surely, that will be a good enough excuse to get out of dinner with just Dean, at least until the stalker is caught."

Chapter Four

Saturday, June 1, 2019, Heart's Destiny, Texas

Dean couldn't believe how nervous his brother was as they finished putting on their tuxedos for his wedding in the groom's room at the church. James knew Randi loved him, so Dean didn't understand why he was so worried about her not showing up for the wedding. But even with both Dean and Anthony reassuring him that Randi would be there, James was still pacing a hole in the carpet from his nerves.

His third groomsman, Justin, being late, certainly wasn't helping James calm down. Dean was trying to think of something he could do to help his brother chill out, when Justin finally walked into the room. "What took you so long getting here?"

"Ran into Amy's dad on my way and had to introduce him to Mom and Dad, since he doesn't really know anyone else here today," Justin replied.

Dean hadn't met any of Amy's family that week, but he'd heard the stories about her mother and sister's antics when they were at Bobby and Brooklyn's wedding shower from the Burlesons. With Amy being his soon-to-be sister-in-law's best friend, he'd also heard the news about her long-lost father being found after she did a DNA test at Charlotte Burleson's birthday party. So, he had to wonder just how interesting her family was going to make the wedding reception, since Randi had invited all of them to attend.

"Thank fuck, you're here." James pulled Justin in for a back-slapping hug. "I was beginning to worry that Randi had gotten you and Amy to help her run away before the ceremony."

"Dude, I already told you. Randi's not running away." Anthony shook his head at James. "Because if she was, Kay and I would have been the ones she called to help her."

"Naw, if she didn't want to marry you, she'd have her dad help her get away from here," Dean chuckled, trying to lighten the mood.

"Fuck, don't even joke, Bro." James clearly didn't like Dean's version of humor as he glared at his twin. Then he turned to look at Anthony with panic in his eyes. "You don't think Charles is gonna try and talk her out of this, do you?"

"No, he's not." Anthony tried to reassure the anxious groom. "Besides, even if he does, Kay already has a plan to feign labor pains to distract him until the ceremony starts."

"Relax, man," Justin chuckled. "Randi's not gonna let her dad or anyone else keep her from walking down that aisle to become your wife."

"He's right," Dean agreed, slapping a hand on James's shoulder. "She'd have married you the last time we were in Vegas, if you'd have proposed a month earlier. So, I'm sure she'll practically run down the aisle to get hitched with you today."

"Yeah, I'm seriously regretting not suggesting that Vegas wedding back in January." James shook his head. "That would have been much less nerve-wracking than waiting for today."

Dean didn't bother reminding James of the fact that he'd still have had to go through with the wedding and reception today to appease their mother. All a Vegas wedding would have saved James was the anxiety he was suffering through at the moment from worrying about not getting to marry Randi.

Finally, Pastor Harrison knocked on the door to tell them it was time for the wedding to begin. They lined up right outside the room as the processional music changed to the song signaling it was time for the guys to enter the chapel. The pastor led the way through the side door of the chapel to the pulpit, followed first by James, then Anthony, then Dean, and finally Justin.

They took their places at the front of the church and turned with the rest of the guests to look at the back of the room to observe the ladies walking down the aisle. Dean knew from attending the rehearsal the day before that Amy would be the first to walk down the aisle, followed by Allissa, then Kay, then Tia and Maria acting as both flower girls and ring bearers, before Randi made her grand entrance on her father's arm.

But he wasn't prepared for the way he would feel when he saw Allissa walk through the doorway in her red, satin bridesmaid's dress. She took his breath away, and made him long for the day she'd walk down that same aisle toward him in a white dress for their wedding.

Damn, Darlin', I can't wait to officially be your man. Dean sighed, knowing he'd pretty much considered himself taken by Allissa from the first moment he laid eyes on her, and wishing he had the reassurance that she felt the same.

When their eyes locked on one another as she walked up the aisle, he hoped she felt comforted by the love he knew was shining in his for her. Allissa gave him a confused look as she got to the end of the aisle before turning to take her place on the other side of the pulpit. Dean just smiled at her, unable to do anything other than projecting his undying love in his expression.

He couldn't take his eyes off her as the rest of the wedding party walked up the aisle. While Dean knew the bride was supposed to be the center of attention on her wedding day, he couldn't bring himself to turn his gaze away from Allissa to even see what his brother's bride was wearing for the wedding.

"Dearly beloved," Pastor Harrison began the ceremony. "We're gathered here today to join James Stark Hunter and Randi Mae Lee in holy matrimony."

Damn! I can't believe James let Pastor Harrison announce his middle name to the world! His shock at the mention of the middle name he knew his brother hated was the only thing that got him to turn his eyes away from Allissa. He realized he wasn't the only one to be surprised by the declaration as the hushed whispers of the congregation drowned out the words of the preacher and Randi's father as they continued with the ceremony.

Yeah, the guys are gonna rib him like crazy when he gets back from his honeymoon. Hell, what am I thinking? They won't wait that long. They'll start ribbing him as soon as he walks into the reception.

As the murmurs died down, Pastor Harrison continued to speak about love and the sanctity of marriage. Dean's eyes drifted back to Allissa as the preacher explained the declaration of intent the same way he had at Anthony and Kay's wedding.

As James and Randi went through the different parts of their ceremony, Dean imagined his and Allissa's wedding, locking eyes with her once more. He couldn't help but wonder what she was thinking about as he pictured repeating their own vows of love to one another.

Fuck! I hope it doesn't scare her off if the way I'm acting today makes her realize I want all this with her. Dean barely stopped himself from mouthing "I do" to Allissa at the same time his brother said those two little words to Randi, only stopping himself as her eyes widened when he started to open his mouth.

Damn, I need to remember to back off and take things slow. We have to deal with her stalker situation before I can tackle the other issues making her skittish about even dating me. I just hope it doesn't take too long.

Dean spent the rest of the ceremony lost in thought about how to go about earning her affection after her stalker was caught. He finally came back to the moment when Pastor Harrison declared, "I now pronounce you husband and wife. James, you may kiss your bride."

With his eyes still glued on Allissa, he only knew his brother barely kept the kiss PG by the slight blush on Allissa's face at witnessing it. "Hey, James, ya might wanna wait 'til ya'll get out of the church before ya start the honeymoon," he quipped to get his brother to tone it down while in church in front of all their family and friends. He was too eager to get to walk down the aisle with Allissa on his arm to wait for his brother to come back to his senses while kissing his bride.

After a few giggles around the room, James finally straightened, releasing Randi from the inappropriate lip lock.

"I present to you, James and Randi Hunter," the preacher announced as they turned and started walking back down the aisle together.

Tia and Maria quickly followed, along with Anthony and Kay. Dean somehow managed to face forward as he offered his arm to Allissa and walked down the aisle with her.

They stopped in the vestibule, so Kathy Harrison could position them in a receiving line and all the guests could leave the chapel to head to the reception. As their duties at the church were winding down, Philippe snapped picture after picture before ushering the ladies away to the restroom. "Take a moment to dry your tears and freshen your faces, so we can get the rest of these gorgeous photos."

Dean watched as the ladies walked away, specifically focusing on how fantastic Allissa looked in her long, red dress. As soon as they were out of sight, he turned and looked at the other men still standing in the vestibule, waiting on the women to return for the rest of the pictures.

"Dude, you look as nervous as James did before the wedding." Dean slapped a hand on Justin's shoulder.

"No, not nervous." Justin shook his head and took on a thoughtful expression. "Excited maybe? Ready to pop the question, and afraid I won't be able to make myself wait until after the reception to do it. But definitely not nervous."

"Seriously? You want to propose to Amy at our reception?" James grinned at Justin. Dean could tell his brother liked that idea.

"I almost dropped to one knee when Amy got to the end of the aisle before your wedding even started," Justin chuckled. "But I'm trying my best to hold back, so I don't steal the spotlight on your special day."

"Are you kidding? Randi would love it if her best friend got engaged at our wedding." James's smile widened. "And if you're really ready to do it, I say we rig the bouquet and garter toss like Anthony and Kay did. So you can ask her in the middle of the reception."

"You wouldn't mind?" Justin looked at James quizzically, appearing skeptical of the possibility.

"I would consider it a wedding present to be able to include my bride in the plan." James grinned and chuckled.

"Do you have a ring yet?" Anthony asked Justin.

"Yeah." Justin pulled the box from his coat pocket. "Her dad gave me his mother's ring to use so he could pass it down to Amy."

The guys huddled around to look at the ring for only a moment before Justin had to hide it in his pocket again because the women were coming back from freshening up to take more pictures. Dean was happy for his friend, but slightly jealous that he and Allissa weren't as far along in their relationship as Justin and Amy.

"What are you guys whispering about?" Randi raised an eyebrow at James as the ladies joined them.

Leah Mae Wright

"Just telling them about the plans I have for our honeymoon, Angel," James lied, pulling Randi into his arms.

Before Randi could call James out on his lie, Philippe stepped in to direct them where to stand and how to pose for another round of pictures. Dean enjoyed every moment of having Allissa on his arm as they took several shots at the church. And he really enjoyed the few minutes he had Allissa alone as they drove over to the bed and breakfast, even though their conversation was focused on the beauty of the wedding. *And I bet our wedding will be even more beautiful, Darlin'.*

~~~

Since Allissa hadn't ever attended a wedding reception before, she had to follow Dean's lead when they arrived at the ballroom to know where she was supposed to go and what she was supposed to do as a member of the bridal party. She hadn't realized that all that dance practice all week was for them to dance their way into the ballroom, but she soon figured it out when one of the local ladies stopped them from just walking into the ballroom and lined them up to make their entrance.

As Justin and Amy started off the entrances, Rick's voice boomed out, introducing them as if they were making a ring entrance at one of the GWA shows. "First up into the ballroom, we have the scientific tag team of Justin Burleson and Amy Lawton!"

"Oh, I didn't realize Rick was planning to do this again." Kay looked up at Anthony with a hint of sadness on her face. "I hope the girls aren't disappointed to not be included this time."

"Naw, I'm sure they'd much rather be with Antonio to keep him from being overwhelmed by his first experience with the spectacle that is a GWA wedding," Anthony reassured his wife.

Allissa still couldn't believe that in the month they'd been off the tour to prepare for the birth of their baby, Anthony and Kay had adopted another little boy. But she loved seeing their family grow to include the shy child, even if he wasn't quite ready to participate in his new aunt's wedding and the other events of the week that drew a crowd.
~~~

"We're next, Darlin'." Dean grinned at her as he took her hand in his and spun her into his arms to start their two-step into the ballroom.

Allissa tried to focus on the dance steps that she'd finally managed to get right on the last day of their practice sessions the day before, but Rick's announcement of their entrance stole her focus.

"Next into the ballroom, we have the future GWA Women's Champion, Allissa Walters. Following her like a lost puppy, and hoping she'll one day deem him worthy of helping lace her wrestling boots is Dean Hunter, brother of the groom."

"Thanks, Boss," Dean hollered at Rick as Allissa laughed. "I appreciate the way you always put me over in your introductions!"

She wasn't sure how they managed to stay on beat with the music as they made their way to the table, where Justin and Amy were already sitting on the opposite side of the ballroom from the rest of the guests.

"Next into the ballroom, we have the couple trying to single-handedly double the population of Heart's Destiny, Texas, Anthony and Kay Burleson. While we all know how much you both love to fly, please keep the pregnant lady's feet firmly on the ground this time. We don't need to rush that population increase with early labor in the middle of the reception."

"What?" Allissa was confused by Rick's strange request at the end of Anthony and Kay's introduction.

"They did the lift from *Dirty Dancing* during the entrance at their wedding reception," Dean explained as they watched Anthony and Kay dance their way up to the table.

"And without further ado, please welcome the Intergender Tag-Team Champions of the Galaxy, Mr. and Mrs. James S. Hunter. Sorry, James, I'm not risking a lawsuit from Marvel for announcing you with your full name."

"Damn, I didn't even think about the *Iron Man* references I coulda been ribbing him with all these years." Dean dramatically slapped his head. "All this time, I've just been commiserating with him about our fanatical parents giving us bad middle names."

Once again, Allissa was confused. "I don't get it," Allissa admitted as Anthony and Justin laughed at Dean's overdramatization. While she recognized James's middle name of Stark was also the last name used by Iron Man while not in the super suit, she didn't understand why Dean referred to it as a bad middle name. "What's wrong with your middle names?"

"They're named after James Dean, the actor," Anthony chuckled. "I knew James's middle name came from the last name of his character in a movie, but I couldn't remember what it was to pick on him with Tony Stark references."

"And?" Allissa shrugged one shoulder, not understanding what was so bad about the middle name Stark. She kinda thought it was a cool name, but then again, she was a fan of the comic book movies to like that reference without knowing the connection to James Dean.

"Our parents went to a classic movie showing of *Rebel Without A Cause* for their first date," Dean explained with a groan. "They joke around saying James Dean introduced them anytime anyone asks about how they met, even though they actually met at the Independence Day picnic in town. Since they say they fell in love watching that movie on their first date, they planned to name their son James Dean Hunter. Then they found out they were having twins and split the name for our first names. James's middle name was the last name of the main character in *Rebel*, and I got stuck with the actor's real middle name."

"I told ya he'd bitch about our middle names," James pointed out to Randi as they took their seats. "Though I don't know why he's complaining, since Byron is by far the better option."

Dean Byron Hunter. Yeah, I don't know why he doesn't like his name. It's way better than having a misspelled name like mine.

"Oh, I agree I got the better name," Dean acknowledged, nodding at his brother. "I just wish Mom and Dad would have looked up the meanings of our names before we were born. While the story of why they picked our names is kinda cool, I doubt they would have stuck with them if they'd realized what they mean."

"You've looked up what our names mean?" James looked at Dean in surprise.

"Yeah. Dean means 'from the valley' and Byron means 'from the barns,' so my name basically means I'm a hunter from the barn in the valley."

"You should point that out next time you leave the door open, and Ma asks if you were born in a barn," James chuckled.

"Yeah, maybe," Dean laughed with his brother.

"So what do James's names mean?" Randi questioned with a mischievous grin.

"James means 'supplanter' and Stark means 'firm or unyielding'," Dean informed them. "Combined with the Hunter last name, it makes him sound like a poacher who won't quit."

"Yeah, I'm gonna stick to saying it's an *Iron Man* reference," Randi chortled.

"We should probably also make sure Dad doesn't find out what James's name means," Kay giggled.

"Oh, no, now that I've got a ring on her finger and she has my last name, it's too late for him to come between us," James bellowed. "And since that's pretty much what he thought of me from day one, I'm proudly owning that shit now."

"All this talk about name meanings makes me want to look up all our names to see what they mean," Amy chimed in to change the direction of the conversation away from James's father-in-law issues.

"Oh, yeah," Kay agreed, pulling her phone out of Anthony's jacket pocket. "Me, too."

Allissa focused on eating the meal that was placed in front of her as the discussion at the table carried on with wonderful meanings for the rest of their names. Well, except Randi's, which came up as the diminutive form of Miranda or Randall, and her middle name of Mae was a reference to the month of May.

"Allissa, how do you spell your name? There's three different versions on here and they all have different meanings."

"A-l-l-i-s-s-a, but you won't find it on there." Allissa shook her head at Kay, who was looking up the names on her phone. "My mom misspelled it on my birth certificate, but claims she did it on purpose so I wouldn't have one of the three more common versions. Unfortunately, all she really accomplished with the strange spelling was to make it difficult for me to learn to spell my name in school because my teachers kept trying to correct it to one of the more common spellings."

"Oh, well, okay," Kay sputtered before coming up with another option to include Allissa. "What's your middle name then?"

"Victoria," Allissa replied.

"Is that why you use Victoria for your ring name?" Dean arched an eyebrow at her.

Allissa nodded at Dean as Kay filled them in on the meaning of her middle name.

"Oh, you definitely got the most appropriate middle name," Kay giggled. "Victoria means 'winner or conqueror,' which seems like the perfect name for a professional wrestler."

Allissa had to laugh at the irony of how she'd decided on her ring name because of not liking any of the other options she'd been pitched when she first started training with VPW. Little did she know at the time that the meaning behind her middle name would be so appropriate for her wrestling gimmick.

Their conversation quickly died down as Randi's father started off the speeches for the evening. When he handed off the microphone to Anthony to give the next speech, he whispered just loud enough that the wedding party could hear him. "Ya'll might want to keep the speeches short, so we can get through everything the kids want to be a part of before Antonio reaches his limit with being amongst the crowd."

"Definitely," Anthony agreed before he and Kay combined their congratulatory speeches.

Dean and Allissa followed the other couple's lead, as did Justin and Amy, so it didn't take long at all before they were going through the special dances. Allissa and Dean only had to participate in the last of those, which she was grateful for, since it would be the last time this week she had to dance with Dean.

Thank you, Randi, for picking bridesmaid dresses that allow for a padded, strapless bra, Allissa mentally thanked her friend as her nipples pebbled once again at being in Dean's arms. *I'd have never survived the embarrassment of him noticing my response to him if she'd gone with the backless dresses she was originally looking at.*

As soon as the song was over, Allissa started walking back to her seat, needing a reprieve from listening to Dean's deep voice as he serenaded her during their time on the dance floor. She didn't get far when the emcee announced it was time for the bouquet toss.

"Oh, no, if I have to go, so do you," Amy insisted, grabbing her hand, and pulling her away from the head table to join the other single ladies gathering on the dance floor.

"Fine," Allissa agreed before turning to point at Randi as she walked backward toward the crowd. "Don't you dare get any ideas about throwing that thing at me, Leigh, or I'll get even next time we're in the ring."

"I wouldn't dream of it," Randi laughed, holding her hands up in surrender.

Once they were standing amongst the crowd, Randi looked around as if she was trying to decide whom to aim for before she turned and fast-pitched the bouquet straight at Amy. Amy had no choice but to catch it before it smacked her in the face.

Guess Amy should have also warned her not to target her.

"Jeez, Randi," Kay shouted while laughing. "I wasn't nearly that blatant when I threw my bouquet to you. Or as deadly with the toss."

"Sorry, Ames, didn't mean to almost poke your eye out with the roses," Randi yelled across the room, laughing with her sister.

"I'm just glad you had the foresight to have the thorns removed," Amy hollered back, laughing along with the rest of the people in the room.

"And now it's time for the single gentlemen to line up for the garter toss," the emcee announced.

Allissa went back to her seat, passing between Dean and Justin as they joined the single men on the dance floor.

Randi sat down in a chair that Allissa hadn't seen placed in the center of the dance floor as James got down on his knees at her feet. James lifted the hem of Randi's dress and bent even further, looking as if he was going to dip his head under her wedding gown.

"Remember there are children present!" Anthony shouted from his seat at the head table.

"Guess that means I have to use my hands and not my teeth to remove the garter," James quipped, wagging his eyebrows up at his bride.

"Please don't slobber on it before you toss it at us, Bro," Dean yelled from his place in the middle of the crowd of men, inciting a round of laughter throughout the room.

"For real," Crockett, the wrestler with a lumberjack gimmick, hollered. "Randi's the only one who wants your bodily fluids flying at her."

"Dude, I don't want him to spit on me either!" Randi squealed over the roar of laughter.

"I don't think that's what he meant, Angel." James chuckled as he slid his hands up under Randi's dress. "But I promise I won't be sharing any bodily fluids, even the ones I know you do want shooting at you, while we're here in front of an audience."

Randi's face turned beet red, as Allissa realized what James was referring to. *Wonder what sexy romance novel scenes they're gonna emulate later tonight?*

"Oh" was all Randi said before covering her face with her hands and folding down to touch her forehead to the top of James's head.

I'll have to ask her later. Along with a few questions I have about whether those scenes really feel as amazing as they're described in books. Or if I'm right in thinking they sound like more of a mess than they're worth.

James pulled his hands out from under Randi's dress, holding the garter in one and reaching up to move her hands away from her face with the other. He whispered something unintelligible before pressing his lips to hers briefly.

"Now, let's get this show on the road!" James stood up and looked around the room. "I'm ready to get started on our honeymoon!"

Without any warning, James wrapped the garter around his fingers as if they were a slingshot, aimed directly at Justin, and let it fly. Justin couldn't have missed catching the garter if he'd tried. Not that he would have, since he and Amy were already a couple.

Allissa had to smile at how obvious Randi and James were in picking the couple to catch the bouquet and garter.

"Fabulous! Time for the bouquet and garter photo!" The flamboyant photographer, Philippe, clapped his hands to get their attention before pointing at Justin and Amy to direct them to the center of the dance floor, where the chair was now sitting empty. "Miss Amy, if you would please have a seat."

"Oh, I thought Justin was supposed to sit first with me on his lap, like at Kay and Anthony's wedding." Amy looked confused at the photographer's instructions.

"Oh, but that pose is so last year." Philippe waved his hand around, dismissing her comment. "The trend now is for him to make it look like he's going to put the garter on you, as if you're getting ready for your own wedding."

"Oh, okay." Amy still looked slightly confused as she sat down in the chair for Philippe to arrange the bouquet in her lap the way he wanted it for the pictures.

When he stepped back, Justin dropped down on one knee in front of her. Instead of presenting her with the garter and pretending to put it on her as Philippe directed him, Justin put the garter in his pocket. When he pulled his hand back out, he was holding a small box instead. He took her left hand in his, opening the box with his right hand before presenting it to her.

"That's not a garter!" Amy pointed out the obvious before Justin could utter the first word of what Allissa assumed was going to be a proposal.

"No, it's not," Justin chuckled. "But I still hope you'll let me put it on you tonight."

Amy opened her mouth as if to speak, but quickly closed it and nodded at Justin to continue.

"Amy Edwina Lawton, I fell head over heels in love with you the first moment I saw you back in November. Getting to know you as a friend and coworker just made me fall deeper and deeper in love with you. Dating you these past few months has only shown me that I was right to give you my heart from day one. I know this is sooner than you expected, and I'm willing to wait through a long engagement if that's what you need. But I can't wait a moment longer to call you my fiancée. Please, Sweetheart, will you marry me?"

"Yes!" Amy shouted, dropping the bouquet on the floor as she threw her arms around Justin's neck.

Allissa looked down at the table in front of her, not wanting to broadcast her inexperience to the world by blushing at witnessing their kiss, the same way she had when James kissed Randi at the end of their wedding ceremony earlier.

Shouts of "congratulations" spread around the room, alerting Allissa that it was safe to look back up at the happy, newly engaged couple. She saw Justin place Amy back down on her feet before taking the ring from the box.

"How did you get it to fit?" Amy asked as Justin slid the ring on her finger.

"That was actually the work of your dad and Ashlyn," Justin confessed.

"Yeah, Dad called me and asked our ring size, since you wouldn't tell Justin." Amy's sister, Ashlyn, whom Allissa had met earlier that day, pushed between Justin and Amy to hug her sister.

"It's not that I wouldn't tell him," Amy protested while hugging Ashlyn. "I just don't know it and haven't had the chance to visit a jewelry store to have my finger sized."

As more people crowded around Justin and Amy to offer their congratulations, Allissa sat there feeling awkward for not knowing how to respond to the situation. She'd just met the couple a week before, so she didn't want to intrude on their time with their close family and friends to offer her congratulations. But she also felt rude for not joining the other members of the wedding party who were among the revelers.

Luckily, it was only a few short moments before the crowd dispersed from the dance floor and most of the wedding party rejoined her at the head table. James and Randi walked over to the table on the other side of the band to cut the cake.

Allissa laughed along with the rest of the room as her friends smeared cake across one another's faces. But with Dean back by her side, her heart wasn't in the laughter. She'd been fighting her attraction to him all evening, and the feelings only got more intense the more she tried to fight them.

When she'd first seen him in his tux as she'd stepped into the church to walk down the aisle, she'd been blown over by how gorgeous he was in the all-black attire. Oh, she'd thought he was hot from her first glimpse of him in gym shorts. And he was equally attractive in his ring attire and the business casual slacks and button-downs he wore as they traveled with the GWA. Seeing him in casual wear of cargo shorts and t-shirts this week was equally enticing.

But there was something about Dean in the tuxedo that did something to Allissa's insides that even the suits he'd worn in the winter hadn't caused. The flutters in her belly were more intense than normal and every part of her was turned on in ways she'd never even imagined possible. The way he'd looked at her during the ceremony in that tux had caused her to start picturing what it would be like if she married him.

And I couldn't even smell him during the ceremony. Now that they were seated side by side, she couldn't escape the cloud of pheromones that he had to have mixed with his cologne to amp up her libido so much. All through the reception, his masculine, woodsy, leather scent kept messing with her senses, making her want to find the same kind of loving relationship with him that Randi had with his twin.

But there's no way that'll ever happen, so I've gotta quit dreaming about it. Hopefully, now that this week of forced proximity is almost over, I can go back to my normal routine of avoiding him as much as possible on tour. And maybe, one day, this irrational attraction I feel to him will eventually go away.

Chapter Five

Monday, June 3, 2019, 9 a.m., Flying out of San Antonio, Texas

As he boarded the company plane to fly out of San Antonio on Monday morning, Dean scoped out the people already on board so he could grab a seat in the same quad as Cage Dalton. After the updates Allissa got from Byron Avington the previous week and shared with the GWA crew in attendance for the wedding events, he knew Cage would be the person he needed to get in good with to be able to help protect Allissa while they were on tour. Though he still didn't think he'd have any better luck getting Cage to agree that she'd be safe alone with him for a date than he had when dealing with Byron Avington.

I still can't believe the Burlesons have a cousin who shares my middle name and runs a security company. Talk about a sign from God that he was the right person to trust with Allissa's safety.

Dean hadn't told anyone how the shared name had helped ease his worry about hiring an outside security company to look into her stalker situation. He didn't want to give the guys any more fodder for ribbing him, especially about the middle name he disliked.

He also hadn't been completely honest with everyone about why he disliked the name when they discussed it at the wedding reception. But since he hadn't let anyone outside of his immediate family know about his dyslexia, he couldn't exactly tell them that he hated the name because it was the first word he kept reversing letters in to make his diagnosis obvious.

As a child, he hadn't known exactly what was wrong that caused him to keep trying to write the name as Bryon instead of Byron. He'd just stopped writing the name altogether to fix the problem. Not that it really helped when he kept bombing his spelling tests.

His parents had tackled the problem early, as soon as his teachers pointed it out. He had some extra tutoring sessions and was able to eke out decent grades in school, but he was still a slow reader and scribbled his signature when he gave autographs, so nobody would notice if he transposed a couple of letters.

He'd actually done well in college, thanks to being able to use a word processing program with spellcheck for all his written assignments. But knowing that some people already saw him as a dumb jock for working as a professional wrestler, he wasn't about to publicly admit to a learning disability. He also had a degree in finance, and knew he needed to maintain his image as competent and intelligent to be able to put it to good use once he retired from the ring.

Not that he had to find another job if he were suddenly injured and couldn't continue wrestling sooner than he planned to retire. He'd already used his degree to invest his income and was financially set for life. But he couldn't imagine being very happy if he wasn't getting out of the house and working in some capacity. So he had plans in place to open his own investment firm, once he retired from wrestling, and he couldn't do that if his potential clients thought less of him for having a learning disability like dyslexia. *It doesn't seem to affect the way I see numbers the way it does words, so it shouldn't matter.* Dean unconsciously scowled at the thought.

"Is that your scare-off-the-stalker face?" Cage nodded at Dean when he took the seat in front of him.

"No," Dean chuckled, glad to change gears in his head, even if it was to Allissa's stalker. "This is my thinking-about-nothing-important face. My scare-off-the-stalker face is a lot meaner."

"Good to know," Cage chuckled as Liam and Dion joined them in the aisle seats in their quad. "I take it you guys are all here to offer your services guarding Allissa?"

"No, Deano is the only one putting in for a close-cover bodyguard job," Liam quipped, slugging Dean in the shoulder. "We just wanna know what to watch out for whenever we're all out in public together."

"At this point, there's not really any specific threat for any of us to look out for," Cage huffed. "From what I've learned so far, there aren't any notes with the gifts to even indicate that this guy is anything more than the typical appreciative fan sending her presents. Granted, they're creepy presents, but other than the black roses, nothing that could be construed as sinister."

"Yeah, our typical appreciative fans come up and ask for autographs and pictures," Dean disagreed, shaking his head. "They don't hire someone else to deliver presents, so we don't know who they're from."

"True," Cage conceded, holding up his hands in surrender. "But it's because he's not showing his face anywhere near the company that we're less concerned about him actually trying to hurt her. At this point, all we can do is keep an eye out for anything unusual going on, either package deliveries or someone trying to get close to one of the crew, and let the Avington Security teams do all the leg work with checking out the main suspects and following the leads to figure out what's really going on."

Dean wasn't completely convinced that was all they could do, but he bit back his frustration at not being able to do more to protect Allissa. None of this was Cage's fault, so he didn't deserve to be on the receiving end of Dean's anger at the situation.

"So, we're just supposed to keep watch for anything out of the ordinary and make sure nobody but Dean gets close to Allissa?" Liam grinned mischievously at Cage.

"Something like that," Cage chuckled, shaking his head from knowing how badly Dean had bombed every time he tried to get close to Allissa in the past. "But seriously, guys, keep an eye out for all the ladies. Allissa's the only one who's gotten black roses, but all the women have gotten lingerie and other gifts from fans in the past. So we constantly have to be vigilant in case the gifts go past creepy into dangerous territory."

"Yeah, we will," Dean agreed, knowing the rest of the roster would gladly step up to protect every member of their GWA family.

And I'll make sure everyone else knows to make sure none of the women and children ever go off somewhere alone, Dean thought as they continued chit-chatting on the flight. *Though, I should probably wait until we're all in the men's locker room before the show tonight to mention it, so none of the ladies get upset about us planning to walk them to and from their hotel rooms from now on.*

It wasn't just his inner caveman coming out to make him want to protect Allissa. He wanted to make his family proud by being the gentleman they raised him to be, and that meant protecting all the women and children around him, not just the woman he wanted to be his for the rest of his life, regardless of whether they were capable of defending themselves.

Yeah, I know they're also professional wrestlers and just as capable of defending themselves in a fight as any of us guys. But Meemaw would tan my hide if I didn't behave like a gentleman and step in to defend a lady. And I'm much more afraid of Meemaw bein' mad at me than Allissa or any of the other women who work with the GWA bein' irritated by us guys walking 'em to their rooms or steppin' between them and anyone who might threaten their safety.

~~~

Monday, June 3, 2019, 10 p.m., Jackson, Mississippi

Allissa was so glad to feel like she was getting back to normal after wrestling on the first show after the Memorial Day break. She'd managed to convince Cage that she was just as safe riding in a car with her girlfriends and caravanning to the hotel with the rest of the guys as she would be actually riding with a couple of the guys, so she felt like she had the space she needed between her and Dean. While she knew he was still keeping her in his line of sight as they made their way back to the hotel after the show, at least with the guys following her and the Precious Stones, he wasn't all up in her space like he'd been the previous week while they were paired together for James and Randi's wedding events.

"Ms. Walters," the front desk clerk flagged her down as they made their way toward the elevators. "I have something for you."

Allissa had a sinking feeling that the clerk wasn't going to give her the laundry she'd dropped off that morning when she'd checked in. *I guess the vacation from having to see the stuff from my stalker is over.*

She stopped in her tracks and changed direction, walking to the front desk instead of the elevators. Emerald and Amethyst surprised her by flanking her as she went. "You guys can go on to your room.
~~~

I'm just gonna call Cage to come get whatever this is and send it to the security company."

"Oh no," Emerald protested, shaking her head. "If this guy's gonna blow one of us up, he's gonna blow all of us up."

"I highly doubt he's sending me a bomb," Allissa chuckled wryly, not wanting to even let herself think of the possibility of something deadly being in one of the packages.

"Hey, you never know," Emerald shrugged. "It could be just like that show last week when the unsub was sending bombs to kill his enemies."

"I think she's been streaming too much *FBI* this last week." Amethyst pointed at Emerald with her thumb. "Those shows just feed her warped sense of humor that none of us appreciate."

Allissa tuned out her friends' conversation about laughing instead of crying and how realistic TV crime dramas could be as she took the small box from the front desk clerk. She thanked the woman with as much of a smile as she could muster before turning and running into a wall of muscle.

"You alright, Darlin'?" Dean gripped her shoulders, keeping her from stepping back too far from him.

"I'm fine," Allissa sighed, knowing she wasn't going to like whatever Dean had to say about the box in her hand. "Just ready to go to my room and call Cage, so he can handle this."

She held the box up between them to make her point. "Hopefully, it won't take him too long to come and get it, so I can get some rest to look my best for TV tomorrow in Tupelo."

"If you want, I'll take it to Cage for you," he offered, surprising her that he wasn't insisting on taking care of the package himself.

"Oh, damn, you know it's true love when he offers to take a bomb for you," Emerald quipped, earning eye rolls from everyone around her.

"It's too light to be a bomb." Allissa shook her head at her friend as they all started making their way to the elevators once more. Looking down at the size and shape of the box that was wrapped in plain brown paper, she thought it looked about the same size as a Barbie doll box. Realizing that they were five weeks out from the last pay-per-view, she thought she had an idea of what was in the box. "I bet it's another doll dressed in an outfit similar to my ring attire."

"Another doll?" Dean arched an eyebrow at her as they got on the elevator, nodding his head down at the package in her hand. "You've gotten one of these before?"

"I've gotten three of these before," Allissa confirmed with a half-shrug. "Well, if it's what I think it is, anyway. I know the timing is right since the **No Remorse** pay-per-view, but I don't remember how the others were packaged to say for sure."

When they got to the first floor of rooms that were booked for the GWA crew, the Precious Stones and Bennington brothers got off the elevator, leaving only Allissa and Dean to go up to the next floor. She wasn't surprised when he followed her all the way to her room, just as he'd started doing every night they were in Heart's Destiny.

"So, you want me to take that to Cage or wait here with you for him to come and get it?"

Allissa wasn't sure how to respond, fumbling with her keycard as she tried to open her door. *Oh, gawd! What's he going to want to do in my room alone while we're waiting on Cage? And am I strong enough to resist whatever he suggests?*

Seeing how flustered she was, Dean deftly took the card from her hand and opened her door. He ushered her into the room, dropping his gear bag by the door before taking her gear bag off her shoulder and the package out of her hand to set them on a table.

"Relax, Darlin'," Dean instructed, turning her toward the bed, but not pushing for her to actually move in that direction. "I'm gonna call Cage and let him tell us what we should do next. But you need to take a few deep breaths and not let this stress you out."

Allissa wasn't sure what he thought caused her to freak out and freeze up, but she was glad he didn't seem to realize it was him being in her hotel room alone with her. She took a couple of deep breaths before she walked over to the bed and sat down.

Stop! Stop! Stop! Allissa mentally told herself to calm down while Dean pulled out his phone and placed the call. *I can't freak out about being alone in what's essentially my bedroom for the night with the only man I've ever been attracted to. He's not here to kiss me, or teach me about the pleasurable aspects of sex. He's here to make sure I'm safe from the stalker sending me weird gifts.*

"Hey, Cage. Allissa got another package tonight and is having a bit of a panic attack about it. Can you come to her room to get it and send it on to Avington?"

A panic attack? Is that what that was? Allissa wondered as Dean gave Cage her room number and asked if the athletic trainer on staff was at the hotel yet. *Oh, geez, no! I don't need anyone else seeing me freaking out and possibly realizing it's not because of the stalker.*

"You don't need to call Doc," Allissa protested as Dean hung up the call with Cage. "I'm fine, just needed a minute to process everything."

"You sure, Darlin'?" Dean arched an eyebrow at Allissa, just as there was a knock at her hotel room door.

"Yeah, I'm sure." Allissa nodded and started to stand to answer the door, thinking Cage was awfully fast at getting there from his room.

"You sit back down," Dean ordered, waving her back as he walked to the door. Without even thinking about it, Allissa sat back down on the foot of the bed, feeling all her erogenous zones light up with excitement at Dean giving her instructions.

I should really stop reading those BDSM romance novels. They've apparently seeped into my brain to somehow make me respond to the dominant tone of Dean's voice.

He looked through the peephole before opening it to let Cage in the room. "Damn, dude, that was faster than I expected."

"My room's just down the hall." Cage motioned over his shoulder with his thumb, presumably in the direction of his room from hers. He then walked over and squatted down beside Allissa, getting to her eye level before starting to ask her about the package. "Where's the package? And what is it about this one that has you freaked out?"

"I'm not freaked out about the package," Allissa confessed, inwardly cringing at almost giving away her real reason for freezing up a moment before. "I'm just tired and felt a little overwhelmed by realizing just how long I've been getting these same packages. But I'm fine now, and it's on the table behind you."

"You've been getting these longer than the last couple of months that you told Avington?" Cage stood back up and turned around to examine the box.

"Maybe?" Allissa shrugged, relaxing a little now that she wasn't alone with Dean and could focus on the stalker issue, instead of the way Dean taking charge had just turned her on. "I haven't opened it to verify, but if it's a doll in my ring attire from the *No Remorse* pay-per-view, then I've been getting them since our first day back from Thanksgiving break."

Cage didn't respond. Instead, he pulled out his phone and dialed a number, placing it on speaker and setting it on the table beside the box.

"Avington Security," Byron's voice bellowed from the phone when he answered the call.

"Hey, Byron," Cage spoke as he pulled a pair of rubber gloves from his pocket and put them on before picking up the box. "It's Cage Dalton, and I have you on speaker. I'm here in Allissa's room with her and Dean Hunter. She got another package tonight that triggered her to remember getting similar packages as far back as November."

"And you think these are from the stalker?" Allissa wasn't sure if Byron was asking her, or Cage, so she kept her mouth shut to allow the security experts to talk until they specifically directed their questions to her.

"Well, it's wrapped in brown paper and has her name written in the same block script as the ones sent to her mom's place last week," Cage explained, nodding even though Byron couldn't see him through the phone.

"Okay…" Byron drew the word out to multiple syllables before clearly addressing his next question to her. "Allissa, what is it about this box that makes you think these started coming back in November?"

"I don't remember how the others were packaged, but the box is about the same size as a Barbie doll box," Allissa explained. "And I've gotten a doll dressed in my ring attire approximately five weeks after every pay-per-view I've worked, since I started with the GWA back in October. In November, it was the black catsuit I wore at the *Halloween Horror* pay-per-view. Then in January, it was the red Mrs. Claus outfit I wore at the *Christmas Chaos* pay-per-view. In March it was the pink outfit I wore on the *Saint Valentine's Day Massacre* pay-per-view. So, I'm guessing this will be the lavender outfit I wore at the *No Remorse* pay-per-view at the end of April. I can't say for sure that they're from the stalker, but they are the only things I got at the hotels before we got back from the European tour in March."

"Yeah, I agree that it sounds like the same person sending them. Cage, carefully open the package to preserve the paper and any fingerprints on the tape, and let's see if we need to look a little farther back for Allissa's stalker," Byron instructed.

Cage pulled out a pocket-knife and sliced through the paper along the side of the box, avoiding the seams where it was taped down. He then cut the paper up and over the top of the box at both ends before slicing along the other side of the box, essentially cutting out a rectangle to be able to slip the two pieces of paper off the box without tearing it or cutting the tape.

Allissa stood and looked around Cage as he set the paper aside and opened the box. "Yes, that's what I wore at the *No Remorse* pay-per-view," she confirmed as soon as the contents were revealed. "So, this person has definitely been sending me gifts since my first pay-per-view appearance with the GWA in October."

"Okay, that still doesn't rule out Ron Langston, but it does seem to rule out anyone who started working with the company this year." She heard the sound of typing in the background from Byron's end of the call, and assumed he was making notes in her file for the cyber team he had working on the case. "That'll save a little bit of work for my guys doing background checks on all the new hires Rick sent us to check into. Oh, one more question, Allissa. When and where did this package show up?"

"It was waiting at the front desk of the hotel when I got back after the show tonight," she replied.

"Damn, I was afraid of that," Byron grumbled. "They should have notified us when it was dropped off, so you wouldn't have to deal with it tonight. I'm gonna hafta make sure the guys are making it clear to every hotel manager they're talking to that they are to call us immediately when one arrives."

"I can have Rick send a statement to all the hotels we use to let them know we're dealing with a stalker issue to maybe scare them into being a little more diligent," Cage suggested.

"Maybe add Emerald's bomb theory to that statement if ya wanna really scare 'em," Dean quipped with a grin.

"Emerald's bomb theory?" Byron was obviously confused by Dean's reference to their friend's earlier warped idea.

"One of our friends has a morbid sense of humor and a fascination with TV crime shows," Allissa explained, shaking her head at Dean. "She was joking around earlier about the box containing a bomb, like one of the shows she watched last week. But none of us actually think this guy is gonna send me a bomb."

The room got eerily quiet, with nobody backing her up in saying the stalker wasn't going to send her a bomb. She looked back and forth between Dean and Cage, hoping one of them would agree with her to help set her at ease. "Right guys? He's not gonna send me a bomb, right?"

"We don't know what he's gonna do, Darlin'." Dean reached out and took both her hands in his, trying to comfort her as he freaked her out even more than she'd been freaked out earlier at being alone in her room with him. "That's why we're all so worried and doin' everything we can to keep you safe while the Avingtons track him down."

"But on all those shows that Emerald and Kandi like to watch, the stalkers go through steps to escalate from creepy gifts to actually trying to kill someone. So, surely, this guy is gonna do something to forewarn us he's escalating before we have to start worrying about him actually coming after me, right?" Allissa argued while trying to sound more confident than she felt. She didn't normally believe there was any accuracy in the cases depicted on television, but she hoped that part of the shows was at least partially true. If not, then she wasn't sure how she was going to get through her days constantly in fear of what might show up from the psycho stalking her.

"Possibly," Byron sighed through the phone. "While some of those shows are fairly accurate in depicting the stages of stalking, they often gloss over the fact that real perps don't always go through all the stages. Or that they can jump back and forth between the various stages, without always making sense to the rest of us who aren't privy to what's going on in their head."

"So, yeah, right now your stalker is in what we'd classify as stage one, where he's trying to prove his love by sending you gifts, with the black roses being the only thing that could be classified as stage two, uncomfortable contact. And he could stay in these stages for the whole time he's stalking you without jumping to the other stages at all. Or he could skip over the intimidation phase we call stage three and jump to stage four by making threats. Or he could skip both of those stages and go to stage five, where he shows aggression or violence against inanimate objects by sending you a decapitated doll, or breaking into your home or hotel room when you aren't there and trashing the room. Or he could skip all of those stages completely and jump to stage six with no warning. That would be sending you a bomb or trying to grab you to physically harm you."

"And unlike those television shows, in real life, we can't predict which stage he's going to jump to next, or if he's just gonna stop bothering you altogether for no apparent reason. Just like we can't magically get DNA results instantaneously, or solve the case in an hour the way they do on TV."

Allissa couldn't stop herself from sobbing, though she tried to fight back her tears as best she could. She suddenly felt even more frightened about the whole situation, with Byron's words making the threat seem more real than it had previously.

"Oh, Darlin'," Dean consoled her, pulling her into his arms to hold her as she cried into his chest. "Don't cry. We're not gonna let him get close enough to you to hit stage six."

Her mother was the only other person who had ever hugged Allissa to comfort her the way Dean was right then, and it had been years since she'd experienced the same sense of security and support. She didn't know how to handle the strange combination of feelings she was dealing with at the moment, so she wrapped her arms around Dean's waist and clung to him for the strength to let it all out through her tears. She didn't think about sending him mixed signals by clinging to him. She just blindly followed her gut instinct to trust Dean and let him take care of her for a few minutes.

For the first time in her life, she felt safe and protected in the arms of a man. *It's almost like he's acting as my real-life superhero. Maybe that Aquaman comparison isn't so far off after all.*

At that point, their drastically different backgrounds and his player status didn't matter. None of her memories of seeing her mom and her mom's friends battered and bruised from dating the wrong guys infiltrated her brain. The only thing that sunk in for her right then was that Dean was there for her to lean on when she needed him. The walls she kept trying to put up between them started to crumble as she started to trust him with more than her safety.

I just hope these feelings I'm developing for him aren't just my fear of the stalker combining with my attraction to Dean to make me think we can be more than friends and coworkers.

She didn't know how long they stood there as she cried with him rubbing her back soothingly the whole time. But when she finally lifted her face from his chest to see the giant wet spot she left on his shirt, Cage had left the room, taking the package with him.

"I'm sorry," Allissa apologized as she pulled back from their embrace and wiped the tears from her face, feeling embarrassed by the unusual show of emotion. "I don't know what came over me. Normally, I don't let stuff get to me like that. I'm not normally such a crybaby."

"You're not a crybaby, Darlin'," Dean reassured her with a smile as he reached out and swiped his thumb over her cheek, wiping away a tear she'd missed. "We've all gotta vent from time to time. And you're welcome to cry on my shoulder whenever you want."

"Thank you, Dean," Allissa choked out, not feeling like the words were adequate to express how grateful she was for him being there as a friend when she needed it.

"No thanks necessary, Darlin'," Dean grinned. "Now, do you want me to stay until you fall asleep? Or do you want me to call the Stones to come crash with you tonight, so you don't have to deal with this alone?"

Allissa just shook her head, not wanting him to do either. She didn't want her friends to see her in such a vulnerable state. And now that she realized she was alone in the room with Dean again, her lustful thoughts were coming back, so she didn't think she could trust herself alone with him for much longer.

"Neither," she finally stated in a much stronger voice than she felt. "I feel better now that I've cried it out, so I can handle being alone until morning. No point in waking the girls up to rehash all this tonight, and I know you need to get to your room to get some sleep for tomorrow, too."

Dean eyed her skeptically before finally nodding and stepping back toward the door. "If you're sure, Darlin'."

"I'm sure," Allissa declared adamantly, trying to get him to leave before her resolve to not fall for him crumbled to dust. "Goodnight, Dean. Go get some rest."

"Goodnight, Darlin'," Dean grinned as he bent to pick up his gear bag before reaching for the door handle. "But come lock up behind me as soon as this door shuts. I'm not leaving until I hear you put the chain on."

"It's a hotel room," Allissa chuckled as she walked over to the door just as he stepped through it. "The door locks automatically as soon as it shuts."

She let the door shut behind him without even touching it.

"Put the chain on!" Dean bellowed just as she reached up to do exactly that.

How on earth am I going to keep resisting him when he's being such an overprotective sweetheart?

~~~

Monday, June 10, 2019, Cedar Rapids, Iowa

Allissa was still struggling with her conflicted feelings for Dean a week later as she entered the women's locker room to change into her wrestling gear for the show in Cedar Rapids that night. He hadn't hugged her again the way he had their first night back on tour, but he always made sure he was the one to walk her to and from her hotel rooms and made sure there was always a group of people around her throughout the day to make her feel safe. He continued to be his flirty self, but his flirtatiousness wasn't limited to just her. Seeing him with the ring rats, who hit on him anytime they were out in public, was the only thing helping her keep him in the player box she'd stuffed him in when they first met. Anytime they were just among their coworkers, he acted more like a supportive friend than she'd ever experienced with another guy, which only amped up her attraction to him.

Her friends' continued efforts to play matchmaker with the two of them didn't help. As soon as Randi and James rejoined the tour after their honeymoon, Randi started back in with wanting Allissa to complete their foursome wherever they went. On the plane. In the gym. At the hotel restaurant for lunch. Even eating dinner in catering. It was all beginning to feel like too much, and making Allissa wish for some time off by herself.
~~~

Not that she would get any alone time in the near future, other than her stolen meal times in her hotel room. With Rick and Fiona planning their wedding for the week they'd be off for Independence Day, Allissa knew she'd be going to Heart's Destiny once again. At least this time she'd be there as a guest and not actually part of the wedding, so she was hoping for a little more freedom from the forced proximity of the various activities scheduled that week.

Guess I finally understand that old saying about being careful what you wish for, she sighed as she finished changing into her black lycra ring attire and stepped out of the bathroom stall. *All those years I hoped and dreamed about becoming a wrestling star, so I could get Mom and I out of the trailer, and now I just want a few days to lay in my bed there and chill out with nobody but Mom to keep me company.*

"What was that sigh for?" Randi arched an eyebrow at Allissa from her seat on the bench in front of the lockers.

"Just stressed and feeling a little homesick," Allissa admitted as she picked out a locker to put her things in and sat down to put on her wrestling boots. "All this stalker stuff makes me worry about my mom and want to go home for a few days to check on her. But at the same time, I'm also afraid to go home, where the stalker would have easier access to me and possibly put her in more danger."

"Have you talked to her about traveling with us for a while?" Holly suggested, shutting her locker after getting dressed in her street clothes since she wasn't wrestling that night. "I know it's not the same as being at home, but at least you'd get to see her and know she's safe."

"No, I hadn't even thought about that possibility." Allissa shook her head, not wanting to admit it was because she was afraid her mom would embarrass her and put her job in jeopardy by talking about her former profession with the people making decisions about her future with the GWA. "But I doubt she'd go for it."

Windy Walters still refused to quit her job, even though Allissa made more than enough money to provide for the both of them. *You'd think the fact that I now make twenty-five times her average yearly income would be enough for her to realize she doesn't need to keep working. But no, she's too stubborn to quit and let me take care of her, even though my monthly take-home pay after taxes is way more than she makes in a year.*

   Because Windy Walters was notoriously bullheaded, Allissa knew her mom would use her job as an excuse for why she couldn't leave town anytime soon. That was why she hadn't agreed when Allissa wanted to send her on a vacation to get away from the danger of being in Dead End, Nevada, where her stalker knew their address. Not to mention how much she was enjoying the eye candy of having the hot bodyguards from Avington Security watching over her for the last couple of weeks. Between her determination to keep working and getting to show off the beefcake bodyguards to all the girls at work, trying to convince her mom to leave their home for a little while would be an impossible task.

   "At least you have an Avington team there to keep her safe," Randi reassured her with a slight smile. "And hopefully, they'll catch your stalker soon, so you won't have to worry so much anymore."

   "Not about Mom at least," Allissa whispered under her breath, hoping nobody heard her since she was bent over and focused on the laces of her boots. She knew the biggest worry she had after what her stalker might do next was fighting her growing attraction to the Aquaman look-alike who seemed determined to break through her walls. "Just resisting Dean."

   "I knew it!" Randi squealed. "You do like Dean!"

   "No," Allissa groaned, mentally berating herself for not keeping her thoughts in her head.

   "You may as well admit it, Vic," Emerald chimed in. "We've all seen it since day one."

   "What you've seen is me being annoyed by him since day one," Allissa protested, pointing a finger at Emerald.

   "Yeah, I still say you keep calling him a player to cover for how much you want him," Amethyst smirked.

   "No, I call him a player because he's a player," Allissa argued with her friends. "You saw him earlier with the rats in the gym. I guarantee you he left there with no less than four phone numbers in his pocket."

   "Take it from us old married ladies," Shauna interjected, pointing between herself and Holly. "Just because they gave him their numbers, doesn't mean he's gonna call them. He probably does the same thing with them that Vaughn does — toss them in the trash as soon as he gets out of the public eye."

"They just stick them in their pockets, so they don't alienate a fan," Holly added, nodding her agreement with Shauna. "Same as we do."

"But that boy hasn't taken a rat to his room since before your try-out match." Emerald pointedly looked at Allissa. "And he can't take his eyes off the monitor whenever you're in the ring."

"Face it, Vic," Amethyst grinned at Allissa. "You turned that badass player into a smitten kitten. And it's only a matter of time before you start reaping the benefits of the friendship you've developed with him lately."

"No, absolutely not," Allissa protested, holding her hands up, as if they would ward off the statements of her friends. "I don't do friends with benefits."

"Good thing," Randi chuckled, then shrugged when everyone turned to look at her. "Ya'll might have met in Vegas, but Dean's from Heart's Destiny — the love-at-first-sight capital of the world. He's not lookin' for friends with benefits from you. He was being a hundred percent honest when he told us all at the wedding shower how he fell head over heels for you before ya'll even said a word to one another. And I know you fell for him too, no matter how many times you try to lie about being interested in James instead of Dean until you knew he was taken."

Allissa felt guilty for having said that during James and Randi's wedding shower, blushing at remembering the awkwardness she'd felt at the time. She was just about to apologize to her friend for the things she'd said at the wedding shower when Randi held a hand up to stop her.

"See, you're blushing at being called out on the lie," Randi pointed out. "And I guarantee, though he probably won't ask anytime soon since you won't even go on a date with him, Dean's planning for marriage and babies and happily ever after with you."

"He is not," Allissa vehemently disagreed, shaking her head at her friends. "He just wants a roll in the hay 'cause I won't give him the time of day. If I were to give in one night, he'd drop me before the sun came up and have one of his ring rats in his bed the next day."

"You only believe that because you're still young." Holly sat down beside Allissa, bumping their shoulders together. "But trust me, a man doesn't get as protective as Dean's been of you lately, unless he's in love."

Leah Mae Wright

"Oh, yeah, he's definitely giving off that same caveman-claiming-his-mate vibe that all our guys have shown over the years." Shauna nodded in agreement.

"He has been acting weird the last couple of weeks," Allissa admitted while shaking her head to disagree with the other women. "But it's more like he's backing off on the flirtatiousness with me to be a friend."

They didn't have a chance to continue the discussion as one of the production assistants knocked on the women's locker room door. He barely cracked the door open, just enough for them to hear him as he hollered from the hallway, "Shauna and Allissa, you're up next."

Allissa was relieved to escape to the ring before her friends realized she kept turning their discussions about Dean to his player status to keep from admitting she was attracted to him, and that she was afraid his attraction for her would wane as soon as he found out about her history. She was so thankful for the mental break from the constant loop of thoughts about Dean while she did her job. Being in the ring required too much concentration to keep from getting hurt for her to keep dwelling on the things he made her feel.

If only I could spend all my time in the ring, then I wouldn't have to worry about the girls figuring out just how right they are about my attraction to Dean. Or that I've started developing feelings I'm not sure I'm ready for yet. Unfortunately, she didn't know how much longer she could keep her growing feelings for him to herself, especially with her friends being so observant.

Chapter Six

Friday, June 21, 2019, San Francisco, California

As soon as they got checked in at the hotel for the pay-per-view weekend, Dean made sure Allissa was safe in the hotel spa with his sister-in-law, Randi, and the rest of the GWA women, so he could go have a talk with Rick and Cage. While the Avington team had done a much better job with intercepting the packages her stalker kept sending to the hotels, he wanted to know what the plan was for the things the fans would undoubtedly bring her at the fan expo the next day.

"Hey, Dean, come on in," Rick greeted him as soon as he opened the door to his suite where they planned to meet. "Can I get you something to drink while we're waiting on Cage?"

"Naw, I'm good. Thanks." Dean walked in and took a seat on the sofa, wanting to be comfortable while talking to his boss and the head of the GWA's security. Having seen Cage going into the spa as he was leaving, Dean knew he wouldn't be that far behind him in getting back upstairs to the family suites. *Unless Jax convinces him to stay down there for that couple's massage*, Dean thought, remembering how the history teacher was flirting with the head of security as he passed them in the hall outside the spa.

Dean had never seen Cage show any kind of interest in relationships, either with men or women, so he couldn't tell if he returned the other man's attraction or not. But Jaxon Nolen had made it obvious from his first day on the job that he was a proud gay man with a huge crush on Cage Dalton. Jax was such a happy-go-lucky guy that Dean thought he could be the perfect balance for Cage's broody seriousness. That is, if Cage returned his attraction.

Rick's known Cage longer than I have, though, so maybe he knows what Jax's chances are of landing his dream man.

Just as he was about to ask Rick about the possibility of another love match among the GWA crew, there was a knock on the door. Rick opened the door for Cage to enter.

"Sorry I'm late," Cage apologized as he walked over and took a seat in one of the chairs across the coffee table from Dean.

"Don't apologize for doing your job and making sure our crew is safe in the spa," Rick insisted as he took a seat in the other chair.

"Sorry, dude," Dean apologized, holding up both hands in a surrender position. "I didn't mean to pull you away from using a massage as cover for pulling bodyguard duty."

"You didn't." Cage shook his head. "Jax just doesn't understand that I don't do massages, which is why I have the Avington team down there on guard duty."

Guess the Avingtons have already set up extra security for this weekend. Dean relaxed a little, knowing that the security company would be around all weekend.

"You need to at least fill Jax in on your issues, man," Rick pointed out to Cage. "Even if you decide you're not interested in him the same way he's into you, he deserves to know why."

"Yeah, I know," Cage groaned, looking up at the ceiling before turning his head to look at Dean. "But we can talk about that after we deal with whatever Dean needs to discuss."

Dean got the impression that Cage didn't want to discuss his love life, or lack thereof, while he was still in the room. Since he didn't feel comfortable discussing his feelings for Allissa with most of his coworkers, he understood and decided to give the man an easy out to the conversation. "I just wanted to know what extra precautions are being taken to deal with the gifts the fans are likely to bring to the fan expo tomorrow. But since you just mentioned there being an Avington team downstairs in the spa, I'm guessing they'll be handling that tomorrow. So, I can bug out to give ya'll some privacy to talk about other stuff."

"Yeah, they'll be working with the arena security to screen any gifts the fans bring in and specifically watching anyone near Allissa all weekend," Cage confirmed.

"Perfect, so we're done with what I needed." Dean started to stand to leave.

"Actually, Dean might be the best person in the company to give you some advice about how to move forward with Jax," Rick suggested, motioning for Dean to stay seated. "Allissa's got him in pretty much the same position you have Jax, so he might be able to give you an idea of how he'll respond to your issues."

"You feel comfortable discussing relationship issues between gay men?" Cage arched an eyebrow inquisitively at Dean.

"Dude, love is love," Dean shrugged and grinned. "I don't care who ya love as long as you're not tryin' to poach my girl. As for talkin' about relationship issues, I'm totally cool with it. Though I have to warn you, I don't have much experience with anal play, so I might not be able to give you much advice there."

"I don't need advice about anal," Cage grumbled.

"Actually, I do have some anal advice," Rick chuckled. "Always wear a condom, so you don't embarrass your partner when your cum works as an enema."

Dean and Cage both looked at Rick in shock for a moment before responding to Rick's oddly specific statement.

"That's actually pretty good advice," Cage chuckled.

"But since you're engaged to my preacher's daughter, I don't wanna know anything about how you learned that lesson," Dean added, laughing along with the other two men as he pushed the unwanted image of Fiona shitting the bed from his mind.

He also stopped himself from thinking about what it would feel like to fuck Allissa in the ass. *Fuck, as little as she is, I'm sure her pussy will be a tight fit for my cock. So there's no chance in hell I'd be able to fit in her tight little ass.*

"Alright, so back to Cage and Jax," Rick prompted when their laughter died down, pointedly looking at Cage to share his story with Dean.

"Yeah, how can I help?" Dean looked from Rick to Cage.

"I know you're really into Allissa," Cage started, looking up at the ceiling for a moment before continuing. "But would you still want to be with her if you found out she had issues in her past that prevented her from being comfortable with certain intimate acts?"

"Of course," Dean replied. "I may flirt with her like crazy, possibly to the point that I'm pushing the limit of it being too much. But I'd never pressure her to do anything she wasn't comfortable with. Hell, I haven't even tried to kiss her 'cause I know she's not ready to act on our mutual attraction."

"But if she admitted she was attracted to you and you guys started making out, how long would you be willing to stop with just kissing?"

"Dude, if I got to kiss Allissa, I'd be over the moon," Dean admitted. "And more than willing to wait forever for her to be ready for more."

"But what if the scars from her past prevent her from ever wanting more?"

"There's nothing she could tell me about her past that would make me stop loving her and wanting to be with her. Even if we never progress to more than the friendship we have now, I'll always be there for her without pressuring her for more than she's willing to give to the relationship." Dean wasn't sure he understood what Cage's issue was with Jax. With Jax barely hitting the six-foot-tall mark and Cage matching Dean's six-foot-four stature, Dean couldn't imagine the smaller man intimidating badass Cage into sex, which seemed to be what he was implying.

"I think you should explain your scars to Dean," Rick suggested, pointedly looking at Cage. "Because he doesn't seem to understand what you're really trying to ask him."

Cage closed his eyes and groaned. "If I felt comfortable talking to him about them, I'd be able to tell Jax about them."

"You don't have to tell me about your scars, man." Dean held up a hand and shook his head, finally getting the picture. "I don't even need to know if they're physical or mental to know how I'd respond to them on someone I care about. They don't matter."

Cage opened his eyes and locked them on Dean's, obviously confused by his statement.

So, Dean elaborated. "When a person really loves someone, they love who you are, not how you look or what happened in your past. If your scars change the way you have to be intimate, then someone who truly loves you will adapt to meet your needs."

Dean might have the image of a player who never took life seriously, but he meant every word of what he was saying to Cage.

And he planned to apply it to his relationship with Allissa because he loved her enough to adapt the way he showed his love in whatever manner she needed from him.

"If Allissa were to tell me that we couldn't ever have sex because she'd been raped in the past and had mental scars that prevented her from feeling comfortable with any kind of sexual contact, then I'd be happy to settle with holding hands and hugs for the rest of our lives. And if she told me she was born a man and had no intention of ever having gender reassignment surgery, then I'd learn to take it in the ass if that's how she wanted us to be intimate."

Cage finally cracked a smile and nodded at Dean.

"Just be honest with Jax about whatever your issues are, and if he loves you, he'll adapt and show you in the ways you need him to," Dean assured Cage, even more certain of how he was going to always put Allissa's needs first in their relationship.

"I told you the kid's smarter than he looks," Rick smirked.

"Hey, just 'cause ya'll have at least a decade on me, doesn't mean I'm a kid," Dean protested. "And when it comes to matters of the heart, I'd say I have the advantage over ya'll because of growing up in Heart's Destiny."

"Since you're still single and can't even get Allissa to go on a date with you, I don't think your advantage is working all that well for you," Rick retorted with a smirk.

"Ah, but I've known she's *The One* since I first laid eyes on her and have adapted to take our relationship at her pace," Dean shrugged and cocked his head to the side. "So, I'm fine with savoring every step and not ruining things by rushing to the finish line."

Before they could continue their verbal sparring, Cage's phone blared with an alert. "Fuck," he cursed when he looked at his screen.

"What's wrong?" Dean and Rick questioned him in unison.

"Someone leaked our hotel information," Cage explained as he stood. "So now I need to reconfigure our security plans for the weekend, while helping hotel security clear the lobby of loiterers. Thanks for your help, Dean."

"Anytime," Dean replied, also standing to leave.

The men shook hands before Cage rushed off to deal with the security issue.

Leah Mae Wright

"How about we go double-check that everything's still good at the spa?" Rick suggested, obviously worried about his fiancée and daughter being there with Allissa and a good portion of the GWA crew while their more rabid fans were infiltrating the hotel.

"Absolutely," Dean agreed, eager to make sure his girl was safe and sound. "And we can reconfigure the schedule for tomorrow, so I can keep a little closer eye on Allissa when she's interacting with the fans, while we're on our way down there."

~~~

Allissa was irritated after the notification that popped up on her tablet that morning, alerting her to an update to her schedule for the fan expo leading into the ***Gateway to the Gold*** pay-per-view. Instead of having a booth to herself for the autograph signing and being able to spend time in the ring doing a Q and A with the kids interested in learning about the wrestling profession, as she had at every other fan expo that she'd been a part of since joining the GWA roster, she was being lumped in with the Dangerous Twins and Leigh for the autograph signing and to play video games with the fans.

It's like I've been demoted to their second manager, instead of being pushed for a shot at the women's division title tomorrow.

And what's up with the whole video game thing, anyway? After almost nine months on the roster, you'd think it would be evident that I don't play video games. Hell, I don't even play games on the tablet I bought with my first GWA paycheck. Like most of the other women, I only use it as an e-reader and to keep up to date on our schedule, not to play games on the plane like a lot of the guys. So making me play the GWA video game against the fans is going to be a humiliating experience. As if having a stalker isn't bad enough...

Wait! Is the stalker why I'm stuck with Dean today? So he can play bodyguard while I'm at the fan expo? Is that what he and Rick were talking about when they came to the spa yesterday?

Allissa fumed about Dean interfering with her career by going behind her back to the boss to set this up as she got dressed for the
~~~

day. She might not have any proof that Dean was behind the last-minute schedule change, but she was pretty certain he'd made it happen.

Is he also the reason why I'm booked to job to Holly again tomorrow? I thought the whole point of us continuing our feud was for me to finally win the title when we met for the third pay-per-view in a row. That was the whole spiel Ethan and Stone fed me back in February, when they told me I'd be jobbing to Holly at both the **Saint Valentine's Day Massacre** *and* **No Remorse** *pay-per-views. I was supposed to win the title at* **Gateway to the Gold** *with that whole third-time-is-the-charm gimmick. So this new booking sheet that has me jobbing to Holly again tomorrow doesn't make sense.*

Then again, neither does Dean convincing Rick to have me job again. It's not like he'd get anything from me continuing to lose out on the title.

As she put the finishing touches on her hair and makeup, she decided to go ask Rick about the changes as soon as she got to the arena for the fan expo.

And I'll make sure he knows Dean has no say in my life. About my career or my security.

With that thought in mind, she sent Cage a text to get an earlier ride to the arena, instead of waiting to ride with Dean the way he'd insisted the night before. She lucked out that her ride ended up including Rick and his family, along with Jax and Cage in a limo.

"You know Dean's gonna lose his shit when he goes to get you and you're not in your room," Jax leaned over to whisper to Allissa, so Britney didn't overhear him.

"You know you can speak loud enough that the rest of us can hear you," Fiona prodded Jax before Allissa could reply to him. "Britney's wearing noise-canceling headphones."

Allissa looked over to see the preteen with her eyes closed and bobbing her head like she was listening to music. *If only we could all be as carefree as Britney.* Her lips lifted in the slightest bemused smile.

"I was just telling Allissa that Dean's gonna lose his shit when he goes to get her and she's not in her room," Jax reiterated for the group.

"No, he's not," Cage disagreed, shaking his head. "I already texted him to let him know she's with us, so he doesn't blow up my phone, or cause a scene at the hotel by breaking down her door to make sure she's safe."

"You know he'd break down the door before he blew up your phone," Rick chuckled.

"I'm glad you guys think his caveman behavior is funny," Allissa fumed when the others joined in with Rick's laughter. "But he's driving me nuts with the way he's playing bodyguard. And I'd appreciate it if you guys would quit encouraging it."

"We're not really encouraging it," Rick corrected her. "More like taking advantage of the extra eyes on you, since you refused a protective detail from Avington."

"No? Whose idea was the schedule change for today?" Allissa arched an eyebrow at her boss, not caring that she was acting insolent to the man who signed her paychecks. "Why am I now stuck in the same booths as Dean all day, when I'm normally on my own at the fan expos? And while we're on the subject of changes that affect my career, why am I jobbing to Holly again tomorrow, instead of going with the third-shot-being-the-charm gimmick Stone and Ethan sold me on back in February?"

"Okay, yeah, the schedule change for today was Dean's idea." Rick held his hands up in surrender, obviously trying to placate her. "But it was after we found out the hotel had been leaked yesterday, and the extra security we have on hand this weekend needed to be stretched a little thinner to protect everyone and couldn't exclusively shadow you during the Expo."

Allissa remembered back to the day before when Dean and Rick had shown up at the spa. They'd taken the places of the two security guys Cage had set up there earlier, so they could go help with the unruly crowd in the lobby. Thinking about the danger her coworker's children could have been in from the mob scene helped her realize that the change in security plans had definitely been warranted.

Damn it! I'd much rather be stuck with Dean for the day than risk anyone else in the GWA family getting hurt. Allissa nodded her acceptance of the reasoning behind the schedule change.

"As for the booking change for tomorrow, that call was all mine. That third-time-is-a-charm gimmick has been played out so much that the fans expect you to win tomorrow, and you know I prefer to swerve the fans a little to keep the shows exciting. Besides that, I realized it would be more meaningful for you to win your first title in front of your hometown crowd at the *Sin City Showdown* in August."

"Oh," was her only response, feeling really stupid for thinking Dean had tried to interfere with her career by requesting the booking change.

"I understand that you're overwhelmed with this whole stalker thing, Allissa." Rick leaned forward in his seat to make eye contact with her. His position and the earnestness of his tone of voice made her feel like he was about to impart some sage, fatherly advice. So, she pushed aside her earlier anger and really listened to his words. "And Dean can go a little overboard when he gets his mind set on something. But I promise you, I'm the one making the final decision on how our shows are booked and what's best to keep everyone in the GWA safe."

"You are one of the most talented wrestlers I've ever seen, and I'm not going to let this stalker derail the long and illustrious career you have ahead of you. So, I need you to trust me and the people I'm surrounding you with to act in your best interest, even if that means you have to put up with Dean's gregariousness a little more than you'd like."

"Okay, yeah, I can do that," Allissa sighed and nodded at her boss, not really wanting to explain to him why she had issues with trusting most men.

Even though she hadn't worked for him for very long, Rick Robertson had already shown her that he could be trusted by the way he'd taken care of the Ron situation as soon as he was made aware of it. She might not completely believe the other men she worked with weren't just out for themselves after some bad experiences earlier in her life, but she knew she could count on Rick to act in the best interests of his employees, even if it wasn't always the best thing for his company. Several of the people who worked for the GWA called the company and all its employees their GWA family, but the belief that they were all chosen family originated with Rick Robertson.

While she knew Rick wasn't nearly old enough to have fathered her, Allissa was really starting to look up to him as a father figure. She got the impression that he took on that role with several of his employees, not just her.

Fiona reached over and gripped her hand, giving it a reassuring squeeze as the men in the vehicle discussed the changes to the security plan for the day. Allissa returned her friend's comforting gesture. But instead of talking about her feelings like Fiona seemed to be prompting her to do, Allissa tuned into the guys' conversation to make sure she was being proactive about her own safety.

Maybe one of these days, I'll finally feel comfortable enough with everyone in the GWA to let down my guard and open up the way the girls are always trying to get me to do.

~~~

Sunday, June 23, 2019, San Francisco, California

Dean felt like he had royally fucked things up with Allissa the past couple of days. While everything seemed fine between them on Friday, she'd apparently gotten pissed about him suggesting to Rick to change her booking for the fan expo on Saturday. After getting a ride to the arena with Cage, instead of waiting on him to go for their scheduled appearance at the fan expo, she'd basically ignored him all day while they were there. She was bright and bubbly when interacting with the fans, though he could see that her smile never reached her eyes. Yet when he tried to talk to her, she only gave him curt, one-word replies. Then, she'd refused to go out to dinner with the rest of the crew, saying she needed to catch up on some of the rest she'd been missing lately due to their hectic schedule.

On Sunday morning, she refused his offer to check out the sights of San Francisco before they had to go to the arena for the pay-per-view. From what he could tell, she'd stayed in her room all morning, waiting until the last group of GWA performers were leaving the hotel before riding with them to the arena. She hung out with her girlfriends as usual backstage during the show, but she was even more quiet than usual whenever the guys were around.

Fuck! That can't all be because I pushed to be the one by her side to protect her yesterday. Dean tried to figure out what else was going on, as he watched her on the monitor during her match with Holland Everett. Her performance wasn't up to her normal standards. Not that
~~~

it was a bad match, but her moves weren't nearly as sharp as they normally were, making him keenly aware that she was off her game for some reason. *Something else must have happened that nobody's bothered to tell me about.*

He looked around until he found Cage and Rick both keeping a close eye on the monitor set up closest to the classroom area. He knew they were both over there to split their focus between the teachers they'd both started falling for this year and the women in the ring in case the extra security guards from Avington Security needed backup at ringside. Dean decided it was best to go talk to them right then, while they were together and near a monitor, so he wouldn't miss a moment of Allissa's match.

He didn't waste time with pleasantries or warning them that he'd walked up behind them, speaking as soon as he was close enough that they'd hear him without him having to speak loud enough for the rest of the crew to overhear the conversation. "What happened that's thrown Allissa off her game tonight?"

"Fuck, Dean," Rick jumped in his seat and glared at Dean over his shoulder. "Don't sneak up on someone like that."

"Sorry, Boss, didn't realize you're gettin' too old to hear me walk up behind you," Dean quipped, causing Cage to chuckle before he pointed to the monitor he hadn't been able to take his eyes off of since he turned in their direction. "But seriously, what happened? Allissa's not herself today."

"She got another delivery this morning," Cage sighed, running a hand over his military short hair. "One that didn't get stopped at the front desk."

"What do you mean it didn't get stopped at the front desk?" Dean's voice rose in anger, drawing the attention of several of their coworkers and their families.

"I mean, somehow, a flower delivery person was allowed to take a bouquet of black roses to her door," Cage elaborated.

"Oh, fuck, no!" Dean shouted, his fists balling up involuntarily.

"Chill out, man." Cage tried to calm Dean down by placing a hand on his shoulder. "She looked through the peephole, saw the roses, and immediately called me. I intercepted them and questioned the delivery guy. Turns out they were an online order, so the stalker probably isn't even in town. That's how the delivery got past the front desk. The guy didn't even stop because the order had her room number listed."

"How the fuck did this psycho find out her room number?" Dean bellowed, wishing he could find the guy. *If I could just get five minutes alone with this fucktard with no witnesses and no repercussions, he wouldn't be able to stalk Allissa or anyone else ever again.*

"We're not sure yet." Cage shook his head. "But Avington has people investigating it. And the San Francisco PD filed a report on the incident. They can't really do anything about it, since the card didn't have a specific threat to Allissa, but at least we have another incident on record with the authorities for when they finally catch him."

"There was a card with them?" Dean was shocked, since the previous flowers and gifts didn't include one. "What did it say?"

"Knock 'em dead tonight," Cage quoted, shaking his head. "Since it was worded to seem like someone trying to wish her well in her match, we're lucky we were able to convince the cops to even file a report. But hopefully, ordering them online is his first fuckup, making it easier for Avington to track him down through his credit card."

Hearing that Avington Security finally had a lead they could use to track down Allissa's stalker allowed Dean to release the breath he hadn't realized he'd been holding. Unfortunately, he didn't get a chance to ask if there were any changes to Allissa's security plan due to this incident because his earlier shouting had incited a panic among the rest of the crew.

They were instantly surrounded by worried wrestlers and frantic family members, all shouting questions over one another. By the time Allissa and Holly's match was over and it was time for the main event defense of the Galactic Heavyweight Title, Cage had taken charge of the situation and had everyone sitting down in catering for him to debrief the whole GWA family, minus the crew finishing out the show.

When Allissa and Holland made it backstage and joined the rest of them in catering, Dean got up and moved to sit right beside Allissa, who wrapped her arms around herself and seemed to shut down before his eyes. Dean wished he could pull her into his lap and hold her to comfort her when she was obviously in distress. But he knew she wouldn't accept his soothing gesture in the friendly way he meant it with how he'd recently fucked things up between them.

There's no fucking way I'm lettin' her outta my sight right now, even if she won't let me hold her to comfort her at the moment.

Cage updated everyone on the morning flower delivery, explaining in a little more detail the steps he was taking to ensure everyone's safety while working with the GWA.

"Based on the profile the Avington team has put together on this stalker, we believe our standard security measures are sufficient for our house shows and weekly televised events. If this stalker should escalate to more threatening behavior, we expect it to happen during one of our more highly anticipated events, which is why we've added additional security on staff for pay-per-view weekends and our Independence Day break next week."

"You think this guy might show up at one of our wedding events?" Fiona looked frightened as she looked back and forth between Rick and Cage.

Allissa gasped beside him, making Dean wish he could do something to ease her fear of everything going on. But all he could come up with to offer her at the moment that she couldn't reject was a sympathetic smile.

"We don't know, Fifi." Rick consoled his fiancée by reaching over and taking her hand in his, the way Dean wished he could console Allissa. "That's why we're bringing extra security with us to Heart's Destiny."

"After talking to Byron Avington this morning, we think it might be best to make some kind of public announcement about your wedding to lure the stalker to Heart's Destiny." Dean wasn't sure how Cage managed to maintain his stoic, expressionless demeanor as he laid out the reasoning of the security team for the rest of them. "It's such a close-knit community that any outsider coming into town would stand out, making it easy for the HDPD to apprehend the stalker. And with their police chief being the one who first recognized the black roses as a threat, they would be the best law enforcement agency for us to work with to prosecute the perpetrator. So, Byron thinks issuing a press release about the wedding plans is our best play to tempt the stalker to try to make a personal delivery when he thinks we'd all be too preoccupied with the wedding festivities to catch him."

Dean wasn't sure he liked the idea of luring the stalker to his hometown, where they could put his family at risk in the crossfire while trying to catch him. He could see that Allissa was struggling with the same worries about the plan, but he agreed with the security team's rationale that it would be the best place to catch him. *Unless they can track him through his credit card before then.*

Realizing that was a possibility, he pointed it out to the group, hoping to put Allissa and the rest of the GWA family at ease. "But that's only going to be necessary if they can't track him through his credit card before then, right?"

"Yeah," Cage nodded, then closed his eyes for a moment before shaking his head. "But with all the red tape Avington is gonna have to go through to get access to the credit card records, they may not be able to track him down before Friday when we go to Heart's Destiny. Not to mention the very real possibility that he used a prepaid card that they can't trace back to him."

"Okay," Fiona sighed, her shoulders slumping as she leaned over into Rick's side. "What do we need to do to issue a press release?"

"I already have it written and sent to Patrice to release first thing in the morning," Rick informed them, wrapping Fiona in his arms to comfort her. "And in the meantime, we're just asking everyone to continue being vigilant in watching for anyone who seems to be out of place."

"Besides everyone keeping an eye out, I'm going to check Allissa's room at every hotel," Cage added. "Since he was able to find out her room number here, I don't want to take any chances on him doing the same thing elsewhere and lying in wait for her."

"Should those of us who normally get our own room start doubling up?" Jax gave Cage a pointed look, obviously wanting to double up with him. "That way, none of us go into a room alone in case this stalker gets the wrong room?"

"We can definitely do that, if it'll make you feel safer," Cage agreed, smiling at Jax.

Oh, yeah, those two are definitely gonna be workin' out their issues and hookin' up soon. If they haven't already. Too bad I can't convince Allissa to bunk with me so easily.

"We don't have to, though, right?" Allissa's words were barely audible, but he heard the quiver in them indicating that she was just as leery of rooming with one of their fellow performers as she was of getting another delivery from her stalker.

"What was that?" Rick arched an eyebrow in their direction, indicating that he heard Allissa but couldn't make out what she said.

"I don't think it's necessary to double up in our rooms," Allissa asserted, her voice coming out stronger than before. "I mean, it's not that hard to call and pretend you're a family member to get a room number to send flowers. But it would be quite a jump in difficulty for this guy to actually break into my room, so I think just having Cage or one of the other guys check my room before I go in is more than sufficient for now. So it's not necessary to give up the few hours of alone time we get each night just yet, right?"

"No, you don't have to double up in a room if you don't want to," Rick reassured her with a slight shake of his head. "But we want to make sure everyone knows that's a possibility if they would feel safer."

"Hey, Cage, can you walk us all through the procedure for checking the rooms?" Dean wanted to make sure he was adequately trained to check over Allissa's room, in case Cage or one of the other security guys wasn't available. Ideally, he'd be the only one checking her room, but he knew she wouldn't go for that just yet. "I know it's just Allissa that's being targeted right now, but it's always possible that someone else could pick up another stalker. And I know you can't check every room, so I'd like to volunteer to help you check all our rooms."

Dean almost screwed up and volunteered to check all the women's rooms, barely catching himself to correct his wording. He knew his fear for the women and children being the most vulnerable to a stalker would be perceived by the women in the room as seeing them as incapable of defending themselves and their children, instead of him being the gentleman his family raised him to be.

Damn, keeping from sounding like a caveman when all I want is to protect my girl is gonna be a challenge of epic proportions now that Allissa's brought my inner caveman to the surface.

Several of the other guys agreed, offering to assist in keeping everyone associated with the GWA safe. As Cage walked them through the process of checking a room for intruders, Dean paid special attention to the steps, knowing he didn't want to miss something that could potentially put Allissa or one of the other women he worked with in danger.

Damn. With everyone else volunteering, I probably won't ever need to check anyone's room but mine and Allissa's. I just hope she doesn't think I'm only planning to check her room. I don't want her to feel like I'm taking advantage of this situation to pressure her into anything because that's not my intention. And if nobody else had volunteered, I'd have gladly checked the rest of the ladies' rooms, too.

Fuck! Now I'm gonna have to make sure Cage checks her room while I check someone else's, so she doesn't think I'm being a creep and takin' advantage of the situation.

Chapter Seven

Allissa was going stir-crazy after several days of hiding out at the boutique hotel the Hunters ran in Heart's Destiny. After making obligatory appearances at the bachelorette party and wedding shower the previous weekend, she'd decided it was safer to stay in her room when she couldn't hang out with her friends in one of the rooms in the massive hotel building or the grounds surrounding it. Since Cage had insisted on the GWA making a public announcement about the wedding events to try to draw out her stalker, her anxiety about going out in public, where he could possibly find her, had amped up to epic proportions. But with him not making a move yet, not even sending her more gifts or flowers to the bed and breakfast where it was announced they'd be staying all week, she was starting to lose patience with the plan.

At least she had full run of the huge estate, including the kitchen Dean's cousin Ashley, who was the head chef at the restaurant in the B and B, had shown her around the last time she was in town. While she liked not having to place a room service order when she wanted a snack in the middle of the night, she could only spend so much of her time exploring the hundred-thousand-square-foot mansion before she got bored. And she was most definitely bored after spending the last three days in the library, which is why she found herself cornering Cage just after breakfast to see if he thought it would be safe for her to venture out to San Antonio with some of her friends.

"The girls are going to the RiverWalk to watch the fireworks tonight and I'd really like to go," Allissa pleaded with the broody security chief. She hoped having come out about his relationship with

Jax during the meeting at the last pay-per-view had softened him up enough to agree, even if it was only so his boyfriend could also enjoy a night out in San Antonio. "Will you and Jax please come with, so you know I'm being safe?"

"You realize the whole point of releasing the location of the wedding events is to lure your stalker here to Heart's Destiny, right?" Cage arched an eyebrow and pointed down at his feet to indicate the spot where he wanted to lure the stalker. "Not San Antonio. Here. Where we can catch him and have law enforcement backing us up to arrest him. I know you're bored without a lot to do in this town, but I still need you to stay put until we head out on Monday."

"Bored doesn't even begin to describe it," Allissa groaned, barely resisting the urge to roll her eyes at Cage. "There's not even a gym here. I've had to resort to dancing in my room to get my cardio in each day. I can't even go over to Randi's and use their gym because every time I've called to try, they're off with their family. I'd go see Kay and the new baby, but I can't even do that until she's released from the hospital."

Kay had given birth to baby Sam a couple of days ago, and Allissa was as eager to see the newest Burleson as everyone else in the GWA. But when he went to see the new baby the day he was born, Rick sent a message to everyone in the company to tell them that the small birthing center in town limited their visitors to only family members. So, James and Randi were the only people from the GWA that were allowed to visit.

I wonder if Dean could get away with going up there as Anthony and Kay's brother-in-law's brother? Not that it would do me any good for getting to go see the baby while everyone else is off in San Antonio, but maybe he could Skype me while he's there so I could at least see more than the picture that was texted to all of us.

What the hell am I thinking? Dean doesn't have to go up there to do that. I'll text Randi to have her Skype me next time she's up there to see baby Sam. No point in giving Dean any more opportunities to break down my defenses against him.

"If you need a gym, Darlin', you can come use mine," Dean interjected, startling her as he walked up behind her. "We have plenty of time for a workout before the cookout and fireworks in town this evening."

Allissa blushed at the image that instantly popped into her head at the thought of working out with Dean. *Oh, no! Going to Dean's house is not a good idea, even to use his home gym. Being alone in his space would be too much for me to resist.* She imagined what could transpire between them in the seclusion of his home, picturing her and Dean acting out the love scene she'd read the day before because it was set in a gym.

Would his lips feel super soft against mine? Or would they be hard and demanding? Would his facial hair be rough and scratchy against my skin? Or soft and tickly? Would we just kiss? Or would he push for more? And if we did do more, how would we do it while balancing on a weight bench? And would we do it before or after one of his killer workouts?

While she knew firsthand that he always came up with the best workouts from her time helping with Randi's training to start wrestling, she still didn't trust herself to spend any time alone with him. More and more often she found her thoughts wandering to what it would be like to be with Dean, no matter how hard she fought to shut them down.

She'd been more successful avoiding him between meals and wedding events, by burying her nose in a book in the massive library at the B and B or heading to her room, this week than she had been the week they were there for James and Randi's wedding. *And I need to keep maintaining that distance between us, even if my traitorous body clamors to give itself to him.*

"We'll be at the cookout and fireworks with Rick and Fiona later," Cage interrupted her thoughts to inform her. "So we can all sit together if it makes you feel safer."

"Yeah, okay." Allissa wasn't sure what all she missed in the conversation between Cage and Dean while she was lost in her fantasy about being *with* Dean, but she didn't think she was agreeing with anything more than going to the cookout and fireworks with him and the others from the GWA later that afternoon. "What time do I need to meet you guys to get a ride over there?"

"You'll be ridin' with me, Darlin'," Dean grinned, putting his arm around her shoulders. "Cage and Jax are goin' now to help Fiona set up the church's food tent in time to start cooking the burgers before lunch. But we're gonna grab a few of the guys to go workout beforehand."

Allissa opened her mouth to protest as Dean steered her away from Cage and over to the tables where several of their coworkers were still eating breakfast with their families. She quickly closed it when she realized that it wouldn't be just the two of them going for the workout. Since his invitation to use his home gym before going to the cookout and fireworks extended to a mix of their single and married coworkers and a few of their children, she couldn't find a reason to decline. Even if she was the only single woman in the group, at least having Holland, Shauna, and Sarina come along with their children meant she wasn't the lone woman in the group.

Somehow she ended up riding in Dean's truck with him, Liam, and Dion, with the families each taking their own vehicles, and Crockett, Surfer Josh, Sawyer Owens, and Blade Braddock bringing up the rear of their caravan in one of their rentals. They drove past a couple of houses that Allissa had been told were family homes that weren't included in the buildings used for the bed and breakfast. She kept watching out the window while the guys talked, paying more attention to the route they were taking and the beauty of the land than the conversation around her.

After passing the house that his Meemaw had previously pointed out as hers, Dean turned down the wooded lane that she remembered from her last time there led to James and Randi's home. She wasn't surprised, when they got to the turnoff for James and Randi's place, that Dean turned in the opposite direction, remembering Randi pointing out the turn to Dean's house when she'd taken Allissa to her house back in May.

Thankfully, she'd already seen the "cabin" James had built on their family land, so her jaw didn't drop at her first glimpse of Dean's huge log home. It was clearly a different floor plan than James and Randi's house with the garage on the right side of the home as you drove up to the front, as opposed to the left side at James and Randi's place, but it was obviously just as spacious.

Dean pulled into the garage, which contained a couple of muscle cars in addition to his truck with space for at least one more vehicle, leaving the wide expanse of his driveway for the other four SUVs behind them to park. When he opened her door and extended his hand to help her out of the backseat of his truck, Allissa begrudgingly accepted the assistance, not wanting to cause a scene in front of their coworkers and their children by informing him that she didn't need his help.

"Dude, your house is huge!" Sarina and Donovan Kirby's son, Dillon, shouted, running up beside Dean and looking up at the house in awe as they all started walking toward the front porch with a beautiful double-door entry. The French doors matched the warm medium-brown color of the logs, and each had etched glass inlays with a woodland design to accent the rustic style of the home.

"It's not that big," Dean chuckled, shaking his head as he ruffled the kid's hair. "It's only a tenth of the size of the Heritage House."

"Yeah, but that's not really a house," Dillon objected. "It's a hotel, so it has to be a lot bigger than a house. But this makes our house look like it was built for one of Laci's dolls." Dillon pointed with his thumb over his shoulder at his sister as he said her name. Then he turned to look up at his dad. "Dad, why don't we have a house this big?"

"Because we live in hotels ninety percent of the time," Donovan explained. "So there's no point in building our dream house until I retire, and we can actually be home to enjoy it."

"Need a tour, Olympus?" Dean smirked as he opened the doors and ushered them into his home. "Since you're getting up there in years, maybe it'll give you some ideas to get started on that dream home when you retire next year."

"I'll be thirty-two this year, asshole." Donovan slugged Dean in the arm as he walked by him into the house. "And I don't plan on retiring until I hit forty."

"But we'll still enjoy a tour of your house to start getting ideas," his wife, Sarina, added as she followed her husband and kids into the home.

"Then let's get started with the great room, here in the center of the house. If you turn to the west wing, you'll find the casual dining room." Dean pointed around the spacious open floor plan area they'd just entered.

The warm brown color of the logs on the outside of the home spread inward with accent beams outlining the planks of wood on the ceiling and encasing the windows. The flooring was a mix of brown and gray tiles that matched the rockwork on the fireplace on the wall to the left of the great room and the section of the kitchen island that was lined with wooden director's chairs as barstools. The walls were a creamy beige and not as dark as she expected since they weren't the other half of the logs on the outside of the home. The artwork and furnishings were all rustic but elegant, making Allissa wonder if Dean had hired an interior decorator when he built his home.

"Next to the casual dining room is the kitchen, only separated by the island. Just past the casual dining room, that little room off to the left is the breakfast nook, with the formal dining room through those doors straight ahead. If you go through the door off to the right, you'll find the pantry, laundry room, a half-bath, and the garage."

As they all gathered in what Dean called the great room to watch Dean point out the rooms on the right side of his home, Allissa realized just how vastly different her life was from Dean's. Oh, she'd realized he came from money before then, but none of his family seemed to flaunt it the way his house did.

Geez, you could fit our trailer twice over in just the space he's calling the great room and casual dining room.

"And if you turn to look at the east wing, you'll find another half-bath, the stairs, and dual master bedrooms." Dean started ushering them toward the stairs, continuing the tour by having them walk up first.

Allissa was in awe of the beautiful woodwork throughout the house. The stairs were just as stunningly well made as the cabinetry and other built-ins, including log boxes near the fireplace, presumably to hold firewood.

Once they all made it upstairs to gather on a balcony that overlooked the great room, Dean continued. "There are two bedrooms up here, one on each end of the house, with full baths attached to each of them. In addition to the two loft areas right outside each of the bedrooms, there's also a reading nook and a hallway to the room over the garage that will one day be a giant playroom for my kids. For now, I've only furnished the bedrooms as guest rooms and the rest is all just open 'cause I can't decide what to put in there yet."

Allissa followed along with the other ladies as they peeked into the rooms to see the spaces. The bedroom closest to the stairs and over the master bedrooms was octagonally shaped, making her think of a castle turret the way Randi described her nieces' bedrooms in the house Anthony and Kay had recently built. The other bedroom was a more traditional rectangular shape, with both of them having full bathrooms attached that included glorious claw-footed soaker tubs.

She had to admit that the home was exquisite, even with the upper level being sparsely furnished and the main floor appearing to have been decorated by someone other than Dean. She could easily see Dean raising a family in the space one day. But she stopped her wandering thoughts before she pictured herself as those children's mother.

"How many square feet is this place?" Tanner waved a hand around as the ladies rejoined them to go back downstairs.

"Right at ten-thousand," Dean replied. "With five bedrooms and seven bathrooms. Well, four full bathrooms and three half-baths."

Holy shit! That's more than twelve times the size of the trailer I can't get Mom to move out of, Allissa realized as Holland pulled her away from the rest of them going down to the lower level just as they got back to the main floor.

"Are you okay? You look shell-shocked from seeing this place," Holland whispered as she opened the first door closest to the stairs and pulled Allissa into one of the dual master bedrooms.

"It just seems like a lot for a single guy," Allissa shrugged as she followed Holland down the short hall between a closet and bathroom to enter the main area of the octagonal room.

"No, *this* is a lot for a single guy," Holland squealed, pointing at the baby furniture that filled the room.

"What the…" Allissa's words trailed off as her jaw dropped at the sight before her. The room wasn't completely decorated as a nursery. But the crib, rocking chair, and changing table in the octagonal room made it obvious that it was designated as such, even without the brightly painted walls or any of the other decorations she associated with a nursery. "Why?"

"Oh, the guys are gonna give him so much shit once they see this," Holland cackled with laughter as she pulled out her phone and snapped a few pics. "But now I know why he didn't give us a chance to look into the rooms on this level."

Allissa laughed along with her friend as they backtracked out of the room and joined the others on the lower level. This space was obviously where Dean spent most of his time when he was at home, with wrestling memorabilia decorating the walls of the bar area, which was the first thing visible when they stepped off the stairs. Beyond that, under the main floor master bedroom that she and Holland hadn't explored, was what looked like a second living room, where Dean was getting the younger kids set up with a movie to keep them occupied while the adults worked out.

Allissa glanced into the octagonal room under the nursery that she assumed was the fifth bedroom, noticing that Dean currently had it set up as a home office. *I wonder what he does on his time off to need an office?*

When she turned around, Allissa saw the older kids and some of the guys playing old-school arcade games in the space under the great room that was also decorated with more wrestling memorabilia. Holland pulled her husband Tanner aside, obviously showing him the pictures she'd taken.

"Um, Dean, you got something to tell the rest of us?" Tanner fought to keep a straight face as Dean rejoined them.

"There's water, soft drinks, and protein shakes in the fridge behind the bar." Dean waved a hand in the direction of the bar as he walked toward the open doors leading to the gym set up in the area of the lower level under the dining rooms and kitchen. "Feel free to help yourselves to whatever you need while we're working out."

Allissa followed Dean and Tanner into the gym area as Holland's phone made the rounds among the other adults, who quickly joined them. She was glad the tile stopped in the space being used as a game room, feeling more comfortable with her sneakers on the specialized padding used as the gym flooring.

"Dude, is this baby furniture in your house 'cause you're gonna have a kid?" Liam inquired, turning Holland's phone around for Dean to see the picture of the crib.

"Or do you have a fetish you never told us about?" Sawyer Owens quipped, arching an eyebrow at Dean.

"I don't have a baby fetish, you freak." Dean flipped Sawyer off, shaking his head as they all started picking pieces of equipment to use for their cardio warm-up. "I just have a mother who thinks setting up the baby furniture she used with me and James will motivate us to give her grandkids. And it's much easier to let her set it up in a room I don't use than to convince her she's gonna hafta wait a few years before I'll be ready to start thinkin' 'bout havin' kids."

"Why is it at your place and not James and Randi's? I mean, it makes more sense to push them to have kids first since they just got married. Unless she thinks you're more likely to knock up a ring rat before Randi's ready to have kids." Allissa spoke without thinking, not realizing her jealousy at the thought of Dean having sex with one of the hundreds of ring rats she'd seen hit on him was emblazoned on her face. She just hoped the rest of the crew thought her flush was from jogging on the treadmill and not her embarrassment when she realized what she'd said aloud.

"Oh, his crib and stuff is at their place too," Dean assured her. "But since he didn't have his lower level finished out and has all three of his bedrooms furnished, it's being stored in the basement."

"Why didn't he finish out his basement?" Vaughn gave Dean a confused look from his spot on a recumbent bike.

"Because the floor plan he picked out had an indoor basketball court and theater room on the lower level with only one more bedroom than the three he has on the top floor," Dean explained. "And he wants to wait until he knows how many kids he'll have to know if he needs to modify the plans to include more bedrooms before he finishes it out."

"And you've already decided to stop with four rugrats, so you're happy with the five bedrooms you already have?" Liam gave Dean a suspicious look.

Allissa wasn't sure what the looks they were exchanging meant, but she couldn't deny her curiosity about Dean's thoughts on children. At least, not to herself. She wouldn't exactly broadcast it to the world that she'd had a couple of dreams at night about making babies with Dean, but his next words could be just what she needed to hear to stop herself from having those dreams when she was wide awake.

"I actually haven't thought about how many kids I'll have one day," Dean shrugged as he got off the stair stepper and moved over to the free weights. "That'll be up to fate and my future wife. I'll be happy with whatever we're blessed with, whether that means having a dozen or not having kids at all, if that's what my lady love wants. But if we have more than two, we'll have to remodel the space over the garage for the extra bedrooms. I'm still gonna need my office in the bedroom down here to manage my investments. And once we're done using the room that shares the master bathroom as a nursery, I want my wife to convert it to whatever she needs for her favorite hobbies, or just someplace where she can relax without me and the kids drivin' her nuts."

Damn it! Why couldn't he have had a set plan that he refused to budge from, so I could use his answer to reinforce my walls? But no! He has to have the perfect answer of leaving it up to fate and his future wife. And why do I suddenly want to be that future wife to help him plan how to fill those bedrooms?

"Oh, I didn't realize the two rooms shared the master bath." Holland looked mortified as she covered her mouth and got off the spin bike she'd been using for a warm-up. "Yeah, you definitely don't want that room used for one of your kids once they can walk in on you."

"Though your future wife might prefer you take that room as your office and let her have the space down here," Shauna interjected with a grin. "If it's really meant as a space for her to escape from you and the kids, then she won't want to walk in on you in the master bath either."

"Nobody wants to walk in on him in the bath," Blade teased. "Some things just can't be unseen."

"Haha, very funny," Dean deadpanned, shaking his head at Blade. "Just for that, it's sandbags and kettlebells for the next hour."

Allissa finally slowed the treadmill and joined the rest of them as Dean opened a door off to the left of the room, under the breakfast nook on the main floor. Apparently, it was a storage room for the equipment that didn't fit into the space with the cardio machines and free weights. Dean started handing out sandbags and kettlebells until they all had at least one piece they could use for the most intense workout Allissa could ever remember attempting.

This is perfect, Allissa thought as Dean started instructing them on the moves to do for each circuit. *Maybe I'll be too sore from this to get out of bed the rest of the time I'm stuck here in town, so I won't have to see more of Dean's sweet, charming, fun-loving, boy-next-door side that tempts me to give in when he flirts with me.*

~~~
~~~

Dean wasn't doing as good a job at spending time with Allissa during this holiday and wedding week visit to his hometown as he had when his brother got married. He knew the biggest reason for that was that they weren't paired together in the wedding party, but he couldn't help but think she was also intentionally avoiding him.

Even when she was at his house to work out, she stayed with the other women there and didn't let him get within an arm's length of her except on the ride to and from. Then later, at the cookout and fireworks, she ended up sitting with the local women she'd met at the various wedding events since that was where Randi and Fiona were when they first arrived. And Friday she was back to hiding out in the library or her room at the Heritage House, not even giving Dean a chance to ask her to come to his house for another workout with the rest of the GWA crew.

As he sat through Rick and Fiona's wedding, Dean couldn't take his eyes off of Allissa. She was sitting a couple of rows up in the church and perfectly in his line of sight. He was so focused on her that he couldn't remember if any parts of the ceremony were different than the other weddings he'd recently been in at the Heart's Destiny Community Church.

He hoped to at least worm his way into sitting beside her at the reception, but before he could follow her to her table, his mom asked him to help the band with an issue they were having getting their microphones to connect with the speaker system in the ballroom. By the time he got that fixed and made it over to the tables, Allissa's table was full.

Thank fuck, I know I can trust the Benningtons and Protection Detail to watch over her without hitting on her.

After his jealousy the last time they'd all been in town and he'd thought the Canadian wrestlers were flirting with her, he'd taken them aside in the locker room to make sure they knew she was his. Since their friendship was so new, neither Harrison nor Cameron had wanted to take a chance on pissing him off, so they stopped flirting with her immediately.

Had it been any of the locals filling up the seats at the table with the single GWA women, Dean would have probably made a scene to take the seat beside her. *The Walkers woulda flirted with her just to get a rise outta me.*

Dean ended up sitting a couple of tables over with James, Randi, his parents, Meemaw, and PopPop. They had an empty seat at their table, but thankfully, his family all knew how he felt about Allissa, so they didn't try to put anyone else in the seat beside him. Meemaw even saved him, when his cousin Ashley's friend Kenzie came to ask him to dance, once the special dances were over and the dance floor was opened up to everyone.

"Sorry, Kenzie," Meemaw apologized as she reached over and patted the young woman's hand. "Dean's dance card is already full for the night. And I've got dibs on his first dance of the night."

"Oh, well, maybe later," Kenzie smiled sadly at him before turning to walk away.

"That wasn't very nice, Mom." Dean's dad, David, admonished Meemaw. "Kenzie's a nice girl and a good friend of Ashley's. There's no reason Dean couldn't dance with her."

"And maybe seeing Dean dance with someone else is what Allissa needs to get jealous enough to finally give him a chance," PopPop added.

"Oh, no, that'll never work." Meemaw shook her head. "If jealousy were enough, then she'd have responded to hearing about all the local girls who like him when she was here for James and Randi's wedding."

Dean had a feeling his family had already filled Allissa's head with ideas about him that he wished they hadn't, but he couldn't stop himself from asking for clarification. "Oh, no, what did ya'll tell her last time we were home?" Dean rubbed his temples, trying to ease the headache he knew he'd develop from their answers. "Please tell me ya'll didn't give her more reasons to think I'm a player."

"Of course not," his mother defended herself and Meemaw. "We didn't say anything about you being interested in anyone at all." Mandi took a deep breath before finally admitting, "But we did make sure she overheard a conversation about how the local girls would all focus on trying to get your attention now that James is off the market."

"In our defense, we did it before Randi filled us in on how some of your fans being too flirtatious with you causes Allissa to fight her attraction to you," Meemaw elaborated with an apologetic expression on her face. "Which is why I turned Kenzie down for you, so you can show Allissa that you're not interested in any other women by only dancing with her and your doting family members tonight. No woman can resist a man, who spends his time dancing with his mom and grandmas, instead of trying to get frisky with half the girls in town."

Dean couldn't help but chuckle at the misguided way his meemaw tried to help him out. "Thanks, Meemaw." Dean smiled at his grandmother as he stood and extended his hand to her. "But now you've gotta follow through by dancing with me all night."

"Of course, I'm following through," Meemaw chided as she took his hand and stood. "It's my plan, after all."

"Is showing her that I'm a good guy and not a player ya'll's only plan?" Dean arched an eyebrow at Meemaw as he squared up their position to start dancing, knowing his mom and grandmothers were all in cahoots with the other Matchmaking Mommas around town.

"We may have a few more plans," Meemaw shrugged. "But they're all innocent things, like rigging the bouquet and garter toss to go to a couple like you and Allissa, who just need a little push."

"Thanks, Meemaw," Dean chuckled, remembering back to how Justin had proposed to Amy after catching the bouquet and garter at James and Randi's wedding. "But it's a bit early for us to be talking about marriage and forever. I need to wait until her stalker is caught before I even try to get her to agree to go out with me. I don't want to scare her off by pushing for too much, too soon, especially when she's so vulnerable because of the stalker."

"That's a load of horse hockey if I've ever heard one," Meemaw admonished him. "What better way to help her stop worrying about the stalker than to show her that you're gonna be there to protect her? And there's no better way to convince her that you're not just playing her than to let her know you want forever with her. Trust me. She needs to know you're serious about her and not just gonna break her heart after you get her in bed. Maybe don't actually propose while you know her answer is still gonna be no, but start letting her know you want more than she thinks you want."

"If you say so, Meemaw." Dean wasn't sure listening to the advice of his eighty-year-old grandmother would help him earn the heart of a more modern woman like Allissa or not. But he knew it wouldn't fail any worse than the other things he'd tried to get her attention. Nevertheless, he was still sure he couldn't get too serious in his pursuit of her until after her stalker was caught. He didn't want to do or say anything that might make Allissa think he was as obsessed with her as the psycho sending her unwanted gifts. *Hopefully, she'll realize my obsession with her is different, since I only want to make her happy for the rest of our lives.*

They continued dancing in silence as he pondered the ways he could act on Meemaw's idea to show Allissa he wanted more than a hookup with her without coming off as a creep. *The only way I can talk about marriage and forever with her right now is if I joke around about it. If I sound too serious, she won't believe it's real from me and I'll just piss her off.*

Just as he was about to ask Meemaw if she thought joking about planning their wedding would work or not, the song they were dancing to ended, and the emcee took to the mic. "If we could please get the gentlemen to clear the dance floor, it's time for the single ladies to gather for the bouquet toss."

Dean escorted Meemaw back to their table and watched as Emerald pulled Allissa out of her seat. He wasn't close enough to hear their conversation, but he kept his eyes on Allissa as she took her place along the edge of the crowd.

I wonder what Amethyst and Emerald said to make her back away from them, Dean thought as he watched the ladies making faces at each other while Fiona got set up to toss the bouquet. Dean took his eyes off of Allissa just long enough to watch as Fiona looked around at the crowd, making it obvious that she was looking for someone specific to catch the bouquet. *Guess the Matchmaking Mommas really did convince her to rig the bouquet and garter toss the same way James and Randi did.*

He couldn't tell if Fiona was aiming for Allissa as his Meemaw suggested, or if she was aiming for her best friend Charlotte, since they were standing so close together. But, when Allissa either had to catch it or get hit in the face with the bundle of pink roses, Dean had to turn and grin at Meemaw, knowing she'd take credit for the setup.

"And now let's get the single gentlemen on the floor for the garter toss," the emcee announced as Meemaw winked at Dean.

As he walked back out on the dance floor, Dean watched as Fiona whispered something to Rick before taking a seat for him to remove the garter from under her gown. *Oh, yeah, Fiona's definitely in on rigging this.*

Unlike at past weddings, none of the guys joked around with Rick about what he was doing under Fiona's skirt. Dean assumed it was because half the guys who'd previously made those jokes respected their boss too much to do something like that at his wedding reception, and the other half of the jokesters in the room had grown up in town listening to Fiona's father preaching every Sunday.

Since Dean fell in both of those categories, he kept his mouth shut. While Pastor Harrison didn't scare him so much now that he was a grown man, Rick still had the option of tossing that garter to anyone but him. And Dean wasn't taking a chance on not being the one to take the bouquet and garter picture with Allissa by pissing off his boss.

When Rick stood and looked around the room, Dean took a step forward, making sure his boss knew he was front and center and the only option for catching that garter. When their eyes met, Rick smirked like he wasn't going to go along with the plan before slingshotting the garter straight at Dean. *Thank fuck!* Dean let out a sigh of relief as he caught the garter and held it up victoriously. He looked around the room for Allissa, as Philippe started setting up for the pictures.

"Hey, Darlin', you need to come back up for pictures," Dean hollered across the room, twirling the pink garter on his finger, and grinning at her, as the crowd of men shuffled off the dance floor.

Allissa looked at him with exasperation before finally walking back to the dance floor and sitting in the chair Fiona had vacated.

There were numerous catcalls from their coworkers and Dean's local friends, as Dean got down on one knee in front of her at the direction of the photographer. Dean tuned them all out and hoped to relax her a little with a smile as he reached out and clasped her ankle.

As soon as he touched the smooth skin of her ankle, Dean felt a jolt of lightning run through him, straight to his cock, which rapidly engorged. He lifted her leg and stretched the garter with his other hand to fit it over her sexy-as-fuck stilettos, while trying to convince his dick not to embarrass him too much in front of practically everyone he knew.

They locked eyes, as Dean lightly brushed his hands over her leg from her ankle to her calf to put the garter in place just below her knee. He could tell from the way her eyes dilated that she was feeling the same tingle of electricity that he felt any time he touched her. *Thank fuck! She's not as immune to me as she tries to appear.*

Dean wished he could stay lost in the moment of connection with her for the rest of forever. But he couldn't pass up the opportunity to start implementing Meemaw's suggestion when he heard Liam shout, "Guess this means you're next to get married!"

He turned his head and grinned at the audience before responding in what he hoped sounded like a joking manner. "Yeah, well, if this means we're the next to get married, then ya'll can all plan to come back here for our wedding on our Labor Day break in September."

Allissa looked shocked at his declaration, opening her mouth as if to object. But she didn't get the chance when Charlotte shouted from the audience, "Sorry, Dean. That week is already spoken for, so Fiona can be here as my matron of honor!"

Damn, I can't even jokingly claim our next holiday break. Dean had to laugh at the way everyone seemed to take him seriously all of a sudden. *Should I drop it and let them all in on the joke? Or should I carry it out to the point of absurdity, so Allissa starts to understand that I really do want to marry her one day?*

Realizing the whole point of the joke about getting married so soon was to start planting the seed in her mind, Dean answered his own questions before he even finished thinking them.

"Guess that means we'll have to plan a Thanksgiving wedding, Darlin'." Dean wagged his eyebrows suggestively as he turned back to gaze into Allissa's blue-gray eyes.

Allissa's jaw dropped, showing Dean that she wasn't sure what to think of his declaration. *Fuck! Should I tell her it's a joke, so she doesn't completely freak out? I knew I should have thought this through a little more before I tried to follow Meemaw's plan.*

Worried his Meemaw was wrong about the timing of when he should let his intentions be known to Allissa, Dean grinned at her as he backtracked. "I'm jokin', Darlin'. I figured you'd realize that and laugh at me, so Philippe can get your real smile in these pictures."

"Oh, thank gawd!" Allissa relaxed in the chair, rolling her eyes at him before turning to Philippe to follow his directions for the pictures.

Apparently, he'd gotten several of them looking at one another, so he had them look at the camera and smile for a couple next. When that was all Philippe wanted, Dean thought about suggesting a couple where they kissed each other on the cheek. But Allissa bolted back to her table as soon as Philippe said he was done.

Dean thanked Philippe and made sure he had his email address to send those pictures to before walking off the dance floor. He got back to his table just as Rick and Fiona started to cut the cake.

"Oh, Dean, that was the perfect way to let her know you're serious about her," Meemaw assured him, reaching over to pat his hand as he took his seat.

I hope you're right, Meemaw, Dean thought, but didn't have the heart to say. He didn't want to hurt her feelings by letting her know he was skeptical that her plan would work.

Dean mingled with the rest of the guests as the night went on, but he only danced with his mom and grandmothers. He wanted to ask Allissa to dance, but since she was only dancing when the ladies filled the dance floor for some of the faster songs and a few line dances when she didn't need a partner, he wasn't sure she'd agree to dance with him.

When he noticed the seat beside her was free, Dean made his way over to her table to chat for a bit. It took a few minutes of ribbing from Trojan and Magnum before he worked up the courage to finally ask Allissa to dance. "Hey, Darlin', how 'bout you save me from more ridicule from these guys by spinnin' 'round the dance floor with me?"

"Sorry, Dean," Allissa declined, shaking her head at him. "My feet can't handle these shoes any longer. I'm going to call it a night and head up to my room."

"Oh, yeah, I guess it is getting kinda late," Dean nodded and looked at his watch to see it was nearing midnight. "I should probably head out to get some sleep before our flight in the morning, too. So, I'll walk you to your room and check that it's clear."

"You don't have to," Allissa protested, looking around the room. "I'm sure Cage is still here and can do it."

"Cage is on the dance floor with Jax," Dean pointed out, lifting his chin in their direction. "There's no point in interrupting their night when it'll only take me a couple of extra minutes before heading home."

"Oh, um, okay," Allissa stammered, reaching down to pick up the shoes she'd just slipped off.

"Want me to carry any of that for you?" Dean offered, nodding at the shoes, clutch purse, and bouquet she held in her hands as they stood.

"No, I think I can handle it." Allissa rolled her eyes at him before starting toward the door of the ballroom.

Dean caught up with her in just a couple of strides. They walked silently, side by side, out of the ballroom and up the stairs to the third floor. She stopped to pull her key out of her purse before handing it to Dean.

Allissa waited in the hallway as Dean opened her door and checked her room. He also checked the bathroom, but couldn't check the other room connected to hers through the shared bathroom because the door between the rooms was locked.

"Do you know who's in the adjoining room?" Dean inquired as he handed her back her key after clearing her room. "They didn't answer when I knocked, so I couldn't check their room."

"Chastity," Allissa replied, glancing just inside her room at the door to the bathroom that led to the room beside hers. "She was still dancing when we left the ballroom."

"Do you want me to stay until she comes up and check her room? Or do you think she'll have someone come up with her to check it?" Dean hoped he could get a few extra minutes alone with Allissa, even if he just sat silently waiting on Chastity.

"Um, do you mind staying for a little bit while I text her to make sure she's got someone coming with her?" Allissa looked nervous as she pulled her phone out of her purse and started typing out a text.

"No, I don't mind at all." Dean smiled at Allissa, hoping to put her at ease. "But let's go in your room instead of standing around in the hall while we wait. If she's on the dance floor, it could take her a while to get back to her phone to get the message."

"Thanks," Allissa smiled tentatively at him as she walked past him into her room. She looked nervous as she started putting her things down on the dresser before turning and putting her shoes in the open suitcase on the table in the corner of the room.

Dean walked in and sat down in the chair beside the table, thinking Allissa might not be comfortable with him sitting on the bed, which was the only other place to sit in the room. He watched her as she fluttered around anxiously, realizing that she only ever appeared flustered like that when they were alone in a hotel room.

Holy shit! Why didn't I see it before? That's not stalker anxiety. That's an inexperienced girl unsure of how to handle our sexual chemistry.

She hasn't been turning down my advances all this time because of not feeling the same attraction for me that I feel for her. Something must have happened to scare her off of men in general and now she's frazzled because she didn't do much, if any, experimenting with her sexuality as a teenager like most people.

Wanting to put her at ease, Dean decided it was best to get her talking about her career, knowing she was most comfortable in a wrestling ring and therefore, most likely to calm down while discussing something wrestling-related. "So, what's your angle leading into the **Sin City Showdown**? Are you finally booked to win the title then?"

"Yeah, that's what Rick told me at **Gateway to the Gold**." Allissa nodded as she stopped scurrying around the room. She sat on the foot of the bed, where she could face him to talk without being too close to him. "Ethan and Stone had planned for me to win my first title at **Gateway**. At least, that's what they told me when I got my first title match back in February. But Rick thought the third-time's-a-charm gimmick was too played out and decided to swerve. And since Vegas is as close as we get to my hometown, he thought it would be more meaningful for me to win my first title there."

"Oh, yeah," Dean agreed, grinning at how much more relaxed Allissa appeared. "It's definitely more meaningful to have family and friends in the audience for big title wins. You just have to make sure you get Rick a list of names and addresses for the comp tickets a month in advance, so he has time to get backstage passes printed and sent out to them on time. James didn't think to do that before he proposed to Randi at the Valentine's show, so it was kinda a mess to get tickets held at will call for everyone, and none of them got to come backstage after the show."

"Yeah, well, I don't have as big a group of family and friends as you guys, so I doubt it'll be an issue." Allissa's shoulders slumped, showing her discomfort at discussing her family.

Fuck! I know she doesn't like to talk about her family. So why the fuck did I bring that up?

"Well, it'll still be more meaningful, even if it's just your mom there to see your first title win." Dean gave her a reassuring smile, glad he didn't have to come up with a new topic when Allissa's phone buzzed on the dresser.

Allissa jumped up and practically ran to the dresser to pick up her phone. "That's Rylie. She's going to have both Cameron and Harrison walk her up to her room now, so you don't have to stick around to check her room."

While Dean didn't think there was much of a chance that Allissa's stalker was hiding in Rylie's room and just waiting for her to be left alone before sneaking over to attack her, he wasn't planning on leaving until he knew all three members of Protection Detail made it up to the room. But he still stood and slowly started walking toward the door.

Just as he rounded the end of the bed to get within arm's reach of Allissa, she reached out and placed a hand on his forearm, stopping him in his tracks. "I just wanted to say thank you, again," Allissa quavered as she looked up at him tentatively. "Not just for checking my room tonight and waiting until I know I'm not alone to go home. But also, for how you've stepped up as a friend to make me feel safe through this whole situation. I don't know how I can ever repay you for everything."

"Oh, Darlin', you don't ever need to repay me for anything," Dean assured her, patting her hand on his arm to try to comfort her. Wanting to lighten the mood, he grinned at her and wagged his eyebrows as he added, "But from you, I'll gladly accept hugs and kisses as rewards."

"Oh, you will, huh?" Allissa giggled and shook her head before surprising him by wrapping her arms around his waist and pressing her face against his chest. "I guess I can handle giving you a little reward then."

Dean bent slightly as he wrapped his arms around her to return the embrace, trying to keep his hips pulled back enough that she wouldn't notice his cock's immediate response to being allowed to hold her for a moment. He brushed his lips over the crown of her head, assuming that would be the only kiss he'd be getting any time soon.

Dean was actually surprised at how much he was thinking about kissing her. Since it seemed like way too intimate an act to share with ring rats, he hadn't kissed anyone in years. Well, except for the cheek kisses he gave his mom and grandmothers, but he didn't think those counted.

As Allissa pulled back from the way-too-short hug, Dean reluctantly released her. When they pulled apart, their eyes locked on one another. He felt a connection with her in their eye contact that he'd never experienced before, knowing it was just another sign of how they were meant for one another.

He desperately wanted to bend down and kiss her properly, needing that intimacy with her that he'd never share with another woman. But he knew it was probably too soon for her to feel comfortable with that. Instead, he just smiled, hoping she could see a little of how he felt about her in his eyes. As he studied her expression, he thought he saw a hint of affection before it became apparent that she was mentally wrestling with something else.

As Dean tried to figure out what Allissa was thinking, she surprised him once more by pushing up on her tiptoes and sliding her arms around his neck. His hands instantly went to her hips as she pulled him down and pressed their lips together in a feeble first kiss.

When she didn't pull back, like she meant to give him a peck, Dean let his desire for her out and took over the kiss, applying more pressure as he moved his lips over hers. He slid his hands up, not stopping until they were both buried in her hair, so he could hold her head in place as he explored her mouth.

While her inexperience was evident, Allissa didn't hesitate to open up for him to delve his tongue between her luscious lips. He relished his first taste of the woman he knew was his soulmate, finally coaxing her tongue out to play for a moment before pulling back to keep himself in check.

As much as he wanted her, he didn't want to make her feel pressured into doing more than she was ready for. So, even as his dick clamored to come out and meet her, Dean released his hold on her and took a step back, smiling down at her bemused expression. "Best reward ever, Darlin'."

Allissa opened her mouth as if to respond, but quickly closed it when there was a knock at her door.

"No need to come to the door, Vic," Magnum relayed before either of them could walk over to answer the knock. "Just wanted to let you know we cleared Chastity's room, so you can get some sleep."

Now that he knew she would be safe for the night, Dean knew it was time for him to leave. "Goodnight, Darlin'." Dean gave her a quick peck on the cheek as he walked past Allissa to head for the door. "Come lock up behind me."

He stepped through the door, closing it behind him, but he stood there until he heard her door lock click and her whispered, "Goodnight, Dean," through the closed door before he made his way to the stairs.

It's already a great night, he thought as he made his way down the stairs. *And it's just gonna get better once I'm home and reliving that kiss in my dreams.*

Hell, I won't even be able to wait to go to sleep to relive that kiss. Kissin' my Darlin' Allissa is gonna be running on repeat in my head as soon as I get in the door and get my pants outta the way to jerk off.

Chapter Eight

Monday, July 8, 2019, Birmingham, Alabama

Allissa was still in a daze from that amazing first kiss as she exited the company plane almost twelve hours after it happened. She couldn't believe she'd actually initiated it. But after another wedding where she saw Dean with his family, and not as the player she kept trying to think of him as being, she just couldn't control the urge to, finally, feel his lips on hers.

After years of thinking the feel of someone else's tongue in her mouth would be completely unappealing, she finally understood the way all the girls gushed back in middle school about kissing their first crush. *Surely, all kisses aren't as wonderful as that, though. If so, then I've been seriously missing out by not wanting to kiss anyone until now.*

I wonder if that means sex isn't nearly as painful as I've heard, too? It's certainly described as a wonderful experience in all the romance novels. But can I really believe those works of fiction are accurately describing the same act Mom told me was so painful? I mean, with her former profession, she's kinda an expert on the subject.

Allissa was so lost in her own head that she ran into one of the guys when the group seemed to stop in front of her, just outside the rental car office, as they walked through the airport in Birmingham. "Sorry," she muttered, looking up at Dion, whose back she had bumped into, and trying to shake off her wandering thoughts.

"Oh no, I'm sorry." Dion gave her one of his trademark affable smiles. He was one of her favorites of the people she worked with, which was surprising considering his gimmick had him behaving like a rich ladies' man on all the GWA shows, which was exactly the same behavior she'd tried to ascribe to Dean since the day they met. He was always smiling and happy-go-lucky when not performing, and not as outrageously flirtatious as some of the guys, so Allissa felt safe with him. "I'm the one who stopped suddenly and caused a traffic jam. But I didn't think about you being behind me and too short to see past me that the office is full."

Allissa leaned to the side to look around Dion, finally seeing for herself why the hallway was suddenly filling up with people. "Guess it's a good thing we share rides, so we don't actually have to wait in that line to get our own cars."

"Geez, we must have landed at the same time as one of the airlines," Chastity pointed out as she motioned to the crowd around them that was more than half made up of people not associated with the GWA. "Hope they have enough cars for all of us."

"That's the benefit of the GWA reserving our vehicles," Dion assured them as he positioned himself between them and the crowd of strangers in a protective gesture that Allissa appreciated. "They pay a premium to make sure there are enough cars reserved for all of us to have a ride."

They stood there making small talk about the efficiency of the office staff in taking care of their daily reservations, until a few of their coworkers started exiting the car rental office with keys in hand. Allissa and Chastity followed the Precious Stones out to load up in their vehicle, as Dion and the other guys around them in the hallway did the same with Liam, Dean, and a few of the other wrestlers. Allissa was glad to see that things were going back to normal with her riding with her girlfriends, even though the guys still followed their vehicle to the hotel.

"Alright, Vic," Emerald started, turning around in the passenger seat to look at Allissa. "Now that it's just us, without the guys close enough to overhear anything, you've gotta tell us why you're off in Lalaland today."

Allissa knew it was time to finally come clean and confide in her friends. While she still didn't feel comfortable talking to them about her mother's former profession, she knew she could trust the women of the GWA with more of her personal history. She knew they wouldn't ridicule her for her inexperience. Well, at least, not too much. They were professional wrestlers after all, so they might rib her a little about it. But they'd also be able to help her work through her feelings about her newfound sexuality by sharing their own experiences.

She took a deep breath to shore up her inner fortitude before blurting, "Dean and I kissed for the first time last night."

"It's about damn time!" Emerald shouted.

"I knew you liked him more than you wanted to admit," Chastity stated at the same time, speaking softer from her seat beside Allissa.

Amethyst waited until the other two finished before looking at Allissa through the rearview mirror, where she was driving, and prodding her with, "You can't stop with just that, Vic. You've gotta give us details."

"He walked me to my room after the reception and checked my room," Allissa informed them. "And he waited with me until Chastity came up and we got the all-clear on her room."

"And you guys made out the whole time you were waiting?" Emerald's face lit up with excitement at the prospect of her theory being correct.

"No," Allissa chuckled and shook her head at her friend. "We just talked about our upcoming angles, and didn't even get to finish that discussion because it wasn't but maybe ten minutes before Chastity texted me that she was on her way up with Protection Detail to check her room."

Allissa paused to take another deep breath before explaining how the kiss happened. "Then, as he was walking by me to leave, I stopped him to thank him for the way he's been helping me out with all this stalker stuff. Dean being Dean, he joked around about taking his reward in hugs and kisses, so I gave him a hug. Then the next thing I know, I pushed up on my toes and pulled him down to kiss him. I didn't even think about it. It was like my body just moved of its own accord."

"Wait!" Emerald held up her hand in the universal sign for stop. "You kissed him? He didn't make a move on you first?"

"Of course, she had to kiss him first," Amethyst interjected, reaching over to shove Emerald's hand down. "Dean might've been a man-whore before he met Allissa, but he was always a gentleman. Putting his arm around her is as far as he'd push things until he knew she was ready for more." She looked back up into the rearview mirror at Allissa before adding, "But once you started it, he kissed you back, right?"

"Oh, yeah," Allissa admitted, suddenly feeling warm from the memory of the way he'd taken over the kiss. "I think it was obvious to him that it was my first kiss, and I had no idea what I was doing, so he took over and showed me."

"Hold the phone!" Chastity reached out and grabbed Allissa's wrist. When Allissa turned to look at her friend, her eyes were bugged out in shock at the revelation. "Are you saying that was your first kiss ever, not just your first kiss with Dean?"

"Yes," Allissa admitted sheepishly, shaking off her friend's hold on her arm.

"Holy fuck!" Amethyst exclaimed, slamming on the brakes at a yellow light.

"I think you mean *no fuck*," Emerald chortled before pointing back and forth between Allissa and Chastity. "Maybe you guys should trade gimmicks, since you're living that whole virginal thing that Chas has to fake."

"Oh, yeah, no fuck," Amethyst chuckled with Emerald.

"At least I'm not faking the titty part of my ring name." Chastity cupped her ample breasts and grinned at them.

Allissa couldn't help but laugh at the antics of her friends. Instead of making her feel like an outcast or asking her a million questions about why she was still a virgin, they popped off with a few jokes about their boobs and gimmicks to lighten the mood before going back to the topic of her and Dean.

"So, what happened after Dean knocked your socks off by teaching you how to kiss?" Amethyst continued through the intersection the next time the light changed to green, seeming to use the light change as a signal to get back to the original conversation. "And what does it mean for you guys going forward?"

"Nothing else happened," Allissa shrugged, not sure what it meant that Dean just left right after the kiss. "Magnum knocked on my door to tell me Chastity's room was clear. Then Dean said it was the best reward ever, kissed my cheek, and left. I didn't come back to my senses enough to say anything else until he was already gone. I'm not even sure he heard me return his wish goodnight as I locked the door behind him, so I have no idea what he was thinking or what us kissing might mean."

"What do you want it to mean?" Chastity arched an eyebrow at Allissa.

"I don't know," Allissa shrugged and looked around the car at the three women with her. "I was hoping one of you could tell me what it means. Or at least give me an idea of what to expect next, so I don't look as clueless as I feel the next time I talk to him."

"You should probably talk to Randi," Amethyst suggested. "She's the only one of us to ever be on the receiving end of one of the Hunters' affections, so she's the only one who could possibly have a clue of what to tell you to expect next from him."

"I don't know about that," Chastity disagreed. "I mean, yeah, Randi's probably going to have the best insight into what sex will be like with her husband's twin. But even though I just met Dean in April, I can tell from the way he looks at you that he's probably hoping last night's kiss was just the first step in claiming you as his."

"Oh, no," Emerald laughed. "Dean claimed Allissa as his the first time he saw her. And he didn't have to do anything but look at her for the whole locker room to get the message."

"But yesterday's the first time she's given him any idea that she might actually agree," Amethyst pointed out. "So, Randi would be the one to know what he might expect now that they've both admitted to the attraction."

"Randi and James had sex the first day they met," Allissa reminded them, remembering back to one of the many conversations they'd had with Randi about what dating James was like. "So, while I will definitely talk to her about this in the locker room later, I don't think she'll be able to give me any better ideas for convincing him to take things slow than any of you."

"Is that what you want?" Chastity inquired, turning in her seat to examine Allissa. "To take things slow with Dean?"

"Yeah, maybe," Allissa shrugged, unsure how to answer, since she didn't know what the next step should be in trying to start a relationship with him, or if she was really ready to explore her newfound sexuality, when she wasn't sure it would last once Dean got to know her better. "I don't really know what I want."

"Damn, Vic," Emerald sighed, shaking her head. "If I'd waited as long as you have, I'd be a lot more eager to have him punch my V-card."

"Yeah, well, you didn't grow up hearing the horror stories about how painful sex can be the way I did," Allissa confided. "And while Dean's the only man I've ever been attracted to, and he's shown me I can trust him to keep me safe from this stalker, I'm still scared that he won't be able to stop it from hurting." *Or want to be with me at all when he learns my family history.* "Besides, I can't trust that this attraction I'm feeling is more than misunderstood gratitude for helping me stay safe from the stalker. So, until he's caught, I can't even think about seeing what else could happen between me and Dean."

"Oh, please," Emerald scoffed. "My mom tried to scare me away from having sex as a teenager with the stories about how painful it is, too. And yeah, there's a pinch the first time if you haven't already broken your hymen, but other than that, the only time it's painful is if you're not into the guy, or if he's really hung and doesn't stop when he hits your cervix. While it's obvious Dean's really hung, I'm sure he knows how to use it, so you don't have to worry about that. And I'd be willing to bet you broke your own hymen within the first month of starting your wrestling training, so you don't have anything to worry about pain-wise. And the whole stalker thing is just an excuse you're trying to use that doesn't track. He's not the only one who was attracted from day one, long before that creep started sending you shit. We could all see it written all over your face too, so quit denying it."

"Please tell me your observations about Dean's size and experience aren't from firsthand knowledge," Allissa groaned, feeling a sudden surge of anger at her friend, and not even registering the possibility of having broken her hymen without having sex, or Emerald's observation of her earlier attraction to Dean.

"Oh, no!" Emerald's eyes widened as she shook her head at Allissa. "I've never been with Dean or even seen him in the buff. But his wrestling tights don't exactly hide that bulge, and the ring rats he was with before he met you always left with a smile. So, him being well hung and good in bed are easy conclusions to make."

The reminder of his long line of ring rats was all it took for Allissa to decide she wasn't ready for more than the one kiss with Dean. Her friends all groaned when she said as much aloud, arguing that he'd stopped sleeping around from the first moment he saw her. They continued trying to convince her to give Dean a chance the rest of the way to the hotel, rehashing the same points they'd been trying to make her see for months.

"Fine," Allissa conceded as Amethyst parked the car. "I'll agree that he doesn't seem to be as much of a player as he used to be. But I'm still not ready for more than this sort-of-friends thing we've developed recently. That's all I can handle while stressing about this stalker. So I'm going to pretend the kiss never happened and stick with the status quo."

With the guys surrounding them as soon as they got out of the car and unloaded their bags from the back, her friends finally dropped the subject, much to Allissa's relief. *Hopefully, they won't bring it up again in the locker room when the guys aren't around.* Allissa knew that her chances of that were slim to none, since Randi hadn't been in on the previous discussion. *But maybe I can catch Randi when it's just the two of us to fill her in, so she'll back me up with getting the girls to quit hounding me.*

"Hey, Darlin'," Dean greeted her as he walked alongside her into the hotel, each of them carrying their own bags. "Since Cage is busy with Britney and Rick's parents while Rick and Fiona are off on their honeymoon, I'm gonna go up and check your room this week. So don't leave the front desk until I get checked in, too."

"Oh, um, okay," Allissa sputtered, flustered by his sudden appearance so soon after talking to her friends about him.

Unsure how to act around him after the kiss the night before, and not wanting to let him see how affected she was by his presence, Allissa silently got in line to check in at the hotel. While her coworkers chattered around her, Allissa surfed through social media on her phone as she waited for her turn at the counter.

She'd turned her professional social media profiles over to the company when she started work with them in October, but she still had a private account she used to keep up to date with the news around the world. She didn't have many friends on the app and didn't really post on it, but it was fun to follow favorite authors and other celebrities to keep up on current events while traveling all the time with her job.

After months of going through the same check-in procedures almost daily, Allissa was able to disassociate from her surroundings as she waited in line. She didn't even see what she was scrolling through on her phone, as she mentally compiled a list of reasons why she needed to forget all about the kiss with Dean the night before.

Even if the girls are right and he's not the player he once was, he's got way too much experience for me. Exploring my sexuality with Dean would be like trying to drive a racecar without being able to even ride a bike without training wheels.

Besides that, I can't very well agree to date him if I'm not willing to share anything about my past with him. Even just being friends with him is pushing my limits. Eventually, he's going to start asking more about my family and my childhood experiences. And there's no way I can tell him about Mom's job or how I was ridiculed in school.

Even if he believed the lie that she's only ever worked in the bar of the brothel, his family is too upstanding to ever want him associating with someone like me. While everyone was nice and welcoming the two times I've been in his hometown, I'm sure they'd run us out of town if Mom ever came to visit me there.

So, no, even if what I'm feeling is more than gratitude for him being a friend when I need it, I can't take a chance on getting my heart broken by letting things develop into more of a romantic relationship between me and Dean.

"You're up, Darlin'," Dean drawled into her ear, bringing her out of her mental spiral.

Allissa tucked her phone back in her bag and smiled at the front desk clerk waiting to check her in, eager to get up to her room where she could order a room-service lunch and prep her gear for the show that night. *And maybe I'll schedule a massage at the spa, instead of going to the hotel gym to work out with the guys.*

"Allissa Walters, also on the GWA reservation," Allissa informed the clerk, whose name tag read as Vail, when she asked about the name the reservation was under.

"Ah, yes, Ms. Walters," Vail replied with a perfect customer service smile. "We've already prepared your key cards and assisted the courier in delivering your packages to your room this morning. Let me just go grab the key cards from the office."

"Packages?" Allissa screeched, scared out of her mind at the thought of her stalker possibly getting his hands on one of those key cards before she even checked in at the hotel. She swayed on her feet, suddenly light-headed at the thought of what could be waiting for her in her room. *Why is there more than one today, when he still sent stuff to Mom's all last week while I wasn't there? Unless he was in Dead End and saw that it wasn't me or Mom who received them? Shit, if the stalker was there and saw that Mom has bodyguards with her all the time, could it have triggered him to do more than just send me stuff?*

Thankfully, Dean was right behind her. He supported her weight as she swayed on her feet when her thoughts spiraled with the horrific possibilities.

Allissa felt guilty for letting him take over, worried she was using his attraction to her to take advantage of his protective tendencies. But when she felt like passing out, she couldn't do anything but lean on him, even as she hoped she wasn't trusting him too much because of the stalker.

~~~

Dean tried to back off and not crowd into Allissa's personal space as they waited in line at the front desk, thinking he could still protect her without hearing every word of her conversation with the front desk attendant. But when she shouted something about "packages" and wobbled on her feet like she was going to pass out, he had no choice but to step up and wrap an arm around her to make sure she didn't get injured by falling to the floor or hitting her head on the front desk on her way down.

"I've gotcha, Darlin'," he assured her as he dropped his bags to the ground and pulled her back into his chest.

Allissa turned in his arms, wrapping her arms around his waist as she buried her face in his chest. She wasn't crying or sobbing like she was breaking down, but she clearly needed a moment to get a handle on her fear. And Dean was glad to give it to her by holding her in his arms while taking care of the situation.

He looked at the name tag the hotel attendant was wearing to address her by name. "Vail, can you please tell me where these packages are at the moment?"

"They're in Ms. Walters' room," Vail replied with a smile, as if delivering packages to a room before a guest checked in at the hotel
~~~

was their standard service. "As I was telling Ms. Walters, her key cards were prepared this morning when we helped the courier deliver her packages, and I need to go get them from the office."

"You let a courier into her room this morning?" Dean bellowed, fuming with anger at the possibility of the courier actually being her stalker.

"I didn't personally." Vail held up her hands in a placating gesture. "My assistant manager handled the situation this morning because of the size of the delivery."

"You'd better call your assistant manager and the manager above them to come deal with the situation now," Dean demanded, releasing one arm from around Allissa to get his phone out of his pants pocket.

Allissa pulled back, visibly taking a couple of deep breaths as she released her death grip on him. "Thank you." She smiled up at him, but it didn't reach her eyes. "I think I can handle this now, if you can please get Cage down here to deal with the packages."

"Already texting him, Darlin'," Dean smiled reassuringly at Allissa. He continued to let his thumbs move across his screen as he watched Allissa square her shoulders and turn back toward the front desk. He was glad to see a moment in his arms was all it took to give her the strength and confidence to take care of the situation. While his inner caveman wanted to fix it all for her and protect her from the whole world, Dean knew she needed him to be supportive while letting her assert her independence.

Dean: 911 @ front desk. {Supervillain Emoji}

Cage: On my way.

"Please do as Dean asked and call the general manager of the hotel," Allissa calmly instructed Vail. "Our head of security is going to need to speak with them, as well as the assistant manager who handled the delivery this morning."

"Yes, of course." Vail looked irritated by the request, but she tried to cover it up with a fake smile as she picked up the phone on the desk to call her bosses. "If you would please step to the side while you wait for them, so we can check in the rest of our guests."

Dean just nodded as he and Allissa grabbed their bags and moved over to the wall beside the front counter. While they waited for Cage and the hotel management to arrive, Dean decided to make sure her stalker couldn't find Allissa at the hotel in Birmingham. He opened the web browser on his phone and looked up luxury hotels in the area with two-bedroom suites.

He understood the need to use more mid-grade accommodations to make housing the wrestlers and staff of the GWA cost-effective for the company. But he also knew that Allissa wouldn't feel safe in the same hotel that gave her stalker access to her room before the GWA even arrived in town, even if they upgraded her room, so she wouldn't be staying in the same one. So Dean made a quick reservation for a two-bedroom suite at one of the better hotels in Birmingham.

He'd wait to talk to Cage about changing their reservations at the hotels in the other cities they'd be working in this week while Rick was off on his honeymoon, but he wasn't going to be satisfied with just checking her room for intruders any longer. Allissa might balk at sharing a suite with him, but in Dean's opinion, having the room in only his name seemed like the best way to keep her stalker from finding her.

Just as he was about to inform Allissa of the reservation he'd just made, Cage walked out of the elevator and joined them. "Catch me up."

"Apparently, instead of sending my stalker packages to Avington, this hotel decided to let the psycho deliver them to my room before I even checked in today," Allissa filled him in just as they were joined by two men, one of whom appeared to be in his mid-forties, with the second at least ten years older.

"I'm Daniel Lewis, the general manager of the Birmingham Inn and Suites," the older of the two introduced himself before motioning toward the other man. "And this is Andrew Jones, our assistant manager. Vail has informed us that there was some confusion regarding the packages Ms. Walters sent ahead of her arrival today."

"I didn't send myself anything!" Allissa protested, glaring at the hotel manager.

"Ms. Walters has been receiving packages from a stalker," Cage clarified, giving Dean a look that seemed to say, "calm her down" before he continued. "You should have been notified of this weeks ago to know to forward anything that arrived before we did to Avington Security in Marietta, Georgia, and to call me if anything arrives while we're here."

Dean reached out and took Allissa's hand, hoping to calm her some as Cage took over handling the situation with the hotel management.

"And you are?" Mr. Lewis arched an eyebrow at Cage.

"Cage Dalton, GWA head of security." Cage extended his hand to the older man.

"My apologies, Mr. Dalton." Daniel shook Cage's hand. "I do remember seeing that noted on the reservation about a month ago. I'm not sure why those instructions weren't followed this morning."

He then turned to look at the man beside him, who looked down at the floor rather sheepishly. "Andrew, do you know what happened with this delivery this morning?"

"According to the courier, these packages were things Ms. Walters sent ahead of her arrival, so she would have them in time for the show tonight." Andrew Jones gave off a weaselly vibe that rubbed Dean the wrong way as he explained what happened that morning. "When I saw the sender was Ms. Walters and the return address was the same as the GWA headquarters address we have on file for billing the rooms, I assumed they weren't supposed to be sent to the security company."

"Okay, well, now that Mr. Dalton has arrived and we've been informed that they aren't actually supposed to be delivered to Ms. Walters, I'm sure it will only take a few moments to move them to Mr. Dalton's room and get Ms. Walters settled in her room." Daniel tried to placate them by offering what he thought was a simple solution.

"Not gonna happen," Dean objected, shaking his head at the hotel manager. "Allissa and I will be going to a different hotel for the night."

"We are?" Allissa looked up at him in surprise.

"Yeah, Darlin', we are," Dean assured her, squeezing her hand comfortingly as he gazed into her wide gray eyes, which were darker than normal with her heightened anxiety. "I know you don't want to stay in a room that your stalker has been in, and I don't feel comfortable staying in a hotel that gives anyone off the street access to our rooms."

"I can assure you, we didn't give a stalker access to Ms. Walters' room," Daniel Lewis seethed, his whole face turning beet red in anger at Dean's accusation.

Dean didn't give a shit that the manager was pissed. He was going to make sure Allissa was safe, regardless of whatever pompous asshole he pissed off in the process. "Yeah, well, according to Vail at your front desk, your assistant manager created her key cards this morning before the GWA even landed in town, and helped the *courier*, who might be her stalker, deliver them to her room. So, yeah, ya did."

"Is this true, Andrew?" Daniel turned his irate glare at his employee.

"They were all stacked on a dolly, so it was easiest to just escort him up to the room," Andrew admitted sheepishly. "I knew you wouldn't want a stack of boxes cluttering up the reception area or the office, and it was too much to carry in one trip without the dolly, so it seemed like the best solution at the time."

"Did you personally escort him up to the room?" Cage took over questioning the assistant manager.

"Yes, and helped unload the dolly onto the side table when he had to use the restroom," Andrew confessed, looking much more concerned than he had previously.

"I am definitely not going in that room, and especially that bathroom," Allissa shuddered, squeezing Dean's hand, which he took as her acceptance of his suggestion to change hotels.

"So, you got a good look at the guy and can sit down with a sketch artist to describe him?" Andrew nodded in response to Cage's question. "Great, then we'll let Dean and Allissa go on to find a new hotel, while you take me up to that room and we get the police to come out and make a report."

Dean and Allissa had to stay long enough to give their statements to the police, but thankfully, they didn't have to go up to the room in question to do so. Once they spoke with the local authorities and Cage took over dealing with the situation at the Birmingham Inn and Suites, Dean and Allissa left the hotel to go check in at the hotel he'd secured for the night.

"Are you sure we'll be able to find rooms at another hotel?" Allissa looked nervous as she got into the passenger side of the SUV Dean had rented at the airport.

"I already got us a reservation," Dean assured her as he took the driver's seat. "And since it's just you and me at this hotel, I got a two-bedroom suite in only my name, so your stalker won't be able to call around and find you."

"Okay," Allissa sighed, starting to relax back into her seat as Dean drove them across town.

At least, he thought she relaxed, since she closed her eyes and sat quietly as he drove. He was used to her being the quietest of the group whenever they hung out with the rest of the GWA crew, so he wasn't too concerned by her lapsing into her usual silence. But he could still feel waves of tension coming off of her the closer they got to the second hotel. And they didn't feel the same as the sexual tension he always felt when they were in the same space.

"You okay, Darlin'?" Dean was concerned that he'd overstepped her boundaries by making the hotel change without asking her about it first.

"I'm fine."

Dean knew those two words didn't mean the same thing coming from a woman as they did from one of his male friends. He might not have any firsthand experience in long-term romantic relationships, but he had a best friend with sisters, and had seen enough of his brother and friends' relationships to know that the word "fine" was woman-speak for "pissed."

"I'm sorry if I overstepped by booking this suite and insisting you change hotels," Dean apologized, running a hand through his hair as he turned into the entry to the Embassy Suites. "I didn't mean to take over or make the decision for you. I just wanted to get you out of that place and away from the threat as quickly as possible."

"I know," Allissa sighed once more, opening her eyes, and turning to look at Dean. "And I appreciate it. I don't know how you managed to think of getting another hotel reservation while I was struggling to keep my shit together. But thank you, again, for helping keep me safe."

"You're welcome," Dean replied automatically, while trying to figure out why she seemed pissed when her words didn't match the emotions she was projecting. "But if you're not pissed at me for overstepping your boundaries, why do I still feel your anger filling up the space between us? And how can I help you deal with it?"

"Ugh! It's more like, 'what am I not pissed about?' 'Cause I'm pissed at this whole situation," Allissa started ranting, obviously needing to vent. "The stalker who won't go away. The idiots at that hotel, who let him, or at least his flunky, into my room. Worrying about my mom, who won't let me send her on a vacation to help keep her safe. Now having to change hotels, and not being able to have any time alone to decompress and eat without being embarrassed."

Allissa stopped waving her arms around and slapped her hands over her mouth. Her eyes went wide, making it obvious to Dean that she said more than she intended.

Allissa follows one of the cleanest diets I've ever seen. Why would that embarrass her?

Dean kept his eyes facing forward as he parked, trying to decide how to respond to her unexpected revelation. He decided he had two choices. The first would be to ignore her statement about being embarrassed while eating, which would be the easy way out. But since he wanted to get to know her better and wasn't one to ever take the easy way out, he opted to specifically ask about the issue, hoping to be able to help her deal with whatever problems she had, even something as seemingly innocuous as food.

Finally, he turned to look at her as he turned off the SUV. "Why would you need to be alone to eat without being embarrassed?"

Allissa closed her eyes before dropping her hands and angling her head down toward her feet. "I didn't mean to say that. It's not something I talk about with anyone."

"Yeah, well, I'm not just anyone," Dean retorted a little more forcefully than he intended, suddenly worried that she was fighting an eating disorder that she was trying to hide. "I'm the friend who wants to protect you from anything that could do you harm, no matter whether the threat comes from a stalker, or some internal demon you're battling that could cause you to hurt yourself. So, I need you to tell me what's going on, so I can help you deal with it."

Dean braced himself for her to argue with him, resolving to stay in the car and fight it out until she told him the whole story, even if he was risking his chance for more than friendship with her. *It's better to get her help to keep her alive and only be friends with her than to lose her completely to an eating disorder that eventually takes her life.*

She opened her eyes and looked up to lock their gazes. He tried to make sure he projected his love for her in his eyes, even as he also showed his tenacity to take care of her. In her expression, he clearly read confusion at first, followed by a slow transition to a tentative form of trust.

Allissa took a deep breath and blew it out before finally claiming, "I don't have an eating disorder, if that's what you're thinking. At least, not any kind of eating disorder I've ever heard of."

"Then what's the issue?" Dean wasn't about to drop the subject, more concerned about Allissa than he was about getting checked in at the hotel in time to work out before going to the arena.

"I didn't grow up in a tolerant town like you did," Allissa admitted with a sigh. "I was picked on as a kid for growing up on the wrong side of the tracks. And when I became a teenager, it only got worse."

Dean couldn't imagine anyone ever picking on Allissa, especially as a teenager. No matter what side of the tracks she grew up on, no teenage boy in his right mind would bully a pretty girl. They might be clumsy and awkward as they flirted to try to get into her pants, but Dean couldn't fathom them being malicious with their teasing. *Unless they were little assholes who couldn't handle being turned down by her.* "Then the guys in Nevada are imbeciles. That's the only explanation for pickin' on the prettiest girl around."

"Whatever." Allissa rolled her eyes at him, instead of taking the compliment the way he intended it, but her lips turned up in the slightest smile.

Dean just returned the smile, hoping the silence would get her to finish telling him about her eating issues. He didn't have to wait long before she sighed and continued.

"It was actually the girls who started it, and the guys just followed their lead. But regardless, they were constantly looking for new things to tease me about. And they could be just as brutal skinny-shaming someone as they could fat-shaming someone else. And because I was the thinnest girl in school, they started off accusing me of being anorexic. When I tried to fight back by showing off my high metabolism by out-eating the whole football team at the pancake breakfast to kick off our senior year, the accusations switched to saying I was bulimic. It didn't matter if I ate or not, they ridiculed me about it every day at lunch."

Allissa's shoulders slumped as she paused to take a breath. "Then, after high school, I started modeling, which just led to a whole new group of people finding fault with whatever they saw me eating. So, I finally figured out that if I stuck with what most people think of as clean eating when others are around, they wouldn't say anything bad about it."

"I still get comments about how disciplined I am to stick to a healthy diet, but at least those comments are somewhat positive. I just don't tell anyone that what they see me eat in catering or out in public is only about a third of what I actually need to maintain my energy levels with how active I am. And I eat whatever sounds good at the time, ordering room service or takeout, or raiding a vending machine if those aren't available, at least three times a day when I can eat it alone in my room without anyone around to make comments."

"I don't starve myself. I don't binge or puke. I just don't eat things others might consider unhealthy whenever anyone else is around. So, unless secretive eating is an eating disorder I've never heard of, I don't have an eating disorder. But if I'm going to have to share a suite with you tonight, then I'm going to have to get over it pretty quick, 'cause I'm not going to go to bed hungry either."

While Dean hated hearing how the ignorant opinions of others had affected her, he was relieved to hear that she didn't have a problem that could potentially be deadly. He was also glad to have earned enough of her trust that she'd confided in him, when it sounded like she hadn't even talked to her girlfriends in the locker room about her secretive eating.

Knowing she was still feeling vulnerable about revealing so much to him, and she wasn't ready for him to tell her how serious he was about them as a couple, Dean decided to try to lighten the mood by being his typical jovial self. "Thank fuck!" He sank back into his seat like the weight of the world was lifted off of him. "I was afraid I was gonna starve tonight, trying to stick with your clean eating. Now I know I can still pick up a greasy cheeseburger or pizza instead of more rabbit food on the way back to the hotel after the show."

"Seriously?" Allissa gave him an incredulous glance. "You think I would have made you eat more fruits and veggies after the show, instead of ordering whatever you want? When have I ever pushed anyone to eat the same things I was?"

"You haven't," Dean admitted with a half-shrug. "But I still felt guilty for grabbing a couple of burgers after we finished off the sandwiches at the cookout last week while you kept munching on strawberries."

"Those were good strawberries," Allissa defended half-heartedly.

Dean eyed her dubiously. "Yeah, but they weren't as good as those cheeseburgers. And now that we're here, we should really hurry up and check-in, so we can raid the room service menu before we have to head to the arena. I can't wait to watch you eat real food, instead of just rabbit food."

Dean winked at her before getting out of the vehicle and going to open up the back to grab their bags. He was tempted to go open her door for her and help her out the way he was taught to be a gentleman, but he knew she needed to show a little of her independence at the moment, after the morning they'd had that led to him deciding for her to change hotels.

"You're not going to mention my food issues to anyone, are you?" Allissa looked a little nervous as she joined him at the back of the vehicle to grab their bags.

"Of course not," Dean assured her with a sincere smile. "While I'm sure everyone we work with would be understanding and supportive if you told them what you told me, it's not my place to share. Anything you ever tell me will go in the vault and stay between the two of us. I promise, Darlin'."

"Thank you," Allissa sighed, returning his sincere smile as they turned in unison toward the hotel entrance. "I feel like I'm saying that to you a lot lately, but I really do mean it."

Dean just smiled, not wanting to make her feel bad by telling her to stop thanking him, even though he didn't think it was necessary. *She shouldn't have to thank me for treating her the way she deserves. But that's a discussion for another day.*

Dean was determined not to let anything bring them back down to earth when they were having a good time together. Even if that meant not sharing with Allissa when Cage sent him pictures of the message that had been scrawled on the bathroom mirror, when her stalker delivered a stack of boxes containing a mix of lingerie and wrestling attire that was way too skimpy for her to wear in public.

You're mine! I can't wait to see you wrestle while wearing what I picked out for you.

Dean hoped he concealed his outrage at the stalker trying to claim Allissa, so she didn't have to be scared any more than she already was. Seeing the photo of those words scrawled in black marker on the bathroom mirror bothered Dean for more reasons than just being written by the psycho stalking Allissa. They also made him hate that part of himself that he tried to keep buried deep inside that shared similar sentiments about her.

Oh, he hadn't picked clothes for her and commented on wanting her to wear them. But he had imagined her wearing a few things he'd seen and thought would look good on her. He'd also fantasized more than once about claiming her with the words "you're mine" while his dick was buried deep inside her to instantly come while jacking off.

Fuck! I really need to back off and stay in the friend zone with her until this jackass is locked up. And I can't ever share those fantasies with her, even if we do get together eventually, so I don't remind her of this nightmare.

And hopefully, she won't be too turned off by having a slightly too flirtatious friend, so we can move on to more as soon as this stalker shit is behind us.

~~~

Allissa wasn't sure how to feel about the way the day had gone. On the one hand, she felt like she'd successfully avoided the awkward day-after conversation about the kiss she'd shared with Dean, keeping him firmly in the friend zone where she needed him to stay. But on the other hand, she'd leaned on him when she freaked out about the stalker getting into her room at the other hotel, and unintentionally opened up to him about her eating issues in a way that seemed like they were way more intimate than just friends.

His response to her revelations went a long way toward increasing the trust she had in him as a friend. And his lack of a response to her
~~~

hint about their socioeconomic differences made her wonder if they mattered as much as she thought they would with regard to them being more than friends in the future. *Not that it matters if he doesn't think the fact that I grew up poor factors into our potential relationship. It's more likely that what Mom had to do to earn what little money we had when I was a kid will be what makes him realize I'm not good enough for him.*

Once they got checked in at the new hotel and carried their luggage to their separate bedrooms, Dean ordered room service and acted like it was no big deal that she chose and ate the same triple cheeseburger and fries that he did. She still couldn't believe how he'd just smiled at her and carried on a normal conversation about the feud he and James were working against the Inglemans since they were back on tour.

Allissa was fascinated with Reid and Tait Ingleman and their relationship with their shared wife, Kori. Not that she was brave enough to ask Kori if her relationship was anything like the throuples she'd read about in some of the more risqué romance novels that Kay had recommended. But seeing them together and how they lovingly raised their two kids together certainly made Allissa wonder if some of her other thoughts about things only happening in the make-believe world of books were completely accurate.

If throuples like the Inglemans happen in real life, maybe those books aren't completely off base about orgasms and pleasurable sex, she'd wondered.

Allissa had hidden her sexual thoughts as best she could while spending the day with Dean, trying to block them out completely as much as possible. That had been a struggle during the hour they were in the weight room together before heading to the arena for the show that night. Dean had a problem with keeping his shirt on when he worked out, pulling it off to use as a sweat towel, instead of remembering to bring a hand towel with him the way she did. And seeing Dean Hunter shirtless was a surefire trigger to Allissa's previously dormant sexual curiosity.

Thankfully, he gave her a little space once they reunited with the rest of the GWA crew, leaving her to hang out with her friends, instead of being glued to her side the way he was at the hotels earlier. She appreciated the breathing room, needing the time away from his libido-stimulating woodsy, leather scent to keep from being tempted to go for another kiss.

Now that they were back at the hotel with a pizza for each of them on the table between them, Allissa was having a hard time remembering why she didn't want to explore her sexual side with Dean. Especially when she remembered back to the conversation in the women's locker room earlier, when her single friends had brought the married ladies up to speed on her attraction to Dean.

Randi had been the first to tell her to trust Dean to take things at her pace while pushing her past her previous limits. Then the other women had all jumped on the bandwagon by telling her to trust Dean to take care of her sexual needs, as well as her security issues.

She'd confided in the rest of the women that she was feeling overwhelmed and confused by how much their first kiss, her first kiss, had affected her. She skipped over the history of why she'd avoided romantic entanglements in the past, only saying that she'd never been attracted to anyone before, for why she was still so inexperienced at twenty-three years old. But she had to let them know the full extent of her virginal status to explain why she was so worried about Dean's vast experience being too much for her to handle in her first foray into romantic relationships.

She'd hoped that would help her friends come up with ways for her to keep from giving in to the attraction between her and Dean. Instead, they all seemed to think that having her first time with someone with so much more experience would be way better than the typical fumbling first time having sex with someone closer to her experience level.

For the rest of the evening, Allissa struggled with trying to decide whether or not they were right. As she sat with Dean eating pizza and breaking down their matches from that night, she had to admit, if only to herself, that they were definitely right about Dean being a gentle giant when he wasn't portraying a badass biker in the wrestling ring.

He was flirtatious and a lot more boisterous than his twin brother. He could also be extremely scary when he was acting angry in his promos for the GWA shows. But the only times she'd ever heard him raise his voice in real anger were all on her behalf, not directed at her in any way. So, she didn't think she had anything to fear from him. At least, not that he would turn physically abusive with her, like some of the men her mom and her mom's friends had dealt with over the years.

Just because he's not the type to intentionally hurt me, doesn't mean he won't accidentally hurt me, though. And I don't see how his size alone won't make sex painful.

Although, Randi seems to enjoy sex with Dean's twin, who is the same size as Dean. And she and I aren't that much different in size. I mean, we're the same height and she's barely a size bigger than me in clothes. Surely that extra ten pounds she has on me doesn't make that much of a difference in the size of our vaginal openings to make sex more comfortable for her.

I'll have to talk to her, when I can get a moment alone with her, to ask her some more personal questions about what sex feels like with James. Maybe then I can decide whether it will be worth the risk to try with Dean. If it's anything like that kiss last night, the pleasure might outweigh any momentary pain.

"Earth to Allissa," Dean called out, bringing her back to the moment and out of her head. "You alright, Darlin'?"

"Yeah, sorry, just tired," Allissa lied, feeling herself flush at realizing she was thinking about sex with Dean while sitting at the table with him watching her.

"You sure?" Dean arched an eyebrow inquisitively at her, then smirked. "From the look on your face, I'd have guessed you were thinking about that kiss last night."

Allissa floundered for how to respond, surprised that Dean could read her thoughts so easily. *How did he know that? Did I actually move my lips like I was reliving it?*

"No," she lied, denying her wandering thoughts. "In fact, I pretty much forgot about last night after everything that happened today."

"Sure you did," Dean chuckled. "Probably about as much as I did, which was not at all, 'cause I was thinkin' about kissin' you again every other second since the moment our lips parted last night."

Allissa opened her mouth to refute his statement, but promptly filled it with pizza instead. There was no way she could take the chance of saying what she was thinking. *I only thought of kissing you again about once every hour, not every other second.*

"That's alright, Darlin'," Dean laughed. "You don't have to admit to wanting to kiss me again just yet. I can be patient and wait for you to work through all your thoughts and feelings before rewarding me with another kiss."

Allissa chewed and swallowed her last bite of pizza, washing it down with the last of her soda before finally retorting, "Not gonna happen. I wasn't impressed enough for a repeat, so don't expect more than a hug between friends for your rewards from now on."

With that, she got up and disposed of her trash from their midnight snack before flouncing off to her bedroom for the night. Dean chuckled behind her, but she didn't stick around to listen to his retort, knowing it would be something flirtatious.

After getting changed in the ensuite bathroom, Allissa settled in for a long night of dreaming about Dean.

I wonder if I can find an online tutorial for how to touch myself to deal with this strange sexual need I feel around him without anyone knowing?

She grabbed her phone and did a quick internet search for a "beginner's guide to female masturbation" and settled into the pillow-soft bed for a long night of reading. And a little tentative exploration with her fingers. Unfortunately, she wasn't very successful at following the directions she read on her phone. Even with holding the phone upside down to try to compare her parts to the diagram on the screen, she wasn't sure she was touching the right area to find the magic button of her clit.

Ugh! I swear my female parts are broken! All this is doing is making me feel like I need to go pee. And that's definitely not what all the books say an orgasm is supposed to feel like.

Allissa finally gave up, going to the bathroom and pulling her panties and sleep shorts back on before giving up for the night.

Chapter Nine

After a week and a half of staying glued to Allissa's side practically twenty-four-seven, Dean was more sexually frustrated than he'd ever been in his life. *Thank fuck for ensuite bathrooms in these two-bedroom suites,* he thought as he stepped into the shower as soon as they got back to the hotel after the show that night. If it wasn't for his twice-daily jerk-off sessions, he feared he'd start to pressure Allissa into more than she was ready for between them, no matter how much he wanted to be the friend she needed until she was ready for more. As it was, he was just at risk of making her think he was a germaphobe because of the way he insisted on taking a third shower as soon as they got back to the hotel room each night, even though he'd already rinsed off the sweat of performing in the locker room at the arena right before leaving for the hotel.

They'd settled into a daily routine that seemed to be working for them to build a solid foundation of friendship for their relationship. She let him act as her round-the-clock bodyguard, continuing to share a two-bedroom suite, registered in only his name, even though they were back to staying in the same hotels as the rest of the GWA. And they had meaningful conversations with one another whenever they were alone, instead of just sticking to the superficial talk about their jobs that they'd started out with on their first night sharing a suite.

Dean was thoroughly enjoying the extra time he got to spend with Allissa when they were alone in their suite, feeling like they were really getting to know one another as they talked about their hobbies and favorite things while accommodating her eating habits. But with Allissa still being in her sleep shorts and a tank top most mornings, or already changing into the same styles of sleep outfits before their meals were delivered at night, he was really struggling with keeping his dick in check.

Those fucking thin tank tops, Dean mentally moaned as he palmed his cock and started stroking while picturing what Allissa would be wearing when he got out of the shower to join her for their late-night meal. *If I didn't know how fucking inexperienced she is, I'd swear she's wearing them on purpose to tempt me with those perky tits.*

Picturing peeling one of those tank tops off of Allissa and fucking her tits had quickly become Dean's go-to fantasy while jacking off in the shower. *Fuck, I hope I can convince her to pierce her nipples one of these days. They'd look amazing with my piercings rubbing between them while I fuck her tits.*

He squeezed his cock as he stroked from the base to his frenum piercing, lessening the pressure as he rotated the D-ring to rub on the most sensitive spot on his cock before moving up to the head to lightly flick the balls of his apadravya piercing for the added stimulation there.

Back when he and his twin had gotten their matching family tree tattoos, Dean had seen pictures of various penile piercings in the portfolio of the tattoo and piercing studio. When James wanted to go back for more ink to complete sleeves on both arms and add a back piece, Dean had opted to skip the extra ink in favor of the piercings that had piqued his interest.

While all the different options fascinated him, Dean had picked the two piercings after talking to the tattoo and piercing artist about the sexual benefits of each of them. With the frenum and head being the two most sensitive areas on his dick, even the slightest movement of the jewelry heightened his pleasure. But the piercer had sold him on both when he explained how the two combined were guaranteed to stimulate his partner's G-spot when he fucked her from behind.

With doggie style being his favorite sexual position at the time, the decision for which piercings to get was a no-brainer. It had sucked to have to abstain from any kind of stimulation while they were healing. But once those hellish three months were over, he quickly found out that the piercer had been one-hundred percent correct about the benefits.

As his fantasy morphed from fucking Allissa's tits to having her suck his cock and flick his piercings with her tongue, Dean had to wonder what she would think the first time she saw his dick. *She's so fucking innocent. I hope the piercings don't scare her off.*

Hell, if she really is a virgin like I think she is, just my size might scare her off. It's gonna be torturous to take things slow and be gentle enough not to hurt her the first time.

Dean squeezed his shaft as he continued to stroke himself, imagining how tight Allissa's pussy would feel the first time he fucked her. It didn't take but a few of those really tight strokes while fantasizing about his first time with Allissa before Dean painted the wall of the shower with his cum. "Fuck, Allissa," he groaned, hoping the shower drowned out his cry for her as he came.

As much as he wanted to share a shower with her, Dean didn't want her to come running, thinking he was calling her, only to catch him jerking off when she was obviously not ready to go that far with him.

Dean stood there under the spray of the shower, recovering from the intensity of the climax for a moment before releasing his dick and cleaning up the mess he made. Once his swimmers were washed down the drain, Dean made quick work of cleaning himself up and getting out to get dressed.

He put on a pair of compression shorts to help conceal the erection he knew he'd get as soon as he saw Allissa, knowing he'd have to replace them with a standard pair of boxer briefs later to keep from cutting off his circulation when it was time to go to sleep. He covered the compression shorts with a pair of sweatpants and hid his torso with a t-shirt before joining Allissa in the communal living room area of the suite to place their room service order.

While he knew she was used to seeing him shirtless in his wrestling tights, or a pair of workout shorts, when he was in the ring at the arenas where they performed, or working out at the hotel gyms, Dean didn't want to make her feel uncomfortable by wearing so little when it was just the two of them in their hotel room. He might be eagerly anticipating the day he'd finally get to be naked with her, but he knew she wasn't ready for him to jump that far ahead in their relationship.

"What looks good on the room service menu?" Dean flopped down on the sofa beside Allissa, who was looking at the in-room food guide.

"Nothing, since room service through the hotel closed an hour ago," Allissa pouted with the cutest disappointed expression on her face. "So, I'm trying to figure out which restaurants we can still get delivered through Grubhub or Uber Eats."

Dean looked over her shoulder at the guide listing the different restaurants for the food delivery services. "Whataburger," Dean decided, pointing out the distinctive orange and white logo with one hand, while pulling his phone out of the pocket of his sweats with the other. "They're usually open twenty-four hours and their patty melts are excellent."

"Sounds like you've had them a time or two," Allissa giggled, closing the in-room food guide, and dropping it on the coffee table in front of them.

"Oh, yeah," Dean agreed with a chuckle, pulling up the food delivery app and starting to place their order. "PopPop calls their store sign a Texas stop sign, 'cause anytime we see it a true Texan has to stop for a Whataburger."

"Wait, I thought a Texas stop sign referred to Dairy Queen?" Allissa arched a questioning eyebrow at him.

"Yeah, well, PopPop disagrees with that consensus and taught us it was Whataburger," Dean shrugged. "And I have to agree it's the best burger you'll get from a chain store like that. Though even a Whataburger doesn't compare to the ones from the Burger Barn back home."

"Well, since you're such a burger connoisseur, then I guess I'll trust you to pick out the best thing on the menu for me." Allissa grinned at him as she picked up the remote for the television and turned it on. "And I'll pick us something to watch while we wait."

Dean knew he could trust Allissa with the remote, learning over the last couple of weeks that she usually settled on superhero movies, sports, or stand-up comedians whenever she actually turned on the television. The fact that she never picked sappy chick flicks or ridiculous reality TV shows seemed to Dean like more proof that they were made for each other. He also figured out her love of superhero movies was probably why she'd called him Aquaman when she was drunk a few weeks back.

Once he had their food order placed and Allissa found a comedy special for them to have as background noise, Dean decided to start braving the relationship talk waters. While he knew he needed to stay in the friend zone until her stalker was caught, he also wanted to know what he needed to do to make her more receptive to transitioning their friendship to a more romantic status, so he could be prepared for when the time was right. "So, you trust me to feed you and keep you safe from your stalker, how can I convince you to trust me to take you on a date?"

"What?" Allissa turned and looked at him like a deer caught in the headlights of an oncoming car.

"I wanna take you on a date." Dean gave her a smile that he hoped conveyed the message that he wasn't being lascivious when he suggested a date. "I know you won't be ready for us to take a step up from friends until after your stalker is caught. But I wanna be prepared for when that time comes, and that starts with knowing what I've gotta do to get you to give me a chance to take you on a date. So, what do I hafta do to convince you to go out with me, Darlin'?"

"I, uh, I don't know," Allissa sputtered, obviously uncomfortable with the direction he was leading them. "Wha-what's different about a date from what we're doing now?" She waved her hand around to indicate she meant what they were doing right at that moment. "I mean, with our schedule, this is about as close as we can get to dinner and a movie, so why do we need to call it a date? Can't we just keep hanging out the way we have for the past couple of weeks?"

"The difference is that we'd start doing things like this as a couple, instead of as friends," Dean explained, reaching out to take her hand in his, so he could gauge her reaction to his words by rubbing his thumb over the pulse-point in her wrist. "And we'd go out and do things together in public, letting our friends know we're a couple by holding hands, kissing, and other public displays of affection."

"Dean," she sighed his name as her pulse seemed to quicken under his thumb. "If this is your way of trying to get me to sleep with you, it's not going to work."

"It's not," Dean adamantly defended his intentions. "Don't get me wrong, I want to sleep with you. But not until you want to sleep with me. And I know it's gonna take a while before you're ready for that. I don't know why you're so leery of men that you won't give me a chance to show you that I'm worthy of being your man, but I'm patient enough to go as slow as you want in our relationship. I just want to take the small step of committing to trying for more than friendship between us by starting with a first date as soon as you're ready to let me take you out."

"Dean," Allissa groaned his name, obviously struggling with how to respond.

His phone chimed, alerting him that the delivery driver was leaving Whataburger and on the way to the hotel. "Hold that thought, Darlin'." Dean held up a hand to stop her from starting to speak as he jumped up from the sofa. "Let me go grab our food while you think about how great dating me will be for a few more minutes."

He wagged his eyebrows at her before rushing back to his room to put on some sneakers and grab his wallet. He grinned at her perplexed expression as he confidently waltzed back through the living room of the suite. He made sure the door was closed and automatically locked behind him before he took the elevator down to the lobby to meet the delivery driver. Ten minutes later, he unlocked the door to their suite and found Allissa still sitting on the sofa, looking delightfully discombobulated.

It wasn't until he sat down on the sofa beside her and placed the two bags of food and the drink carrier on the coffee table that she seemed to come back from wherever she'd gone in her head to think. "Geez, Dean, how much food did you order?"

"Four patty melts, two fries, two Cokes, and two shakes," Dean replied with a grin as he started unloading the bags. "Don't worry, Darlin', it'll be enough that we both get full."

"It really doesn't bother you that I eat almost as much as you do?" Allissa eyed him dubiously, as he handed her one of the patty melts before picking one up for himself.

"Nope, not at all, Darlin'." Dean smiled at her as he unwrapped his first burger of the night. "I actually think it's hot that you eat pretty much anything, whether it's the healthy stuff you eat whenever anyone else is around, or whatever we pick up when it's just the two of us. Way more attractive than those girls who only order a salad and then pick at the food without actually eating it."

"Only you would say that eating is hot." Allissa rolled her eyes as she opened her burger and took the first bite.

When she moaned in pleasure at her first taste of a Whataburger patty melt, Dean had to close his eyes and picture his grandmothers, so his dick didn't poke through his compression shorts and tent his sweats. "Trust me, Darlin', I'm not the only guy who thinks watchin' a woman eat is hot. If you pay attention in catering, you'll see that most of the guys are staring at their plates to keep from poppin' a boner at how hot it is, so they don't embarrass themselves."

"Oh, please," Allissa scoffed, rolling her eyes at him again. "You can't really think this is hot." She took another big bite of her patty melt, moaning once more.

"Fuck, Darlin', you've gotta stop making those foodgasm noises." Dean reached down with the hand not holding his food to adjust his cock, losing the fight to prevent his erection.

Allissa's eyes widened as she blatantly studied his crotch.

"You should also stop looking at me like that," Dean suggested, wishing the sofa had some throw pillows he could use to cover up a little more. "When you stare like that, he thinks it's an invitation to come out and say hi."

Allissa's eyes popped up to his as her cheeks turned the prettiest shade of pink. Dean just smirked and took another bite of his burger, fighting to keep his eyes on hers, instead of looking to see if her nipples were hard under her tank top.

They ate in silence for several long moments, eventually turning to look at their food and the television, instead of each other. Dean opened the straws and stuck them in their shakes and Cokes, needing to wash down the first patty melt. Allissa followed his lead when he dove into their fries, drinks, and shakes before going for a second patty melt.

Knowing Allissa needed a topic change from the explicitly sexual turn of their discussion, Dean decided to circle back to their previous topic. He really wanted to know what he needed to do to earn her trust enough that he could take her on a real date, even if it probably wouldn't lead to a date, or even another kiss, at this point in time.

"So, before our food delivery rudely interrupted us, you were about to tell me what I need to do to convince you to go on a date with me." He kept his eyes on his food, only catching her pause in eating as she thought about his words through his peripheral vision.

"I, um, don't usually date," Allissa choked out before stuffing a few fries in her mouth.

Dean waited a moment for her to finish chewing, prompting her to follow up when she didn't elaborate after swallowing. "Why not?"

He expected her to give him an excuse about their schedule, fully prepared to suggest midday dates, since they worked during the evening hours when most people went out.

"I've never seen the appeal of romantic relationships," Allissa confided, her tone of voice turning solemn. "Probably because I'd never seen one that wasn't a disaster until I started working with the GWA. And I still have a hard time believing the couples I've met the last few months are as happy together as they seem."

"Damn, Darlin'." Dean was at a loss for words, unsure of how to respond to her revelation. "I'm sorry." He knew the words were completely inadequate, but it was all he could think of to say.

Allissa shrugged, and they lapsed into another awkward silence as they continued eating. Dean hated that their conversation had turned so somber, but he had to know just how bad the relationships she'd witnessed in her life were to, hopefully, get some ideas for how to show her that not all relationships were that way.

"I take it your parents were the first couple you saw in a disastrous relationship," Dean prodded, trying to get her to open up a little more before sucking down the last of his milkshake.

"No," Allissa laughed ruefully. "I don't even know who my father is, so I couldn't say if my parents had a disastrous relationship or not. In fact, if my mom has ever dated anyone seriously, I wouldn't know about it. She's never brought a man home to meet me, though I did see the aftermath when she got home from a few bad dates over the years. And a few of her friends, who were also our neighbors, had a few live-in losers over the years. None of them ever lasted very long, either turning abusive, or cheating, or both before the women kicked them out."

"Fuck," Dean fumed, hating that any woman had to suffer through the things Allissa had witnessed in her mom and neighbors' relationships. "I hope they had the bastards arrested when they kicked them out."

"Some of them, I'm sure." Allissa nodded, popping the last of her fries in her mouth. When she finished chewing and swallowed, she added, "I remember seeing police cars a couple of times, but I don't know if the guys were arrested or not."

From the sounds of things, being arrested was the least of what they deserved. Dean didn't want to share his thoughts on how he'd have punished the abusive assholes had he been around to witness the same things Allissa had because he didn't want his anger on behalf of those women to scare Allissa into thinking he'd be abusive.

"I hope the time you've spent with the GWA and in Heart's Destiny has shown you that not all men are abusive assholes, but I can see how it would take you more than a few months to believe it."

Fuck! How am I ever going to prove to her that I'd never do anything to hurt her like that? Will she even believe me if I promise never to be that way with her? Maybe not, but making that promise and reiterating it as often as she needs to hear it until the end of time is the only way I can think of to start trying to convince her.

Dean turned in his seat to take her hands in his, looking her in the eyes as he made his vow to her. "I promise you, I will never mistreat you in any way. I will never hit you or touch you in a way meant to harm you. I will never cheat on you. I want to protect you from anything that could ever hurt you. But I understand if it takes a while for you to believe that enough to give us a chance as more than friends. And if all you ever want from me is friendship, then I'll cherish our friendship, and never pressure you for anything more."

"You really mean all that?"

Dean couldn't tell if her softly spoken words came out as a question or a statement, but he reinforced his declaration of his intentions, just in case she questioned it. "Yes, I mean every word. And I never go back on a promise."

"Okay," Allissa smiled, squeezing his hands. "Thank you for being my friend."

"You don't ever have to thank me for that, Darlin'," Dean grinned. "Now, how 'bout we clean this mess up and get some sleep, so we can get up early enough for breakfast before our flight out in the morning?"

"Absolutely," Allissa agreed, smiling as she pulled her hands from his and started picking up the trash from their feast.

Dean assisted in disposing of their garbage before going to his room for the night, resigned to several more months, if not years, of jerking off in the shower while he worked to earn his place in Allissa's heart.

~~~

Monday, July 22, 2019, Columbus, Ohio

After wrestling with her conflicted thoughts and feelings for Dean all weekend, Allissa resolved to confide in her girlfriends a little more, needing their advice on how to reconcile everything in her head. On the one hand, she was still leery of men and romantic relationships, unable to completely banish the memories from her childhood of witnessing the bruises left on her mom, Kandi, and some of the other ladies in the trailer park. But on the other hand, she found herself confiding in Dean about things she hadn't even felt comfortable sharing with her mom in the past.

If I can trust him with knowing about my eating issues and feel comfortable eating junk food in front of him, shouldn't I be able to trust him not to hurt me if we go on a date?

He's been nothing but a gentleman the whole time we've been sharing a suite, so I don't think he'd try to force me to have sex with him if we went to a movie. So why can't I get the words to come out to agree to go on a date with him?

When she really thought about it and tried to be honest with herself, she had to admit that their one kiss only happened because she instigated it. Yeah, he'd taken over and taught her how to kiss, but he also stopped the kiss when she would have kept going all night.

Geez! Talk about giving the guy mixed signals! I went from calling him a player and telling him I'm not interested, to kissing him like I wanted to sleep with him. Then I went back to shutting down his flirting and trying to lock him in the friend zone, while also clinging to him as my hero every time I get scared by my stalker.

I'm so all over the place with him, I'm giving both of us whiplash!

Since she and Randi both had the night off from performing on the show, they hadn't gone into the locker room to change at the same time as the other women, so Allissa didn't get the chance to talk to them all at once like she'd hoped. Instead, she waited until everyone else was either focused on preparing for their matches or watching the show on the backstage monitors to grab her bestie and pull her off to an unused corner of the backstage area to ask her advice.
~~~

"What's going on?" Randi appeared to be concerned about Allissa's unusual request to talk privately. "You haven't been acting like yourself for the past few days."

"I haven't felt like myself for the past few days," Allissa admitted. "Hell, not just the last few days. More like the last couple of months."

"Is it the stalker?" Randi arched an eyebrow at Allissa from across the table where they'd sat down to talk.

"No, not really," Allissa confessed with a sigh. "I mean, that whole situation is stressful, but I know Dean, Cage, and the Avington Security guys are doing all they can to catch him and keep me safe. It's the situation with Dean that has me flustered."

"Girl, when are you gonna give in and let him punch your V-card?" Randi smirked. "Trust me, you'll feel a lot better about everything else once you do."

"I don't know," Allissa groaned, dramatically dropping her head to rest on her crossed arms on the tabletop. "I've started dreaming about doing it every night, but I'm still scared."

She turned her head, resting her cheek on her forearm to look at her friend as she explained, glossing over any details about her upbringing that might clue Randi in about her mom's former profession. "I didn't grow up believing in happily ever after like everyone else. I was raised by a single mom, who got pregnant on a random one-night stand and doesn't even know my sperm donor's name. The only romantic relationships I ever saw before I started working with the GWA were neighbors and friends of my mom, who hooked up with losers who abused them and slept around behind their backs. So, even though Dean has really stepped up to help out with this stalker situation and made great strides in showing me that he's not the player he used to be, I'm not sure I can believe it's real."

"I don't trust men in general, and my judgment of them even less than I trust them. And then when I think about how I've started leaning on Dean to make me feel safe from this stalker, I have to wonder if it's my fear making me think this attraction I feel for him is more than it really is, ya know."

"Oh, wow," Randi whisper-shouted, her eyes widening as her jaw dropped upon hearing the abridged version of Allissa's history. "So, that's why you've hung on to the V-card so long. Now it makes more sense."

While Allissa was glad her friend was starting to understand where she was coming from, she wished Randi would hurry up and come up with some great advice for her. "Yeah, so what do I do to quit feeling like a pinball bouncing around in my head between wanting to try things with Dean and wanting to run away from how he makes me feel?"

"Sorry, Vic, without having walked in your shoes, I can't tell you specifically how to let go of your issues." Randi gave Allissa a sympathetic look. "But I can tell you what helped me most in getting past my sexual hang-ups, after growing up in a household that taught me sex for more than procreation was a sin."

"Yeah, what's that?"

"Therapy," Randi advised with a smile. "And the love of a good man, who somehow, instinctually, knows just how far past my comfort zone to push me."

Randi's grin widened as she thought about her husband. "I'll gladly give you my therapist's contact information, so you can try some telehealth sessions like I do every month. But I think you've already found the man who instinctively knows what you need. And if he's anything like his twin, which I think he is more than they like to let on, then I'm sure you can't go wrong in letting your guard down around him and giving him the chance to show you the things you've previously been too scared to try for yourself."

"You really think I need to trust Dean?"

Randi nodded at Allissa's question. "Absolutely. I know you're afraid the stalker situation is making you feel things you wouldn't feel otherwise, but I don't think so. Ya'll were obviously attracted to one another long before your stalker became an issue. Dean looks at you the same way James looks at me, so I know his feelings for you are real. Now you just need to let him in and trust him to show you how loving relationships are supposed to be."

"And your therapist might be able to help me know how to do that?"

"I can't guarantee you'll get anything out of therapy," Randi shrugged. "But she helped me figure out I trusted James more than I thought I did, so I think she might be able to help you, too."

"Then, yeah, I'll try talking to her," Allissa agreed, adding the contact information to her phone when Randi forwarded it to her in a text. "Thank you. You don't know how much better I feel, just knowing I have a plan for how to deal with my crazy thoughts."

"Good," Randi smiled. "Anytime you need to talk, I'll gladly listen. And nobody has to know…" Randi trailed off as James and Dean sat down beside them.

"Nobody has to know about what?" James gave his wife a curious look.

"About girl talk," Randi grinned before leaning over and kissing James.

"Rick said we can cut out early since we're not working the show tonight," Dean informed Allissa while James and Randi made out on the other side of the table. "And we should probably usher these two out of here before they forget the rest of us are around and start losing their clothes."

Allissa laughed as James flipped Dean off without stopping kissing Randi.

"Go to your room!" Allissa wasn't sure which one of the older boys, who were raiding the catering table for a snack, yelled at James and Randi, but it was all they needed to finally break up their PDA.

"Damn, how did Tia teach them all to be little cock blockers, when she's only seen them the couple of times we've been back home in the last three months?" James chuckled.

"I have a feeling she and Connor have been talking online while they're home with baby Sam," Randi chortled. "But you can't tell Anthony."

"Oh, no, Angel," James objected as they all stood to get their things and leave the arena. "If he can cock block me, it's only fair that I cock block him back by telling Tia's dad. Besides, as Anthony's best friends, it's mine and Dean's job to back him in protecting his daughter from teenage boys."

"Oh, please, Tia is perfectly capable of cock blocking Connor all by herself," Randi laughed, as the couple started walking away. "And since she won't even let him hold her hand, I don't think ya'll have anything to worry about when it comes to protecting her from Connor."

"Ready to head back to the hotel, Darlin'?" Dean leaned his head in the direction of the exit.

"Sure," Allissa agreed, walking with Dean toward the locker rooms, so they could get the things they'd stored there earlier before they knew they had the night off.

"Since we're heading out early, how about we stop off for some wor su gai on the way?"

"Wor su gai?" Allissa looked up at Dean as they walked, trying to figure out what he was talking about. "What's that?"

"It's one of the foods the city of Columbus is known for," Dean explained. "It's a chicken and rice dish, but I doubt it's as healthy as the chicken and rice we had in catering earlier."

"Sure. I'm always interested in trying new foods."

Dean just grinned in response as they went into their separate locker rooms to grab their things. Once they met back up outside the locker rooms and walked out to the rental car, Allissa wondered if they were getting takeout, or actually going to sit down in a restaurant like they were on a date. "Is this your subtle way of getting me to go on a date with you without actually asking me on a date?"

"Um, not intentionally," Dean chuckled. "But since I haven't ever been to the restaurant I read about earlier, I don't know if they do takeout or not, so maybe, accidentally."

Allissa had to laugh at the way Dean was acting like an innocent little boy as he drove them to the restaurant. "Then I guess I have no choice but to agree to go on a dinner date with you."

"No, you absolutely still have a choice," Dean objected, his expression turning serious from the previously boyish charm. "If this restaurant doesn't do takeout, then I'll search online for one that does."

"No, you don't have to do that." Allissa shook her head, and reached over to put her hand on Dean's arm reassuringly. "I think a casual dinner out with you might be just what I need to deal with some of my eating and dating issues without too much pressure."

"Are you sure?" Dean arched an eyebrow as he quickly glanced at her before turning his eyes back to the road. "I'm more than willing to wait if you're not ready for more than takeout as friends."

Allissa took a deep breath as she gathered her courage. *Since he's the only person I've ever trusted enough to share my eating issues with, he's probably the only person I'll ever trust enough to try dating, especially if the date includes going to a restaurant.*

"No, I want to go on a date with you," she finally admitted with a small smile in his direction.

"Then let's go on our first date, Darlin'," Dean grinned back.

It didn't take him long to drive to the restaurant he'd read about earlier in the day, telling her about the article he read about famous foods from Columbus, Ohio. Once they arrived, he escorted her to their table with a hand on the small of her back, making her tingle inside in a way she'd only ever experienced with Dean.

Like the gentleman he was, he pulled out her chair for her and waited for her to sit down before taking a seat himself. Allissa hadn't ever seen a man behave in such a manner in real life, until she'd started working with the GWA. And Dean was the only man to ever show such behavior specifically to her. It might mean she wasn't as liberated as her mother had raised her to be, but Allissa couldn't help but like the way he seemed to take care of her with such thoughtful niceties.

After they placed their order, she circled the conversation back to the article, thinking it seemed odd and out of character for Dean to read a random article like that. "So, why did you read an article about famous foods from Columbus?"

Dean leaned back in his seat and sighed. "So, I told you I'm not really into reading books and stuff when we talked about our hobbies, right?"

Allissa nodded before he continued.

"What I didn't tell you is that I don't like reading books because they're too long and frustrating." He looked nervous as he admitted, "I was diagnosed with dyslexia as a kid, so reading and writing have always been a chore for me. I swear autocorrect is the only reason my papers in college made any sense, and the only reason I do okay with texting now. But if I want a career after wrestling, I have to keep up my reading skill, too. So, I find a few minutes each day to look up an article about whatever city we're in at the time. They're short enough to keep from frustrating me, and long enough to keep me in practice with the skills the therapists taught me as a kid to be able to read in school. And I get to learn and experience a little something different about every place we travel."

Allissa was in awe at how he'd overcome an issue like dyslexia while finding a way to get something more out of his therapy to treat it. "Wow, I would have never guessed that you had to deal with that kind of issue. But I love how you've used it to experience more of the local flare wherever we go. Besides new foods, what else have you learned that the rest of us missed out on?"

"As much as I love to eat, it's mostly been new foods," Dean chuckled. "Some of which I wish I hadn't learned about, like jellied moose nose when we were in Canada."

"Oh, that sounds disgusting," Allissa cringed, trying not to gag at the thought of people eating something with the word "nose" in the title, which sounded like it would be the same consistency as boogers.

"Yeah, I didn't go try that one," Dean shuddered. "But I've also found interesting places to visit that are almost exclusively known about by locals, like the wave organ and secret tiled staircase in San Francisco."

"Wait, we were just in San Francisco last month," Allissa blurted. "Why didn't you mention these things then, so I could have seen them, too?"

"Yeah, well, you were still tryin' to avoid me that weekend, Darlin'," Dean smirked. "But maybe if you agree to keep dating me, I'll show 'em to you the next time we're there."

"Oh," was all she could say, suddenly embarrassed by how she'd kept fighting her attraction to Dean by hiding out in her hotel room to keep her distance. Luckily, the waiter delivered their meals, effectively changing the subject of their conversation away from the uncomfortable topic of her fighting the attraction between them.

After discussing the food and what they each thought of it, Dean asked her about her favorite places they'd traveled to since she started working with the GWA. It turned out that neither one of them could narrow it down to one specific city, but they agreed that the European tour took top billing for both of them, since they had skipped their midday workout sessions to hit up the various tourist attractions with the rest of the GWA crew.

When Dean mentioned that the guys with families did their workouts early in the morning so they could do those same kinds of touristy things at midday back in the States, Allissa agreed to try to get up a little earlier each day, in order to swap over their workout schedule on the days they were in cities with tourist attractions she or Dean wanted to see.

She wasn't sure she'd be successful in training her body to survive on an hour or two less sleep than she was currently getting. But since she'd successfully eaten an unhealthy meal with Dean in public while they talked about their schedules, she hoped she'd be able to shave off some of the time she needed in the mornings by grabbing food on the way to the airport, instead of having to wait in the room and order room service for breakfast.

The rest of the evening seemed to fly by as Allissa enjoyed her time with Dean. Even the tingles she felt when he took her hand to walk her out of the restaurant and into their hotel.

Since we're calling this our first date, I wonder if he's going to kiss me goodnight when we get up to the suite? Or since it's still early with us leaving the arena so early, will he want to spend some time making out on the couch?

Allissa fidgeted nervously as they waited for the elevator, trying to decide if she was ready for more than a single goodnight kiss.

Damn it! If I'd have realized we were going on a date tonight before my talk with Randi, I'd have asked her what to expect for how we're supposed to end the night. Then I wouldn't be so freaked out about possibly doing more than kissing on the couch.

Allissa shuffled along a half-step behind Dean as he scoped out the other people on the elevator before stepping on and positioning Allissa between him and the wall, with him between her and the rest of the hotel guests taking the elevator up to the rooms. Dean released her hand and wrapped his arm around her shoulders, obviously interpreting her nervousness as a wariness about being so close to the group of strangers.

Allissa was surprised to be able to relax a little into his side, thinking she was less worried about Dean protecting her from the men in the elevator than she was about potentially making out with him when they got up to their suite. *I guess my body is on board with more than kissing, even if my mind isn't quite there yet.*

Once they were alone on the walk down the hall to their suite, Allissa's anxiety amped up with each step they took.

"Relax, Darlin'." Dean gave her a reassuring squeeze into his side as he unlocked their suite. "It'll only take me a minute to clear our rooms before we can get you safely inside."

Allissa gave him what she knew was a weak smile as he released her to step into the suite, unsure how much longer it would take before he realized she wasn't stressing about the stalker right then. Since he hadn't closed the door completely behind him, Allissa watched him through the small gap until he left the area of the room that she could see.

Oh, this whole date thing was a bad idea. I probably should have insisted on takeout tonight, and waited until after I talk to the therapist before agreeing to this.

"All clear," Dean announced as he pulled the door the rest of the way open for her to enter.

Allissa didn't reply as she stepped into the suite. She stopped just a few feet in, unsure if she should wait for the goodnight kiss or just flee to her room.

Dean shut the door and loudly engaged the extra locking mechanisms before walking up behind her and rubbing his hands on her shoulders. "It's okay, Darlin'. The stalker's not here and nothing looks disturbed, so you can relax now."

Allissa only nodded in response, still standing there stiffly as she waited for him to show her how a typical date ended.

Dean released his light grip on her shoulders and took a step around her, using one finger to lift her chin, so she had to look into his eyes. "Hey, Darlin', why are you still so tense?"

"I, um, uh," Allissa stuttered before finally babbling, "Is our date over? I'm assuming it is, since we're back in our room. But I don't know how we're supposed to end it. Are we supposed to kiss goodnight? Or just rush off to our separate rooms since we're back to our normal friend zone? Or does dating mean we're supposed to make out on the couch for a little while before going to bed together? 'Cause I'm not ready to sleep with you, even though I wouldn't mind a little kissing."

Allissa closed her eyes and her mouth as embarrassment washed over her from admitting to wanting to kiss him.

"We can end the date however you want, Darlin'." Allissa could hear the smile in Dean's tone as he stroked a finger over her cheek. "I'd kinda like a little kissing. But if you wanna skip it 'til you're sure you're ready, then we can call it a wonderful night and go to our separate rooms."

Allissa opened her eyes again, needing to look into Dean's to verify the truth in his words. She clearly saw patience and honesty in his dark blue-gray gaze. She was fascinated with the way his eyes seemed to change color depending on the emotions he felt.

Having gray eyes herself, she knew they could appear to change color based on the lighting and color of clothing a person was wearing. But Allissa had always thought her mom was wrong when she called them "mood ring eyes" as she was growing up. The only time she could ever see the different appearance of color in her own eyes was when she changed her clothing or makeup to get them to reflect the different colors. But Dean's eyes definitely changed based on his mood, no matter what color shirt he was wearing at the time.

She'd figured out that they were greener when he was excited about something, noticing the color most often when he was in the ring or talking about some aspect of the wrestling business. She'd also seen them so dark brown they were almost black, only seeing that color when he was angry about her stalker. They were a steel-gray whenever he was happy, usually when he was hanging out with his friends or family. But she wasn't sure what the navy-blue she only saw when they were alone meant.

I'll have to ask Randi if she's ever noticed the same thing about James's eyes. Maybe she knows what the blue means.

Whatever it meant, Allissa found the color that seemed to be reserved for only her extremely attractive. So much so that she couldn't stop herself from admitting, "I'd like to spend a little time kissing before we go to our separate beds for the night."

Dean just smiled instead of replying. He cupped her face in his hands, holding her in place as he brought their lips together. The kiss started off soft and sweet, and much less erratic than the kiss Allissa had initiated a couple of weeks earlier.

She followed his lead, as they moved their lips over one another, opening her mouth when Dean did so he could deepen the kiss. Allissa was much less wary of tangling her tongue with his than she'd been the first time, not wasting a second before she licked into his mouth.

She unconsciously wrapped her arms around him, pressing her body into his as they continued to kiss the way James and Randi had earlier backstage. It wasn't until she felt his erection pressing into her belly that she realized what she was doing.

Oh, gawd, what am I doing? I shouldn't be rubbing up on him like a cat in heat. He's going to think I'm ready for more than kissing if I keep this up. But, damn, it feels so good, I can't seem to make myself stop.

Allissa enjoyed the feel of Dean pressed against every inch of her torso for a few moments longer than she thought she should have before finally releasing him from her embrace and stepping back, effectively breaking their kiss. "So-sorry," she stuttered out, closing her eyes in embarrassment at her wanton behavior.

"Nothin' to be sorry about, Darlin'," Dean informed her, not releasing his gentle hold on her face. He placed a quick kiss on her forehead before finally releasing her and stepping back. "Like I said, we can do as much or as little as you want. And I'm happy to call it a night, knowing I'm gonna have some sweet dreams about that kiss."

Yeah, me too, Allissa thought, but couldn't bring herself to say. "Goodnight, Dean," she finally muttered before scurrying off to her room.

"Goodnight, Darlin'. Hope you have some sweet dreams tonight, too."

Yeah, I will. Right after I pull up another article and follow the directions for trying again to masturbate. Maybe thinking about Dean being the one to touch me will make it feel better than it did the last time I tried, so maybe I can finally find out what all the hype about orgasms is all about.

Chapter Ten

The last week was both the best week of Dean's life and the most torturous. It was the best week because he was officially dating Allissa. They had to get up early for workouts and schedule their dates for the middle of the day due to their schedule as they toured around the Mid-Atlantic and South-Atlantic states. But they had come up with a fun excursion each day and called it their date time. Dean loved every minute of the time he spent exploring unusual sights and trying new foods with Allissa. Getting to hold her hand as they explored quirky places like Randyland in Pittsburg and hugging her to his side when they took a picture with the world's largest Rubik's Cube earlier in the day there in Knoxville were the highlights of his days. The torture came into play when they rejoined the rest of the GWA crew at the end of their midday dates and reverted to acting like they were only friends instead of dating.

When they reached the Knoxville arena, they got the news from Cage that her stalker had sent another doll to the hotel that morning, this time dressed in a gold outfit to match the one she'd worn at the *Gateway to the Gold* pay-per-view. Apparently, the stalker didn't care if he could get an actual room number for Allissa or not. He still kept sending things to the hotels the GWA frequently used, assuming the packages would still get to her.

It wasn't just the stalker not going away that was getting to Dean. Not being able to kiss Allissa the way he wanted to start moving them to more than kissing, and the fact that he hadn't gotten more than a chaste peck of a kiss from her in the last week, was what was really killing him.

He knew she wasn't ready for more yet, but he was dying for at least a few more of the long, deep kisses like they'd shared after their first date. Since they hadn't ended any more of their dates back at their hotel room, Allissa hadn't given him any indication that she wanted to really kiss him again.

And even though they still shared a suite and ate a late-night meal together after the GWA shows when they got back to the hotel, she had reverted to acting like they were just friends then, saying "goodnight" and going to her own bed without even the slightest hint that she wanted a goodnight kiss. It was taking every ounce of willpower Dean possessed to keep from pushing her for more than she was ready to give him.

But damn, she was so responsive when we kissed. I don't understand how she doesn't seem to want a repeat performance every night.

Dean rolled over onto his side and watched her sleeping peacefully in her bed, just a few short feet away from his. In the three weeks since he'd insisted on sharing a suite with her, this was the first night they hadn't been able to get a two-bedroom suite at the hotel.

When they first checked in that morning, Dean hadn't been happy and wanted to search for a new hotel. But since the room he was assigned had two queen-sized beds, Allissa had argued it would be fine for one night, so they could hurry up and get started on their midday date.

He couldn't disagree with wanting to get started on their date earlier, so he'd acquiesced. It wasn't until they got back to the room after the show that Dean realized what a bad idea it was for them to share such a small space, and especially only one bathroom.

He hadn't felt comfortable showering, and more specifically jerking off to thoughts of her during his shower, while she was wide awake right outside the bathroom door. So, he'd had to skip his second solo-sex session of the day, and was finding it extremely hard to go to sleep when he could see her in the sliver of moonlight shining through a crack in the curtains.

Fuck! I hope she's actually asleep, he thought as he let his eyes roam over the delicate features of her face. As he trailed his eyes down her form, he could see the swell of her breasts, which weren't exactly hidden under the thin blanket on the bed. *Damn, if I can see her this well, then she can probably see how I'm tenting my sweats just as clearly.*

Dean laid there fighting his need as long as he could, knowing he wouldn't actually die from blue balls, no matter how much it seemed to hurt at the time. But when she made the cutest little cooing noise that wasn't quite a snore, he couldn't hold out any longer.

Dean quietly got out of bed and stepped softly around Allissa's bed to go take another shower, resolving to be as silent as possible while jerking off. *Hopefully, the water running in the shower won't be loud enough to wake her up.*

He softly shut the bathroom door and quickly stripped off the sweats and t-shirt he'd worn to bed out of respect for Allissa being in the same room. Then he turned on the water and stepped into the shower. Instead of grabbing his bodywash, as usual, to slick things up, Dean picked up the bottle that Allissa had left in the shower earlier.

Lavender, he read from the label as he opened the bottle and took a sniff. *Guess this is why she always smells like flowers.*

He squirted a good-sized dollop into his palm before placing the bottle back on the shelf where she'd left it. *Fuck! I'm gonna come on the first stroke like a virginal teenager when I'm smelling her at the same time.*

Dean bit his lip to keep from moaning as he palmed his cock and fought not to blow his load immediately. *Just think about kissing her. Don't think about touching her yet.*

Dean closed his eyes and leaned back against the wall of the shower, as he mentally relived the kiss they'd shared at the end of their first date while languidly stroking his cock. She hadn't been as tentative as she was the first time they kissed after Rick and Fiona's wedding. Instead, she'd followed his lead beautifully, mirroring every movement of his mouth and tongue.

She'd also pressed her body against him, rubbing on him like she was searching for a special touch that he knew she wasn't ready for him to give her just yet. As bad as he'd wanted to wrap her in his arms and thrust his hips against her, Dean had somehow managed to stand still and keep his hands on her face the whole time. A week later and he still wasn't sure how he'd held back.

Remembering the feel of her tits pressed into his chest and her midsection softly cradling his cock caused Dean's balls to start tingling, signaling that he was about to come already. *Fuck, no, not yet! I wanna at least picture her naked before I come.*

Dean opened his eyes, hoping he could stave off the orgasm by seeing his surroundings and not his mental picture of Allissa. But as he peered through the clear shower curtain, his eyes met the blue-gray gaze of the woman he was just fantasizing about. Well, they would have if she'd been looking up at his face. Dean froze in place with his hand covering the head and the first inch or so of the shaft of his dick. He was glad his hand was big enough to hide both his piercings from her view, knowing she wasn't ready to see them just yet. He stood there immobile for the longest time, unsure how to handle her walking in on him in the middle of masturbating.

Fuck! Fuck! Fuck! Fuck! Fuck!

I knew I shouldn't have done this tonight. But fuck, I didn't trust myself not to crawl in bed with her if I didn't.

He watched as Allissa looked up from where he'd stopped stroking his cock, loving the way her eyes dilated as she took in his body before she finally looked him in the eyes.

"I, uh, I'm sorry," Allissa stuttered out, holding up an empty glass in one hand and pointing in the direction of the bathroom sink with the other. "I just wanted a sip of water and didn't realize you were in here."

"It's alright, Darlin'," Dean assured her as he continued fighting not to come from the way she was looking at him. "Go ahead and get your drink and I'll, uh, be out in a minute." *And please turn on the hot tap, so this shower will go ice cold and help me get my dick under control.*

"Oh, um, okay." Allissa turned toward the sink, but even with her back to him, she seemed to be looking at his cock in the mirror.

Dean closed his eyes again, fighting the urge to start stroking his dick once more. Unfortunately, when she turned on the tap to fill her glass with water, she only turned on the cold, so his shower temperature wasn't affected. *Damn it, I really need that cold shower now!*

He heard the door shut and opened his eyes to find Allissa had left the room. He contemplated turning the water to straight cold, thinking it would help him get his erection to go down without her hearing him as he got off to more thoughts of her. But the more he thought about it, the more he knew it wouldn't be enough to keep him from tenting his sweats again the instant he walked out of the bathroom and saw her in those tiny sleep shorts and tank top again.

So, he did the only thing he could that might give him a few minutes to get to his bed and cover his crotch before popping another boner at the sight of Allissa. Dean closed his eyes once more and imagined Allissa standing in the bathroom naked as he slid his hand back down his shaft.

He envisioned her leaning back against the door, touching herself as she watched him jacking off. *Just because she's not ready for me to touch her, doesn't mean we can't enjoy a little mutual masturbation. Even if it's only in my fantasies.*

Fuck! I'd love to see how she touches herself. Watch what she does that gets the best reaction, so I know all her unique trigger points to be able to give her the most pleasure the first time I get to touch her.

He continued to stroke his dick, applying more and more pressure until his grip was as tight as he imagined her pussy would be the first time he fucked her.

Based on the way she couldn't stop staring at my cock, I bet she'd like to watch me jerk off, too. Hell, as quiet as she was standing there watching, I bet she would have stuck around for the whole show, if I hadn't opened my eyes and caught her.

Damn, now I wish I hadn't opened my eyes. Maybe giving her a show would have pushed her into wanting more. Or at least admitting to wanting to watch.

Dean could tell that she was still too innocent to tell him what she wanted, whether it was just a kiss goodnight, or to watch him masturbate like he thought he saw her yearning for a few minutes earlier. But he hoped that she'd eventually feel secure enough in their relationship to be able to share her sexual desires with him. He wanted to be the man to fulfill all her sexual fantasies, no matter how tame or kinky they might turn out to be.

As he continued stroking his cock, Dean went back to the fantasy of her standing there fingering her pussy with one hand, and playing with her tits with the other, while watching him jack off. It wasn't the first time he tried to imagine her naked, and guessed on the color of her nipples and how much pubic hair she kept when she went to get waxed with the other women wrestlers. Considering the bikinis he'd seen her in when they went swimming over the past few months, Dean didn't think she kept much, if any.

Fuck! Dean bit his lip again to keep from groaning as he pictured her fingers playing with her bare pussy. *What I would give for a taste of that sweet slit.*

With thoughts of her coming on her own fingers and then offering them to him to lick clean, Dean let loose, shooting jet after jet of thick, white cum on the clear shower curtain. *Fuck! Yes! Allissa!* Dean screamed mentally, as he clamped his mouth shut to keep from uttering a sound to alert her to what he was doing.

It took a few minutes for the aftershocks to stop and for him to catch his breath after the intense climax. As soon as he felt like he'd partially recovered, Dean pulled the shower curtain under the spray of the water to rinse his cum down the drain. Then he grabbed his own bodywash and cleaned himself as quickly as possible.

Time to go have a talk with my girl, Dean thought as he rinsed off. *'Cause there's no way she's already asleep after that.*

Not that I have any clue what to say to her. But I can't let her go to sleep without addressing the elephant-sized dick in the room. Dean chuckled at his mental quip as he shut off the shower and dried off.

I don't want her to feel embarrassed about seeing me, or think I'm upset about her seeing me. But I also don't want her to feel any pressure to take the next step with me until she's ready.

Hopefully, this won't be as awkward as some of the after-sex talks I've had with ring rats who wouldn't leave when we were done. Dean mused as he put his clothes from earlier back on. *Naw, this won't be that bad. For one, because we didn't have sex. And for two, because I don't want Allissa to leave.*

This is just me repeating what I've already told her about wanting more with her but not until she's ready. So, it'll go fine, and we'll be back to normal before morning. And maybe I can work in something about it being okay for her to watch since I'm her man, so I can convince her to finally admit we're dating to the rest of the GWA.

~ ~ ~

As she chugged the water and put the glass on the table between the beds, Allissa felt mortified at having walked in on Dean masturbating in the shower. She crawled back into bed and buried her face in her pillow, trying to force herself back to sleep before he returned to the room. *Why didn't I think to look over at his bed to make sure he was still in it before I just walked into the bathroom?*

Oh, yeah. Because I was afraid that if I looked over at him asleep, I'd be tempted to crawl into his bed to cuddle with him.

Stupid! Stupid! Stupid!

Waking up in the morning cuddling with him couldn't be nearly as embarrassing as walking in on him in the bathroom and staring at his dick! At least then I could have claimed to have been sleepwalking or something to have an excuse.

But no, I'm stuck with the lame-ass excuse of getting up for a drink of water and not knowing he was in there. While that's true and covers why I walked in there, it certainly doesn't explain why I stood there for several minutes just staring at his dick.

He's never going to believe that I was so shocked at the sight that I froze. No, I think the way I was drooling was a dead giveaway that I was enjoying watching and wanted to stay to see him finish.

And now I have a whole new set of questions for Randi about how something that big fits inside a woman. Plus, the questions for the therapist, Kelly, about whether being fascinated by what he was doing and wanting to watch makes me a pervert.

Allissa made sure she was covered from head to toe and intentionally laid on her stomach, so her hard nipples at remembering every detail about Dean's dick wouldn't be obvious when he walked back into the room.

And what was up with the jewelry I saw before he covered it up when he stopped stroking?

It wasn't her aversion to needles, or even thoughts of how painful it must have been to pierce his dick, that came to mind when she remembered seeing his piercings. She was too focused on trying to remember back to middle school health class to figure out if the jewelry would catch on anything inside her if they ever tried to have sex.

Can he even have sex with that jewelry in? I'm assuming so, because I don't think a guy would pierce his dick if he couldn't have sex anymore because of it.

But even if it's possible for someone as big as Dean to fit inside me, won't the jewelry scraping my insides be painful? Guess that's something else I should ask Randi.

Oh, geez, how embarrassing will it be to ask her about dick piercings, when I can't be sure James is pierced the same way Dean is? I mean, I know they're probably the same size since they're twins and all. But their tattoos don't all match, so they might not both be pierced.

Guess I'll be Googling "sex with a dick piercing" the next time I get a few minutes alone, so I don't have to embarrass myself by asking anyone about that.

Oh, gawd! I hope we can get a two-bedroom suite at the hotel in Nashville tomorrow. If not, then I guess I'll be locking the bathroom door when I go to take a shower, and bringing my phone with me to look it up then, since that's the only way I'll be guaranteed the privacy to do that research.

Realizing her nights alone in her bedroom were her only private moments in the last three weeks sidetracked Allissa from her thoughts about Dean's dick. Having spent so much time on her own growing up, and in the first nine months of her time working with the GWA, Allissa was surprised at how she hadn't missed her alone time since starting to room with Dean. Instead, she'd felt perfectly comfortable spending most of the time she usually spent alone doing things with him.

I'm not sure I want to know what that means about our relationship. I'm sure if I were to mention it to Randi, she'd say it's because we're meant to be together or something sappy about soulmates.

Allissa still wasn't sure she believed in all that soulmates and meant-to-be-a-couple stuff that Randi kept trying to convince her was true for her and Dean. While it seemed to be the real deal for Randi and James, and all the other romantic relationships in the GWA, Allissa wasn't sure she was lucky enough to find that same happiness in life with Dean.

Although I thought maybe mine and Mom's luck improved when I got this job, I think being the only person in the GWA with a stalker shows that it really didn't.

She might have agreed on one of their talks over the last week that they were officially dating, but she still wasn't convinced that the relationship wouldn't end in heartache instead of happily ever after. She also might have trusted him to help her start investing some of her income, since they talked about their plans for after they retired from the GWA. But letting him know that she was clueless about how to manage large sums of money because of growing up with little to none wasn't really the secret from her childhood that she feared would come between them. Her mother's former profession was the one secret she wasn't sure she'd ever feel safe with trusting him to know.

Even if he doesn't think I've done some of the things mom had to do to earn a living for us after seeing first-hand how sexually inept and inexperienced I am, I'm sure he won't want to sully his reputation by being involved with the daughter of a former prostitute and one of her johns. But I can't seem to stop myself from wanting to, at least, enjoy a few experiences with him that I've never wanted from anyone else before he kicks me to the curb.

Allissa let those self-deprecating thoughts drift away when she felt the energy in the room change, as Dean walked out of the bathroom. But she was too embarrassed to face him, so she pretended to be asleep as she heard him click on the light between the beds.

"I know you can't be asleep that fast, Darlin'," Dean chuckled. "So quit hiding and let's talk."

"HHHUUUMMM, SHOOO. HHHUUUMMM, SHOOO." Allissa couldn't bring herself to face him, so she feigned snoring and hoped he bought it.

"That's not gonna work, Darlin'," Dean laughed. "Even James isn't that bad at faking sleep."

Yeah, I knew it the instant I tried it. Allissa sighed as she rolled over and sat up in bed. She pulled her knees up under the blanket and hugged them to her chest to try to cover up her traitorous nipples that made it obvious how aroused she was by seeing Dean naked. She rested her head on her knees, unable to look over at Dean. "Can we just pretend that didn't happen? Or chalk it up to me sleepwalking and pretend we don't remember it happening?"

"Sorry, Darlin', no can do," Dean chuckled. "But until you're ready to see that and a whole lot more, we'll go find another hotel where we can get a two-bedroom suite, if our usual hotel doesn't have one available."

"Yeah, I now understand why you thought a single room was a bad idea, even with two beds." Though she couldn't figure out why the thought of going back to separate bedrooms gave her a sense of disappointment.

Duh! It's because you want to see him naked again. And if you were being really honest with yourself, you'd realize that you'd rather be in a single room with only one bed, so you could lose your V-card and cuddle up to that stud muffin all night, every night. Allissa's inner voice sounded an awful lot like a mix of the women's division of the GWA.

"It's not that I thought it was a bad idea," Dean disagreed, confusing her even more. "I just didn't want you to feel pressured to do more with me than you're ready for. But I honestly thought it would be my tendency to strip in my sleep when I get overheated, and you seeing me in just my boxers the next morning that would bother you."

Allissa wasn't sure she believed him. She had a feeling that the scene she'd witnessed in the bathroom was a regular occurrence for him, and that he had to have expected her to catch him in the act at some point.

Why else would he have waited until after I went to sleep to do that? He certainly didn't take that long in the shower earlier this evening, so I'm guessing he didn't do it when I was awake to try to keep me from realizing what he was doing.

But why didn't he want me to know what he was doing? That's what doesn't make sense to me. If he's really interested in having sex with me, wouldn't he want me to know what he was doing and be tempted to join him in the shower? Unless he really isn't interested, and all his flirtation is just an act?

"Why did you wait until I was asleep to do that, anyway?" Allissa closed her eyes, cringing at how she'd just blurted out her question.

"Because you're not ready for more than an occasional kiss, and I didn't want to make you feel pressured for more than that if you heard me," Dean admitted, sounding a little embarrassed.

Allissa turned her head to look at him and realized he was sitting in the middle of his bed with a pillow in his lap. *So he is interested and just trying to let me set the pace? Then why is he still trying to keep me from looking at his dick?*

"Why would I feel pressured from hearing you do the same thing I'm sure most men do regularly?" Allissa felt irrationally hurt by the way he seemed to be pulling back from her by hiding his bulge under the pillow. Him not wanting her to look at his body reinforced her assumption that he wasn't really interested in her, but had just pursued her because she'd been a challenge. Unfortunately, her pain at that being the case seemed to manifest itself as anger, causing her to tear up, lash out, and rant.

"I might not have had a boyfriend before, but I took Sex Ed in school like everyone else. I know your body produces semen daily and you have to expel it, just like my body goes through the various stages of my menstrual cycle every month. I mean, I don't want you walking in on me in the middle of changing a bloody tampon. But I'm not going to suffer through leaving one in too long, so I only change them when you're not right outside the bathroom. So, I'm not going to be upset or feel pressured by hearing you take care of your normal bodily functions. And maybe if I had heard you, I wouldn't have walked in on you and seen more than you wanted me to see."

"Oh, I wanted you to see a whole lot more than you did," Dean snarked back in response to her pissy tone. "So much so that I fantasized about you watching me while I finished myself off."

Allissa would have believed his admission if he wasn't still covering his lap with a pillow. "Then why are you hiding your dick now? It's like you're repulsed that I might want to look at it."

"Because my dick isn't as much of a gentleman as I am." Dean tossed the pillow to the side, and Allissa got an eyeful of the tentpole in his sweatpants. "I was trying to be considerate and show you that I'm in this for the long haul by patiently waiting while you set the pace for our relationship. But if you wanna see how my cock stands up and tries to get your attention every time we're in the same room, then by all means, look as much as you want, Darlin'."

Allissa couldn't tear her eyes away from the prominent bulge in his pants, even though she felt ridiculous for how they somehow ended up fighting. *Geez, what's wrong with me? How did I go from apologizing for walking in on him to arguing with him? This is, like, the most outrageous case of PMS I've ever experienced. Maybe my hormones are more affected by my newfound libido than I thought.*

"What are we even fighting about?" She somehow managed to lift her gaze to Dean's as she posed the question.

"I have no idea," Dean chuckled, causing her to laugh along with him. "But I'm down with finding out if make-up sex is as good as everyone says it is." He wagged his eyebrows at her as he adjusted his erection.

"Yeah, I'm not sure I'm ready for that yet," Allissa giggled as she shook her head at him and blushed. "But maybe we could try a make-up make-out session?"

"We can definitely do that, Darlin'," Dean grinned as he shifted in his bed to sit with his back to the headboard. "But you're gonna hafta come over here for it. That way, when you feel like we've gone as far as you're comfortable goin', you can go back to the safety of your bed."

"Are you implying that your bed isn't safe?" Allissa slowly crawled out from under the covers on her bed and moved to the edge on her way to Dean's. She was a little nervous about what was to come, but also excited at the possibilities.

"I'll keep you safe no matter which bed you're in, Darlin'," Dean assured her. "But your bed is the no-touch zone. Mine is where all the kissin' and touchin' happens. At least, for now. I'm still only gonna go as far as you're comfortable with and work us up to more gradually. And hopefully, you'll eventually feel safe enough with me to open your bed up to kissin' and touchin', too."

"You make this sound like a game of tag with my bed as the base," Allissa giggled as she stood and took the two steps over to Dean's bed, embracing the excitement and trying to let the nerves go.

"Well, I do wanna tag you, Darlin'," Dean smirked, taking her hand, and pulling her onto his bed. "But only with kisses for now. And maybe having you wear a 'Property of Dean Dangerous' t-shirt during rehearsals tomorrow so everyone knows we're a couple."

Allissa rolled her eyes at how silly Dean was behaving. Though she secretly liked him wanting to claim her in front of their friends and coworkers. "Is that what we are?"

"Yeah, Darlin', we're most definitely a couple. Have been since you agreed to our first date last week. Remember when I first mentioned dating, and told you it would mean we'd be a couple and not ashamed to kiss in front of our friends?"

"Oh, yeah," Allissa remembered back to their first conversation about going on a date. "But we haven't done any of that PDA stuff you mentioned, so I forgot you'd said something about it."

"Yeah, I didn't think it would happen until after your stalker is caught," Dean admitted sheepishly. "So, I've been holding back to keep from making you feel overwhelmed by everything. But I consider you my girlfriend, since we agreed we're officially dating last week, so I wanna start reaping some of those PDA benefits." Dean wagged his eyebrows at her suggestively.

"If I'm your girlfriend, does that make you my boyfriend?" Allissa giggled as she tried to flirt with him, but she wasn't sure she was successful.

"Yeah, Darlin'," Dean grinned. "Now, come sit on my lap and let me kiss you the way I've been dying to kiss you for the last week."

"I think you're trying to get more than a kiss by suggesting I sit on your lap." Allissa arched a skeptical eyebrow at him as she scooted closer to him, the butterflies in her belly flapping up a storm.

"Oh, Darlin', I want a lot more than a kiss, but I'm not trying to trick you into anything. With you on top, you control how much we touch while we're kissin'. You can sit close to my knees and just touch our lips together, if that's all you want. But if you want to scoot a little closer, and use our hands a little more, I'll follow your lead and only touch you as much as you touch me. Deal?"

"Okay," Allissa agreed, her nervousness amping up as she moved to straddle Dean's thighs, just above his knees. Once she was in position, she leaned forward and pressed her lips to his.

Dean did exactly as he said he would, letting her take the lead and set the pace for their kiss. Allissa felt extremely awkward as she moved her lips over Dean's, wishing he'd take over and kiss her the way he had previously, instead of just moving his lips the same way she was. *Guess I'm going to have to do like Mom always says and "show my pussy" by opening my mouth and using my tongue the way he did before.*

Allissa's mom had taught her as a teenager that everyone had it wrong, when they called someone a "pussy" to insinuate they were weak and to "grow a pair of balls" to toughen up and do something difficult.

"Obviously, whoever came up with those terms was an idiot," her mother had declared. "A man's balls can't take nearly as much punishment as a woman's pussy. So we should say we're 'showing our pussy' instead of 'growing a pair of balls' and call a coward a 'ball sack' instead of a 'pussy'."

Allissa felt herself smile at the memory, taking advantage of opening her mouth to progress their kiss to include their tongues. Dean followed suit, tangling his tongue with hers to deepen the kiss the way she remembered from the other times they'd kissed.

As they sat there kissing for several long minutes, Allissa realized she also wasn't sure what to do with her hands, feeling weird for just leaving them resting on her own thighs. *With him leaning back against the headboard, I can't even hug him. So, how am I supposed to show him I want him to hug me?*

Should I pull back and ask him to lean forward, so I can hug him? Or would that just make it obvious how inexperienced I am and cause me to die of embarrassment? Yeah, no, that's too embarrassing. Maybe I can put my hands on his shoulders and slide them around his neck?

She opted to go with her second idea, tentatively lifting her hands and placing them on his broad, muscular shoulders. As she slid her hands up to his neck, Dean seemed to get the hint and leaned forward to give her room between him and the headboard to wrap her arms around him. Again, he followed her lead and wrapped his arms around her upper back and neck.

The embrace seemed to pull their torsos closer, causing her nipples to rub against the firm musculature of his chest. *Gawd, if his chest feels that good touching me there, I bet his hands and mouth would feel even better.*

Eager to find out, Allissa pulled back from the kiss to slide her hands from Dean's back up to his shoulders. She looked him in the eyes as she let her hands trail down his chest. She'd fantasized about touching him since the first time she saw him, and the feel of his hard pecs under her palms was definitely living up to her fantasies.

She felt his nipples pebble under his t-shirt, and felt a sense of awe at being able to make his body respond like that with just a gentle stroke of her hands. She was tempted to lift his shirt so she could run her hands over his bare skin. But even as her hands moved of their own accord over the ridges of his abs toward the hem, she knew she couldn't follow through.

If I do that, then he'll lift my shirt up, too. And no matter how bad my wet pussy and hard nipples might crave his touch, I'm not ready to get naked with him yet.

She stopped her hands just before they reached his waistband, moving them back up his torso, over his shoulders, and down his arms. *Hands, arms, and lips are all the skin-on-skin contact I can handle right now.*

Dean followed her lead, mirroring her movements just as he had with their kiss. Neither of them spoke, as he gently caressed her, making her audible intake of air as his palms ran over her nipples sound much louder than she expected.

Allissa closed her eyes, knowing she was blushing at the way she couldn't stop her body from responding to his touch. She felt herself arch her back and press her breasts into his hands while unconsciously squeezing his pecs, but she didn't realize she'd also scooted up on his thighs until she felt his erection press against her core.

"Oh, Darlin', please let me kiss you again," Dean moaned as he kneaded her breasts the same way she was massaging his pecs.

"Yes, please," Allissa pleaded, unable to verbalize her need for him to take over the lead and kiss her this time.

Dean apparently understood her silent request, sliding one hand up from her breast to circle her nape and pull her lips to his. The passion behind this kiss blew their previous kisses out of the water with its intensity.

Allissa had felt connected to Dean through those tentative first kisses, but this one seemed to strengthen that bond in a way she didn't fully understand. She felt claimed, ravished, and cherished. All from this kiss.

She slipped her arms up around his neck and held on for the ride, as he somehow transported her to another realm of existence. The room around them seemed to disappear, with the two of them making up the entirety of her world.

She didn't even realize that she was grinding her pussy on Dean's dick until the friction sent a jolt of electricity from her pussy to spread throughout her whole body. Allissa shuddered in Dean's arms as she cried out in the most intense bliss she'd ever experienced. Dean swallowed her cries of pleasure as he continued to kiss her through her first-ever orgasm. Not that her brain could function at the moment to realize what had just happened.

As the sensation started to pass, Allissa broke their kiss to collapse into Dean, resting her head on his shoulder, and feeling completely drained of all her energy.

"Fuck, Darlin'," Dean groaned, rubbing his hands up and down her back and cuddling her close. "You are incredible."

Allissa wanted to return the words, but all she could muster at the time was "mmmhum," as she floated on a high she'd never experienced before.

"Fuck, I wish I could hold you like this all night, Darlin'. But I think it's time for you to go back to your bed."

"Goodnight, Dean." Allissa kissed his cheek as she pushed herself up off of him. Her whole body still felt like jello, but she somehow made it to her bed.

"Goodnight, Darlin'. Sweet dreams." Dean got out of his bed and placed a gentle kiss on her forehead as he walked past her bed to go into the bathroom.

Allissa vaguely registered a wet spot on his sweatpants, but she wasn't sure if it was from how wet she'd gotten when she was grinding on him, or if he'd also climaxed when she did.

I hope he came too, she thought as she started to drift off to sleep. *Holy shit! I just came, and we didn't even take our clothes off. And it felt amazing!*

Maybe Mom and our friends are right about orgasms being worth the painful part of sex. I guess if things keep going the way they are with Dean, I'll find out for myself soon enough.

Chapter Eleven

After more early morning workouts and midday dates with Dean had monopolized her time for the rest of the week, Allissa's friends wouldn't let her bail on their Saturday spa day before they all had to be at the arena that evening. Since she'd been tight-lipped about her relationship with Dean and how it was progressing, she knew they were going to grill her once they were alone in the relaxation room between services. While Allissa knew she'd be embarrassed to admit to how they had started making out every night before bed, she also wanted their advice about how to confess to Dean about still being a virgin before going all the way with him.

Even though she knew she was probably setting herself up for a major heartbreak when Dean found out about her mom's former profession, Allissa couldn't resist letting things move forward with him. Since her previously dormant sex drive had been awakened by Dean, she knew she'd regret it if she didn't take her chance to experience all she could sexually handle with him before he found out and broke things off with her.

Since they had gone back to a two-bedroom suite at each of the hotels they stayed at since the previous Monday, they made out on the sofa in the suites, instead of in one of their beds. But Dean had been true to his word about letting her set the pace. As sweet as she thought it was that he didn't want to push her for more than she was ready to happen between them, she was starting to get frustrated with not knowing what to do to progress their relationship past the kissing and over-the-clothes touching that most people moved on from as teenagers.

Hopefully, the girls can give me some suggestions for that today, too, Allissa hoped as the esthetician finished up her facial. When she got to the relaxation room to wait for her turn to get a massage, she found Randi and the Precious Stones already relaxing with glasses of fruit-infused water in their hands.

"Alright, Vic, I know that glow isn't all from the facial." Emerald pointed at Allissa as she took a glass from the side table and sat down on the lounge chairs with them. "So, spill. What have you and Dean been doing to give you an O-glow?"

"An O-glow?" Allissa sputtered, glad she hadn't taken a drink of her water just yet, or Emerald would be wearing it. "I've never even heard of an O-glow, so I doubt I have one."

"An orgasm glow," Emerald explained as Chastity joined them in the relaxation room. "It's that look a woman gets when she's finally getting good dick on the regular. And since you're glowing, I'm betting Dean finally punched your V-card."

"Yeah, well, I hope you didn't put any money on that bet because my V-card hasn't been punched," Allissa chuckled, shaking her head at her friend.

"Pay up, Em," Amethyst cackled, holding out her hand at Emerald.

"No, I'm not buying it," Emerald objected, setting her glass down on a side table and crossing her arms as she studied Allissa. "That's an O-glow if I've ever seen one, and I've definitely seen more than enough of them to know I'm right."

Allissa hid her smile behind her glass as she took a sip of her water and listened to her friends contemplate the reasons for her glow.

"You do realize that we can O without having sex, right?" Randi arched an eyebrow at Emerald. "Granted, the self-induced ones aren't as good as the ones with a partner, but she could still have an O-glow without anything happening with Dean."

"Is that what you're betting happened?" Amethyst looked at Randi with an arched eyebrow. "'Cause that would be my bet, too."

"No." Randi shook her head at Amethyst before turning to examine Allissa. "I'm betting she and Dean have gone to second or third base to give her that glow without actually going all the way."

"What about you Chas?" Emerald arched an eyebrow at their quiet friend. "What's your guess for how far Allissa's gone with Dean?"

"Oh, no, I'm staying out of any bets." Chastity held her hands up in surrender. "I'm not taking any chances that you'll start betting on my love life next by participating."

"You know we're not going to skip over you when we're making bets, even if you don't partake in the other wagers now," Amethyst informed Chastity.

"Yeah, well, I don't want to hear about it if you do bet on me," Chastity laughed.

"How much do you guys have riding on this bet?" Allissa couldn't believe her friends were placing bets on her sex life. She knew they'd bet on some of the other couples in the GWA getting together as a couple or not, but none of them had ever hinged on when they had sex, just when they publicly admitted to being a couple.

"A hundred bucks a piece," Emerald confessed with a shrug. "Same as we did on when Rick & Fiona and Cage & Jax would get together."

"To make sure I'm clear on who's betting what, Emerald thinks we've done the deed, Amethyst thinks I've O'ed on my own, and Randi thinks my O-glow comes from second or third base with Dean?" Allissa wanted to clarify the terms of the bet, so she could settle it for her friends while confiding in them to get their advice.

"Yeah," the three women agreed in unison.

Allissa rolled her eyes at her friends before nodding in Randi's direction. "Then you both owe Randi a hundred bucks."

"Seriously?" Emerald scoffed at the same time Amethyst encouraged her with a "you go girl" and grinned.

"You guys are insane." Allissa shook her head at her friends.

"Agreed," Chastity nodded at Allissa.

"No," Amethyst disagreed. "Just happy for you to finally start enjoying the benefits of being a woman."

"And that you're finally headed toward being my sister-in-law," Randi added with a grin.

Allissa shook her head, starting to object that they weren't anywhere near talking about marriage. Then she stopped when she remembered how Dean had joked about planning a Thanksgiving wedding and had said several times how he wanted their relationship for the "long haul." *I still need to find out what he means by that. And not get my hopes up until after he meets Mom in a couple of weeks.*

Allissa was pretty sure her mother coming to the *Sin City Showdown* would tank her relationship with Dean, and possibly her career with the GWA. She'd already talked to Windy about not mentioning where she worked, but she knew there was no hope of her toning down her appearance or personality to fit in with the family atmosphere of the GWA.

Thankfully, I've been saving most of my income and am already seeing good returns on the investments Dean set up for me. So it'll just be my dreams of a long and illustrious career in wrestling that will suffer if I lose my job because of her. And we'll be able to get by for quite a while on the money I've made in the last few months while I try to get my face back out there for acting and modeling jobs.

"Yeah, I'm still shocked that you're holding out on Dreamy Dean," Emerald quipped with a smirk, bringing Allissa out of her head and back to the conversation at hand. "If I was in your shoes, we'd be burning up the sheets every night since day one."

Allissa knew that her friend claimed to have never slept with Dean, but the way she kept coming up with flirty nicknames for him, and talked about him with multiple references to wanting to have sex with him, still made her feel angry and jealous. "Some of us prefer to focus on our friendship before jumping straight to the benefits, like you and Dane."

"Oh, please," Emerald scoffed, rolling her eyes at Allissa. "There are no benefits with me and Dane. We tried kissing one time and realized we aren't sexually compatible. I just like messing with him when the ring rats are around 'cause he's fun to aggravate."

"Oh, yeah, they're both too alpha to ever hook up with each other," Amethyst laughed. "If they ever did, the angry fuck would be so explosive they'd burn down the hotel."

"Enough talk about Emerald and Dane," Randi interjected, waving her hand at the Stones to shush them. "We don't have time to waste on the way they cockblock each other. I wanna know what's going on with Allissa and Dean before we get separated again for massages and waxing."

"You already know we're dating," Allissa confirmed, knowing she'd already told them about their quirky midday dates to find the most unique places and foods in each city they visited.

The girls all nodded and made motions with their hands for her to continue.

Allissa sighed, trying to work up the gumption to tell her friends about the make-out sessions she'd recently shared with Dean, and ask their advice on how to progress them a little further than they'd gone so far. "Well, we've also started making out some every night before bed."

"I'm guessing by making out, you mean something more than just kissing, since Randi won the bet," Amethyst remarked with a wiggle of her eyebrows.

"Yes, we've also done a little touching, but with our clothes on," Allissa admitted, knowing she was blushing at the revelation. "And rubbing against each other to cause the orgasms."

She wasn't about to tell them about walking in on Dean jerking off in the shower. While the girls would all be happy to hear she'd seen him in all his naked glory, she didn't want to answer any questions about his dick. And she knew Emerald would ask about it, even if the other women wouldn't.

"I'm so proud of you for progressing to dry-humping," Amethyst cheered. "After you told us you didn't think orgasms would be worth the pain of sex, I was afraid you'd never try to find out. So, now that you know how great they are, how long before you think you'll try pushing past your fear of pain to go all the way?"

"I think I'm ready to go farther than we have," Allissa confided, looking around to make sure nobody would overhear them before leaning toward her friends and whispering the rest of her confession. "But Dean keeps letting me lead and only touches me the same way I touch him. And I don't know what I should do to let him know I'm ready to start getting naked but not quite ready to go all the way yet. I feel so awkward trying to set the pace for us when I have absolutely no idea what I'm doing. And I really wish he'd take over and teach me instead. Ya know?"

The ladies nodded in unison, seeming to understand her plight, even though she stopped short of telling them the details of what she was thinking. In truth, she kind of wished he would act more like one of the alpha heroes in the romance novels they all read and start issuing commands about what they were doing when they were making out, so she didn't have to stress about thinking up their next move.

"So, I need you guys to give me some advice," Allissa appealed to her friends. "What can I do to move us to the next level without him thinking I'm ready for full-on sex? And do I have to tell him I'm still a virgin? He's so experienced, I think telling him that would be too embarrassing, and I don't want to make him think I'm a freak and cause him to not want to be with me anymore."

"I've got a few favorite porn sites I can give you to get ideas of what to push him to do next," Emerald joked with a wicked grin. "And we can stop on the way to the arena this afternoon to buy you a dildo, so you can practice solo to keep him from finding out about your V-card."

"No, just, no!" Randi held a hand up to Emerald in the universal sign to get her to stop. "You absolutely have to tell him before your first time. But you don't have to be embarrassed because he's not gonna think you're a freak. With the way he's let you take the lead, I'm pretty sure he already knows you're still a virgin, and he wants to make sure your first time is good for you."

"You think?" Allissa questioned her friend's belief.

"I mean, I could ask James to double-check," Randi shrugged. "But yeah, I'm pretty sure. As for what to do to get him to take the lead and teach you, instead of staying stuck where you are, just be honest and talk to him. If ya'll are gonna make it as a couple, you have to learn to talk to each other about even the most embarrassing things. And if I know Dean the way I think I do, I bet he'll share stories with you that are even more embarrassing for him at the first sign of you blushing at telling him yours."

Their conversation was cut short as the ladies were called back to the treatment rooms for their waxing and massage appointments. As Allissa laid on the massage table for her next spa service, she thought about Randi's advice.

She's probably right about him already knowing I'm a virgin. I'm sure it was obvious the first time I kissed him that I had no idea what I was doing.

But I still don't know how to tell him I want him to take the lead and move us to touching each other without our clothes. And since I know about his dyslexia, I can't even suggest he read some of the sexy scenes I'd like to try. But maybe I could download the audiobook

Leah Mae Wright

versions and let him accidentally on purpose catch me listening to pivotal scenes?

Though, since I have to wait a couple of days after my bikini wax today to let him see me naked, I guess it's not a big deal that I can't figure out how to make myself suggest we do more yet. Surely, I can "show my pussy" and tell him I want to be naked with him before it's time to wax again next month.

~~~

Sunday, August 4, 2019, Sioux Falls, South Dakota

Dean wasn't sure what was going on with Allissa since he picked her up after her spa day with the girls the day before. He'd thought they were progressing nicely with their relationship, even adding in a little more PDA for the last week. But as soon as their eyes met in the lobby of the spa, she seemed to have pulled back from him, leaving space between them that he didn't like one bit. *Fuck! I hope she's not having second thoughts about us because I didn't wait until she's not stressing about the psycho stalking her to move us out of the friend zone.*

Since he was there to pick Randi up at the same time, James had also noticed it. When the brothers got a moment alone in the locker room later, James had offered to talk to his wife that night to find out if something had happened at the spa to spook Allissa. Now that they had a chance to speak in private in the locker room of the arena in the next city on their tour, Dean was eager to find out what James had discovered when he talked to Randi the night before.

"So, what did Randi tell you happened yesterday?" Dean impatiently stared at his brother, instead of focusing on lacing his wrestling boots, praying he hadn't screwed things up by going too fast with Allissa.

"She didn't think anything happened to cause Allissa to pull back," James shrugged. Dean wasn't sure he believed his brother, since James was looking down at his boots as he tied them, instead of making eye contact as they talked. "But she did say they talked a little about the two of you."
~~~

"Okay," Dean grunted, irritated by James not giving him much information. "And what exactly was said?"

"First that Randi won two-hundred bucks for guessing how far ya'll have gone so far," James chuckled and smirked. "Or not gone, as the case may be."

If Dean hadn't already put his kneepads on, he'd have thrown one at James. Unfortunately, the only thing in arm's reach that he could throw at his brother was his phone, and Dean wasn't about to risk damaging it by beaning his brother in the head with it. So, he just sat there glaring to get his point across to James.

"Seriously, they talked about how Allissa's embarrassed to tell you how inexperienced she is," James finally confessed. "In fact, I'm supposed to grill you about what you already know about that, and make sure you know to tell Allissa some embarrassing stories about your teenaged fumblings when she finally feels comfortable sharing with you. That way Randi can reassure Allissa that you're not gonna pull away when she finally tells you she's still a virgin."

"Damn, I thought that might be the case, but I wasn't a hundred percent sure," Dean groaned, finally looking down to lace up his boots as he finished getting ready for their match that night. "That's why I've been letting her set the pace for our make-out sessions."

"Yeah, that's the other thing they talked about," James added. "Randi said Allissa's ready for a little more than ya'll have been doing, but she's not sure how to step things up. Randi wasn't completely sure if she was uncomfortable being in charge, or just too inexperienced to know what the next step is to be able to initiate it."

"Okay," Dean drawled the word out, unsure how to proceed with Allissa based on this new information.

So, should I guess which it is? I don't want to screw things up by guessing wrong. As much as I'd prefer to take charge and step things up, I don't want to do that if it'll scare her into thinking I'm anything like the guys her mom and their friends dated. Guess that means I need to keep letting her lead and gently coax her to do more.

"Randi said to tell you to start pushing the boundaries a little bit." James shook his head, almost like he wasn't quite sure he agreed with his wife. "But I'm gonna tell you to keep going slow and give it a few days before you try anything more. Even if she thinks she's ready, they were just waxed yesterday. So she might be a little too sore for a bit, if you know what I mean."

Ah, so that's why she backed off and didn't even want to dry-hump last night.

"How long does that take to heal?" Dean figured his brother had been with Randi long enough to know the typical time frame he'd have to hold off after the women's waxing days before they wouldn't be chafed and need to avoid any contact down there.

"Four, long, no-fucking days," James groaned, hanging his head. "Makes me wish Randi would go back to shaving instead of going to spa days with the girls to get waxed. Or at least, make sure to get waxed the day before she starts her period, so the no-sex days of the month are all at one time."

Dean almost laughed at his brother's distress, but considering he'd gone a lot longer than four days without sex since meeting Allissa, he could relate too much to James's plight to be able to laugh.

Damn, now I'm gonna hafta figure out when Allissa's period is before I can start trying to get my hands under her clothes, too.

After basically sharing a room with her for the last month, Dean thought he could possibly figure it out by remembering back to when she might have shown some kind of sign that it was that time of the month for her. But as he thought about his time with Allissa over the last month, he couldn't remember a single day when she'd been more irritable than normal or complained of cramping or bloating the way he'd heard from his friends' sisters when they were teenagers.

Unfortunately, the only irritability that he'd noticed was when there was an update from Cage on the packages he and the Avingtons had intercepted. *And I doubt those days coincided with her period, since it was only one day a week that Cage updated us.*

Guess I'll just have to study her a little closer for the next month, Dean finally decided as he and James made their way out of the locker room to watch their fellow performers on the backstage monitors until it was time for their match.

He took a seat beside Allissa, reaching over to hold her hand. She smiled at him and squeezed his hand, as they sat there watching their friends wrestle.

Maybe she's not as distant as I thought, Dean decided as Allissa leaned into his side as they discussed ideas for their matches at the pay-per-view coming up in a couple more weeks. *Guess she was just nervous about the whole virginity thing, and too shy to tell me about being waxed and needing a few nights off from the way we've been grinding on each other recently.*

I'm still gonna give her a few days before I start trying to step things up between us. Both because I wanna make sure it all feels good for her and because I wanna make sure she knows I'm interested in more than just sex with her.

Maybe I'll even back off some on the overtly sexual stuff and focus on doing things to show her how well I know her, and wanna be her best friend and biggest supporter, and not just her lover. While I know she's enjoyed going to try new foods and seeing the strange sights on our midday dates, I think maybe it's time to plan something to really impress her that's geared to more of her interests.

Knowing she was a model and actress before she started training to wrestle, Dean wondered if she might enjoy a set visit when they went to Los Angeles. *Maybe I can call up that producer who met with us last year to discuss that wrestling movie. Or maybe David Daniels, since he's the person Rick referred the producer to, and I actually have his number. I bet she'd love to go watch whatever scene they're filming when we get to town on Saturday. Even if he's not filming yet, we might be able to go work out with the actors he has training for it.*

~ ~ ~

Saturday, August 10, 2019, Los Angeles, California

Allissa wasn't sure what to think about Dean not telling her where they were going for their midday date after checking in at the hotel. With all the extra security precautions being taken since they entered the state of California on Wednesday, she wasn't sure how he managed to get the approval to take her somewhere without a couple of bodyguards following them. Especially since the added security was due to Ron Langston living in Los Angeles. Allissa thought for sure that this would be the city when Cage and the Avington Security team now traveling with them would insist on her staying in the hotel or arena the whole time they were in town. While she was a little nervous about possibly running into Ron if he was her stalker, she was also excited about getting to see whatever Dean seemed to want to surprise her with on this outing.

Since he limited them to straight cardio that morning for their workout in the hotel gym before they left Bakersfield, and insisted she put extra gym clothes in her gear bag to bring with them for the date, she thought he might have planned a second workout at Muscle Beach. But as they left the hotel, Dean didn't turn in the correct direction to go to Venice Beach.

"Why won't you tell me where we're going?" Allissa pestered him as he drove.

"Because it's a surprise, Darlin'," Dean grinned, shaking his head at the way she was pouting like a child.

"But you know I hate surprises," Allissa whined, playing up her irritation to epic proportions, even though she was more excited than irritated. "So, quit being Mean Dean, and tell me where we're going."

"Mean Dean?" Dean chuckled. "You tryin' to change my ring name?"

"Oh, no. Since I don't see a ring hiding in the back seat, it can't be a ring name," Allissa quipped with a grin. "Mean Dean is just who you are, not a gimmick."

"Ha, ha," Dean feigned a laugh. "Just for that, I'm not even gonna give you a hint now."

Allissa only groaned in response, going back to playfully pouting like an insolent child.

"Don't worry, Darlin'," Dean encouraged her with a smile and a brief glance in her direction. "You know I'm only gonna give you good surprises, so eventually you'll quit hating them so much."

She did know that, actually, which was why she smiled at him and quit acting bratty. As they had talked more over the last few weeks, she let him in on why she'd previously hated surprises, glossing over the root cause of the financial issues that started it all.

Her aversion to surprises had started in childhood, when she'd get all excited for her birthday or Christmas, only to be disappointed when her mom could only afford the knock-off version of whatever gift she'd wanted. Her dislike of surprises was exacerbated by the random times throughout her life when she'd come home from school to find one of their utilities had been shut off because her mom was late paying the bill.

Just when she thought she'd taken care of the lack of funds issue by working with the GWA, and could possibly look forward to her birthday and Christmas once again, she'd started getting creepy gifts from her stalker. Now she wasn't sure how successful Dean would be in getting her to like surprises with no sign of those stalker gifts stopping anytime soon.

Thankfully, I haven't had to actually see them since Cage and the Avington Security team have been intercepting them.

Needing to change her mindset off of thoughts of her stalker and back to something positive, Allissa changed the subject. "Okay, if you're not going to tell me where we're going, can you at least tell me about the article you read today?"

"It was **Twenty-Six Really Cool Things To Do in L.A. This Month**," Dean smirked. "And no, we're not doing any of them."

"Well, if we're not doing them," Allissa chuckled at his goofiness. "At least tell me what some of them are."

"There were only three that we could've done today. A taco and beer festival, a tea festival, and a beauty convention."

"Yeah, the only one of those I could see you enjoying would be the taco and beer festival," Allissa chortled, shaking her head at how out of place she imagined him being at a beauty convention.

"Yeah, we probably would have gone there to catch some of the lucha libre show at the same time," Dean admitted with a grin. "But I already had these plans set up, and I think you'll enjoy what we're doing way more than the festival."

"Wait," Allissa exclaimed, turning in her seat to look at Dean in shock. "You passed up food and wrestling for our plans today? Those are our two favorite things in the world, so this is going to have to be a pretty spectacular date."

Allissa suddenly wasn't so sure they were dressed appropriately in their business-casual traveling clothes. *And all we brought with us are our gym clothes and ring attire for going to the arena right after. Surely, he would have warned me if I needed to wear something fancier, though. Right?*

She was just about to ask him to make sure her slacks and blouse were appropriate when he pulled up to a gate for one of the studios in

Hollywood. She promptly closed her mouth as Dean rolled down his window to speak to the guard who stepped up to their vehicle.

"How can I help you?"

"Dean Hunter and Allissa Walters, here to meet David Daniels," Dean told the guard.

Who is David Daniels? And why does his name sound so familiar?

"I need to see your identification," the guard informed them.

"Of course," Dean grinned as he pulled his wallet from his pocket and turned to Allissa. "He'll need yours too, Darlin'."

Allissa grabbed her purse, pulled out her wallet, and handed over her driver's license for the guard to look them up on his list of approved visitors. Once he found their names, the guard gave Dean directions through the lot to the specific studio, where they were going to meet David Daniels, as he handed back their licenses.

"Okay, I think you can tell me what we're doing now," Allissa babbled excitedly as Dean drove to where they were supposed to park. "And who is David Daniels? The name sounds familiar, but I can't figure out where I know it from."

"So, last year, a couple of days before you started with the GWA, we were in L.A.," Dean explained. "There was a producer who met with Rick to get recommendations on who to get to train the actors for a movie he's making about wrestling. I don't know if you remember the Blue Thunder faction from their time in the GWA or not, but that's who Rick referred him to, and also who I called to set this up today. David is Blue Thunder Tornado."

"Remember them?" Allissa squealed with excitement. "Oh my gawd, Lightning was my idol growing up! The guys were cool with their face paint and all, but she was my inspiration for wanting to become a wrestler."

"Then I hope you're ready to meet your idol," Dean grinned at her as he parked the rental car. "'Cause Lightning is Tornado's cousin and business partner in their wrestling school. And they're showing us around the set and arranged for us to be extras in the scene they're filming today."

"Seriously?" Allissa's heart raced with excitement as she unbuckled her seatbelt, leaned over the center console, and kissed Dean in appreciation. "You're right. This is way better than a taco festival."

As they got out of the car and walked into the studio, Allissa remembered back to her childhood, watching Saturday morning wrestling, instead of cartoons, because it was what played at that time on the station their antenna picked up best. Before the GWA moved to a live TV format on cable, they had a syndicated show that aired on one of the national network stations in all the major markets. It was on that show that Allissa first saw the team known as Blue Thunder and felt inspired to one day become a professional wrestler.

The two guys, Tornado and Hurricane, were the tag-team champions at least seven or eight times. But it was their manager that was also a female wrestler, who caught Allissa's attention. Unlike the other women of her era, Lightning didn't use her sexuality to win over the fans. She always dressed like a super classy lady when she was at ringside in her managerial role. Even when she stepped into the ring to wrestle, her ring attire was more like a modest one-piece bathing suit than the skimpy outfits most of the other women wore.

While Allissa didn't always go as extreme as a one-piece for her wrestling attire, she did try to keep the bra tops and skorts she wore in the ring to more full coverage in homage to Lightning's style. Thankfully, all the ladies in the GWA had gone to a similar style and away from the triangle bikini tops, which barely covered their nipples, and butt floss that had been the standard attire for women in the wrestling business in the 1990s and 2000s.

Lightning also had a more athletic style in the ring than the other women of her era. Back then, women's wrestling was more a way for models and actresses to be seen than an athletic endeavor. Lightning refused to participate in the mud matches and dance-offs that used to dominate the women's airtime, actually calling out the guys to give her some competition in the ring.

She led the charge to make women's wrestling seem more legitimate, instead of just a step up from being a stripper. She didn't just bring athleticism back to the women's division and make the women's division title more prestigious. She was also the only woman to hold the lightweight title in GWA history, having defeated one of the guys to win it.

I can't believe Dean set it up, so I get to meet her! I hope I don't fangirl too much and embarrass myself. Or Dean. I'm seriously going to have to think of something special to thank him for today.

~~~

Dean was walking on cloud nine after the day he had with Allissa. He couldn't stop smiling after seeing how excited she got when she met her childhood idol. From one of their previous talks, he'd known she watched wrestling as a kid the same as he did. But she'd only mentioned it in passing as one of the reasons she'd looked into wrestling as a career after one of her modeling gigs was as a ring girl for Vegas Pro Boxing, so he hadn't known which organizations she'd watched or what wrestlers she'd liked back then. He couldn't believe how lucky he'd gotten to have previously met her favorite wrestler to be able to set up the meeting for their date that day.

Fuck, her excitement was contagious today, too, Dean thought as they made their way back to the hotel for the night.

She'd apologized multiple times for fangirling when she first met Lightning. The older woman laughed it off and seemed just as excited to meet Allissa, especially when they got the chance to work together in the ring in the background of the scene being filmed. The two women became fast friends and even exchanged phone numbers to be able to keep in touch after Dean and Allissa left the set.

Once they got to the arena, she'd had to tell everyone they worked with about the "awesome experience" of meeting the legendary wrestler. Luckily, her excitement wasn't diminished in the slightest when Amethyst informed her she'd gone through her wrestling training at the Blue Thunder Wrestling Academy with Lightning as her trainer. The date hadn't given Dean much time alone with Allissa like their normal outings, but he still felt privileged to be able to witness the joy radiating from her the whole day.

After the way she'd been worried when she found out the security staff was increased when they landed in Sacramento, California, on Wednesday, Dean especially felt good knowing he'd taken her mind off the stalker threat while they were in the same city where Ron Langston lived. Even though the Avington Security team hadn't been able to find any evidence that he was Allissa's stalker, they'd still insisted on taking extra precautions while she and the GWA were in the same state with him, just in case. So, they had two Avington
~~~

bodyguards discreetly following them around in all eight of the California cities they were visiting this week.

Not that Allissa knew they were being followed all the time. She got so nervous when she met Lincoln and Wright, and found out they'd be traveling on the GWA plane until the pay-per-view weekend in Vegas that Dean had stepped in to calm her down.

Dean had pulled Cage aside later to discuss protecting Allissa without increasing her anxiety over the stalker. He knew the two Avington bodyguards were discreetly following them at a distance when they went on their midday dates, but he didn't want to worry Allissa by letting her know that. As far as he knew, she had no idea that the bodyguards went anywhere but the hotel and arena. And Dean hoped to keep it that way, so she didn't panic again.

He knew it was probably pushing her limit for how much control of her life she wanted him to take over for her. But after seeing how relaxed she was on set today that she didn't even notice the bodyguards when they stood out like a sore thumb compared to the much shorter actors all around them, he tried to block out any minor guilt he felt for taking that burden off her shoulders.

Hopefully, she'll just think I'm being overly affectionate as usual, he thought as he hugged her to his side and listened to her gushing about how she still felt high on the excitement of the day, as they walked into the hotel and got on the elevator. *And won't realize I'm trying to block her from seeing them behind us again.*

Luckily for him, the elevator doors closed before the security guards could catch up to take the same one. *Thank fuck, Cage agreed that I could keep checking our suite, instead of insisting on one of them doing it every time.*

Dean felt remorseful for keeping her out of the loop on all the extra security precautions they were taking. He knew she was a grown woman and perfectly capable of dealing with the situation. But he still had a hard time controlling his protective instincts with her, and he couldn't hold them back when she seemed to get extra anxious while discussing the security details.

He wanted her to be able to go about her day with a smile on her face like she had right then, not the frown and worry lines he'd seen after every security update. It was bad enough that she felt like she was constantly being watched by her stalker. She didn't need to feel like she was living in a fishbowl with the extra security, too. So, he sucked up the self-condemnation for taking over her choices in life, and did whatever he could to help her feel like she had more freedom than she really did at the moment.

It was his guilty conscience that kept him from stepping up their make-out sessions over the last few days, even though he knew she'd had plenty of time to recover from her waxing appointment the previous weekend. Logically, he knew she was *The One* long before the stalker situation became an issue. But he still couldn't stop himself from feeling like he was taking advantage of the ordeal to get closer to her. Even if he could somewhat justify their rapid relationship timeline by pointing out how fast he'd known his feelings for Allissa, Dean knew that, at the very least, he'd used the perceived risk she was in to his advantage to push them into a relationship faster than they would have started had she not had a stalker.

In his heart, he knew they'd eventually get together, stalker or no stalker. But his brain could see how their accelerated timeline due to his need to protect her might be perceived by Allissa and their peers. So even though his heart and his dick were ready for full steam ahead with the sexual side of their relationship, Dean continued to put on the brakes to keep from being perceived as just as much of a lowlife scumbag as her stalker.

When they got to their suite, Dean quickly searched each room and closet for intruders. Then they were able to drop their bags in their separate bedrooms and settle in for the night. As usual, they went to their separate spaces to clean up and change clothes before meeting back in the living room space to place an order with room service for a late dinner.

Once their order was placed, they sat together on the sofa, but neither of them reached for the television remote. Since they normally ended up talking instead of paying attention to whatever they turned on, Dean didn't mind skipping the distracting noise.

"So, I've been trying all evening to think of something I can do to thank you for today." Allissa leaned into his side, resting her head on his shoulder and her hand on his chest, but not making eye contact as she spoke.

"You don't have to do anything to thank me, Darlin'. Seeing how happy and excited you've been all day is all the reward I need for setting things up." Dean wrapped his arm around her shoulders, hugged her to his side, and rested his cheek on the top of her head, happy to just relax on the sofa with her while they waited on their food to be delivered.

"But nobody's ever done anything that special for me before, and it means so much to me that I want to do something special for you, too." Allissa rubbed her thumb over his nipple, making it harden under his t-shirt.

Fuck! I hope she's not thinkin' 'bout doing something sexual to thank me for setting up a fun date today.

"Since we're gonna be close to your hometown next weekend when we have both Friday and Saturday evening free, how about showing me your favorite place to go when you were growing up?" Dean stopped her hand as she started trailing it down his abs, holding it in his to keep her from getting too close to his cock. He might not be able to stop himself from getting hard at the thought of her touching him, but he could still keep them in the slow lane by holding her hand.

"That would be Death Valley National Park, but it's way too hot this time of year to go out there." She went on to tell him how her hometown was about halfway between Vegas and the national park that was actually in California. "Mom used to take me camping there for Spring break every year. We'd also go for weekend trips in the winter, but March was always the best month temperature-wise to be there. And we'd stay home in the air conditioning between April and October."

"Just how hot does it get out there this time of year?" Dean might not want to get out of their air-conditioned vehicle if they went for a day trip, but he didn't think it would be too hot to drive through and look at the views from inside their air-conditioned vehicle.

"This time of year, the high is somewhere between a hundred-and-ten and a hundred-and-twenty," Allissa informed him. "And the low is somewhere around ninety."

"Okay, so we'll have to table that trip until the next time we're near there in the winter," Dean conceded when he realized the temperatures were a good ten to twenty degrees hotter than he was used to back home. After dealing with the heat of south Texas all his life, he knew the air conditioner in a vehicle wouldn't be capable of dropping the temperature in the car by more than twenty degrees from the outside temperature. So, he agreed with her logic to stay indoors as much as possible. "But I'm sure we can find something to entertain us while we're there all weekend."

Luckily, their food arriving was enough of a distraction that Allissa didn't bring up the subject of trying to thank him again. At least, not until after they finished eating and the room service cart was pushed out into the hall.

"So, I've been thinking about what I can do to thank you for today." Allissa barely let him sit back down on the sofa before she moved to straddle his lap. She ran her hands over his chest, slowly lowering them toward his waistband without making eye contact. "And I'm thinking maybe we can lose a little clothing before we start making out tonight."

As much as Dean enjoyed the feel of her hands on him, and especially the way she watched herself touching him, he didn't want her to associate their romantic endeavors with her thanking him in any way. "No, Darlin'," he objected, stopping her hands with his before she got very far. "As much as I want to get naked with you, I don't want it to happen until you want it as much as I do. I don't want you to thank me with your beautiful body. Like I've told you before, I don't expect thanks of any kind for anything I do for you. Everything I do is because I care about you and want to make you feel safe and happy."

"But you said I could reward you with hugs and kisses before," Allissa pointed out, finally looking up from their joined hands and into his eyes.

"And I shouldn't have said that." Dean shook his head, hating that he'd screwed up so badly with his joking around. "I was trying to lighten the mood with my usual flirtatiousness because I was uncomfortable with you thanking me for being a decent guy and doing what anyone else in the company would've done to keep you safe."

"Oh." Allissa's shoulders slumped as she pulled her hands from his and stood from his lap. "I, um, I guess I'll call it a night then."

"Wait!" Dean reached out and grabbed her hand, pulling her back to him. "That doesn't mean I want us to stop kissin' and stuff. I just don't want it to be out of gratitude. I already feel bad enough for taking advantage of you having a stalker to get you to spend time with me. I don't want to make it worse by pushing our relationship along faster than you want. I know we're meant to be together, so I'm more than willing to wait as long as you need for the rest to happen."

"Oh, Dean," Allissa sighed, throwing herself back down on his lap, and gripping his face in her hands as they locked eyes.

Dean's dick twitched from the slight tug on his beard, and he hoped she wouldn't notice how his cock was contradicting everything he'd just said about being willing to wait.

"Don't you dare feel bad for stepping up to make me feel safe. You may think anyone in the company would have done it, but you were the only one who actually did. If there's a silver lining to having a stalker, being pushed to admit to my attraction to you is it. And you are not pushing me to move things along faster than I want. If you were, and I was really trying to thank you with my body, then we'd have had sex a month ago. If anything, you're holding us back by putting me in charge of when we do more than kiss, since I'm too inexperienced to know what our next step should be."

Dean had to take a moment to let her words sink in from how shocked he was by her response. He felt a little of his guilt for starting their relationship in the middle of her stalker situation lift from his shoulders. He was relieved to know that she, at least, didn't think he was a creep for taking advantage of the situation.

Instead of double-checking his understanding of the first part of her rant, Dean smiled at her before clarifying the meaning of her final statement. "Does that mean you want me to stop holding us back, Darlin'?"

"No, um," Allissa stuttered, her eyes widening slightly. "I mean, yes, but just a little."

Dean couldn't hold back his chuckle at how adorably cute she looked when she was flustered. "You're gonna hafta explain a little better than that, Darlin'."

Allissa sighed and closed her eyes a moment, taking a couple of deep breaths and blowing them out her nose before opening her eyes to look into his as she elaborated. "I'm not ready for full steam ahead, jump into bed, just yet. But maybe you can start showing me the steps between kissing and having sex. Like maybe, one new thing a week?"

"Are you asking me to teach you about foreplay, Darlin'?" Dean hadn't thought about how his insistence that she set their pace could be intimidating for someone as innocent as Allissa. But now that he realized the error of his ways, he was more than ready to take charge of their sexual encounters to correct it.

Fuck, this is gonna be the best form of torture.

"Ye, yes," Allissa stuttered before squaring her shoulders and running her hands over his shoulders and chest again. "I'm sure you've figured out by now that I've never done any of this before. I never thought I'd want to before I met you. But now I want you to teach me."

Dean didn't want to embarrass her by saying anything about her virginal status, so he only nodded his acknowledgment of her statement while thinking about all the things they could do that were a step above kissing, but wouldn't be too much for her. *Oh, yeah, I'm lookin' forward to all the dirty things I wanna teach you, Darlin'.*

Dean knew he couldn't push too fast with any of the dirty things he wanted to do with Allissa, but he had more than a few ideas for how to progress the sexual side of their relationship. Thankfully, most of them were ways he could give her pleasure without removing his pants. He still didn't trust himself to keep taking things slow, if she even lightly touched his bare cock.

"One new thing a week, huh? Yeah, I can do that. But only if you're sure you're ready to start losing your clothes before we make out, and you want me to take the lead."

"Yes, I'm sure," Allissa stated more confidently than he expected.

"Then let's get started, Darlin'." Dean finally wrapped her in his arms as he leaned in to kiss her.

Allissa slid her arms around his neck as she returned the kiss, opening up for him to explore her mouth as she moved to straddle him once more.

Once she was in a better position, Dean trailed his hands down her back until he reached the bottom of her tank top. He broke the kiss to watch her expression as he slowly lifted her shirt. "Tell me to stop if anything I do is too much for tonight. Okay, Darlin'?"

"Oh, okay," Allissa stuttered as she lifted her arms for him to be able to remove the tank top.

Dean let his gaze wander downward as he revealed her perky tits for the first time. His mouth watered at the sight, momentarily stalling his movements. Her breasts were perfect. A natural handful that would fit perfectly in his large hands. Their dusky pink tips taut with need.

"Fuck, you're gorgeous, Darlin'." Dean barely registered that he finished removing her shirt and tossed it away. His only thought was how he needed to get his mouth on her tantalizing tatas. He bent his head as he cupped her breasts, sucking one nipple into his mouth before swirling his tongue around it.

Allissa arched her back, offering her pert peaks up to him for his oral attention. The movement slid her lower body forward, so her pussy rubbed over his engorged cock in the most sensual way.

While Dean loved the way she grinded on him, he kept his focus on her chest, kneading her mounds as he moved his mouth back and forth between her diamond-hard nipples. He suckled and licked as Allissa weaved her fingers through his hair, holding him in place and moaning each time he did something she seemed to especially enjoy.

"Oh, gawd, Dean," Allissa cried out, her wetness soaking through her shorts and saturating his sweats.

That's it, Darlin'. Come from me suckin' your tits. As much as he wanted to say the words aloud, Dean couldn't lift his mouth from her titties to vocalize them. Besides, she only wanted him to teach her one new thing a week. And this week, it wasn't going to be dirty talk.

He continued playing with her breasts as she rubbed her cunt up and down the length of his dick. He didn't let up until her whole body convulsed from her orgasm and she went boneless in his arms. Then he lifted his head and pulled her down to rest on his chest as she recovered.

Dean was still hard, though his cock throbbed with the need to join her in orgasmic bliss. *Maybe next week, I'll teach her how she can come multiple times in a session, so we can go long enough that my third shower of the day is just to clean up after coming in my pants like a teenager.*

Chapter Twelve

Dean knew Allissa was nervous about the possibility of her stalker making a move over the pay-per-view weekend, since they were in the nearest major city to her hometown for the **Sin City Showdown**. As they had through all their stops in California and at the last pay-per-view, Avington Security provided more personnel for them at the hotel and fan expo leading up to the big show the next day. In addition to Wright and Lincoln, the two bodyguards that had been traveling with the GWA for the last couple of weeks, the Avingtons brought in at least a dozen more men to keep Allissa and the rest of the crew safe. But even with the extra security, Dean wasn't letting Allissa out of his sight if he could help it.

They had actually met with Byron and his sons, Barrett, Blaine, and Brady the night before, when they first arrived at the hotel to get an update on the case. Byron, Barrett, and Blaine had flown in, along with several of their employees to be on hand for the long weekend when the GWA would be in Las Vegas. Brady had driven over from where he was staying in Dead End, Nevada, while the other two men on Allissa's mom's security detail watched over her.

After hearing from Brady that the packages had started arriving at her mom's home again on Friday, Allissa had called and insisted her mother come to Vegas for the weekend. She'd already been invited to the show on Sunday to see Allissa win her first GWA women's division title, but hadn't taken off work on Friday and Saturday night to be able to be there before Sunday morning. Luckily, she was at work when Allissa called her Friday night, so she couldn't get away with not asking for the next night off, as Allissa anticipated. So, now they were expecting Windy Walters and her entourage to show up any time before the fan expo started.

Dean wasn't sure what to expect when Windy arrived. Over their time together, Allissa shared stories about her mom and the things they did together over the years. While those tales painted a picture of a loving mother, who obviously shared a close bond with her daughter, Dean still felt like Allissa was leaving something out about her mom.

The night before, she'd finally warned him that her mom could be a bit outrageous and over the top, but he still wasn't sure what exactly that meant. Allissa had distracted him with kisses and another topless make-out session, so he hadn't asked any follow-up questions to get a better idea of what to expect.

"Should we have left someone from Avington at her house in case there's another package delivered today or tomorrow?" Allissa paced the backstage area as they waited for her mom.

"Don't worry, Darlin'. I'm sure Byron has it covered," Dean assured her, reaching out to take her hand and pull her to a stop in front of him. "He's not gonna take a chance on missing one of the delivery drivers when he wants to compare their descriptions of the stalker to the ones he has from the other times the packages went to your mom's."

"You're right," Allissa sighed, stepping in to wrap her arms around his waist and lean her head on his chest. Dean had come to love the way she always hugged him to calm herself down whenever she got exceptionally worked up with worry over things. He enfolded her in his arms and kissed the top of her head to reassure her that he'd always be there for her to lean on whenever she needed him. "I'm just overly nervous because of being so close to home when he knows where we live. Which reminds me, I need to ask Byron what we're doing security-wise in two weeks when we take our Labor Day break."

Dean didn't like the thought of them going to their separate homes for their time off. It wasn't just the thought of Allissa not being safe from her stalker yet that caused his trepidation. After the last few weeks of exploring their relationship and spending all their free time together, Dean knew he'd miss her like crazy the whole time they were apart.

"I was thinking about that actually," Dean drawled as he rubbed her back. "I'd like you to come home with me for our Labor Day break."

"Really?" Allissa leaned slightly back and looked up into his eyes.

"Yeah, Darlin'," Dean smiled at her. Hoping to take her mind off the stalker situation, he decided to steer the conversation in a different direction. "I'm not just bein' an overprotective boyfriend who doesn't want to let you out of my sight, either. I need you to be my plus one at Charlotte's wedding, so Meemaw doesn't have to single-handedly run off all the local girls who ask me to dance like she did at Rick and Fiona's wedding."

"Seriously? You're asking me to go to a wedding with you while flaunting all the girls who want you in my face?" Allissa shook her head at him as she pushed against his chest, trying to get out of his embrace.

"I'm not flaunting anyone in your face, Darlin'," Dean objected, not releasing her. "I'm askin' you to do your job as my girlfriend and protect me from the unwanted advances, the same way I'm protecting you from any guys who want to hit on you."

"Oh, is that what that glowering was during our first autograph session this morning? You protecting me from flirty fans?" Allissa arched an eyebrow as if she disapproved, but she couldn't hide her smile that told Dean she liked his overprotective side.

"Absolutely," Dean nodded before pecking her lips with his. "Seriously, though, I can't go nine days without seeing you. So if you're not gonna come to Heart's Destiny with me for our Labor Day break, then I'll skip the wedding and crash on your couch instead."

"No!" Allissa's eyes widened as she shouted her objection before she straightened her features and smiled at him, making Dean wonder what caused her strange reaction. "Trying to sleep on our couch would end your wrestling career with how bad it would wreck your back. And since I don't want to be responsible for ending your wrestling career prematurely, I'll go to Heart's Destiny with you for the break."

"Good, now let's see if we can find Byron to make sure he knows where you'll be for whatever security precautions he wants to take," Dean suggested before pressing his lips to hers once more.

Dean didn't get a chance to deepen the kiss the way he wanted, as they were interrupted by an ear-splitting squeal of "Lissie!" from just a few feet away.

He barely lifted his lips from Allissa's before she was ripped from his arms by two overly excited women. He would have been concerned had he not seen the two Avington Security bodyguards standing right behind them.

As they bounced around and hugged Allissa, he quickly recognized the brunette as Allissa's mom. *So the blonde must be her mom's friend, Kandi.*

Windy Walters looked exactly as he imagined Allissa would look in twenty years. Well, except for the fact that Windy and her friend were dressed way less conservatively than he'd ever seen Allissa dress when going out in public outside her time in the wrestling ring. They were both in short skirts, low-cut tops, and mile-high stilettos that looked more fitting for walking along the strip trying to pick up a john for the night than going to the family-friendly fan expo put on by the GWA.

Now I see why Allissa's avoided dating and all that comes with it for so long. It's her way of rebelling against her overtly sexual mom.

During one of their many conversations over the past few weeks, Allissa had told him that her mom managed a bar. He'd assumed it was someplace like Tully's Roadhouse back home, since Allissa was also from a small town. But after seeing Windy and her friend for the first time, Dean wondered just what kind of bar they worked in.

I bet it's a strip club, Dean decided just as the enthusiastic greetings finally died down. *And that's why Allissa's been so on edge about everyone meeting her mom this weekend. I'll have to make sure to show her that whatever her mom does or says won't change how I feel about her. Or what everyone else we work with thinks of her.*

"Mom, Kandi, this is Dean," Allissa introduced him, stepping back over to his side.

"We already figured that when we saw you kissing him," Windy grinned.

"Nice to meet you, Ms. Walters." Dean extended his hand to Allissa's mom.

"Oh, none of that," Windy protested, launching herself at him for an unexpected hug. "Makes me feel old, and I'm not old. You call me Windy."

"Oof," Dean coughed from the impact and looked at Allissa for help just as her mom squeezed his ass. "Okay, Windy."

"Mom, quit molesting my boyfriend, please." Allissa extracted her mother. Thankfully, she pulled the older woman off him before she could get a handful of anything else.

"I'm not molesting him," Windy objected, shaking her head at Allissa. "I was just checking to make sure he's built right to take care of you."

Dean stepped behind Allissa, using her as a human shield, so her mother's friend couldn't likewise accost him.

"So, what's going on today if you're not wrestling until tomorrow?" Kandi waved an arm around as if to point out the arena around them.

"Today's the fan expo," Dean explained. "Where we sign autographs and hang out with the fans while giving them the chance to feel a little of what it's like to be a professional wrestler."

"In fact, we've got to go back out for another autograph session in a couple of minutes," Allissa added. "But your passes allow you to come out to the arena floor and hang out, too."

"Oh, fun!" Kandi squealed and grinned. "I'm looking forward to meeting a few of the hunky wrestlers you get to work with all the time."

"Great," Allissa smiled, but it clearly didn't reach her eyes. "Let's head on out there, then."

They walked through the backstage area, leading Windy and Kandi through the passageway beside the ramp that allowed them to enter the arena without disrupting the performers and fans using the ramp for the ring entrance experience. When they separated, the two bodyguards who had shown up with Windy and Kandi followed them around the various booths, while the two that had traveled with them for the last couple of weeks shadowed Dean and Allissa.

As soon as they were far enough away that they wouldn't be overheard, Dean leaned down to whisper in Allissa's ear, "Don't worry, Darlin'. I doubt they'll broadcast their ages to any of the guys they hit on by mentioning that Windy is your mom."

"You obviously don't know them that well," Allissa laughed. "Otherwise, you'd know that they're proud cougars on the prowl for cubs."

"In that case, we should probably point them in the direction of Crockett, Surfer Josh, and Red," Dean quipped, imagining how the biggest players in the locker room would react to a dose of their own flirtatious medicine.

"Oh, gawd, that's a train wreck just waiting to happen," Allissa laughed. "And while I'll be mortified to witness it, I'm not sure I'll be able to look away when it happens."

Dean enjoyed laughing with Allissa as he escorted her to the booth where they were set to sign autographs for the next hour. It might not be the way he wanted to alleviate her anxiety, but making her laugh was quickly becoming his second favorite reaction he was able to elicit from Allissa. Allissa in the throes of orgasm was clearly number one.

<p style="text-align:center">~~~</p>

Allissa was relieved to get back to their suite after surviving the first day of her mom interacting with the GWA crew. While her mom and Kandi hadn't been as outrageous as she knew they could be, she'd still been thoroughly embarrassed by their behavior all day. In addition to dressing like they were still working as prostitutes and on their way to work, they flirted with every man they met and groped a lot more than just Dean.

I guess, at least, they didn't invite them all back to the brothel for the night.

Dinner out with her mom talking about her childhood with Dean and all her friends had been embarrassing enough. She'd regaled them with stories from as far back as when Allissa first learned to walk, through her elementary years when she excelled in math and struggled with spelling, and up through her awkward teenage years before she mastered the art of hair and makeup to catch the eye of a modeling agent and start her career. Allissa was only able to tolerate the embarrassing stories because none of them alluded to the bullying of her peers or were in any way sexual in nature.

Thankfully, her mother finally seemed to understand and respect the boundary Allissa had been trying to set for years regarding announcing where she worked when meeting people her daughter had to interact with daily. *If only she'd learn to start dressing and acting like my mom, instead of my party girl best friend.*

Allissa was surprised by how Dean had taken her mom and Kandi's appearance in stride, and hadn't said anything yet about calling things off with her because of how embarrassing they were. In fact, he'd seemed to enjoy siccing them on his flirtatious friends to give them a taste of their own medicine.

But he doesn't know where they work yet. Or that they both started working as hookers as teenagers. He probably thinks they're just going through a midlife crisis, and trying to recapture their youth by dressing younger than they should and flirting outrageously. I'm sure his opinion will change when he learns the truth. And his opinion about me will change when he finds out I'm the product of Mom's former profession.

Allissa pushed her mom from her thoughts as she changed into her favorite red and black plaid sleep shorts and a red tank top. She had a dozen of these same sleep sets in a rainbow of colors and loved how comfortable they were to sleep in. But as she looked at herself in the mirror while washing off her makeup for the night, Allissa wondered if she should go shopping for sexier lingerie to wear for Dean until he learned her secret shame and ended things.

Although, as quickly as he seems to strip my top off every night, maybe sexy lingerie would be a waste of money to just have him throw it on the hotel floor. Allissa smiled at the thought as she finished her nightly routine, eager to find out what new form of foreplay Dean would teach her that night.

It had been a week since they'd come up with the plan for him to teach her one new semi-sexual technique each week. After that first night when he'd taken her shirt off and kissed her breasts, it had taken her a couple of days to convince him that taking his shirt off for her to kiss his chest wasn't a new thing, just her continued learning of the same form of stimulation. Since they now spent their evenings with both of them topless and teasing each other with their mouths, she hoped he'd opt to remove their pants this week, even though she wasn't sure she was ready to try blow jobs just yet.

Unlike everything else he was teaching her sexually, Allissa wasn't leery of giving him a blow job because of her obvious inexperience. She was pretty sure that all the bananas she'd eaten as a child provided plenty of experience for her to expertly suck his dick. But from what she'd seen of him in the shower a couple of weeks back, she knew he was a lot bigger than a banana. Besides not being sure she could fit much of him in her mouth, she wasn't sure she was prepared for when he came.

Maybe we can just touch each other below the waist? Then I know I won't choke on his cum. I mean, Mom always said guys don't like to give oral as much as receive it. And since he doesn't ever expect me to do anything to him that he hasn't done to me, I'm sure Dean won't expect me to suck his dick, if he's only using his hands on my pussy.

Allissa was both excited and a little nervous at the prospect of what was to come between her and Dean. *Time to get over the nerves and embrace the excitement.* Allissa gave herself a quick pep talk before leaving her room to go see what Dean had planned for them, since they were back in their room early with no GWA show that night.

"You don't mind if we wait a little bit before ordering food, do you?" Dean was toweling off his hair as he leaned in the doorway to his bedroom. "Since we came here straight after dinner, it's a bit early to eat again already."

"No, I don't mind waiting." Allissa couldn't take her eyes off the sight of Dean in just his gray sweatpants to even focus on walking over to the sofa to sit down. She let her eyes trail over his ripped torso and the tattoo of his flowery version of a family tree on his left shoulder and arm until he turned to go back into his room. She watched his firm ass walk away, having the strangest urge to rush over and take a little bite of his buns. When he walked far enough into the room that she could no longer see him, Allissa shook off her lustful daze and flopped down onto the couch.

Dean soon returned, having brushed out his hair, but he hadn't donned a shirt, leaving his chest and abs on display for her visual enjoyment. Allissa couldn't stop her eyes from following the lines of his pecs as they converged into a line down the middle of his abs, leading to the happy trail of hair that dipped into his sweats.

He sat down beside her and gave her a curious look. "So, now that we're alone, wanna tell me the real reason why you insisted on an early night tonight?"

Allissa should have known that Dean would see through the lie she told her mom about needing to get her rest before her big title match the next day. He was so observant and noticed even the little things about her that nobody else had ever seen, so she wasn't surprised she hadn't been able to hide her mixed feelings about hanging out with her mom.

She was pretty sure he already knew she'd had her fill of her mom's embarrassing behavior for the day, so she wasn't sure why he was bringing it up now. "You didn't really want to spend the night out clubbing with my mom, did you?"

"No," Dean chuckled, shaking his head. "But with as often as ya'll call and check on each other, I thought you might want to spend more time with her tonight."

Allissa sighed and slumped back against the back of the sofa, looking up at the ceiling instead of at Dean. "If she'd have suggested a girls' night hanging out in one of our rooms, I'd have gladly spent the whole evening with her. The mom I've told you about is who she is when it's just the two of us. That's the mom I miss and enjoy spending time with. But as I'm sure you noticed today, she's a whole different person whenever there are men around."

Allissa knew her mother's behavior stemmed from years of having to flirt and flaunt her sexuality to earn a living. She'd come to terms with loving her mom but hating her profession and the effects her years of working in a brothel had on her years ago, but she didn't really want to explain all that to Dean. So, she decided not to give him the chance to ask any more questions about why her mom and Kandi were dressed like street walkers and flirted with every man they met.

Allissa stood up and stripped off her shirt. "And, honestly, I've been looking forward to my next foreplay lesson from you all day. So, I didn't want to risk getting drunk and missing it by going out."

She hooked her thumbs in the waistband of her shorts, thinking she'd take them off, too, in order to be ready for what she hoped was the next step for them.

"No, Darlin', leave the shorts on," Dean commanded, gripping her hips to pull her onto his lap.

Allissa wasn't sure if it was his dominant tone, or the feel of his hands on her body, that instantly hardened her nipples and flooded her pussy with arousal. But regardless of which it was, it was obvious her body liked both, so she wasn't going to take the time to analyze the reason for her response right then.

Once she was straddling him, he kissed her, basically stopping their discussion before informing her of his plans for the evening. Not that

Allissa was going to complain about that. She was more than ready to stop talking. And pretty sure she was going to enjoy whatever he surprised her with in their lustful lesson of the night.

As always seemed to happen when their lips met, Allissa's world shrank down to just the two of them. She closed her eyes as their tongues tangled, but even if she hadn't, she wouldn't have been able to see her surroundings.

Dean overwhelmed all her senses. She could only see his navy-blue eyes looking into her soul, even with her eyes closed. She could only hear their panting breaths and guttural moans of pleasure. She could only smell his woodsy musk and leather scent. She could only taste his minty kiss. And she could only feel the sensual touch of their bodies rubbing together in erotic exploration.

Her hands seemed to have a mind of their own as they roamed Dean's body, reveling in the hard planes of his musculature only softened by the light dusting of hair across his pecs and down the very center of his lower abs. Dean's hands mirrored hers, rubbing from her hips up her back before coming around to her chest. Dean broke their kiss to trail his lips down her jaw and neck on his way to her breasts once more.

"I thought you were going to teach me something new tonight," Allissa implored him, as she trailed her hands back up his abs and pecs to cross his shoulders and play with the slightly damp hair at his nape, while arching her back to offer him her breasts. "That's why I thought I needed to lose the shorts."

"Don't worry, Darlin'," Dean crooned as he licked between her boobs. "I'm gonna show you something new tonight, but I'll be touchin' without lookin', so I'm not tempted to jump ahead in your lessons."

Allissa wasn't sure exactly what he meant, but she was glad it sounded like they wouldn't be venturing toward oral sex just yet. Although, with as decadent as his soft beard felt on her breasts, she was kinda curious what it would feel like between her legs as he licked her pussy, and worried that another day with her mom hanging out with the GWA crew would negate her chances of ever finding out.

I wonder if beard burn down there would be better or worse than what I've had to cover up with makeup on my neck and chest?

As Dean latched onto her nipple and slipped his hand in the back of her shorts, Allissa pushed her curiosities from her mind to enjoy the new sensations he was showing her. His large hand covered the majority of her butt, making her feel dainty in comparison to him.

"A fucking thong," Dean groaned against her skin, as he moved his oral attention to her other breast, while rocking his hips to rub his cock against her clit. "Now I'm gonna hafta rethink my plan to teach you about dirty talk next week, so I can strip you out of your shorts to see them."

Allissa knew she blushed at him mentioning the style of panties she wore. Since they were the only style she could wear under the leotards she'd originally worn as ring attire without risking them showing, she'd switched to the T-backed panties at the same time she started training to be a professional wrestler.

Geez, you'd think after wearing them for four years that I wouldn't be embarrassed about them, Allissa admonished herself before changing the subject.

"I don't think dirty talk counts as a lesson," Allissa panted breathlessly, as Dean trailed a finger down the strip of material between her ass cheeks until he reached her pussy. "Since you've been doing that all along."

"Oh, no, Darlin'," Dean disagreed, shaking his head, and tickling her breasts with his beard while he teased his fingers over her pussy through her panties. "Tellin' you how sexy you are while we're makin' out isn't dirty talk. But maybe that lesson will be better in a couple of weeks when we're in Heart's Destiny, so I know you'll be safe stayin' in the B and B, and we can have phone sex to show you the difference."

"You're the teacher, Dean," Allissa moaned, as he slid her panties to the side to run his fingers over her lower lips. "So I'm trusting you to schedule my lessons in the correct order. But I still think you might want to consider dirty talk as an add-on for another lesson."

"Don't worry, Darlin'," Dean smirked and wagged his eyebrows at her. "I might have called it phone sex, but I'm planning on a Skype call, so we can watch each other get off at the same time."

Allissa assumed he meant they'd watch each other masturbate and started worrying that her fumbling recent efforts in that area wouldn't be appealing to him. But then he slipped the tip of his finger inside her and she decided to pay special attention to what he did during this lesson to try to emulate it later.

Hopefully, I'll figure out what actually works with his fingers in the next couple of weeks, so I won't look like a bumbling idiot who can't make herself come if we last long enough to get to that lesson.

"Fuck, you're so tight and wet," Dean groaned as he worked his digit in deeper. "You're gonna strangle my cock when I finally get inside you."

Allissa couldn't respond. She was too carried away by the strange sensations he was causing. Dean continued to slowly move his finger in and out of her opening in small increments, wiggling it around inside her to stimulate nerve endings she never knew could feel pleasurable before.

Holy shit! His finger feels way better than a tampon.

Allissa released his hair to grip his shoulders, needing to ground herself as her orgasm built with each thrust of his digit deeper inside her. "Oh, gawd, Dean," Allissa moaned as her desire spread from her core throughout her body. "What are you doing?"

"It's called finger-fuckin', Darlin'," Dean chuckled before going back to suckling her nipples.

She meant to ask him how to find that spot he stroked over to cause her inner walls to spasm in the first waves of orgasmic bliss, but she couldn't form the words as her climax crashed over her. All that came out when she opened her mouth was, "yes, Dean, yes," over and over.

Instead of backing off and holding her while she recovered the way Dean usually did when she came from dry-humping and nipple stimulation, he continued to finger-fuck her through the orgasm. He stretched her out to insert a second digit along with the first, making her feel fuller than she'd ever experienced, even with an ultra-absorbent tampon, which was the biggest size on the market. Allissa barely felt like she was starting to come down from the first high before he worked her back up to a second.

"That's it, Darlin'. Keep comin' for me. Soak my fingers, so I can get you opened up enough to eventually take my cock."

Allissa wasn't sure if it was the added dirty talk, the increased fullness, or the fact that they were both rocking their hips to rub her clit over the thick bulge of his dick, but she finally understood what her girlfriends meant when they talked about "coming like a freight train" when talking about achieving multiple orgasms with their partners.

The pleasure was so intense that she couldn't think straight to worry about anything but what they were doing right then. She literally lost count of how many times she orgasmed before she finally collapsed from exhaustion. She only stayed upright because Dean's arm supported her back with her head resting in his free hand.

Even though she was totally spent and satiated from the experience, Allissa groaned at the loss when Dean slipped his fingers from between her folds. He lightly chuckled as he sat back and hugged her to his chest, so she could enjoy cuddling with him while she recovered.

With her eyes closed, she missed seeing him stick his fingers in his mouth to suck off her juices. But when he moaned at the taste, she opened them just in time to see him pull his fingers from his mouth. She blushed at the realization that he was licking her essence from his fingers.

"Fucking delicious," Dean grinned at her. "Yeah, we're definitely gonna hafta rearrange the schedule to swap eating your pussy to next week and dirty-talking Skype sex to the week after."

Allissa felt a flutter of nerves at the thought of reciprocating the experience the following week, but she also felt excited about how she imagined it would feel to have his mouth on her most intimate body part.

"I think we need to finish this week's lesson before we start planning next week's," Allissa redirected the conversation, sitting up to slide her hands back down Dean's torso.

"Oh, no, Darlin'." Dean stopped her hands just before she reached into his sweats. "I can't handle you touchin' my cock without the barrier of my pants until we get far enough along in our lessons that you're ready to make love. I don't wanna take a chance on losing control and pushing you too fast."

"But you didn't come," Allissa protested, feeling bad for not reciprocating. "And I want to make you feel as good as you make me feel every night."

"You do, Darlin'," Dean smiled reassuringly. "Trust me, I enjoy makin' you come more than anything. And we'll get to the point where we're both comin' together. But for now, it's gonna hafta be a solo act for me, so I don't lose control."

"But what if I want to see you lose control?" Allissa teased him with a playful pout. Though in the back of her mind, she was secretly relieved that she wouldn't be giving him a blow job anytime soon.

"Sorry, Darlin'," Dean smirked before lifting her off his lap. He placed her on her feet before reaching for her top to hand it to her. "You're just gonna hafta be patient and wait a couple of weeks to watch it on Skype."

"I think you're a giant tease, Dean Dangerous," Allissa quipped as she put on her tank top. "But that's okay because I think I'm way more patient than you, so we'll see which one of us really suffers with waiting two weeks before you let me watch you come."

Dean closed his eyes and groaned before jumping up from the sofa. "I'm gonna go get another shower before we order food."

Allissa giggled as he walked into his room, feeling a little lighter at being able to tease him about something sexual without feeling awkward or embarrassed.

Chapter Thirteen

Allissa paced nervously in the backstage area, where everyone was gathered around the monitors to watch their coworkers wrestle. She wasn't sure why she was so anxious for this pay-per-view appearance when she hadn't been for the previous five, three of which had also included her wrestling against Holly for the women's division title. Yeah, the pay-per-views drew larger crowds than their other shows, but she'd already appeared on shows with crowds just as big as the one in Las Vegas for the **Sin City Showdown**.

She didn't think it was because of the stalker situation, since she'd also dealt with that at the **Gateway to the Gold** pay-per-view two months earlier. There were only two things different about this show from the other big events she'd worked with the GWA in the past ten months — she was scheduled to win the title, and her mom was sitting at ringside. Since she was more excited than nervous about winning her first GWA women's title, she was left with only one idea for why she felt uneasy before her match.

Oh, shit! This anxiety is because I'm worried about how Mom is gonna embarrass me on a show broadcast around the world! Please, please, please, don't let her seat be visible on the hard camera.

Allissa stopped pacing to get a better look at the monitor, watching the crowd instead of the wrestlers in the ring to see if she spotted her mom. *Surely, after meeting her and Kandi yesterday, Rick warned the camera crew at ringside to keep them out of their shots to maintain the family-friendly reputation of the GWA.*

Just as she started to sit down in the only empty chair by the nearest monitor, Dean came back from the locker room, where he'd rinsed off and changed clothes after his match. Allissa wasn't sure how someone as large as Dean was able to sneak in behind her to steal the seat, but he somehow managed it, so she didn't realize he was behind her until she sat on him. She jumped up in surprise, turning to glare at him.

"Oh, no, you're still gonna sit here, Darlin'," he assured her as he pulled her down to sit sideways on his lap and wrapped his arms around her. "Where I can hold you for a few minutes to help you chill out before you go out and wow the crowd."

"How do you know I need to chill out?" Allissa slipped her arms around Dean's neck, returning his embrace and watching his eyes turn from their typical steel-gray to the navy-blue she'd come to learn was reserved for his time with her.

"Because I know you, Darlin'," Dean chuckled. "I knew the whole time I was in the ring that you'd only stay sitting down long enough to watch my match, and then you'd be up pacing until it's time for you to go to the ring. That's why I rushed through rinsing off and changing as soon as our match was over, so I could help you relax enough to really soak in every moment once you step through the curtain."

Allissa was amazed at just how well Dean knew her. But then again, when she looked back at the whole time they'd known each other and not just the last month that they'd officially been a couple, she realized just how observant he was every time they were in the same space. And since the whole company spent so much time together as they traveled around the world, he'd had ample opportunity to observe all her moods and idiosyncrasies.

With anyone else, the thought of them keeping such close tabs on her would be creepy, much like her stalker. But since she'd watched Dean just as closely as he'd studied her from day one, she couldn't fault him for the attention. In fact, she rather liked the way he used his knowledge of her to show his affection.

Hoping to show her appreciation for his thoughtfulness, Allissa leaned in and kissed his cheek, just above his beard. "Thank you," she smiled at him as she lifted her lips from his skin. She would have kissed him properly, or maybe improperly considering they were surrounded by the rest of the GWA at the moment, but she didn't have time to redo her makeup before her match.

"Always, Darlin'," Dean grinned at her. She didn't have to tell him what she was thanking him for because getting closer over the last few weeks meant they'd started to be able to read their feelings in one another's eyes and feel a calming peace in one another's arms.

They hadn't said the big L word just yet, but Allissa thought that was what she was seeing in Dean's eyes, when they turned that deep navy-blue that made her think of looking at the ocean in the middle of the night. She was also pretty sure he could see the same in hers, even if she wasn't quite ready to even admit to herself that she'd fallen for him. She just hoped having her mom hanging around until they left Vegas the next morning wouldn't kill that emotion in his eyes.

They didn't have time to say anything else as Joel Baker, the production assistant who kept them all on schedule, called out, "Victoria and Holly to the gorilla position," alerting them that it was almost time for their match.

She and Dean hugged one more time before she jumped off his lap. Allissa grabbed the gray and white feather cape to match the silver glitter, spandex leotard, and white feather miniskirt she was wearing for the show. At least, she thought of it as a cape, since it attached around her neck like the capes she wore with her other ring attire. In actuality, the feathers stuck out more like wings from her shoulders and up above her head, making it reminiscent of the costumes and headdresses worn by Vegas showgirls. She quickly put it on before practically floating over to the curtain that led out to the arena floor.

Allissa bounced on the balls of her feet and took a few deep breaths to get in the right mindset for her match. Then she followed the advice she'd heard from Dean and her friends all day to take a moment to look around and soak it all in, looking at the smiling faces of her GWA family backstage one more time before her music hit and she stepped through the curtain.

She took another moment to stand center stage and let her eyes roam around the eighty-thousand fans there to watch her win her first title belt. She knew as the heel, she wasn't supposed to smile as she sauntered down the ramp to the ring. So Allissa hoped the smile she couldn't wipe off her face came across as more of a cocky smirk to the fans watching on TV as she made her ring entrance.

Since she couldn't go through the ropes with the flashy feathers sticking out at least three feet above her head and to each side of her torso, Allissa climbed to the top turnbuckle from outside the ring and jumped down into the ring as if she was doing a diving stomp onto an opponent. She then hammed it up, raising her arms and taunting the fans as she looked out of the ring from each side.

Her mom and Kandi gave her the loudest pop when she faced the fans on the side of the ring with the hard camera. *Ah, that's why I couldn't find them on the monitors earlier.* Thankfully, they didn't scream anything inappropriate, other than cheering for her when her character was supposed to garner heat from the fans.

As much as Allissa felt embarrassed by her mother flaunting her sexuality and dressing like she was twenty years younger than she was, she loved her mom more than anyone else in the world. Well, except maybe Dean, but she wasn't ready to admit that even to herself just yet.

Like pretty much everyone in the world, Windy Walters had her faults, but her love for her daughter was most certainly not one of them. Allissa felt like her mom was her best friend from the day she was born. She had made several more friends since working with the GWA, but other than Dean, none of them were as close to Allissa as her mother.

Windy supported Allissa in everything she ever tried in life, regardless of how their interests differed. Allissa knew when she looked down from the ring to see her mom cheering her on that she wouldn't have felt like she'd really won anything without her mom there at ringside for her first title win.

When her ring entrance music ended, Allissa went to her corner and removed the feather cape, handing it over to the production assistant who would take it backstage for her while the fans were focused on Holly's ring entrance. Once Holly made it to the ring and was introduced, the bell rang for them to start the twenty-minute match.

Allissa couldn't take any more mental snapshots of her surroundings to memorialize the night, as she had to focus on performing each maneuver with precision to ensure neither she nor Holly would be injured by a botched move. As was always the case when Allissa faced Holly in the ring, the two women put on a wrestling clinic that would be hard for Crusher Cooper and Tank of Heavy Artillery to top in the main event for the heavyweight title.

When the time came for her to hit her finisher, a backflip splash, which the ring announcers called a "Vicious Victory" because of how she raised her arms in a V for victory while standing on the top turnbuckle facing out at the fans before doing the backflip and landing torso-to-torso perpendicular with her supine opponent to pin them, Allissa went to the corner closest to her mom. She climbed to the top turnbuckle and pointed at her mother. "This one's for you, Mom!"

She raised her arms in her signature V and grinned at her mom before floating through the air to land the move perfectly. She hooked Holly's leg as the referee counted the pinfall. As soon as the ref's hand hit the mat for the third time, Allissa jumped up to soak it all in again.

The referee handed her the title belt before raising her hand as the winner. The ring announcer, Chad Westbrook, climbed into the ring, holding a microphone in her face, just as all the heels in the company filled the ring to help her celebrate.

"Victoria, how does it feel to win your first GWA women's title?"

"Like the title is finally where it belongs," Allissa smirked, embracing her bitchy gimmick as her friends surrounded her. They gave her several pats on the back and congratulatory hugs as Chad continued the interview.

"After Holly won the last three times you've faced her for the title, I was beginning to think she was on too much of a hot streak for you to be able to pull it off. What made the difference tonight?"

"Holly may have been on a hot streak earlier in the year," Allissa laughed as Dean hoisted her up on his shoulder, causing Chad to have to hold the mic up for her to continue her after-match promo. "But I think I just proved that hot streaks don't last. The house always wins in Vegas. And as a Vegas girl, I couldn't lose with the match happening in my house."

They only spent a few more minutes celebrating in the ring before heading to the back, so Tank and Cooper could finish off the night with the main event. Once she was backstage, she was surrounded by all the babyfaces who couldn't come out and congratulate her in front of the fans during the show. They might break kayfabe by hanging out together backstage and outside the arenas where they performed, but they weren't about to do it during a show.

Part of her felt like it was silly for them to congratulate her, since the show was scripted. But even though her title win was a work, Allissa still felt accomplished because she knew giving her the title was a sign of Rick's respect for her as a performer. She may not have had to legitimately fight for the championship, but she earned it with her high workrate. And she relaxed a little, knowing that even meeting her mom the day before hadn't changed his opinion of her enough for him to flip the script and take her title win away from her at the last minute.

"No getting out of it tonight, Vic," Emerald insisted as Holly hugged her backstage. "We're all going out after the show to celebrate your first title."

"I don't know," Allissa protested, looking to Dean to save her from their friends. She was looking forward to a private celebration with him in their suite and wasn't sure she wanted to risk missing out by going out drinking with their friends.

"Don't fight it, Darlin'," Dean grinned and shook his head at her. "I already reserved a VIP room big enough for the whole GWA, and got it cleared with Avington to have the place crawling with security."

"We've even got childcare set up, so we can all go," Holly assured her.

"And since we're just going to Reno tomorrow, we're not flying out until noon," Rick informed them with a shrug. "That way us old folks who aren't used to being up all night can sleep in tomorrow morning."

Allissa couldn't argue with the boss, especially when he was pushing back their flight time by two hours to accommodate their celebration. "Fine, but you guys really should've given me more warning, so I'd have time to shower and redo my hair and makeup."

"Ya might wanna hurry then, Darlin'," Dean smirked, lightly swatting her ass as she walked toward the locker room.

Hopefully, having to air this show on Eastern Time and finishing so much earlier than normal means we'll stop partying earlier in the evening than if we weren't in the Pacific Time Zone. I mean, getting done with the show three hours earlier than normal should make it okay to stop partying three hours earlier, too, right?

Who am I kidding? Not with my mom and Kandi going to party with us.

Oh well, then I guess we'll just move our make-out session to the early morning hours, when we finally get back to our hotel suite, instead of as soon as we can get there after the show. Well, if our relationship survives a night of partying with my mom, who I'm sure won't be able to keep from mentioning where she works once she has a few drinks.

<center>~~~</center>

Dean couldn't believe what a difference there was in their time out in Vegas after just a few months. The first time Allissa had joined their group at a Vegas nightclub back in October, she'd completely blown him off every time he tried to get her attention. Then in January, when their married colleagues had spearheaded a casino outing to push Rick and Fiona together, she'd avoided him completely by sitting at a blackjack table on the opposite side of the room from him. But now, they were side by side, whether seated for drinks with the rest of the group, or out on the dance floor in the middle of the club.

Dean was immensely thrilled with the change of circumstances as they celebrated in the VIP room of the club in their hotel after the **Sin City Showdown**, especially when it involved a little bumping and grinding as they danced. Since they were in a club that played the current popular dance music that Allissa liked instead of the country they'd danced to back in Texas or the classic rock that Dean preferred, she sang along more than he did while they were on the dance floor. Dean couldn't stop himself from laughing at how she bungled the lyrics.

"Can't make no promises, I'll still get hard," Allissa sang as she rubbed her body against the appendage that Dean couldn't stop from getting hard at the contact.

"While your lyrics aptly describe me right now, Darlin'," Dean chuckled as he rocked his hips against her while pulling her into him with his hand on her low back, so she felt what she did to him. "I don't think they're correct."

"How would you know? You don't even like this kind of music to know the lyrics." As Allissa ran her hands over his shoulders and chest while they danced, she lightly pinched his nipple to make her point.

"I might not choose dance music to listen to while I'm doing other things, but I like to dance enough to have heard it a few times," Dean argued with a grin at her impishness. "And as the lead singer of the

244

band my brother, Anthony, and I started in high school, I learned to listen closely to lyrics, so I could sing them when we got a gig. And they're singing 'be home,' not 'get hard,' Darlin'." He leaned his head toward the nearest speaker to indicate he was talking about the original artists singing the correct lyrics to the song they were dancing to at the moment.

"Are you sure?" Allissa stopped dancing, concentrating on listening closely to the music. "Let's go check with the girls, 'cause I'm still hearing 'get hard' every time they sing that line."

Dean escorted Allissa off the dance floor and back to the VIP room he'd reserved, noticing the bodyguards mirroring their movement between rooms. As soon as they were in the private area, Allissa darted over to the table where her mother was leading the Precious Stones, Bennington brothers, and Protection Detail in a round of shots. "Hey, listen to this song and tell us which one of us has the right lyrics. Are they singing 'I'll still get hard' or 'I'll still be home'? Dean says I have the lyrics wrong again."

There was a definite divide between the group in what they heard, with the guys surprisingly hearing Allissa's version and the women hearing Dean's.

"Since you always sing the wrong lyrics, I'm sure whichever Dean picked is right," Emerald slurred, obviously having consumed the contents of more than a couple of the empty shot glasses on the table.

"She gets that from me," Windy shrugged. "We Walters women always sing our own tune."

"At least Lissie's don't seem to be as bad as yours," Kandi teased her friend. "Remember back when we first met, and you kept singing 'Penis' instead of 'Venus'?"

"I do not need to hear this story." Allissa shook her head and held her hand up in the universal sign for stop at her mom and Kandi. But she was smiling and not blushing, so Dean considered it a less embarrassing memory than some of the stories they'd shared previously about Allissa's childhood.

"Oh, but we do," Emerald disagreed, leaning over toward Windy to the point that she looked like she might fall out of the chair. Luckily, Magnum was seated on her other side and reached over to pull her back into an upright position.

"Fine, I'll ask everyone else which one of us is right." Allissa turned her back on the conversation to shout her question to the whole group.

Soon the rest of the group was giving their opinions from around the room, until Fiona looked it up, probably because she was one of the few people in their group still sober. "It's 'be home'," Fiona informed them.

"Seriously?" Allissa's shoulders slumped at the realization that she was wrong.

Dean hated seeing her so dejected, even over something so inconsequential. "Don't worry, Darlin'," Dean comforted her by wrapping his arm around her shoulders and hugging her into his side. "I think your made-up lyrics are cute." Dean leaned down to whisper-shout the rest of his thought in her ear, so only she could hear him over the music. "Especially when they show off that dirty mind you keep trying to hide."

Allissa slapped his stomach and rolled her eyes at him, but she still smiled, which made Dean feel like he'd done alright with cheering her up.

"So, what does Dean win for being right?" Liam interjected, assuming they'd placed a bet on which of them was right, since most of the locker room tended to wager over the stupidest of things like that.

"Nothin'," Dean sighed in an overdramatic fashion. "No time to come up with any bets when we had to get in here to find out who was right before the song ended."

"Damn, dude, I thought for sure you'd take advantage of winning a bet with Vic in Vegas to get hitched," Liam taunted them.

"Who's getting hitched?" Windy Walters stuck her head between Allissa and Dean, wrapping an arm around each of them as she wormed her way between them. "I know where you can go to have an Elvis impersonator as the officiant."

"Not us!" Allissa's eyes went wide as she pulled away from her mother and waved her hand between her and Dean. "We just started dating."

"And we have to wait until our Thanksgiving break to get married, so my family can be there," Dean quipped, stepping away from Windy to pull Allissa back into his side.

"Well, somebody should get married tonight," Windy insisted, turning back to the table of people she'd been sitting with when Dean and Allissa walked back into the room. "Or at least go take some pictures outside one of the wedding chapels to create a buzz with your fans."

"Yeah, I don't think a drunk Vegas wedding fits with the family-friendly image of the GWA," Rick objected, shaking his head.

"It might work with our gimmick," Trojan disagreed, pointing between himself, Magnum, and Chastity. "And could make for an interesting angle, depending on which one of us is in the pretend wedding pictures."

"Oh, yeah, we'd have to have one of the heels trying to corrupt Chastity," Magnum suggested, nodding in agreement with his tag-team partner.

Crockett, Blade, and Red all volunteered to be the heel to pose for pictures at a chapel with Chastity.

"And why wouldn't it work if one of us was trying to corrupt you?" Amethyst protested, pointing between herself and Emerald.

"I mean, it could," Magnum shrugged. "But our gimmick is that we always wear condoms, while Chastity supposedly never has sex. So marrying her to get into her pants just seems more logical."

"How did we go from figuring out the correct lyrics to a song to booking a Vegas wedding angle while drunk?" Rick rubbed his temples, obviously trying to stave off the headache the guys were going to give him long before the hangover kicked in the next morning.

"I have no idea, Boss," Dean chuckled. "But I'm gonna leave wrangling the drunk half of the roster away from the wedding chapels in town in your capable hands and call it a night."

"Yeah, we should definitely leave before my mom drags us to a chapel," Allissa agreed, taking his hand, starting toward the door, and waving at their friends with her free hand. "Night everyone."

Dean just laughed and followed along, waving goodnight to the crew as they left. Since the nightclub was in the hotel where they were staying all weekend, they just had to walk to the elevator to go back to their suite. That had been intentional when planning the celebration after the show, so they could all cut loose and have a few drinks without having to drive.

But now that they were on the way back up to the room where they could have their normal make-out session before bed, Dean was second-guessing how much both he and Allissa had imbibed. While he didn't feel too inebriated to perform or at risk of losing control and going farther than intended, he didn't feel right sexually touching Allissa when she was under the influence of alcohol.

But fuck, I wanna feel her come on my fingers again tonight.

Unfortunately, the way she swayed on her feet as they stepped off the elevator sealed their fate for the evening. So, ever the gentleman that his family raised him to be, Dean quickly cleared their rooms before giving her a relatively tame kiss goodnight and sending her off to her own bed alone.

"But I thought we'd make out and do that finger-fuck thing again," Allissa pouted, slightly slurring her words.

"Not when we've both been drinking, Darlin'," Dean informed her. "I want us both to remember every minute when we're intimate, not let alcohol cloud our judgment and cause us to push past your boundaries."

"You are a very good man, Dean Byron Hunter. You don't just look like Aquaman. You're my real-life superhero." Allissa pushed up on her tiptoes and pressed her lips to his once more, but only for a quick peck of a kiss. "And I hope you still find me worthy of your goodness when you… get to know… what's deep inside me."

The way she paused to try to form the right words made Dean think she might have skipped a couple of them in her drunken state. *But I wouldn't mind being what's deep inside you, Darlin'.* "I'm sure I will, Darlin'. Now go get some rest."

He brushed his lips over her forehead before she turned and staggered to her room. Dean wondered if he should go help her to bed the way he had after James and Randi's bachelor and bachelorette party. But since she was actually awake and able to get there on her own, he didn't think it would be a good idea.

Back in May, he'd had to carry her to her room. He'd removed her shoes and placed her in bed before going to get her a bottle of water and some acetaminophen to place them on her bedside table. He'd sat in the chair in her room watching her sleep for most of the night, just to make sure she didn't vomit in her sleep. When she started to stir in the early hours of the next morning, he slipped out of her room, so she wouldn't think he was some kind of demented pervert for watching her sleep when she wouldn't even call him a friend, much less give him a chance at being her man.

Now, he waited in the living room of their suite until he heard her stop moving around in her room and the light went out under her door before going to his room to go through his nightly routine. But when he got to his bathroom, he couldn't take care of his own needs until he knew he'd taken care of hers.

He grabbed the ibuprofen from his bathroom bag before going out and grabbing a bottle of water from the mini-fridge in the kitchenette portion of the living room area of the suite. He lightly tapped on her door, waiting a minute with no response before opening it to see her already asleep. He quickly crossed the space to put the water and over-the-counter pain relievers on her bedside table before brushing his lips over her forehead once more. "Goodnight, Darlin'. Sweet dreams."

Once he retreated to his room, he handled his own needs in the shower before going to bed to dream of the day he'd finally get to make love to his Darlin' Allissa.

~~~

Saturday, August 24, 2019, Calgary, Alberta, Canada

After a week of struggling with his self-control to keep from stripping Allissa completely and doing way more than just fingering her pussy under her clothing, Dean was eager to move on to the next level in their plan to gradually ease her into sex. He'd thoroughly enjoyed starting to stretch her pussy with his fingers for the last week, and couldn't stop the smile that spread across his face every time he thought about their nighttime activities. While he assumed she'd somehow broken her own hymen since he couldn't feel a barrier when he finger-fucked her, she was still so tight that it was obvious she hadn't had anything bigger than a tampon in her cunt before. So, he was determined to spend as much time as she needed massaging her inner walls with his fingers to open her up enough to be able to take his cock without even a moment of discomfort. But finger-fucking her
~~~

wasn't the only way he planned to prepare her to be able to take his big dick deep inside her. He'd planned to take a couple more weeks before he introduced her to oral sex. But since he started tasting the remnants of her arousal on his fingers at the end of their encounters, he was positive he couldn't wait another day, much less a week, to eat her pussy.

Considering he hadn't gone down on a woman since he was in college, he was surprised at how eager he was to lavish Allissa with his oral affection. Though when he really thought about it, he supposed he shouldn't be so surprised at his desires when it came to Allissa. Much like kissing, he'd considered oral sex too intimate an act to do with the ring rats who had frequented his hotel beds over the last few years. But with Allissa, he wanted every possible intimacy they could conceive to physically show the connection he felt with her.

Thinking of the times he'd licked her cream from his fingers over the past week made his mouth water at the memory of how sweet and tangy she tasted, making him wish they hadn't wasted time stopping for burgers on their way back to the hotel after the show. Though they tasted delicious, it was Allissa's flavor he craved.

Once they finished eating, Dean rushed through his nightly routine, too excited about getting back to the sofa to get his mouth on Allissa to even bother jacking off in the shower. *Fuck, I'm probably gonna come in my shorts as soon as I see her bare pussy the first time.*

Once he finished brushing his teeth, Dean was rethinking his time-saving measures as he released his hair from the man bun he'd put it in to keep it dry during his second shower of the day. He quickly ran a brush through his long locks before removing the towel around his waist and throwing it over the shower door to dry.

He walked naked from the ensuite bathroom to his bedroom, grabbing a pair of boxer briefs and workout shorts from his suitcase. Once those were on, he went back out to the living room, surprising himself by being there before Allissa.

Damn, I really should have taken the time to jerk off in the shower, he realized as he sat down on the sofa and saw just how bad he was tenting his shorts from thinking about what he was planning to do with Allissa. *But I didn't think about her possibly taking extra time to get ready for tonight.*

Dean leaned back on the couch and closed his eyes, imagining what Allissa might be doing to prepare for him to eat her out for the first time. Based on what he'd felt for the last week when he got his hands down her pants, Dean didn't think her wax job would require a touch-up shave, but he couldn't think of anything else she might need to do outside her normal routine. Picturing her spread eagle on the side of the bathtub as she shaved her pussy caused Dean to unconsciously start rubbing his cock over his shorts.

"I thought we were waiting until next week to watch each other on Skype," Allissa teased him as she walked into the room, wearing his second favorite color of her sleep sets. While his favorite color on her would always be red, he also loved the way royal blue made her eyes shine in a bluer hue of gray.

"We are, Darlin'," Dean grinned at her as he opened his eyes and released his grip on his dick. "I just can't keep my hand off my cock whenever I fantasize about you."

"Just how long do you think it'll be before you let me get my hands on your cock?" Allissa cooed the words as she moved to straddle him. "I mean, using my hands over your shorts like you were just doing isn't that much different than the way we've been grinding on each other the past few weeks, so I don't think that should be a separate lesson."

"Fuck," Dean groaned as his dick throbbed in anticipation of her touching him. He gripped her hips and pulled her closer before running his hands up her back. "I love the way you keep coming up with ways to combine lessons, Darlin'. But that's gonna hafta wait until after I eat your sweet pussy, so I can go wash my cum out of my boxers immediately after. I don't wanna send 'em off to be laundered with the inside covered in a dried-up mess. That would just risk a hotel employee starting online rumors about me coming in my pants like a teenager."

"Oh, no, we definitely don't want to start any online rumors like that," Allissa giggled, wrapping her arms around his neck as she pressed her terrific tits against his chest. "Rick's got his hands full with all the Vegas wedding rumors from last week, and I'm sure he wouldn't appreciate us causing him even more internet headaches."

The fiasco their friends caused the week before was a classic example of why Dean was glad he'd turned his social media over to the company from day one. He still had a private account with his name reversed (listing him as Hunter Dean instead of Dean Hunter), so he could keep up with his family and friends back home, but he never posted pictures of people (himself or his family or friends) on it to keep the fans from figuring out it was him if they could get past his privacy settings. Instead, his feed was filled with pictures of the unusual foods and sights he'd seen on his travels.

But Dean didn't want to think about social media or the rumors their coworkers had started by posting Elvis wedding chapel pictures on their public profiles. He wanted to focus on getting Allissa naked and spread out for him to lick every square-fucking-inch of her delectable little body.

With that thought in mind, Dean slipped a hand up into Allissa's hair to cradle the back of her head and pull her mouth to his. He tried to keep things gentle at first, but when she speared her tongue into his mouth, he let loose with all the passion he felt for her. Their kiss instantly became carnal. He claimed her mouth as she dug her nails into his upper back. Allissa kissed him back with equal fervor, matching his movements and grinding her pussy on his cock.

Dean couldn't wait any longer, needing to taste her more than he needed air to breathe. When they broke the kiss to suck in a little air, Dean wasted no time in stripping off her tank top and lifting her off his lap to stand her up in front of him, so he could strip off her sleep shorts. Before he could move to start sliding them down her legs, though, he had to double-check that she was really ready for them to take this next step. "Are you sure you're ready to go a little farther, Darlin'? I can still stop if you're not ready for me to see you naked or eat your pussy. But I need you to tell me now if I need to slow things back down."

"I'm sure, Dean," Allissa smiled as she reached out and slid her fingers through his hair, pushing it back from his face.

Thank fuck!

Dean didn't say a word, only smiled in response as he tugged the hem of her shorts to move them down her legs without disturbing her panties. Under the blue and white plaid shorts, he found the sexiest royal blue thong in the same shade as her solid color shirt.

"Turn around, Darlin'," Dean commanded, needing to see the full picture of the tiny panties on her body before he stripped them off of her, too. Allissa followed his direction, showing off the most perfect heart-shaped ass he'd ever seen. "Fuck, Allissa, you're the sexiest woman on the planet."

He reached out and palmed her ass cheeks, squeezing the firm globes before slipping a finger under the thin strip of material over each hip to slide the thong down her luscious legs.

Once she stepped out of her panties, Allissa turned around, exposing her bare pussy to him for the first time. Her outer labia were only slightly darker than the rest of her complexion. But once he reached out and spread them open with his fingers, Dean could see that her lower lips were the same dusky pink shade as her areolas and already glistening with her arousal.

Unable to resist a second longer, Dean leaned over and lapped up her cream straight from the source. He started by flattening his tongue to lick up through her slit. Then he clamped his lips around her clit and lightly sucked.

"Oh, gawd, Dean," Allissa whimpered, reaching out to grip his shoulders, as if she felt off balance from the sensation.

Not wanting to risk her falling over when she went limp as she came, Dean wrapped his arms around her, picking her up and twisting their bodies to lay her out on the sofa. He shifted to where he was laying on his stomach with his legs hanging off the end and his face at the apex of her thighs with her on her back. He draped her legs over his shoulders as he traced random patterns with the tip of his tongue over her pussy, trying to find every one of her most sensitive spots.

The new position dislodged her hands from his shoulders, so she weaved her fingers through his hair as he savored her. Allissa rocked her hips, moaning in pleasure as she writhed beneath him, guiding him to each of the places she especially liked him licking.

"Oh, yes, Dean! That's, oh, yes, there!"

Dean couldn't stop himself from thrusting his own hips in response to her cries of pleasure, grinding his cock into the arm of the sofa. He continued to mimic fucking her while tightening the muscle of his tongue to plunge it inside her tight channel.

As he fucked her with his tongue, Dean reached around her thigh to circle the pad of his thumb over her bundle of nerves, sending her into her first orgasm. Her inner walls clamped down on his tongue as she pulled his hair to hold his head in place while she thrust her hips up to fuck his face.

"Oh, Dean! Yes!"

Dean matched her rhythm, swallowing down her release as she continued to shudder in ecstasy. When her creamy cunt finally released its vise-like grip on his tongue, Dean pulled it from her body to lap up the juices that had escaped his mouth. He replaced his tongue with his fingers, starting with two and scissoring them inside her to open her up.

He knew it would probably be a while before he'd actually get to make love to her, but he wanted to make sure she was opened up enough to allow him in without hurting her when it finally happened. So, he planned to take his time over the next few weeks, gradually working her up to where she was able to take his long, thick cock in the most pleasurable way possible.

With that thought in mind, he crooked his fingers to find her G-spot while sucking on her needy nub. The combination of stimulation both inside and out was enough to take her over the edge once again.

Allissa cried out her orgasm with mostly incoherent sounds. Only his name was clearly understood as Dean continued to devour her. He sucked down her sweet cream as her inner walls clamped down on his fingers with each wave of her release.

Dean kept his eyes focused on her face as he continued lavishing his oral attention on her perfect, pink pussy. He needed to see her expression to know when he'd taken her to the limit of how much she could endure. When she screamed his name once more and squeezed his head in the grip of her thighs as her third orgasm crashed through her body, he felt like he could barely hold back his own release.

Fuck! Seeing Allissa come is the hottest thing I've ever watched. And knowing I'm the only person to ever witness it, to ever touch her, taste her, is such an awesome feeling that it's indescribable.

As Allissa's climax waned, her whole body went limp. She released him from the headscissors, her legs falling to the sides, now simply dead weight on his shoulders.

Dean watched as her eyes fluttered closed, knowing she was floating in another realm for a moment while she recovered. He gentled all his movements, slowly pulling his fingers from her body as he softly licked up the last drops of her release. He extracted himself from under her legs, pushing up to stand, so he could go get a washcloth to clean her up.

"Just relax, Darlin'. I'll be right back," he informed her as she opened her eyes and reached for him, looking confused as to why he was walking away.

He turned on the water to warm up as soon as he got to his ensuite bathroom. Then he grabbed two washcloths from the stack of towels he hadn't used earlier. He wet one, ringing it out before turning off the water and returning to the living room.

Allissa was still laying on the sofa, looking like an angel with her eyes closed and her lips turned up in a satiated, beatific smile. Dean felt ten-feet tall and bulletproof from being the man responsible for her blissful state. He didn't care if they ever got around to taking care of his sexual pleasure, wanting only to see her so well-satisfied every day for the rest of his life.

He knelt down on the floor beside the couch and gently wiped the wet cloth between her legs. Allissa's eyes popped open at the first touch of the warm washcloth over her mound.

"What are you doing?" Allissa pushed up on her elbows, watching him intently as he continued to wipe between her legs.

"Just cleaning you up, Darlin'," Dean grinned at her. "Don't want you to feel uncomfortably sticky while you sleep."

"I can do that." Allissa's hand covered his, trying to extract the rag from his hand.

"I know you can, but I want to take care of you." Dean smiled at her as he moved her hand out of the way to finish what he was doing. Once he felt like he'd thoroughly removed all of his saliva and any remnants of her arousal he'd missed licking up from between her folds, he used the dry washcloth to pat up any water left behind. He then laid the wet washcloth on top of the dry one on the coffee table to put away later. "How ya feel, Darlin'?"

"Amazing," Allissa smiled up at him, slowly moving to sit up. "But you always make me feel amazing."

Allissa wrapped her arms around his neck and pressed their lips together. Dean returned both the kiss and the embrace, lifting Allissa into his arms as he stood. She wrapped her legs around his waist, just as he turned to sit on the sofa with her straddling him.

They continued to kiss for several long minutes before Allissa pulled back, wiggling her legs out from behind his back so she could slide her ass toward his knees. "Is it finally my turn to make you feel as wonderful as you just made me feel?"

"You don't owe me anything for that, Darlin'," Dean assured her, not wanting her to think of their sexual encounters, or any other part of their relationship, as transactional. "Believe me, I enjoyed every second of watching you come more than I enjoy being the one to get off."

"I know," Allissa rolled her eyes at him. "You've been telling me that for weeks. But now I want to make you come, so I can find out firsthand what you get out of watching me come."

"Fuck, I can't say no to that," Dean moaned, releasing his hold on her to lace his fingers behind his head. He only hoped having his head in his hands would be enough to keep him from giving in to the animalistic desire he had to claim his mate in all ways when she started touching his cock with her delicate hands for the first time. "But you absolutely have to keep your hands on the outside of my shorts, so I can maintain a little self-control."

"I promise I'll be a good girl and leave your shorts in place." Allissa gave him a mischievous grin as she tentatively reached out and pressed her palm to his hard-as-steel shaft. "But you've gotta tell me how to touch you to make you come."

"Fuck," Dean groaned at the exquisite feel of her hand against his dick. "Wrap your hand around it and slide it up and down the length. And squeeze as hard as you can."

She did as he instructed, moving to sit beside him on the sofa when she found her position on his thighs too awkward to get a good grip. Dean moaned from the pleasure of feeling her stroke him, though the expression of awe on her face as she watched what she was doing to him was just as enticing as her touch.

Allissa released the pressure when she felt his piercings under her palm, looking up at his face with slight trepidation as she bit her lip. "I'm not gonna pull the jewelry out by rubbing it too hard, am I?"

"No, Darlin'," Dean chuckled. "Not as long as you stick to the amount of pressure you're using now. If I'm squeezing hard when I jerk off, I have to lessen the pressure when I get to them, but you're not being too rough with them. And honestly, the piercings healed a few years ago, so I don't think there's much risk of pulling 'em out unintentionally now. In fact, it actually feels good to rub over 'em. You might want to let up just enough to flip the D-ring in the frenum piercing, though, but that might have to wait until we're doing this when you can see what you're doing."

"Which one's that?"

"The one on the shaft, just below the head, with the D-ring that flips up and down," Dean explained as she continued to stroke him. "The one through the head with a straight barbell that has balls on both ends is called an apadravya."

"When and why did you get them?" Allissa released her grip to feel the jewelry with just a couple of fingers before covering the head of his dick with her hand and stroking him from tip to base once more.

While it was a little odd to have this conversation in the middle of a hand job, Dean was glad she was asking questions right then. He needed the distraction to keep from coming too soon as she sped up her chirapsia.

"Back when I was in college," Dean replied as his respiratory rate increased with each pass of her hand up and down his length. "When James and I went to get our matching family tree tattoos. Since we wanted them to be identical, we had to use the same artist. So, while James was in the chair getting his tat done, I looked at all the books in the studio. In addition to pics of all kinds of tattoos, the artist was also into piercings and had books with pics of the piercings he'd done over the years."

Dean couldn't keep thinking about the past to finish his explanation. Allissa jerking him off in his shorts felt too amazing to allow his brain to function. He unconsciously thrust his hips, matching his movements to her rhythm as he felt the first tingles in the base of his spine to signal his impending release.

"Fuck, Darlin', I'm…gonna…" Dean couldn't finish his sentence as his balls tightened and the first spurt of his cum shot into his shorts. "Allissa! Fuck! Allissa! Darlin'!"

She continued to stroke him as he shuddered with each jet of his ejaculation. Her continued ministrations pulled more of his cum from him than he'd ever released from using his own hand. His orgasm was so intense that Dean saw stars and had to take a minute to catch his breath.

"Fuck, Darlin', you've gotta stop," he groaned, reaching down to still her hands before lifting them to his lips to lightly kiss her palms. He wanted to worship the hands that had just given him the greatest orgasm of his life. "While you keep me in a constant state of arousal, I need a little more time than you do to recover before I can come again."

"Oh, sorry," Allissa giggled as she looked down coyly. "I just assumed you kept going and made me come more than once to show me how you wanted me to take care of you."

"I wish," Dean chuckled. "But unfortunately, multiple orgasms in one session are your superpower, not mine."

Allissa looked at him like she wanted to ask a question, but was a little too shy to say it out loud. Luckily, Dean knew his girl well enough to figure out what she wanted to know. "Mine is the stamina to hold off my orgasm until I've given you several before I finally come."

Allissa blushed at his revelation and reached for her clothes. "Are you going to finish telling me about getting your piercings? Or do you want to go clean up and call it a night?"

He hated to see her get dressed, but was happy to know they weren't done spending time together for the night just because she felt the need for that barrier between them while they continued talking. "Give me a few minutes to clean up and change, and then I'll finish telling you all about it."

She smiled up at him as he stood, continuing to put on her clothing. "Deal."

Dean quickly went to his room to clean up and change, looking forward to spending the rest of the evening cuddling on the couch with Allissa while talking about whatever she wanted.

Chapter Fourteen

Saturday, August 31, 2019, Heart's Destiny, Texas

Allissa had just sat down for lunch with Dean in the dining room of the restaurant at the Hunters' Bed and Breakfast on their first full day of the Labor Day break when she was surprised by seeing her mom walk into the room. Windy Walters was led through the dining room by Mandi Hunter and followed by her friend Kandi King and the two bodyguards assigned to her by Avington Security. *Shit! I thought I'd dodged that bullet to mine and Dean's relationship by getting out of Vegas without him hearing about her history.*

"What are they doing here?" Allissa couldn't believe her mom had not only shown up in Heart's Destiny, but had also come with a full entourage. Seeing her brash and bold mom side by side with Dean's prim and proper mother was a shock to Allissa's system, causing her a moment of stunned silence at the obvious dichotomy of their families.

"Lissie, honey!" Windy squealed with excitement at seeing her daughter, running through the dining room as fast as she could on five-inch heels.

Allissa found herself engulfed in a cloud of Primo and her mother's arms before she could even come up with a reason for her mom's sudden appearance. She returned her mom's embrace while trying to figure out the reasoning behind her unplanned trip. "What are you doing here, Mom?"

"Oh, I overheard Dean inviting you to come here for a wedding this week and didn't want to miss seeing you on your break again," Windy explained as she released her daughter and took a seat at their table. "Imagine my surprise when Brady told me he'd be taking a trip back here for his cousin's wedding the same week. Since he's here this week and I didn't want to stay home and deal with any more of those dreadful packages from your stalker, we took our vacation time to spend it with you. But that was before I realized there's not a cheap motel in town. So, now I'm just stopping by to let you know we're close, but going back to San Antonio to find someplace affordable to stay."

Allissa was mortified at her mother's declaration in front of Dean and his mother. She was also torn as to how to smooth over the situation. On the one hand, she wanted to argue that she'd cover the cost for her mother and her entourage to stay at the B and B to save face. But on the other hand, she was worried that prolonging her mom's time in town would only lead to even greater embarrassment for her with Dean's family. And would lead to the ultimate downfall of her relationship with him.

"Nonsense," Dean interjected before Allissa could decide what to do with her mother for the next week. "Mom, I'll cover everything for Allissa's mom and her friends to stay here."

"No," Allissa protested, gripping his forearm, and shaking her head at Dean's kind offer before looking directly at Mandi. "You can bill their expenses to me." She then turned to look at her mom. "Although there should be plenty of money in your account to cover it."

"I'm not going to spend the money you put in there for our household bills to pay for a vacation," Windy argued with her daughter. "And our last-minute plane tickets completely wiped out my last check from the brothel, so I have to go cheaper with the motel."

Allissa cringed at the mention of her mother's place of employment. Thankfully, nobody around them seemed to notice what her mom had said, so Allissa quickly replied to keep them from having a chance to ask about it. "But you're not spending nearly what I've been putting in your account each month to cover the bills, so you should still have plenty of money in there to cover the cost of a hotel for a week."

Since she had started working with the GWA, Allissa had been putting a quarter of her pay each month directly into her mom's checking account to cover the household expenses. Having set up her direct deposits from the GWA to split the money with fifty percent going into a savings account and twenty-five percent to each of her and her mother's checking accounts, she knew her mom's portion of the deposit was over seven-thousand dollars a month — the same as went into her own checking account.

She also knew that their household expenses were under two-thousand dollars a month. So there should be over fifty-thousand dollars in her mom's account that she hadn't needed to spend on bills in the last eleven months, which would easily cover a week at the boutique hotel for her mom and Kandi, as well as the two bodyguards.

Since Allissa's only expenses, while she traveled with the GWA, were her upgraded electronics, extra food, toiletries, and monthly spa trips, she'd had even more than that in her account when Dean helped her start investing it the previous month. And with what she'd seen so far of the stocks he'd helped her invest in, she was expecting that money to grow exponentially as she continued to invest a portion of her monthly income.

"But I'm saving all that to make sure we can still cover everything if something happens and you don't keep earning that much," Windy explained, giving her daughter an exasperated look. "I learned from my mistake of not saving back when I was young and hot enough to earn the big bucks. And now I'm gonna make sure that nest egg is there for you by not using more than I absolutely have to from what you've been giving me."

"Mom," Allissa groaned, knowing she'd already informed her mom about the amount she was saving every month, as well as how Dean was helping her invest to earn more. "How many times do I have to tell you I'm saving most of my income before you understand that I've got our future covered and the money I put in your account is for you to live a better life now?"

"But I'm happy with my life as it is," Windy maintained, frustrating Allissa with the same argument they'd had repeatedly.

It always went back to Windy not making as much money after the hormonal changes during pregnancy made her gain weight that she couldn't get rid of after having Allissa, but she still went back to her job because it paid better than any other job she could get without even a high school diploma back then. She'd eventually gotten her GED and took some community college classes to be able to move over to managing the bar, but before that limited education, Windy always saw her prospects as limited by the changes in her body over the years. She knew her mother didn't mean to send her on a guilt trip, but

Allissa still felt like those initial hormonal changes were her fault for being born.

At least she can't blame me for getting a little thicker every year she gets closer to menopause.

"I know that!" Allissa hadn't meant to raise her voice, but her mother's stubbornness was driving her to the point of insanity and making her react irrationally. "That's why I stopped trying to get you to quit your job and let me buy you a nicer house! But even though I've given up hope that you'll retire and let me take care of you, I still don't want you to go stay in some roach motel to save money, when we can afford to stay someplace a hell of a lot nicer!"

"How about we take this conversation someplace a little more private?" Dean rubbed a hand down her back to calm her down, somehow realizing how best to soothe her without her even thinking it was possible.

Allissa turned to look at Dean and then around the room to notice all eyes on them. *Shit! I didn't mean to cause a bigger scene by losing my temper with Mom.*

"Yes, please." Allissa nodded at Dean before reaching down for her purse.

Mandi waved over a server to box up their meals and deliver them to Allissa's room as Dean stood and pulled out her chair.

"How about you keep them in the warmer instead," Dean suggested with a smile as he passed a few bills to the server who was collecting their plates. Allissa hadn't even realized their food had been delivered to the table right after her mom arrived. "And we'll pick them up on our way out in a little bit."

Once the server confirmed their meals would be boxed up and waiting for them in the kitchen, Dean ushered them all out of the dining room. He held Allissa's hand as they walked down the hall to the elegant lobby, stopping the party just as they reached the base of the stairs.

"Mom, since I'm sure you have Allissa's card on file from where she checked in, why don't you get everyone else checked in and settled in their rooms?"

"Of course," Mandi agreed with a smile.

"And we'll be up to check Allissa out, just as soon as we collect her things from her room and our food from the kitchen."

"Wait!" Allissa turned her surprised gaze on Dean. "Why am I checking out?"

"Because I think you're gonna wanna stay in my guest room, so you have access to the heavy bag in the gym at all hours this week," Dean grinned at her before turning to look at her mom. "And I'll have Allissa call you to talk after she's calmed down from her workout."

Allissa started to protest, but then decided that Dean was probably right about her needing a little distance between her and her mom to be able to get through the week. *And if this goes as badly as I expect it to this week, then I'd better take advantage of staying with Dean for as long as I can before he shatters my heart when he breaks up with me.*

Damn, I'm gonna miss all the little things he sees and takes care of for me that nobody else even notices when we have to go our separate ways.

She quickly confirmed the plan before going up the stairs to her room with Dean. It didn't take long for her to pack the few things she'd removed from her bags since arriving the night before. Dean insisted on carrying the majority of her things to his truck, only letting her carry her purse and the food they picked up in the kitchen.

When they got up to the front desk in the other building of the bed and breakfast, Allissa was glad to see that her mom and her security team hadn't gone to their rooms yet. She needed to check with the bodyguards to make sure they still had everything covered in case any packages arrived at her mom's trailer while they were out of town.

"Since Brady wasn't going to be there to back us up, we pulled one of the guys doing surveillance in L.A. to take his place already," Miller assured her. "And he's staying in Dead End while we're here, so we won't miss any deliveries."

"And now we have all five of the Avingtons as backup this week," Knight added, his lips turning up in the closest thing to a smile she'd seen from the serious bodyguards.

"Five? I've only met four." Allissa was confused, thinking she'd met all of the Avingtons when they were in attendance at the last pay-per-view weekend. "Byron and his three sons."

"Byron has four sons," Knight informed her.

"Yeah, you haven't met Blake," Dean explained. "He's the cousin Bobby knew from his time in the Navy before they found out they're related."

Leah Mae Wright

"Blake is still in the Navy," Miller informed them. "So he's here for their cousin's wedding this week, but he doesn't normally work with us."

"But since he'll be at all the wedding events, he's going to help his three older brothers with watching your back this week," Knight continued.

"There's more than just the wedding that we're going to this week?" Windy inquired, turning away from the desk where she was speaking with Mandi to look at Allissa and the three men she was talking to.

Oh gawd, no! After she instigated the Vegas wedding debacle, Rick will be ready to fire me for sure if I take her along to the bachelor and bachelorette party tonight, and she gets into more mischief anywhere near his new in-laws. Or worse, the wedding shower tomorrow at his father-in-law's church!

"Mom, I'm just Dean's plus-one to this wedding," Allissa protested. "I can't bring a whole group of people to any of the festivities."

"Don't worry about that, dear," Mandi interjected. "The Burlesons have invited the whole town, so your mom and her friends are all welcome to join the parties. I put a list of them in with the information about local restaurants and things to do that I just handed you, Windy."

"Excellent," Windy beamed over at Mandi. "We'll go get our things put in our rooms and look over the list while we're freshening up to figure out what we're doing this evening."

Allissa just stood there dumbfounded at the exchange as Mandi called one of her employees to show Windy Walters and her entourage to their rooms. She then quickly checked Allissa out of the hotel, so she and Dean could go to his house to eat their lunch and have a workout.

"It'll be okay, Darlin'," Dean assured her as they drove to his house.

Allissa wasn't so sure, so she didn't respond. She just kept looking out the window as her worries spun out of control. *Mandi didn't go to either of the bachelorette parties at the last two weddings here, so surely, she wouldn't list that as one of the wedding events to suggest to Mom. Right?*

Of course, she also doesn't know Mom or how much trouble she can cause at a bar, so she might not think listing it as an option for tonight is a big deal.

Fuck! Shit! Damn! Mom's gonna get in on the rounds of shots tonight and probably tell the Burlesons and their friends all about her career as a prostitute! Hell, she'll probably get one look at the men in this town and invite them all out to visit the brothel!

And if she goes to the wedding shower tomorrow, she'll meet the older men in town and have a whole new crop to flirt with mercilessly. Rick is absolutely going to fire me if she hits on his father-in-law!

Allissa got so lost in her thoughts that she didn't remember getting to Dean's house, carrying in her things, or sitting down at the table while Dean microwaved their lunch to reheat it. It wasn't until Dean sat down beside her and put a plate in front of her that she started to come back to her senses, but not by much. She was just going through the motions of eating the roast beef sandwich on her plate, not even bothering to dip it in the au jus that Dean had heated up for them, when he mentioned the one thing that was guaranteed to shock her back into focus.

"So, your mom works in a brothel?"

~~~

Dean wondered if he should have continued to pretend he hadn't heard her mom mention working in a brothel when Allissa's head snapped up for her to glare at him. He hadn't meant to blurt it out and shock her. But since she hadn't responded to anything else he'd said to her since they left the B and B, he figured he'd need to address the reason she was most likely to be embarrassed by her mom being in town as soon as he finished eating, so it wouldn't be an issue at the bachelor and bachelorette party that night. Seeing her response now, though, he was thinking maybe they'd skip the party. *Yeah, we'll be better off if we spend the night alone here with me reassuring her that neither her mom nor her mom's profession will have any effect on our relationship.*

Allissa's eyes went as wide as saucers as she dropped her sandwich back to the plate without taking her next bite. She opened her mouth
~~~

as if to respond, but only closed it again, floundering for words like a fish out of water.

Dean reached over and took her hand, squeezing it lightly to reassure her that he was there for her. "It's okay, Darlin'. None of my friends or family will judge you based on what your mom says or does while she's in town. Hell, if Kay or Brook find out where she works, they'll probably press her for stories to add to their books."

"I doubt Mom's stories will fit in the historical romance series they started this summer," Allissa sputtered, lightly laughing, and shaking her head.

"I don't know," Dean teased her, glad to get her to smile and not look like the worried zombie she'd turned into since her mother's arrival in town. "Didn't you say it was set in the Old West? I'm sure they can work in some brothel stories in the rooms above the saloon in their Old West town."

"Randi said they're based on the history of Heart's Destiny." Allissa rolled her eyes at him. "I doubt the town, whose first community building was a church, also had a brothel over a saloon, even in the eighteen-hundreds."

"How do you know the first community building in town was the church?" Dean hadn't even known that tidbit of information about his hometown, so he couldn't imagine Allissa had heard it from any of his local friends in the two short visits she'd had to town before this week. "I always thought it was the train depot."

At least that's what PopPop told us when James and I were growing up. But he also said it was supposed to be called Hunter Depot, so each of the founding families would have something named after them like Rogers and Walker Roads. But then after the town was named by Jonah Burleson, the depot that hadn't been built by the railroad took on the town name instead.

"Building the church was in the first book in the series," Allissa explained, pulling her hand from his, and finally picking up her sandwich again to go back to eating. "And according to the book, the train depot had been there since the railroad was built and predated the founders of the town moving to the area. So, it wasn't really something the citizens decided was important enough to build."

I guess Kay and Brook didn't talk to PopPop or Lincoln Walker about the history of the town before Jonah Burleson got here while writing that book. Not that it matters. If they get some of the history wrong, then maybe it won't be as obvious to the people who know the area that they're writing about our town.

"Okay, fair enough," Dean conceded, grinning at her. While he was glad to get back to their normal easy conversation, he still needed to deal with the information her mother had let slip, which he had a feeling was the root cause of Allissa's inability to completely trust people. He wanted nothing more than to show her that whatever embarrassment her mother's profession had caused her in the past, she could still trust in his feelings for her to keep that history from being a wall between them. "But since this town was also founded by a bunch of lonely cowboys, I'm sure a bar and brothel were just as important to them as the church was to the married folks."

Allissa glared at him once again, obviously turning over thoughts in her head about his opinion on brothels. Not wanting her to think he'd personally ever been to one, but also not wanting her to think he looked down on anyone who worked in one or had visited one for whatever reason, he quickly raised his hands in surrender.

"No, I haven't ever been in one or paid for sex," he adamantly informed her. "But I don't have any issues with the people who partake or make their living in that manner. I was raised not to judge others or discriminate for any reason. I'm curious about things that I haven't personally experienced or witnessed, but it's not because I'm being judgmental or negative about those different experiences in life. When I'm asking about things like the brothel where your mom works, it's because I want to get to know you better, and how her choices in life influenced you growing up. I promise, no matter what you tell me about anything that you might have felt embarrassed about with others in the past, my feelings for you won't change. I'm still gonna want you in my life."

Dean had to stop himself from telling her he was still going to love her. He knew the emotion was heartfelt and would last for the rest of his life, but he also knew she was still skeptical and not ready to believe it. So, no matter how much he wanted to tell her he loved her, he wouldn't say those three little words until she was receptive of them.

"She actually manages the bar there now," Allissa finally whispered, looking down at her plate as she made the admission. "We don't really talk about what she did before, or when she moved over to working in the bar for me to be able to say for sure when she changed jobs. But even once I was old enough to know the difference in the jobs to be able to tell the kids at school that she just served drinks, they never believed me. From the time I started school, none of the other kids were allowed to play with me because their parents knew where she worked. That's why I never really had friends growing up and the number one reason I was picked on as a kid."

"Damn, Darlin'," Dean cursed, hating that she'd suffered through such torment as a child. "Didn't the other women who worked there have kids you could be friends with?"

"No," Allissa shook her head, still not making eye contact with him. "If they got pregnant, they usually quit working there and moved away. Apparently, my sperm donor was the only man who used their services that didn't care enough to provide for his mistress and child."

Dean had a feeling that there was more to the story than just her biological father not wanting to man up and provide for his child. But having only taken the one psychology class required to get through college, he wasn't knowledgeable enough on the subject to recognize anything to feel prepared for delving deeper into her past. Well, other than recognizing the abandonment and bullying issues her mother's history had caused Allissa, that is. So, all he knew to do to help her deal with her feelings and heal her heart was to love her through it and show her he would never leave her or betray her in any way.

He reached over and took her hand again, needing some form of physical contact to show the emotional connection he felt with her. "I'm sorry, Darlin'. I can't go back in time and fix all that for you. But hopefully, I can show you that none of that stuff matters now, and make our future together much happier for you."

She looked up at him then with tear-filled eyes that had turned a muddy brown with her sadness. "You really mean that, don't you?"

"Absolutely, Darlin'," Dean assured her, as the first tear started to slip from the corner of her eye.

Dean pushed his chair back and pulled her over into his lap, wiping her tears away before they had the chance to streak down her face. Allissa wrapped her arms around his neck, burying her face in his chest as she sobbed for a few minutes. Dean just held her, rubbing her back to soothe her as she let all the emotions out. He hated seeing her cry, but knew she'd feel better once she released all the pent-up pain from her past.

"Thank you," Allissa sniffled when she finally lifted her head and wiped the last of the tears from her face. "I don't understand how I feel safe enough to open up to you and cry on your shoulders all the time, when it took several sessions before I could talk to the therapist I started meeting with about all of this, but I really appreciate you being there to let me."

"Anytime, Darlin'," Dean reassured her, pressing his lips to her temple to give himself a moment to think about how to address the subject of therapy. "But I'm not knowledgeable enough to be able to help you heal the way a therapist can, so maybe we should try a session together. That way, you can lean on me when you need a little support to help you open up to them, and I can get a professional's opinion on how to help you better."

"Um, okay." Allissa nodded in agreement, but she looked skeptical. "But, um, before I schedule my next telehealth appointment, you should probably know that I've been talking to her about, um, sex stuff, specifically my fear of sex being painful, without mentioning Mom's former job."

"Oh." While Dean had known she had a couple of appointments with a therapist over the last month, he was surprised to hear what she'd been talking to the therapist about. His shock only momentarily delayed the fear that he'd done something to hurt her in the time they'd been messing around every evening for the last few weeks. "I haven't done anything to hurt you or cause that fear, have I? 'Cause I never want to hurt you, especially when we're in an intimate moment."

"No, you haven't hurt me in any way, shape, or form." Allissa cradled his jaw in her palms, locking their gazes on one another as she reassured him. "But my mom, in her infinite wisdom of trying to keep me from following in her footsteps," Allissa explained sarcastically, "decided to scare me away from having sex the first time we talked about it when I was ten. She told me every horror story she could think of about how painful sex is for women. That's why I've always avoided men, even after I graduated from high school, and started to meet guys who didn't know about her job to make lewd offers, thinking I was in the same line of work."

Dean involuntarily growled at the thought of the guys in her high school offering to pay her for sex. "If we ever run into any of the jackasses you went to high school with…"

Allissa interrupted his declaration of how he would punish the bullies who had tormented her in school by covering his mouth with her thumbs. "I won't tell you, so I can keep you out of jail."

Dean had to chuckle at how well she knew him to be able to anticipate what he was about to say. While the moment of levity was nice to break up the otherwise uncomfortable topic, Dean wanted to make sure she knew he was serious about making sure he never hurt her.

"Seriously, though, Darlin', I know the first time can be painful for a woman if the guy doesn't know what he's doing. That's why I read up on how to prepare you, so it won't be."

"You read extra articles besides the ones to give us places to visit each day?" Allissa's eyes widened, obviously realizing the additional effort it took for him to read some of the longer articles with his dyslexia. "Just so you could keep from hurting me?"

"Of course," Dean nodded and grinned at her. "In case ya haven't figured it out yet, Darlin', I'll do anything for you."

"Anything, huh?" Allissa arched an eyebrow as if considering his words a challenge to come up with something he wouldn't do for her.

"Yep, anything," Dean confirmed. "Reading a few extra articles to learn how to make sure you enjoy our first time making love is just the tip of the iceberg of what I'll do for you."

"Can you also come up with a way to keep me from being embarrassed by my mom at the bachelor and bachelorette party tonight?"

"Easy-peasy, Darlin'," Dean grinned and wagged his eyebrows suggestively. "We'll skip the party and stay home watchin' each other masturbate while teachin' you how to talk dirty."

"Oh, gawd, that might be just as embarrassing," Allissa groaned, smacking his chest with her palms as she pushed off his lap to go back to her seat.

"No, Darlin', it won't be," Dean assured her, shaking his head. "There is absolutely no reason for you to ever be embarrassed by anything we do together. Although, I don't think you should worry so much about your mom embarrassing you either. Everyone already knows you're not as flirtatious and open about your sexuality as she is, so they aren't going to judge you for anything she does or says. Hell, the people whose opinions actually matter won't even judge her for it, I promise."

"You really think so?" Allissa looked at him skeptically as she picked up her sandwich to finally finish her lunch.

"I know so, Darlin'," Dean reassured her. "Anyone who judges her for doing whatever she had to in order to provide for you growin' up is a jackass whose opinions don't matter. Do I hate that either one of you had to go through such a struggle in life? Hell yeah! But without walking in her shoes, none of us can say we wouldn't do the same things she did to survive. Hell, I'd probably do a lot worse to make sure you're taken care of 'cause I'm pretty sure she hasn't killed anyone, which I'm more than willing to do to protect you."

"I don't want you to kill anyone." Allissa shook her head at him as she took her last bite.

"Yeah, well, I'm not actively looking for someone to take out, but I'm not gonna hold back if your stalker escalates to trying to hurt you," Dean shrugged. "But instead of getting worked up about that right now, how 'bout we plan our Skype session for this afternoon before going to our separate bedrooms?" Dean gave her what he hoped was a comically lustful look to lighten the mood in the room.

"If we have to," Allissa sighed, rolling her eyes at him. "But I'm warning you that this won't be as successful as the other lessons you've given me."

"Why do you say that, Darlin'?" Dean couldn't understand why she seemed so worried about their plans for the evening when she hadn't seemed nervous about the times they actually made out before. It couldn't be about seeing each other naked, as they'd already done that in person. No, she hadn't actually touched him when she walked in on him in the shower, but he'd touched and seen her naked several times. So, he couldn't figure out what was so daunting about doing some of the same things over Skype.

"Because you're going to be disappointed when I can't come," Allissa confided softly, not making eye contact as she spoke.

Fuck! Dean mentally cursed himself for not thinking about how inexperienced she was to predict this issue. *She's not worried about seeing me naked again. She's stressing about touching herself with me watching.*

"Is that because you can't make yourself come, or because you haven't ever tried to?" He wasn't sure which issue might be easiest for him to help her with, but he had to know which it was to have an idea of how to help her. Not that he had any experience with helping a woman come on her own hand in the past, but the articles he'd read about preparing her for sex had given him several tips on ways to make a woman come on his fingers, which he was pretty sure would work just as well with her own fingers doing the job as they had with his.

"I didn't even want to try until recently," Allissa confessed, blowing out a breath before elaborating. "When I turned twenty-one and Mom realized I was still avoiding men and sex, she changed her tune and started telling me all about how great orgasms are. But I didn't believe her until the first one happened with you when we made out on your bed the night we only had the one room."

Fuck! That was her first orgasm ever? I wish I'd have known that then.

"I thought maybe I should try touching myself when I realized the ache I'd been feeling the last few months was arousal. I read a few articles online about how to do it, but when I've tried, I just feel stupid for not knowing what I'm doing."

"Don't feel stupid," Dean admonished her, reaching over to take her hand to comfort her. "Some of those articles can be confusing without diagrams to follow."

"Yeah, well, even with a diagram, I couldn't figure it out while trying to contort to look at it upside down to be able to compare the real thing to the diagram," Allissa chuckled.

"Yeah, I guess that would make it harder to relax and get out of your head to be able to enjoy it," Dean laughed with her. "But luckily, tonight you won't have to worry about that 'cause I'm gonna tell you exactly what to do and where to touch yourself, so you can lay back, relax, and enjoy it."

"Yeah, we should probably do this before that heavy bag workout," Allissa teased him. "Otherwise, if you're wrong about this working for me, then I might have to go for a second one. And I'd rather get all my frustrations out at one time."

"Darlin', if I can't talk you through it over Skype, then I'll come upstairs and give you a hands-on lesson," Dean assured her, hoping he could control himself if he ended up having to stop jacking off to take care of her. *Fuck! I'll just wait until after she's taken care of before I pull out my cock and show her what I do while thinking of her every day.* "Now, go upstairs to the first bedroom where I put your bags, and do whatever you need to do to prepare for our Skype session. When I call you in fifteen minutes, you need to be undressed and relaxing in the middle of the bed."

"Yes, Sir." Allissa playfully saluted him before taking off through the house, shaking her ass at him before running up the stairs.

"Fuck," Dean groaned, palming his cock through his pants as it twitched in anticipation of their next foreplay lesson. "That woman is gonna kill me with anticipation."

<div align="center">~~~</div>

Allissa was nervous as she rushed through stripping off her clothes to get ready for her first experience of Skype sex with Dean. While the short prep time was slightly nerve-wracking for her, it also helped her put the other things weighing on her mind out of her head for a little while. *Only fifteen minutes to get ready? It's a good thing I shaved this morning, instead of trying to get with Randi to find a place to get waxed while we're off this week.*

She laid her clothes on one of the chairs in what she considered a sitting area on the opposite side of the octagonal room from the ensuite bathroom. She then rushed into the bathroom to double-check that her crying jag earlier hadn't destroyed her makeup too horribly.

So glad the girls introduced me to their favorite waterproof mascara! After a quick touch-up of her face to hide the minimal streaks from her earlier tears and reapply the lipstick that had come off while she ate, Allissa ran and jumped in the bed, grabbing her phone from her purse before dropping it off the side of the queen-sized bed.

"Shit! How am I supposed to pose for him? What does he consider *'relaxing in the middle of the bed'* and how am I supposed to make it look sexy on camera?" Allissa tried a couple of different poses,

273

holding her phone up to snap a few selfies to find the most flattering of the options.

"Oh, this is a nightmare," she grumbled, trashing the pics as soon as she looked at them. "Straight on and propped on the pillows makes my boobs look best, but it creates that weird roll in my belly that I don't have in any other position. But on my side makes my boobs look lopsided, and completely flat on my back makes them look way farther apart than normal. Ugh! Why can't we do this with me sitting on his lap like we've done everything else? Maybe I can get comfortable sitting up and still look my best."

You were flat on your back when he ate your pussy, her subconscious reminded her as she sat up to take another selfie.

"Oh, yeah," she replied to the voice in her head as she started to rearrange the pillows on the bed once more. "Guess he didn't really mind the whole wide boob thing."

She didn't have time to finish rearranging the pillows and get laid down because the phone chimed in her hand, alerting her that he was calling her over Skype.

"Shit," she cursed, dropping her phone, and accidentally swiping over the green button to answer the call in her attempt to catch it.

"You okay, Darlin'?" Dean chuckled as she picked up the phone and aimed the camera at her face.

"Yeah, just clumsy," Allissa replied, mortified at how awkward she felt doing this. *Why am I so nervous about him seeing me naked on Skype when he's seen me naked in person so many times already?*

"Relax, Darlin'," Dean instructed her. "No need to be nervous. Just lay down and let me take care of you, okay?"

"Okay," Allissa sighed, turning to adjust the pillows and follow Dean's directions.

"Good girl," Dean crooned through her phone, the words sending tingles through her body. "Before we get started, I want you to take a few deep breaths and clear your mind, kinda like you would in a yoga class."

Allissa arched a skeptical eyebrow at his image on her phone, thinking it sounded silly to prepare for masturbation like she was preparing for yoga.

"Trust me, Darlin'," Dean smirked. "From everything I've read, the secret to the female orgasm is eighty percent in your head, and only twenty percent in the physical acts performed to get there. So, we're gonna start by clearing your mind of any negative thoughts that could be preventing you from achieving it on your own."

Allissa thought about what he was saying and reminisced over the past few weeks. When she really examined the times Dean had easily made her climax, and compared them to the few times she'd fumbled with trying masturbation with no success, she had to admit that his belief had merit.

Any time he kissed her, her mind emptied of all her other thoughts and worries. So when they made out, and she came from whatever they were doing, her mental focus was solely on him and the sensations he was pulling from her body. But when she'd tried to masturbate, she'd still been worried about her stalker, her mom, and all the little things she had to do each day, on top of trying to read an article to figure out if she was touching the right places to make herself come.

Dean gave her a moment to think it all through before prompting her once more to breathe, focus on his voice, and push everything else out of her head. She followed his instructions, inhaling and exhaling on his count until her eyes started drifting closed of their own accord.

"Before you close your eyes, Darlin', I want you to spread your legs and prop your phone up between your thighs, so I can see your pretty, pink pussy."

Allissa wasn't sure how pretty or pink her pussy was before Dean described it that way, but she was pretty sure her whole body was pinker than before from blushing as she tried to follow his request. *Hopefully, he won't be able to tell I'm flushed from head to toe if all he can see is my pussy.*

When the ring on the back of her phone wouldn't stay pushed out enough to act as a kickstand to hold the phone in position, she grabbed one of the extra pillows on the bed and put it between her knees to prop her phone against it.

Guess I didn't have to worry too much about how to pose, after all, Allissa realized as she looked at the phone screen one last time before laying back and closing her eyes.

Dean praised her once more with a reverently whispered, "good girl" before starting to give her instructions on how to touch herself. Allissa was pretty sure her positive reaction to those two words was at odds with the independent woman she strived to be, but she couldn't dissect her thoughts on that at the moment when she was supposed to be clearing her mind of anything but the sound of Dean's voice.

"Start with a gentle exploration of your body, Darlin'. Use one hand on your tits and the other on your cunt."

Allissa cringed at the term she'd always considered too vulgar to use when describing a woman's vagina. She'd hated it since it was one of the three slurs her high school classmates had called her most often, with the other two being whore and slut.

"You don't like that term, do you?" Dean had obviously picked up on her slight flinch, even though he couldn't see her face from the angle of the camera.

"No, I don't." Allissa shook her head even though he couldn't see it.

"Then I'll try to remember not to use it anymore, Darlin'," Dean assured her, allowing her to relax and push the negative thoughts from her mind once again. "And I'll apologize in advance if it accidentally slips out at any point in the future."

"Thank you." As she refocused on his voice and what they were doing, she followed his directions, taking her left hand to her breast and her right hand to her mound.

"That's it, Darlin'. Just run your fingertips lightly over your skin, both on your tits and your pussy. Don't stay in one spot. Really feel every peak and valley to find the most sensitive places you like to be touched. Fuck, Darlin', watchin' you play with your pussy is so fuckin' hot."

Allissa followed his directions, basking in his dirty words of praise for her actions. His commanding tone was reminiscent of the scenes she'd read described in some of the BDSM romance books she'd read recently, giving her lots of ideas for things they might try in the future, if he was serious about not holding her mom's history against her and really meant what he said about them being together for a long-term relationship.

Pushing any wandering thoughts from her mind, Allissa found her folds wet with her arousal, making the swipe of her fingers over them much more pleasurable than it had been when she'd tried masturbating before, when she was as dry as a bone. *I wonder if that's because I'm not trying to focus on reading an article at the same time?*

Or is it all because Dean is the one telling me what to do?

"Now cup your whole twat and tit in the palms of your hands and feel the difference in the sensations. Squeeze just a little to find the amount of pressure you like best. Fucking perfect," Dean growled out the last two words, as she followed his directions without continuing to ponder why she liked submitting to his dominance so much.

Allissa was torn as to whether she liked the new sensations or not. She loved the squeeze on her breast, finding it more pleasurable than a single finger trailing around anywhere but her nipples. But she didn't really get anything out of the same squeeze between her thighs. So she continued to use her whole hand on her breasts, moving to the other side to see if the sensations were even from side to side, while lifting the hand on her pussy to go back to using her fingertips.

"Just use your fingernails now," Dean commanded, his voice sounding deeper than normal, more gravelly. Allissa wished she could see him right then, wanting to see his arousal in his eyes, but the position of the phone made that impossible. "Don't scrape too hard on the inner lips, just lightly on the outer ones to feel the difference in sensation from your fingertips. Oh, fuck, yeah. Right there on your clit, too."

Wait! That's my clit? I thought it was lower than that.

As Dean continued to direct Allissa's movements, she started to think some of his instructions sounded weird, but she tried to follow them, anyway. Again, she liked the feel of her fingernails on her breasts but not on her pussy. So she quickly reverted to doing what felt best, circling the pad of her finger over the area Dean had referred to as her clit. *No wonder I didn't like it before, and just felt like it made me need to pee when I tried it by myself. I hadn't moved up far enough from the opening to find my clit, and was probably stimulating my urethra.*

"Now I want you to pinch lightly," Dean directed. "Not just your nipples and clit, but all over. Pinch each pussy lip separately and vary the amount of pressure, so you can figure out what you like best and where. You can pinch with just your nails on your titties, but just use the pads of your fingers on your pussy."

Again, Allissa thought Dean's directions were strange, but she followed them anyway, unable to come up with any reason to object to his controlling tone. She found she really liked having her nipples pinched, but pinching produced mixed results on her labial lips.

"Fuck, that's so sexy, Darlin'," Dean growled from her phone between her legs. "Now pinch your clit. Not too hard, just enough to feel the right amount of pressure, like when you're grinding on my cock. Fuck, yeah, just like that, Darlin'. And rub your fingers up and down like you're jackin' your clit as if it was a tiny little dick."

Allissa giggled at the imagery of Dean's words, but she stopped as soon as she started doing as he instructed. She instantly got wetter, enjoying this form of stimulation more than she had any of the other things he'd directed her to do to her pussy.

"Fuck, Darlin', I need you to spread your pussy lips for me, so I can see this better. I know you like havin' your tits played with, but you need both hands on your wet pussy now. Use one to hold your outer lips open and the other to keep jackin' that hard little clit."

Allissa reluctantly released her breast and moved her other hand down to spread her labia open for Dean to get a better view. She would have felt self-conscious of her actions, but the way she was rubbing her clit felt too amazing for her to notice anything else at the moment.

"Oh, fuck, yeah, Darlin'," Dean groaned. "Be my good girl and make yourself come while I watch."

"Dean," Allissa moaned his name, feeling the quivers in her core that she'd come to recognize as a sign of her impending release over the last few weeks of foreplay lessons with Dean.

"That's it, Darlin'. Come for me. Now."

Her body responded to his command, convulsing in orgasmic bliss as he barked the last word. She let her hands fall to her sides as the waves crashed over her, too sensitive to be able to handle even the lightest touch.

"Oh, no, Darlin', we're not done yet. I know your clit's probably too sensitive right now, but you can still spread those lips for me to watch while you finger-fuck your pussy. Since your hands are so much smaller than mine, you can start with your first two fingers. Lube them up in all that cream on your soaking wet cu- uh, snatch."

While Allissa wanted to lay there and catch her breath, she pushed herself to follow his directions to show her appreciation for how he'd changed his wording at the last second out of respect for her wishes.

She only had to run her fingers over her folds a couple of times before they were thoroughly coated in her juices and easily slipped inside her.

"Such a good girl," Dean crooned, causing more tingles with his words of praise. "That's it. Pump them in and out. Go a little deeper and feel around your inner walls. Fucking perfect. Now that you're opened up a little, push them in as far as you can. Fuck, Darlin', it's so hot to see your fingers knuckle deep in your pussy, especially how shiny and wet they are with your cum when you pull them out a little."

Allissa continued to finger-fuck herself, enjoying the feel almost as much as she was enjoying hearing Dean's voice deepen with his arousal at watching her.

"When you feel like your clit can handle the pressure again, press your thumb down on it. On the front wall, like right behind your clit, you should be able to find your G-spot. If you move your fingers like you're trying to touch them to your thumb, it might make it easier to find. But you'll know it's the right spot when you find the spot where it feels best when you rub against it. Once you find it, it's like your internal orgasm button. So if you rub it and your clit at the same time, it'll be more intense when you come."

Allissa tried to find the spot Dean was describing, but she wasn't sure her fingers were long enough to reach it the way Dean's fingers could. "I don't think I can reach it," Allissa moaned, crunching up to try to get her fingers deeper.

"Then just imagine it, Darlin'," Dean advised, his breathing sounding choppy, like he was fighting his own release to help her achieve hers. "Pretend it's my fingers in your sweet little pussy. Spread your fingers in a peace sign, so you feel fuller like you do when I'm finger-fucking you. Gotta massage your inner walls to get that tight little slit to open wide, so my big cock will fit in your pussy."

"Oh, Dean," Allissa whimpered his name as her body started to quiver with the first waves of her next orgasm.

"Yeah, Darlin'. I wanna hear you screaming my name when you come with my long, thick dick stretching your tight little twat. My piercings rubbing on your G-spot with every stroke of my cock is gonna make you come so many times you're gonna lose count."

Allissa chanted his name repeatedly as she came hard from imagining the scene he described.

Leah Mae Wright

"Fuck, Darlin', I can't hold off," Dean growled, obviously reaching his climax at the same time Allissa did. "Fuck, Allissa."

She was too lost in her own nirvana to look at her phone to see if he was giving her a show or not, as he cried out her name repeatedly. Once again, her hands fell from her body as she floated on a cloud of bliss and waited for the aftershocks to pass.

"Guess we're gonna hafta have a redo after a little gym time, so you can watch me next time," Dean chuckled, still sounding slightly out of breath.

Allissa gave him a thumbs up, resting her fist on her mound, so he could see it, since she was too wiped out to sit up and grab her phone. "Or maybe after a nap…"

Chapter Fifteen

Allissa was nervous once more as she walked into the Heart's Destiny Community Church with Dean, his family, her mom, her mom's best friend, and the two bodyguards tasked with protecting them. The night before hadn't gone as planned, but she thought missing out on a second Skype session with Dean was worth the time she spent talking to her mom to set her mind at ease that the rest of the week would go smoothly. Unfortunately, the trade-off for her mom not going to the bachelor and bachelorette party wasn't playing out as she'd hoped when they spoke the night before.

After a short nap and the boxing workout Dean had promised her, Allissa had called her mom to talk to her about how she needed to behave while visiting in the wholesome small town surrounded by Dean's family, as well as the new in-laws of Allissa's boss. At one point, they'd devolved into an argument, stemming from Windy believing Allissa was ashamed of her. Allissa had finally thought she'd explained to her mom that she wasn't ashamed of her as a person and was actually appreciative of everything her mother had endured in life to raise her as well as she could, but she didn't want to deal with the possible ramifications to her career that other people's opinions of Windy's former profession could cause.

When she finally opened up to her mom about the bullying she'd endured growing up because of everyone in town knowing where her mother worked, she thought her mom understood that she was only trying to avoid another uncomfortable situation similar to her treatment in school now impacting her career. Windy had specifically said she understood and would be on her best behavior for the rest of the week, opting to skip the bachelor and bachelorette party and planning to blend in with the more conservative women of her age group in town at the other events. But Allissa wasn't so sure her mom was really going to blend in, when she chose to wear a miniskirt to church.

Not only had Windy chosen not to find a more conservative dress to fit in, but when they walked into the church, she also started flirting with every man she met. Allissa couldn't get her mom and Kandi seated in a pew for the services fast enough. *Oh, I hope Pastor Harrison gives a scathing sermon about the sins of the flesh today. Maybe that will help Mom understand why she needs to keep her sexuality hidden behind closed doors.*

It wasn't that Allissa had a problem with her mom having sold her body in the past. She didn't think it was morally wrong as long as her mom had enjoyed the acts when they happened. She didn't even have a problem with people having various fetishes and desires that weren't considered normal behavior as long as they were consensual among their partners. She even enjoyed reading some of the kinkier romance novels Kay had recommended over the last eleven months and was even starting to wonder if she and Dean might explore some of those kinks.

Her problem was with the assholes of the world. The sanctimonious scumbags who judged people for their sexual choices. The mean girls who treated her with disdain because of her mother's choices. The bully boys who thought it was appropriate to proposition her when she was still a young teen because to them, "like mother, like daughter" meant she'd give it up for anyone with the right amount of money. The entitled jackasses who thought they could hurt her mom or other women like her because of their jobs as sex workers.

The sadistic bastards who thought paying for sex meant they could use the women as punching bags were the worst. But as she'd only seen their abusive aftermath secondhand, and had firsthand knowledge of the bullying behaviors of judgmental jerks for most of her life, Allissa's fear of other people's opinions was most prominent in her daily life.

As Pastor Harrison preached about loving their neighbors regardless of their choices in life, Allissa started to wonder if Dean was right when he told her that her mom wouldn't be judged for her former profession by the people who mattered in their lives. She started to really pay attention to what the preacher was saying and realized this wasn't just a sermon about love because of the wedding shower scheduled for after the service.

I guess Mom wasn't the one of us who needed a divine message this morning, Allissa realized as the pastor's sermon sank into her heart. *Asking her to hide who she is and what she's had to do in life isn't being a very loving daughter. And I love my mom, so I need to start showing her that I love all of her, even the parts I wish other people would quit looking down on us for. And that's gonna have to start with an apology for asking her to be anyone but herself this week.*

Since her mom was sitting right beside her, Allissa reached over and took her hand to get her attention. She then leaned over and whispered, "I'm sorry, Mom. I love you and appreciate everything you've ever done to take care of me. I shouldn't have asked you to pretend to be anyone but yourself this week. And I'm never going to try to change you in any way because I love you just the way you are, even if you won't let me take care of you now that I can."

"Oh, Lissie, I love you, too." Windy squeezed her daughter's hand in hers before releasing it to hug her close. "And you don't need to apologize. I know you love me flaws and all, same as I'll always love you."

Allissa returned her mom's embrace, unable to control the tears silently flowing down her face as any residual animosity she felt left her body with them. When they let go of one another to listen to the rest of the sermon, Dean handed her a handkerchief from his pocket to wipe her tears. He then slipped his arm back around Allissa's shoulders and bent down to brush his lips over her temple in a silent show of support. She wasn't sure if he realized just how much his thoughtful gesture meant to her.

As soon as the service was over, Allissa excused herself to go to the ladies' room to freshen up after the tears she'd shed during the service. She didn't want to go to the wedding shower with a streaky face from crying. While she was determined to start showing her mom that she loved her unconditionally, she still didn't want to have to explain the catalyst for her tears to the Hunters or Burlesons in the middle of a wedding shower in their church.

Unfortunately, she underestimated the perceptive natures of the women in Dean's family tree. As she was blending her makeup over the streaks on her face, she was joined in the ladies' room by Dean's mom and two grandmothers.

"You alright, hun?" Mandi rubbed a hand over Allissa's back in a comforting gesture that she'd obviously taught her son over the years.

"Yes, ma'am, I'm fine," Allissa assured Dean's mom.

"I thought I broke you of that ma'am stuff the first time you came to town," Mandi jokingly scolded Allissa. "It's Mandi or Ma. Ma'am makes me feel old and I can't be old when I refuse to grow up until I can do so with my grandkids."

"Sorry, Mandi," Allissa chuckled, smiling as she finished fixing her face. "But as I said, I'm fine. Just a little overly emotional during this time of the month."

"Are you sure?" Dean's Grandma Joan gave her a curious look. "The sermon seemed to resonate with you and your mom a little more than the rest of us."

"Is that because of what your mom had to do to provide when you were little?" Meemaw smiled sympathetically.

How does she know about that? She wasn't even in the room yesterday when Mom mentioned working at a brothel.

Allissa opened her mouth to respond, but she was so flustered by the knowing looks of the women around her that she couldn't put her thoughts in order to say a word. She shut her mouth almost as fast as she'd opened it.

"You know her former profession is nothing to be ashamed of, right?" Mandi spoke softly, her tone even more soothing than her words. "Moms will do anything we have to in order to provide for our kids."

"And sometimes that requires making a few hard choices and breaking a few laws," Joan added to her daughter Mandi's words.

"But with you being from Nevada, I don't think your mom had to break any of the laws my momma did back in the day." Meemaw shook her head and reached over to take Allissa's hand. "Brothels aren't legal in New York where I grew up, so my momma had to sneak around and do her business in motels or bring her gentlemen callers in the back door of the boarding house where we stayed when I was a little girl."

Allissa's eyes went wide as she realized what Dean's grandmother was implying. "Your mom had to…" Allissa let her words trail off, unable to vocalize the words "prostitute herself" while standing in a church.

"Oh, yes. And it was much more scandalous back in the nineteen-forties than it is now. But after my daddy died while off fighting in the war, she still had to find a way to feed us all. We were doin' all right when I first started school and she was able to work in the factory while the men were off at war. But then when the war was over and the men came home to take all the factory jobs, she had to go to work in the world's oldest profession to get by until she married my step-dad."

"Since it is the world's oldest profession, I still don't understand why it was so scandalous, even back then," Joan scoffed. "Just because a bunch of holier-than-thou prudes can't handle the fact that nobody wants to have sex with them, doesn't mean they get to dictate what's socially acceptable for other people to do with their bodies. If a woman enjoys sex and can get paid for doing what she loves, then I say more power to her."

Allissa was stunned speechless by the three matronly women basically advocating for legalized prostitution while standing in the ladies' room of the local church.

"In case you haven't figured it out, Allissa," Mandi giggled lightly as she continued to soothe Allissa with a motherly back rub. "We're a lot more open-minded here than the reputation of our state portrays to the world. And our family history of openness and acceptance about sexual matters is just a drop in the bucket to all the stories you'll hear around town. Back in the fifties, sixties, and seventies, there was actually a nudist colony here. And I'm sure with the hippie movement at the time, there was a lot of *free love* being shared, if you know what I mean."

"We had some fun there back before raising kids took up all our free time," Joan grinned, looking over at Dean's Meemaw. "Didn't we Patty?"

"Oh, yes, and we weren't the only ones in town," Meemaw laughed.

Allissa quickly realized Dean's meemaw's name was Patty when she replied to Joan. When she'd first been introduced to her back in

May, she'd been instructed to call her Meemaw like everyone else in her generation and hadn't been told her given name. And somehow, she hadn't thought to look closely at Dean's family tree tattoo to figure it out.

"So, even though most of the kids in your generation and probably a few of our kids' generation don't know about it, we remember all the people we used to party with there. And we're not afraid to out them to their kids and grandkids if anyone decides to get uppity and not accept you and your mom into our family."

Allissa's jaw dropped at the implication that these women would start a fight with their neighbors to defend her and her mom.

"Don't worry, hun," Mandi reassured her with a head tilt toward her mother-in-law. "They won't have to scandalize the town with stories of their antics back in the swinging sixties. We'll just have Kathy talk to her husband about his next sermon and make sure he puts in John eight-seven. That's the Bible verse that says, 'He who is without sin should cast the first stone'. And then we'll ask about the latest book they're reading in book club."

Allissa arched an eyebrow in confusion, not knowing what books the local book clubs were reading.

"We might be divided up by age group," Mandi giggled with a mischievous glint in her eyes. "So we don't talk about the kinky books we're reading with our kids, but we're all getting our book recommendations from Kay."

Allissa had to cover her mouth as she snorted out a laugh at the implication that the older women of the town were also reading the same raunchy romance novels Kay had recommended to the younger generation.

"Oh, you've read some of the same books Kay recommended to us!" Joan's eyes lit with excitement as she examined Allissa's expression. "Do you have a favorite? I like all the ones by Lexi Blake, but I can't pick a favorite."

"That's because you keep picturing Charlotte's fiancé, Ian, as Ian Taggart from her books," Meemaw Patty chortled.

"Don't we all?" Mandi arched an eyebrow at her mother-in-law and grinned mischievously.

"I can totally see that," Allissa chuckled, recognizing the physical resemblance between the man scheduled to get married the following weekend and the book character. She then turned to smile at Joan. "To answer your question, no, I don't have a favorite book. But Lexi is one of my favorite authors. Though I think Kay and Brook will soon surpass the others for my top author spots."

With the subject changed, they talked about the other authors and books they all liked for a few more minutes before finally heading out to join the rest of the people in attendance to celebrate Charlotte and Ian's upcoming wedding. As they left the restroom, Allissa felt like a weight had been lifted from her shoulders. She resolved to relax and enjoy her time off, planning to show the people she loved how she felt more than she had in the past.

That doesn't just go for Mom. I need to show Dean how much I care about him too, even if I'm still a little scared to admit I'm falling in love with him.

<div style="text-align:center">~~~</div>

Monday, September 2, 2019, Heart's Destiny, Texas

Dean realized the drawback to switching Allissa's foreplay lessons to Skype sessions for the week after not getting the chance to actually make out with her for the past two days. Oh, he'd gotten a few chaste kisses when they were out and about with their family members and friends, and a few deeper kisses when they were home alone for a workout or about to go to bed for the night. But she cut him off before anything else happened, so she could go to her room for their sexy Skype sessions. And on Saturday night, he didn't even get a second Skype session because of going to the bachelor and bachelorette party after Allissa talked to her mom to confirm she wouldn't be going to the bar that night. He'd gotten the privilege of carrying his drunk girlfriend to bed once again, but he was too much of a gentleman to allow more than a chaste kiss goodnight when she was inebriated.

Now that she's seen me jerk off on camera, though, maybe I can convince her to go back to making out and practicing her dirty talk in person instead of on Skype when we get home from the Labor Day picnic today?

As he drove them toward the park downtown where the Labor Day picnic and Maria's birthday party were being held, Dean remembered back to the night before when she insisted she got to watch him before she followed his directions to get herself off. *Fuck, she was adorable in her attempt to take charge and tell me how to jack off.*

She had been so unsure of what she was supposed to direct him to do that she'd pulled up a book on her tablet to find a scene with the woman in charge in the bedroom, trying to get ideas of how to talk dirty to him the way he had her the day before. Unfortunately, she couldn't find a scene where the woman commanded her man to masturbate while she watched. So her attempt to top him turned into her reading some of the sex scenes to him over the phone after they'd both gotten off and cleaned up.

While he hadn't really been into the scenes with the Domme tying up her male sub, he'd thoroughly enjoyed the scenes from the other books in the series that she'd read to him. Allissa had explained that the majority of the series had the male characters in the dominant roles, but the female characters were just as badass as the men. She also told him that the stories were less about the kinky sex scenes and more about the love between the characters that developed while dealing with international spies and stopping criminal activity all around the world.

Dean could see how the books might be interesting enough to entice him to want to read, even with his dyslexia issues making reading frustrating. But if he was being totally honest with himself, he imagined reading the same books Allissa was reading, and comparing notes about the sex scenes, would give him a greater insight into her sexual preferences. He thought it might be a good way to find out if she was interested in exploring some of the dirtier desires he'd only dreamed about in the past.

"What are you thinking about?" Allissa gave him a curious smile from the passenger seat.

"Those books you read last night," Dean confessed, grinning over at her. "I've always avoided reading long books because they've always frustrated me more than the stories interested me. But if they're as hot as what you read to me last night, then maybe I should try again. And if I go with the same books you're reading, we can maybe act out a few of the scenes we both really like."

Allissa blushed as he wagged his eyebrows at her suggestively after parking at the lot beside the park on Angus Avenue. "Are you thinking about reading romance novels because you're running out of ideas for my weekly lessons? 'Cause if that's the case, you can get them as audiobooks to get through them faster, so you'll have a new idea before next Saturday."

"No, Darlin', I've still got plenty of ideas for things I wanna do with you," Dean smirked before jumping out of the truck to rush around and get her door. He wanted to whisper his next thought in her ear, so nobody else would hear him. "But since the characters in those books go a lot farther than we have so far, I'll gladly get the audio versions of any of them you're ready to try out now, if it means I finally get to fill your tight pussy with my cock."

Allissa's jaw dropped and her eyes widened as Dean backed away from her, so she could get out of his truck. She didn't get a chance to respond to his lewd suggestion as her mom and Kandi appeared beside them. Dean knew they had followed him with the two bodyguards, but he hadn't realized they'd parked so close that he wouldn't have a second alone with Allissa.

"Oh, Lissie, this is gonna be so much fun," Windy gushed, grabbing her daughter's hand as Dean moved to get the picnic basket and blankets out of the back of the truck. "It's been so long since we went to a festival like this."

Seeing mother and daughter side by side, Dean realized that it was the first time he'd ever seen Allissa's mom when she wasn't wearing heels and a miniskirt. While Windy's shorts were shorter than Allissa's and her top lower cut, the casual look with more natural makeup emphasized just how much Windy looked like an older, curvier version of Allissa.

Damn, I'm gonna hafta keep up my fitness routine even after I retire from the ring, so I can keep up with how smokin' hot my wife will be when we're old. Hell, not just to keep her attention, but also to be prepared to fight off all the guys who'll try to steal her from me. And I can't do either of those things if I get paunchy like Dad and PopPop.

"Barrett texted to let us know they're set up by the playground with the Burlesons, so we can set up nearby for them to help us watch over

Allissa and Windy," Miller informed him as he grabbed a couple of the blankets from the back of Dean's truck.

Once they were loaded down with everything they needed, they followed the ladies into the park. Dean then looked around and realized that Knight was walking in front of the ladies to lead them where they wanted, while he and Miller guarded them from behind.

Since he had a few minutes to talk to the bodyguard alone, he decided to ask the question that had been bugging him since he first met the security teams. "Why do ya'll just go by your last names when all the Avingtons use their first names?"

"Actually, Miller is my first name," the bodyguard chuckled. "But since my last name is James and Knight's first name is James, it got too confusing to know which one of us anyone was talking to when they just called out James on our coms when we were on missions."

"Yeah, I can see how that could cause issues," Dean chortled, imagining a comedy skit for a wrestling promo against Miller James and James Knight. "It'd be even worse this week with my brother James around, too. But if the two of you ever want to give pro wrestling a try, I can totally see ya'll using a James gang gimmick."

"Yeah, I'll keep that in mind," Miller grinned. "As for the other guys, they use whatever name they were used to using in the military, which is usually their last name or a call sign, unless it's too similar to someone else on the team. Like Linc uses his first name because his last name is Beckett and it's too close to Barrett to use in the field."

Now it all made sense to Dean as to why the security guys had only introduced themselves with one name, instead of a first and last like the Avingtons, so there was no chance of confusion when they were all on-site during the big events with the GWA. He didn't get a chance to clarify that the man Miller referred to as Linc was the Lincoln, who had traveled with the GWA through California leading up to the weekend in Vegas for the *Sin City Showdown*, because they met up with the Burlesons and Avingtons.

Allissa bounded over to him and took the blanket from his arms to spread it out. As soon as it was laid out so they could sit down and start pulling things from the picnic basket, Allissa slid over to whisper in his ear. "You remember the scene I read you last night where the couple was talking about training another couple before they got into their dirty talk?"

Dean nodded in response, not wanting to interrupt whatever she was about to tell him by speaking.

"You remember they referenced another character they called 'Big Tag' who owns the club they went to?"

Again, Dean nodded, wondering why she was referring to a character that wasn't actually a part of the sex scene she'd read to him.

"Well, Big Tag's name is actually Ian Taggart, and he's the main character in one of the earlier books in the series," Allissa whispered before nodding in the direction of Charlotte Burleson and her fiancé, whose name was also Ian. "And I thought you might find it interesting that your grandmothers pointed out to me yesterday that Ian Campbell looks almost exactly like Ian Taggart is described in the books. And in a crazy coincidence, he also marries a woman named Charlotte. But his Charlotte is a redhead." Allissa kissed his cheek before leaning back and grinning mischievously.

"Are you tryin' to keep me from wanting to read this series of books, Darlin'?" Dean couldn't think of another reason why she'd want to put the image in his head of his best friend's sister and her fiancé having sex like in one of the book snippets she'd read to him. While Dean had always considered Charlotte attractive, he hadn't ever had any desire to imagine her in a sexual situation, especially since he'd met Allissa. And he really didn't want to think about Ian naked to picture him in those book scenes.

"No, just thought you'd think the similarities between the couples are interesting." Allissa shook her head before her grin widened and her eyes gleamed with mischief. "And if pointing those similarities out gets you to thinking about the scenes I read last night to motivate you for when we get back home tonight, all the better."

As soon as it registered in his brain that Allissa had just referred to his house as "home," Dean could no longer think about the reasoning behind Allissa mentioning the similarities between the book couple and their friends. All he could think about was how it seemed she was finally starting to take their relationship more seriously.

He might have convinced her to be his girlfriend and publicly acknowledge that they were dating, but he knew she wasn't all in with him just yet. That was why he was taking his time with all the foreplay lessons, instead of pushing to make love to her sooner rather than later.

He knew if she ever decided to stop dating him, he'd end up with a heart so shattered that he'd never recover. So, in addition to trying not to push her for more than she was ready for, he was trying to protect a sliver of his heart by not making love to her until he knew she was all in. He didn't trust the beast that lived inside him to let her walk away once he knew the ultimate pleasure of mating with her.

If she were to break things off with him now, he'd be devastated, but he could still live a semi-normal life. After completely connecting with her — heart, body, and soul — he knew he'd have to be locked in a padded cell in a straitjacket to keep him away from her. So, to protect them both, he was doing everything he could think of to hold off making love to her until he knew she was seriously going to give them a chance at forever together.

Hearing her call his house "home" made him think that day might come sooner than he expected. *Fuck, yes! Maybe that Thanksgiving wedding is possible after all.*

"Oh, I've got plenty of ideas for when we get *home*, Darlin'." Dean could only grin when Allissa gave him a beaming smile in response to his words.

Unfortunately, they couldn't continue their conversation at the moment because the crowd around them infringed on their bubble. Dean focused on setting out their feast for lunch while Allissa joined in on the conversation going on around them. When he pulled out the bananas, Dean cursed under his breath, knowing they were the one fruit Allissa didn't eat. "Fuck, I thought I told them not to put bananas in the basket this time."

"What was that?" Allissa turned to him and arched an eyebrow, obviously hearing him.

"Just me being a grump." Dean shook his head, not wanting to get into a discussion about his failed attempt to cater to her culinary choices. While he knew she'd understand his irritation if he explained it to her, he knew he couldn't do so without bringing attention to her issues with eating in front of others. And he wasn't about to do anything to embarrass her, knowing she had enough of that from her mother the past couple of days.

While he'd gotten her comfortable eating anything in front of him and when they were out in public with strangers, he still hadn't made her comfortable eating anything not considered healthy in front of people they knew, who might actually mention something about what she ate. So, he tried to help her relax when they ate with their friends and coworkers by providing the healthy options she was comfortable with eating in public, and picking the foods she seemed to enjoy the most from those healthy options. It annoyed him that his request to leave out the one fruit he knew she didn't like was ignored, but he didn't want to bring down the mood of the day by explaining that to her right then.

"Are you getting hangry, Dean?" Allissa grinned at him, picking up a sandwich and unwrapping it before holding it out to him. "How about we feed your inner beast, so he can quit growling?"

"Thanks, Darlin'," Dean grinned at her before taking a bite of the sandwich she was still holding.

"Hey, now, no food play in public," JJ Burleson chuckled. "It's not fair to those of us without a partner here to be able to participate."

"I'll partner with you if you wanna play, sugar," Kandi cooed at JJ.

Dean choked on the sandwich he accidentally swallowed before he finished chewing. Allissa quickly moved to wrap the sandwich back up before dropping it beside him and scooting over behind him to pat him on the back, helping to clear his airway.

"I don't want to know what they're implying, do I?" Allissa whispered when Dean's coughing fit died down.

"Probably not right now." Dean cringed at the thought of JJ, who wasn't but three years older than him, and Kandi, whom he estimated to be about twenty years older than him, getting together for food play. Even if the rumors he'd heard about JJ being an active participant in the San Antonio BDSM scene were true, he didn't think he was looking for a Mommy.

To get that image out of his head, Dean imagined how he might incorporate a little food play into his naughty naked time with Allissa. *Fuck, I'd love to lay her out on the island in the kitchen and make a buffet out of her naked body.* "But when we get home, I might give you a little demonstration to see if it's something you'd enjoy when it's just the two of us."

Dean could see the flare of interest in Allissa's eyes as she moved back to sitting beside him to start eating. *Oh yeah, Darlin', we're definitely gonna stop at the store on the way home for some ice cream, chocolate syrup, and whipped cream, so I can make you into my dessert tonight.*

Thankfully, the topic had already changed around them to who was partnering with whom for the three-legged race and cornhole tournament that afternoon, so Dean didn't have to help Allissa deal with another potentially embarrassing topic in public. He picked up the sandwich he'd already taken a bite out of and unwrapped it, enjoying the food and comradery with friends for the afternoon. At least, he was, until Windy pointed out Allissa's eating habits.

"Lissie, honey, why aren't you eating those bananas? I thought they were your favorite fruit."

Favorite fruit? Does she not know her daughter at all? Strawberries are her favorite fruit. With the way she actively avoids bananas, they're obviously her least-liked fruit. Definitely not her favorite.

"Oh, um, no," Allissa sputtered, shaking her head, and looking close to panic. "I, uh, must have outgrown my childhood food preferences. Now I only eat them when they're mixed with something else in a smoothie, so I don't really taste them."

"Oh, well, they're still my favorite," Windy shrugged, not seeming to realize Allissa was uncomfortable with the topic for some reason. "So, if you're not going to eat them, then I'll gladly take them to make sure they don't go to waste."

"Sure, Mom." Allissa awkwardly handed over the bananas, standing and dusting off the back of her shorts. "If you'll excuse me, I need to step over to the ladies' room for a minute."

"I'll walk you over, Darlin'." Dean jumped up and took a couple of brisk strides to catch up with Allissa as she walked away from the group. He dropped his arm over her shoulders and pulled her into his side so nobody else could hear their whispered conversation as they walked through the crowd. "What's wrong, Darlin'?"

"Nothing's wrong," Allissa blatantly lied. "I just need to use the restroom."

"Am I gonna hafta start withholding orgasms to punish you for lying to me, Darlin'?" Dean arched an eyebrow as he looked at her expectantly, waiting for her to answer him honestly.

"You wouldn't dare." Allissa glared at him.

"It's either that or spanking your bare ass," Dean retorted with a smirk before turning more serious. "Or you could just be honest with me and tell me what's wrong. I think by now, you've learned that you can trust me with whatever's bothering you. I might not always be able to fix it immediately, but I'll do whatever I can to make you feel better about whatever's goin' on."

"It's just another of my eating issues," Allissa groaned, closing her eyes, and shaking her head, as if that would help her shake off the issue.

"I'm sorry, Darlin'. I actually asked the staff to leave the bananas out of the picnic basket today because I noticed you don't eat them. I'm sorry they didn't listen and made you uncomfortable just now." Dean might not understand what her aversion to bananas was at the moment, but he didn't want her to feel uneasy because of their presence when he'd tried to prevent it.

"That's what you were grumbling about earlier, isn't it?" Allissa kept walking as they passed the park building that housed the restrooms, so Dean kept pace beside her.

I knew she was lying about needing the bathroom.

"Yeah," Dean admitted with a nod. "I was pissed that they didn't listen to me when I just thought you didn't like them. If I'd have known they were some kind of trigger for you with your other eating issues, I'd have double-checked the basket before I left the kitchen at the B and B, so you wouldn't have even had to see them."

"Thanks, that's really sweet of you. But they're not really a trigger so much as my mom eating them in front of other people is a trigger," Allissa explained. "It was actually the way she taught me to eat bananas that caused the first incident in school with the other kids picking on me about food."

Dean was curious about how Windy ate bananas and how she'd taught Allissa to eat them as a child, wanting to know how the way they were eaten caused a bullying incident. But he didn't want to make Allissa even more uncomfortable, so he waited patiently for her to be ready to elaborate further.

Allissa took a couple of deep breaths and looked around to make sure there wasn't anyone nearby to overhear her before she continued. "Apparently, she practiced her oral skills on them so often when she first started working at the brothel that she can't eat them now without fellating them. And not knowing any better as a toddler, I learned to eat them the same way my mom does. No matter how hard I've tried, I can't seem to break the habit either. So, now, even though I love bananas, I only eat them once they've been cut up and put in other things."

It took all of Dean's willpower to maintain a straight face as she told him the reason behind her aversion to bananas. While he understood how fellating a banana in the cafeteria at school had led to a traumatic event in Allissa's childhood, he couldn't help but think about how fabulous it was going to feel when she finally gave him a blow job after practicing the skill regularly from such a young age.

"Go ahead and laugh," Allissa huffed. "I can tell you want to."

"No, Darlin'," Dean refuted her statement, shaking his head. He wanted to smile at the thought of the blow jobs he'd get sometime in the future, but he had no desire to laugh, not knowing how traumatic the kids bullying her in school had been for Allissa. "I don't want to laugh. I'm sure the kids were merciless and traumatized you, and that's no laughing matter. How old were you when this happened?"

"It was in eighth grade, so like thirteen or fourteen," Allissa shrugged.

"Did you quit eating them altogether that day? Or just quit eating them in public?" Dean wondered if it had been almost a decade since she'd eaten a banana. If so, then it was possible she could relearn how to eat them now without reverting to sucking them.

"I just quit eating them in public," Allissa admitted sheepishly. "That's why Mom was confused today by me not eating them. Because I've never had to hide my freakish way of eating them from her."

"You don't have to hide the way you eat them from me either, Darlin'," Dean assured her. He couldn't stop his lips from turning up slightly then. "But maybe you should hold off on eating them with me around until you're ready for the things watching you eat them will make me want to do with you."

"Oh, my, gawd!" Allissa whisper-shouted and playfully smacked his arm off her shoulders as she turned to look at him incredulously. "You weren't about to laugh at my trauma earlier. You were fighting a smile because you were thinking about getting a blow job!"

"I'm sorry, Darlin'." Dean held his hands up in surrender, hoping she'd accept his apology. "I'm tryin' to be a gentleman the way I was raised to be. But even gentlemen love blow jobs. So, I can't help but think about them when you're talkin' about fellating anything, even an inanimate fruit. But havin' you suck my cock is only one of the things I'm eagerly anticipating doin' with you, Darlin'. So, we don't gotta rush to do it."

"Yeah, well, you'd better be prepared to keep anticipating that for a long-ass time. 'Cause I doubt I'll ever get over all my issues to ever do it." Allissa looked close to tears before she shut her eyes and tilted her head down toward the ground.

"Oh, Darlin'," Dean crooned, feeling like an ass for his lame joke and pulling her into his arms to comfort her. "I didn't mean to upset you even more. I was trying to make you laugh by joking around. But I never want you to do anything with me that you're not just as into as I am. So, I'll happily leave blow jobs in the realm of fantasy for the rest of our lives. And I'll cut up all the bananas from now on, so you can eat them without being triggered."

"Promise?" Allissa whimpered into his chest, her arms going around his waist.

"I promise, Darlin'. I'll formally write it up in an agreement between us if you want," Dean assured her. *Or add it to my part of the vows at our wedding.*

"Deal." Allissa nodded into his chest before pulling back. "But we should probably head back now to see how many of your friends have turned green from watching my mom blow a banana."

Dean just nodded and put his arm around her to turn them back in the direction they'd walked from earlier. *And hopefully, it won't be obvious how many of the guys got hard from witnessing the blow job skills of a pro.*

Chapter Sixteen

After spending a few days with her mom and Kandi hanging out with her, Dean, and Dean's family and friends, Allissa was surprised to realize just how well their families got along. For people who had such drastically different backgrounds, they had a lot more in common than she ever imagined possible. Then again, she still had a hard time fathoming Dean's wealthy family having a former prostitute in the family tree.

Meemaw Patty had spent hours over the past few days talking with Allissa and Windy about her experiences as a child. Allissa had been surprised at how some aspects of life hadn't changed all that much in the last seventy years. While growing up poor didn't always limit determined individuals who were willing to work their way up, single moms with little education still had few choices for how to rise above their circumstances.

Patty's mom had only spent a few years in the world's oldest profession before she married one of her wealthiest clients. But if she hadn't met the man who adopted Patty and her siblings when Patty was a preteen, Dean's great-grandmother would have lived a life of poverty and continued prostitution to provide for her family, much like Allissa's mom had decades later.

In addition to the similarities between Patty's and Allissa's situations as children, they also found that Windy and Mandi had a lot of common interests. It wasn't just their taste in music and reading material that they shared, either. Having managed the bar in the brothel for the last decade, Windy had experience in dealing with the issues Mandi had been having since expanding the bed and breakfast to include a full-service restaurant open to the public. The two women spent almost as much time discussing business and how Mandi could add a winery to the property as they had gushing over how cute a couple their kids were together.

Allissa had to admit, if only to herself, that she was starting to agree with them when it came to the possibility of her relationship with Dean being more long-term than she'd previously thought it could last. She'd been so certain that he would dump her as soon as he learned about her mother's former profession that she hadn't let herself hope their attraction to one another could turn into more.

Now that she knew that neither her past, nor her outrageous mother, had any effect on Dean's affection for her, Allissa was starting to wonder if his jokes about getting married could possibly be based on what he really wanted for them as a couple. Granted, the Thanksgiving wedding he kept teasing her about planning seemed highly unlikely, but that was mostly due to the holiday being only two-and-a-half months away. With each kiss, caress, and toe-curling orgasm they shared, Allissa was starting to think a Thanksgiving 2020 wedding might be possible.

She could definitely see herself being happily married to Dean in the future. She pictured them continuing to wrestle for at least the next decade before she'd be ready to take some time off to have kids. Not that they would wait that long to raise a couple of children. Allissa could easily see them adopting first, knowing she'd be ready to have a family long before she was ready to take time off from the ring. Plus, the more she saw Dean with the kids from Heart's Destiny, who weren't too afraid of the character he portrayed in the GWA to approach him whenever they were out in public, the more she knew he'd make a great dad one day.

She doubted he realized just how attractive it was to see him joining in on the children's games at the Labor Day picnic and Maria's birthday party a few days before. Allissa hadn't been the only woman there who noticed either. She'd heard more than one woman comment on how he made their ovaries tingle when he helped the little girls defeat the boys in their Nerf gun war.

While she'd been jealous when she first realized they were all drooling over her man, she also felt a sense of pride to be the only woman he seemed to notice while they were surrounded by the beautiful residents of his hometown. He'd kissed her more than once at the town picnic, not caring that his family and friends all witnessed their public displays of affection. It almost felt like he was claiming her as his in front of everyone, so there was no doubt in anyone's mind that they were a committed couple.

Now that she was thinking about it while soaking in a bath after going horseback riding earlier in the day, Allissa realized that she was ready to fully commit to him. Yeah, she'd agreed to be his girlfriend and had shared more of herself with him than anyone else. But until this week, she'd still been holding back a piece of her heart because of being afraid of not being good enough for him to want more than a roll in the hay before tossing her away.

Now that he knew her deepest, darkest secrets, and still seemed to care for her just the same as he always had, she finally felt ready to let him have that last piece of her heart that she'd been fighting so hard to hold back. While Allissa still wasn't sure she'd be able to tell him how she felt, she was finally ready to admit to herself that she'd fallen hopelessly in love with Dean Hunter.

Realizing how much she loved him prompted her to face her greatest fears — that he was still just saying what she needed to hear so he could get in her pants, and that he would dump her once they finally had sex. *It's going to hurt like hell if he changes his mind about me once we go all the way. But even with that possibility, I still want my first time to mean something by being with the only man I've ever imagined could be* **The One**.

Deciding that she didn't want to live through another day of worrying about the possible heartbreak of breaking up right after her first time having sex, Allissa finished up her bath, making sure she was fully primped and ready before walking downstairs wearing nothing but a smile.

If he breaks my heart in the morning, so be it. But I'm tired of waiting to know what it feels like to make love with the man I love.

When she didn't find Dean in the great room, kitchen, or dining room, she checked the lower level to see if he'd already gone down to start warming up for the workout they had planned for the afternoon. Since he wasn't in any of the lower-level rooms, she went back up to the main floor to search for him in his master bedroom and attached bath.

Allissa hadn't braved venturing into this sacred space before, so she took a moment to appreciate the rustic red and brown décor of the room. Considering the classic rock music playing through the recessed speakers around the space, Allissa was surprised by the classic country style of the room. Instead of a solid color comforter like she's slept under on the bed upstairs in his guest room, Dean had a patchwork quilt in all shades of red and brown covering a king-sized four-poster bed in his master bedroom.

Wow! I knew these rooms were big, but I didn't realize they were so big that a king-sized bed would fit against one of the eight walls in these octagonal bedrooms. Although, I guess there is a lot of wall space on either side of the queen-sized bed in the room I'm using upstairs and it's about the same size as this room.

"What are you doin' in here, Darlin'?" Dean startled her from her thoughts as he spoke from behind her.

Allissa turned to see he'd come from the master bathroom that she now realized was as big as the bedrooms and in the same octagonal shape, since it was directly under the bedroom she was using. Seeing him standing there with a towel wrapped around his hips, she realized she'd obviously caught him on the tail end of his shower. She was momentarily speechless at the sight of his muscular body on display for her visual perusal.

She let her eyes roam from his bare feet up past the tented towel to his rippling six-pack abs, powerful chest, broad shoulders, and finally stopping when their eyes met. She unconsciously licked her lips as she thought about exploring every inch of him with her hands and mouth, the way he'd done with her several times since they'd started making out nightly.

"Darlin', unless you're ready to jump ahead to the main event in your lovemakin' lessons, you should probably go in the other room while I get dressed." Dean's voice was deep and gravelly, giving her a hint of just how aroused he was without her even needing to see how he tented the towel.

"And what if I'm here because I'm ready for the main event?" Allissa put a hand on her hip as she grinned up at him sassily.

Dean's eyes widened and his nostrils flared at her words. "Are you sure, Darlin'? 'Cause once we take that step, there's no goin' back. Once I know what it's like to be buried deep inside you, I won't ever be able to let you go. So, you've gotta be sure you're ready for forever with me first."

Forever? That certainly doesn't sound like he's gonna break up with me the way I thought. Allissa concentrated on examining Dean's eyes, trying to read the sincerity in his expression. They were that dark navy she'd come to recognize as the color they turned whenever he was focused solely on her. *Holy shit! He really does mean he wants forever with me!*

"Yes, Dean, I'm sure." Allissa's words came out sounding much more confident than she felt. Oh, she was confident she wanted to make love with Dean right then. She just wasn't as confident as he seemed to be that their relationship could last the test of time. *Hopefully, making love with him will show me if forever is possible for us or not.*

"Then get up on the bed, Darlin'," Dean instructed before turning to walk back into the bathroom.

She wasn't sure why he walked away, but she followed his directions and laid down on his bed.

"Fuck!" Dean barked a few seconds later, startling her with his vehement expletive, followed by a slamming door.

Allissa didn't know how to take his explosive outburst, unsure if it had anything to do with her or not. *Surely, he's not pissed at the thought of having sex with me. His erection was obvious under his towel, so I doubt he's mad about actually getting to use it.*

"Darlin', I hate to tell you this, but I'm gonna hafta go to the store before we can do this." Dean's head hung as he leaned against the doorway between the bedroom and bathroom with his hands resting on the top of the doorframe, like he was trying to hold himself back from walking into the bedroom. "The condoms I stashed in my medicine cabinet last year when I was home for the first time after meeting you have expired. So I need to go get some new ones."

Allissa giggled, realizing he was upset because he didn't have a condom and not because he didn't want to have sex with her. *Guess we should have talked about whether we need a condom or not before now.*

"It's not funny, Darlin'," Dean huffed. "I'm tryin' to figure out how I'm gonna walk into the H.E.B. when I'm too hard to put on pants right now."

That made Allissa laugh even more. Dean shook his head at her, but he chuckled along with her.

"I guess we should have discussed things sooner to be able to plan better," she finally choked out when her laughter started to die down. Since she'd been able to switch her pills to the online pharmacy to have them sent to the GWA office and out to her with the other medical supplies that were regularly sent to their athletic trainer, and knew they were all tested regularly for anything that could be passed between them if they accidentally bled in the ring, Allissa was pretty sure they didn't need condoms. "But I'm clean and on the pill, so if you're clean, then we don't necessarily have to have a condom."

Dean's face popped up at her words. "I'm clean. I haven't been with anyone since the week before we met, and I've always worn a condom, so going bare would be a first for me, too."

Allissa liked knowing that her first time would be a first for him, too. So she blocked out any thoughts of the women he'd been with before they met and opened her arms to beckon him to the bed. "Then come make love to me, Dean."

Dean didn't have to be asked twice. He dropped his towel before he stepped out of the doorway, running across the room, and jumping on the bed beside her. He didn't give her a chance to say another word, covering her mouth with his as he moved over the top of her and held a plank position above her, resting the weight of his upper body on his left elbow. His left hand delved into her hair to hold her head where he wanted her, while his right hand started to explore her body.

Allissa wrapped her arms around Dean's neck, returning the kiss with equal fervor. She lifted her hands to pull out the rubber band holding Dean's long hair up into a man bun for his shower. She needed his hair free, so she could run her fingers through it, the same way he ran his through her tresses.

Dean didn't even stop kissing her to shake his hair out like he normally did whenever she'd seen him taking it down in the past. He kneaded her breasts for a few moments before moving his hand down to cup her mound. She knew from some of their earlier intimate talks that he was going to finger her first to make sure she was opened up and wet enough to take his large member.

Allissa smiled through the kiss, knowing Dean was doing everything he could to lessen the chance of her first time being painful for her. *I probably should have told him about figuring out during one of my therapy sessions that the doctor broke my hymen when I was sixteen, so he's probably not going to have to be as gentle as he is to make it good for me.*

That had been an exceptionally enlightening session with the therapist that Randi had referred her to a few weeks back. She had talked to Kelly about her fear of sex being painful, especially the first time if it was with Dean because of his piercings tearing through her barrier. She'd also had to explain to the therapist about the stories her mom had told her, Emerald's theory about her possibly breaking her own hymen during her first month of training to become a wrestler, and the painful gynecological exam when she was a teen.

Kelly had listened patiently through all of that before giving her an impromptu anatomy and physiology lesson to clear up her misconceptions. She'd found out that while Emerald's theory was plausible, it was more likely that the doctor had ruptured her hymen during that first painful exam. Apparently, gynecologists were supposed to use a smaller speculum when they had to do pelvic exams on young women, and didn't normally do them on women under twenty-one without a medical reason.

Allissa had cried through the therapy session, finally starting to open up to Kelly about her mom's job managing the bar in the brothel — conveniently forgetting to mention that it wasn't the first position she'd held in the establishment — and how everyone in her hometown had treated her as if she was sexually promiscuous because of it. She realized then that the doctor had assumed she was already sexually active and used the larger speculum because she hadn't believed Allissa was still a virgin. It was because of that realization that she hadn't told Dean about her therapy session back when it happened, even though Kelly had also informed her of the sexual benefits of his piercings at the same time. She hadn't wanted to tell him about her mom's work history to fully explain her reaction to the session. But now that he knew, she could have probably told him at some point this week.

Allissa tensed up as he pushed his fingers inside her, feeling guilty for not explaining why he probably wouldn't feel her tissue tear when he first pushed his dick inside her. *Oh, gawd, is he going to think I'm lying to him about being a virgin?*

Dean lifted his lips from hers, peering down into her eyes with concern. "Are you okay, Darlin'? We can still stop if you're not as ready as you thought."

"No, please don't stop," Allissa pleaded, hating that her nerves were about to ruin the experience. "I just probably should have told you before now that I think my doctor broke my hymen when I had the exam to start the pill. I don't want you to think I'm lying about it being my first time when you don't feel the barrier as you push inside me the first time."

"Oh, Darlin', I know." Dean smiled down at her. "I knew it was already broken the first time I slipped a finger inside you. I also know that it's not a very strong barrier and can break from roughhousing as a kid without you even realizing it. So not having an intact hymen doesn't mean you aren't a virgin."

"Oh." Allissa was surprised by his understanding. "Then why have you been so focused on massaging me down there to prepare me for sex?"

"Because poppin' your cherry isn't the only way I could hurt you," Dean chuckled. "In case you haven't noticed, I'm kinda a big guy and you are tiny. While I'm sure you'll stretch to accommodate me, it's still gonna be a tight fit and require a little pre-stretching and extra lubrication to keep from hurting you. And since my number one goal is to make sure you enjoy every second of the time we spend makin' love, I'm gonna take extra time getting you off a few times, so your pussy is nice and wet and ready for me to give you my cock."

"Oh," was all Allissa could say before Dean kissed her once more.

True to his word, Dean used his fingers to make her come the first couple of times before kissing his way down her body to use his mouth to pull a couple more orgasms from her body. For someone who claimed he hadn't been into oral sex before he met her, Dean had more than proven to her that he was an oral sex expert.

The way he was so giving with his oral affection made her want to reciprocate, even though she'd previously thought the teasing she'd endured in school would prevent her from ever wanting to give a blow job. If there was a chance she could overcome the trauma of her teen years to enjoy the act of giving oral affection to anyone, it would be with Dean. *Maybe one of these days I'll ask him to help me get over that issue, the same way he's been helping me get over my other eating issues.*

But it won't be tonight. Now I need him to make love to me too bad to waste time trying to suck his cock.

As Dean used his fingers and tongue to work her up to yet another climax, Allissa started to lose patience with how Dean was making her wait to finally feel him inside her. "Please, Dean," she begged, pulling his hair to try to get him to move up her body. "I don't wanna come again until you're inside me. Please, don't make me wait any longer to feel your cock in my pussy."

"Damn, Darlin', I never thought I was into begging," Dean crooned, as he lightly trailed his lips over her abdomen while crawling up her body. "But hearing you beg for my cock might quickly turn into my new favorite fetish."

When Dean paused in his upward movement to spend some time sucking on her breasts, Allissa begged some more. "Dean, please, I need you to fill my tight pussy with your big dick."

Allissa had never felt such desperation in her life. It felt strange to go from being afraid of sex being painful to craving it with an almost manic need, especially since she still wasn't sure what it would feel like when he finally joined their bodies together in that ultimate manner.

"Fuck, I need it too, Darlin'," Dean moaned as he kissed his way up her neck. He rested his body weight on his elbows with both hands in her hair, planking above her as he joined their lips once more.

Allissa tasted her own arousal in his kiss, causing her core to gush with even more of her cream. While she'd previously been embarrassed to even think about the taste of bodily fluids, Dean had shown her that swapping them with him was the best kind of dirty experience. And apparently, her constant daily munching on fruit had the unexpected side effect of making her taste sweeter than she'd thought possible.

She didn't have the chance to wonder if the same would be true for Dean if she ever got brave enough to taste his semen, because he rubbed the head of his cock through her lower lips. All thoughts of potential future acts between them fled her mind as she felt him start to slide inside her.

Dean kissed her the same way he was making love to her, slowly sliding his tongue along hers as he languidly pushed the head of his cock through her slit. She definitely felt like he was stretching her wider than he had with his fingers, but it wasn't a painful sensation as she'd previously feared.

Dean took his time, rocking his hips to push in a little more before pulling back out to let her inner walls relax a second. He repeated the process for what seemed like forever, gradually feeding her a little more each time he pressed inside her. The sensual sensations she felt as he joined their bodies for the first time were overwhelmingly amazing. And in her inexperience, all Allissa could do was lay there and enjoy them as Dean continued to work his way inside her body one tiny millimeter at a time.

He continued to kiss her through the whole process, not giving her the chance to beg for more when his leisurely pace started to feel torturously sedate. Unable to verbalize her desire for him to up the intensity, Allissa wrapped her legs around him, hooking her heels on the backs of his thighs and using her lower body strength to pull him in deeper. She also thrust her hips up, trying to get him to speed up the pace.

When Dean didn't seem to understand her non-verbal cues, Allissa trailed her nails down his back until she reached his ass. She grabbed a handful of each cheek to pull him down as she thrust her hips up once more.

"Fuck, Darlin'," Dean growled, breaking their lip lock as he finally bottomed out inside her. "You're makin' it hard to keep goin' slow and gentle."

"That's because I'm tired of you teasing me with slow and gentle," Allissa moaned, unable to control the rocking of her hips any longer as her hands ran over the muscular planes of his back. "I want you to show me what it really feels like to fuck. Please, Dean, it doesn't hurt. You don't have to keep being gentle. So, please, fuck me like I know you want to."

"On one condition," Dean groaned, obviously fighting to hold still inside her while they talked. "You have to tell me if I get too rough, so I can stop before I hurt you."

"I will, I promise," Allissa assured him, grinding her pussy on his cock to try to motivate him to move. "Just fuck me already."

"Make that two conditions," Dean demanded, grinning down at her with pure love shining in his navy blue gaze.

"Anything," Allissa vowed, willing to agree to whatever he wanted at that point.

"You have to know I'm always makin' love to you, even when it's in the form of a wild, kinky fuck." Allissa nodded in agreement as Dean pulled almost all the way out of her. "Say the words, Allissa. I need to know we're both on the same page every night for the rest of our lives, Darlin'."

"Yes, Dean," Allissa agreed. "Whether it's slow and gentle or a wild, kinky fuck, we're always making love."

At her verbal agreement, Dean slammed his hips forward, shoving his cock in all the way to the hilt at the same time he speared her mouth with his tongue. He seemed to have taken her request to fuck her seriously, speeding up his strokes with both his dick and his tongue as he pounded her into the mattress, even as he maintained a tight rein on his control to keep from hurting her.

Now I know what the girls mean when they talk about "goin' to pound town" with their men.

Allissa matched his rhythm with the rocking of her hips, reveling in the feeling of fullness she had each time he was balls-deep inside her. She closed her eyes and tried to keep up with the passion of his kiss while noticing every sensation she felt while making love for the first time.

She vaguely recognized the ball of his piercing jewelry rubbing over the same spot inside her that he'd directed her to stimulate when he talked her through touching herself. *Holy shit! That feels amazing,* she thought as her whole body started to tingle with her impending orgasm.

Dean broke their kiss and lifted his weight slightly off of her without breaking the tempo of their lovemaking. "Open your eyes, Darlin'," he commanded. "I wanna see everything you're feeling the first time you come on my cock."

Allissa followed his instructions, loving the submissive feelings only his deepest, dominant voice brought out in her. Their gazes locked on one another as her inner walls started to flutter with the first waves of her climax. She wondered if he was seeing as deep into her soul as she felt like she was seeing his through their eye contact.

Neither of them spoke as their bodies started to shudder with the most intense orgasm she'd ever experienced. She opened her mouth to scream his name as her body convulsed in pleasure, but the release was so forceful it stole her breath, making her unable to utter a sound. Dean must have been feeling the same strong grip of his climax as he barely made a grunting noise at the same time she felt his seed shoot from his cock to flood her womb.

Looking into his eyes and seeing the love she felt for him reflected back at her made their connection feel much deeper than just the physical joining of their sexual organs. While she floated in that other realm only Dean could take her to, she realized she wasn't as alone there as she'd previously felt. Dean was floating there with her, still joined in both body and soul. It was almost as if they had spiritually combined into one being, leaving Allissa to wonder if she'd ever feel whole when they weren't intimately bonded.

As the aftershocks slowly subsided, Dean rolled them over so he could relax into the bed without crushing her under his weight. Allissa felt a sense of peace like nothing she'd ever known before as she laid atop his resting form, still intimately connected to him.

She knew they should probably talk about what had just happened between them, and how it would change their relationship going forward. But she couldn't think of what to say as she floated in the afterglow of orgasmic bliss. So instead of talking through their feelings, Allissa drifted off to the most peaceful night of sleep she'd had in all her twenty-three years of life.

~~~

Friday, September 6, 2019, Heart's Destiny, Texas

Dean awoke with Allissa in his arms for the first time, and vowed to wake up every morning the same way for the rest of his life. He wasn't quite sure how they ended up spooning when they fell asleep with her draped over him, but he loved the feel of her firm ass cradling his cock. He still couldn't believe how she'd sleepily rolled back on top of him when he came back to bed after cleaning them both up. Thinking of her mumbling about "missing my comfy bed" as he
~~~

maneuvered her under the covers and then pushing him to his back and rolling on top of him brought a smile to Dean's lips. *Fuck, she's cute, even when she's incoherent.*

After they'd made love the night before, he'd rolled them over, so he didn't crush her under his weight. He'd held her on top of him while he laid on his back as they recovered for several glorious minutes of basking in the afterglow. Apparently, she liked the position as much as he had and somehow determined he was her "comfy bed" in her sleep.

Dean had only meant to lay there while he caught his breath, but he enjoyed the feeling of holding her while still buried inside her so much that he couldn't make himself move until he felt her breathing even out in sleep. Then he rolled her onto the bed, so he could get up and grab a few washcloths to clean up the mess they'd made.

He just thought he'd enjoyed cleaning her up when he got her so worked up while eating her pussy that she was dripping wet afterward. Repeatedly having to wipe between her thighs after watching his cum leak from her pussy where he filled her up was even more enticing. He would have sat there staring at the sexy-as-fuck sight all night if it didn't feel creepy while she was asleep.

Guess I'll have to learn to back off on how many times I make her come, so I don't fuck her into another orgasm coma. But, damn, I love being able to make her come so hard and so many times that she has that out-of-body experience.

Maybe I'll just make sure she's okay with my creepy new fetish of watching my cum leak from her pussy while she sleeps. If she's okay with it, then I won't have to put off completely pleasuring her until after I've seen that glorious sight while she's still awake.

Dean laid there reveling in the feeling of holding Allissa in his arms, not wanting to disturb her sleep with even the slightest movement. He wasn't completely certain that she regularly had issues sleeping, but the night before was the first night since they'd started sharing a suite almost two months ago that he hadn't heard her get up at least once in the middle of the night. So he suspected she had some trouble sleeping, probably due to stress about her stalker.

Since they weren't in the same space for him to know about her nocturnal activities, he didn't count the previous Friday night when she'd stayed at the B and B while he stayed at his house. Even if she had slept through the night that one night when he wasn't close enough to notice it, he still knew she'd been up at least once during fifty-eight of the last sixty nights. So, he laid there as still as possible, not wanting to disturb her when she was finally getting some good rest.

Once she started wiggling in his arms, rubbing her tight ass against his morning wood in the most decadent way, though, he lost the fight with his patience. He couldn't stop himself from rocking his hips to grind his cock against her bare ass, burrowing the shaft between her cheeks.

"I think that entrance is reserved for the advanced Sex Ed class that I'm not ready to take yet," Allissa giggled, rolling over to face him.

"Yeah, anal's a little outside my scope of knowledge, too, Darlin'," Dean chuckled, knowing the closest he'd come to anal was watching it in porn, and the one brief discussion he'd had with Rick and Cage a few months back. "But maybe one day we can work up to learnin' it together."

The look she gave him let him know that any fantasies he had of fucking her ass would have to stay locked in his head as only fantasies for quite a while yet. Not that he cared all that much. *Fuck, as good as her pussy felt last night, why would I ever want to put my dick anywhere else?*

"Yeah, don't hold your breath waiting for that day to come."

"I'm not, Darlin'," Dean chuckled at her incredulous look. "I've got too many other ideas for how I wanna stick my dick in your pussy to ever need to think about puttin' it in anywhere else."

"Oh, really?" Allissa snaked her arms around his neck, as he hugged her closer, pressing his hard-on into her belly.

"Oh yeah, Darlin'," Dean grinned, feeling his precum wetting her soft skin. "I'm thinking we'll start in the shower, so I can clean you up better than I was able to last night while you were asleep, and then get you dirty all over again. After that, we'll go around the house, christening every surface until I fuck you into another orgasm coma. Rest and repeat until we hafta stop long enough to go to the next wedding event."

"An orgasm coma?" Allissa laughed. "Is that why I slept so well last night?"

"Absolutely," Dean grinned at her. "And I'm plannin' to make sure you sleep just as well every night from now on. That is, if you're not too sore this morning for the all-day fuck fest I have planned."

"I'm not sore at all," Allissa assured him, wrapping her leg over his hip to grind her slick pussy along his shaft, coating him in her cream.

"You sure, Darlin'?" Dean needed to know he hadn't hurt her in any way. "I got a little rougher than I intended there toward the end."

"And I loved every second of it," Allissa grinned. "Though I now understand why you insisted on doing all that prep work you did beforehand, and will probably need you to do that every time to be able to handle your size."

"Fuck, yeah, Darlin'," Dean agreed, licking his lips at the thought of eating her pussy for breakfast before fucking her in his shower.

Dean leaned in to kiss her, planning to pick her up and carry her to the bathroom. But Allissa gripped his shoulders and pushed him away, arching her back to keep their mouths apart.

"No, I have to go upstairs and brush my teeth first," Allissa protested, squirming out of his arms.

"I have an extra toothbrush in the bathroom, so you don't have to waste time going upstairs for yours," Dean informed her as he pulled her back into his arms. They playfully wrestled around on the bed for a moment, until he finally pinned her down. "And I don't care about morning breath. Hell, Darlin', I wouldn't even care if you'd just eaten one of those garlic and onion burgers Randi insists we find every time we go to Oklahoma. I still wanna kiss you."

He pressed their lips together then, though he was nice and didn't deepen the kiss. While he didn't mind her morning breath, he didn't want to torture her with his. As quickly as he kissed her, he released her, jumping up to get out of bed.

"Now, come on, Darlin'," Dean grinned as he extended a hand to help her out of bed. "Let's go brush our teeth, so I can kiss you for real before we start tryin' to come up with our own modern version of the *Kama Sutra*."

"Yeah, I think I'll leave the writing to Kay and Brooklyn," Allissa laughed as she took his hand and allowed him to pull her up, even though she didn't need his help. "But I suppose we could try to recreate the shower scene from Kay's first book."

"Yeah, you're gonna hafta describe that scene for me." Dean wagged his eyebrows suggestively, wishing he'd have already gotten the list of recommended books Allissa was planning to compile for him.

As they walked into the bathroom, Allissa gave him a brief overview of the scene she was referring to. "He basically sets her up on a ledge around the top of the shower, so he can eat her pussy without having to squat down or sit on the floor of the shower due to their height difference."

"Yeah, I probably should have opted for ten-foot ceilings instead of eight," Dean groaned, not thinking there was enough room for Allissa to sit on the highest shelf cut into the rock walls in his shower as he tried to picture it while looking through the glass door at the small cut-out in the wall that held his shampoo and conditioner.

"Ya know, come to think of it," Allissa backtracked as she opened the shower door and poked her head in to examine the shower with him. "She had to bend over the top of his head to keep from touching the ceiling in the book, too, so maybe that's not a good scene for us to try to recreate. Especially since you don't have a ledge around the top of your shower. Besides, it wasn't really a sex scene. After she came three times on his tongue, she had to touch herself for the fourth while he fucked her boobs instead of her pussy. While it was really hot in the book, I don't think it matches up with the all-day fuck fest you promised me a few minutes ago."

Dean imagined Allissa on her knees, touching herself while he fucked her tits the way she described the book scene. "Fuck, Darlin', that is a hot fantasy we'll have to try one day soon, but I want your tight pussy too bad to do it now."

"Then you'd better hurry up and find me a toothbrush, Aquaman," Allissa taunted him, practically skipping over to the sink on the other side of the room from the one he used regularly.

"Aquaman, huh?" Dean chuckled and opened the cabinet that held his extra supplies, pulling out an unopened toothbrush and tossing it across the room to her.

"Well, you do kinda look like him, and we're planning on starting this fuck fest in the water," Allissa smirked and shrugged after catching the toothbrush he tossed her.

She opened the package and sauntered over to his side, so she could get some of the toothpaste he was putting on his own toothbrush. Instead of going back to the other sink as he'd expected, she stayed right by his side as they brushed their teeth, rinsing and spitting into the same sink before putting her new toothbrush in the holder beside his.

Fuck, she can leave that right there to always have it available without having to unpack when we're home from touring with the GWA.

As soon as their teeth were brushed, Dean picked Allissa up and sat her on the counter between the sink and the jacuzzi tub built for two that took up one of the eight walls in the octagonal room, so he could kiss her properly. Allissa wrapped her arms around him and returned the passionate kiss.

Needing to be inside her and knowing he had to prepare her to be able to take him, Dean broke their lip lock to trail his lips down her body as he knelt down in front of her. He spread her thighs and dipped his head, spreading her labia with his thumbs, so he could lick the slit of her creamy cunt. He mentally reminded himself not to say that word in her presence as he devoured her pussy. He wished he could retrain his brain to not even think it, so he never offended her by accidentally uttering it in the heat of the moment.

She tasted a little saltier than normal, making Dean wonder if it was because his precum had already leaked onto her that morning, or if it was his cum that hadn't fully evacuated her body from the night before. *Either way, we taste great together. The perfect combination of salty and sweet.*

After lapping up the mix of them from her folds, Dean moved to suck her clit while pushing two fingers into her still-tight opening. He finger-fucked her until she cried out his name as she came, pulling his hair as she pressed his face into her pelvis.

Fuck, yeah, Darlin'. Take what you need. Dean swallowed her release as her body convulsed in pleasure, hoping that one orgasm was enough to prepare her to take his cock. As she came down from her high, he kissed his way back up her body, standing and pulling her legs around his waist when he finally joined their lips once more. *Fuck, I hope she likes our combined taste as much as I do.*

He lined up the blunt head of his dick with her snatch before pushing in slowly. Allissa responded by wrapping her arms around him as she rocked her hips, trying to coax him in deeper.

"You're fucking perfect," Dean growled into her mouth as he picked her up and carried her to the shower, lightly bouncing her on his cock the whole way.

"No, you're perfect," Allissa teased him, hooking her feet together over his ass to use her legs for leverage to try to control their coupling, as he closed the shower door behind them.

"How 'bout we're perfect together," Dean conceded as he held her up with one hand on her ass and her back pressed into the river rock wall, so he could turn on the water and set the temperature. As soon as the water splashing on his back felt warm but not scalding, he moved his hands back to grip her firm ass, so he could control the way her body moved up and down his long, thick length.

He was glad he'd opted to upgrade the shower to solid walls all the way around, so he could have the river rock to make his shower feel almost cave-like. The original design of the home called for glass panels similar to the door on three sides, with only the wall separating the water closet from the rest of the bathroom at the back of the shower being a true wall. But as he started to thrust into Allissa while having her pressed against the wall to the side of the glass shower door, he realized those glass panels wouldn't have been able to handle the pounding the wall was about to endure, even though he wasn't about to give her more than a quarter of the power behind his thrusts that he was capable of unleashing.

Allissa moaned into his mouth as he kissed her once more, mimicking the way he was fucking her with his tongue thrusting into her mouth. He took her soft whimpers of pleasure as her agreement, hoping she would soon be ready to admit that they were destined to have a long and lasting love.

As the water beat down around them from the two oversized rain shower heads in the ceiling, Dean started to up the intensity of their lovemaking, adding both power and speed to each stroke of his cock into the tight sheath of her sex. Allissa rocked her hips in perfect time to his rhythm, digging her nails into his back as she bucked and writhed.

When she broke their kiss to take a breath, Dean dipped his head to suckle her neck. He desperately wanted to mark her, but knew she'd fuss about having to cover it with makeup the same way she had when he'd given her a hickey during one of their first make-out sessions. *But surely, it'll fade by Monday night when she has to worry about sweating off the makeup while wrestling.*

"Oh, yes, Dean, just like that," Allissa panted as her inner walls started to clamp down on his cock.

Guess that's a green light to put a little mark right here, he thought as he sucked hard on her pulse point just as she shouted his name in orgasmic bliss. The feel of her pussy convulsing around his cock was more than he could handle, milking Dean of his own orgasm in less than a second.

"Fuck, Allissa," Dean roared as he filled her with jet after jet of his cum, basking in the paradise he only found while buried deep inside his soulmate.

They took a moment to come down from their mutual high before Dean took a step back from the wall. He lifted Allissa off his still half-hard cock and placed her gently down on the bench built into the side wall of the shower. Then he knelt down to watch as his semen slowly oozed out of her body, holding her thighs open so he could see the whole show.

"What are you doing?" Allissa's nose crinkled as she looked at him in confusion.

"Something I didn't know I liked until last night," Dean admitted with a smile, unable to lift his eyes from the sight between her legs.

"Staring at my pussy to watch it close back up after sex?"

"No, watching my cum drip out of your pussy," Dean confessed. "Apparently, it's a fetish I didn't know I had until I was cleaning you up while you were in your orgasm coma last night."

"How 'bout you fuck me into another orgasm coma before you watch next time," Allissa suggested with a giggle. "That way, I don't have to feel self-conscious while you're being a pervert."

"You'd be okay with that?" Dean looked up at her then, needing to see her expression to gauge her reaction to his new obsession. He hadn't yet figured out why he liked watching it so much, but he didn't want to keep doing it at all if it bothered her. "I felt kinda creepy doing it last night while you were sleeping. But until I figure out why it fascinates me so much, I don't think I'll be able to stop looking if you're not awake to tell me it bothers you."

"It doesn't really bother me." Allissa shook her head before grinning at him. "It makes me think you're a weirdo. But you're my weirdo, so it's cool whether I'm awake or not."

Dean could only grin as his gaze drifted back down to Allissa's pussy and the puddle of his cum filling the grout lines between the river rocks of the bench.

"And who knows, maybe this fuck fest you have planned for today will show us that I have a weirdo fetish, too," Allissa quipped. "So we'll be creepy perverts together."

"I look forward to discoverin' all your perversions, Darlin'," Dean grinned before standing up to actually start trying to clean them both up. He had a long list of ways for them to get dirty again running through his head that he couldn't wait to get started on doing with Allissa.

Chapter Seventeen

Allissa was having a surprisingly good time at Charlotte and Ian's wedding reception. When she got there and found out that Rick had insisted on Liam and Dion joining them at their table with Byron Avington and his wife Blair, she'd worried that something was up with her stalker. When she looked across the room to see her mom and Kandi sitting with Byron and Blair's four sons, along with the two bodyguards they'd been assigned since the whole stalker thing started, she really got worried. But once Dean, James, and Randi started picking on Liam and Dion about needing the head of Avington Security to babysit them, she quickly realized it was Rick's way of preventing another scandal in his company by keeping the GWA wrestlers from being negatively influenced by her mom and Kandi the way they had in Vegas. That eased her fears and allowed her to relax and enjoy the party.

"I don't know why I need a babysitter," Dion grumbled. "I wasn't involved in that whole drunk wedding disaster."

"No, ya just egged us on to take the pics before sneakin' off to your room for the night." Liam shook his head at Dion. "Ya shoulda helped a brother out by draggin' my arse outta da bar wit ya."

Allissa wasn't sure if Liam's Irish was coming out because he was still pissed over the fallout from that drunken night, or if he'd already started imbibing at the reception.

"Hey, look on the bright side," Dean interjected, pointing his fork back and forth between Dion and Liam. "At least the whole not-sure-if-anyone-got-married-while-drunk-in-Vegas situation got you out of being set up by the Matchmakin' Mommas this week."

"Oh, no, that's still been happening," Randi laughed, shaking her head at Dean. "Ya'll just missed it by not coming to the rehearsal dinner last night."

Allissa tried not to blush as she remembered why she and Dean had missed the festivities the night before. They had intended to go, but they fell asleep after their extra special workout, where Dean demonstrated a few unique sexual positions atop various pieces of gym equipment. They'd found out that they were both more flexible than they'd realized and could balance on even the thinnest of weight bars as long as it was locked into a Smith machine.

Hopefully, any unusually shaped bruises we have from that adventure will fade before we have to wrestle on Monday.

"Yeah, last night's probably why Rick put ya'll in time out tonight," James chuckled with his wife.

"Do I even want to know?" Dean looked back and forth between his brother and a shockingly pink Liam.

Wow! He might blush brighter than I do, Allissa thought, wondering what had happened to embarrass the Irishman so much that his face turned neon pink.

"When she saw Dion and Liam being set up with Julie and Jen again, Kandi invited the guys to have their bachelor parties at the brothel next time we're in Vegas," James explained with a shit-eating grin. "And instead of turnin' her down, these numbnuts started askin' questions about how it would work. Without realizing that Rick, Fiona, and their family were sittin' right behind 'em."

Allissa suddenly felt lightheaded, worried about the fallout of her boss finding out about where her mother worked. She knew the news had spread through Dean's family and the Burleson family since they'd all been hanging out together all week. But she hadn't talked to Rick or Fiona since they had been otherwise occupied with Fiona's family while they were in town for the week.

While everyone else who found out had been understanding and accepting of her mom's choices in life, Allissa was afraid the pastor and his wife would still be judgmental of a career they could see as sinful. And if Rick's in-laws influenced his opinions, it could mean a setback to her career with the GWA.

"Oh, Allissa, are you alright?" Randi reached over and put her hand on Allissa's arm in a comforting gesture. "You just went as pale as a ghost."

"Yeah, I'm fine." Allissa patted Randi's hand on her arm before reaching out to pick up her water glass and take a drink. She really wished she hadn't finished off her glass of champagne during all the toasts before they started dinner.

"No, you're worried about Rick being upset about where your mom works," Dean clarified, showing everyone at the table how well he knew her.

"You don't have to worry about that," Randi assured her, patting her arm once more. "He was irritated about having to answer Britney's questions, but not about where your mom works."

"Rick's known about your mom's job since you first started working with the GWA, so I'm sure her history has no impact on how he treats you," Byron interjected.

Allissa looked at Byron in surprise, knowing she'd confided in him on the day they first brought in Avington Security to deal with her stalker, and specifically asked him not to share the details of her mother's life with her boss.

Byron gave her a sympathetic smile. "When I gave him my first report on when a team could be in Nevada, he made sure I knew to send a team that would be comfortable escorting her to work. Apparently, part of your HR paperwork with the GWA included authorization to do a background check. And since your permanent residence is still listed as your mom's place, the firm he used for background checks before he switched to us gave him your mother's information as well as yours."

"Oh, um, okay." Allissa wasn't sure how to react to finding out her boss had known all along, and had still bent over backwards to protect her mom as soon as it appeared she might be in danger from Allissa's stalker.

"How 'bout we go to the ladies' room, so you can splash a little water on your face and get your bearings back," Randi suggested, demonstrating what a supportive friend she was to Allissa.

"Yes, please," Allissa agreed, placing her napkin on the table beside her barely-touched plate as she stood.

Dean reached out and took her hand before she was able to step away from the table. He brushed his lips over the back of it before looking up at her with a smile. "Hurry back, Darlin', so we don't miss a single chance to dance."

Allissa smiled back before Randi dragged her out of the ballroom and into the nearest restroom. "You know you don't have anything to worry about with your job, right?"

"Yeah," Allissa agreed, relaxing a little as that realization finally started to sink in. She walked over to the sink and wet a paper towel to run it over the back of her neck to cool herself down. "Well, I do now, anyway. Mom's job has just had such a negative effect on how people see me for so many years that I'm still leery of new people finding out."

"That's completely understandable," Randi smiled, leaning against the vanity. "But since you don't need to worry about it with anyone here tonight, let's change the subject. Tell me where you and Dean disappeared to the last couple of days."

"We didn't disappear," Allissa argued, grinning at her friend. "We just didn't leave the house."

"You didn't leave the house," Randi huffed with a smirk. "That's all you're gonna tell me about why nobody saw ya'll between horseback riding on Thursday and when ya'll arrived at the church for the wedding a couple hours ago?"

Allissa shrugged, but she was unable to hide her grin at how Dean had leveled up her sexual education during the thirty-six hours when they attempted to rewrite the **Kama Sutra**. Or at least, try out a few positions that needed to be included in the modern version.

Randi's eyes widened as she examined Allissa's expression. "You finally gave him your V-card, didn't you?"

"Let's just say that a lot of firsts have happened in the last couple of days," Allissa beamed, blushing at the memories as she opened up to her bestie.

"And now you finally believe me about how amazing it feels?" Randi grinned.

"Oh yes," Allissa agreed, shocking herself as she elaborated. "Especially when his piercings rub across certain spots inside."

"Piercings?" Randi's jaw dropped open as she floundered for words for a moment. "James isn't pierced, but if they're that good for you, I might need to talk him into copying his twin."

"Oh, gawd, girl, I was terrified of them when I first saw them," Allissa admitted with a brief facepalm as she confided in her friend. "But then when I was talking to Kelly about all my fears surrounding sex, I told her about seeing them when I walked in on him in the shower. She assured me that they wouldn't scrape or tear anything in me like I thought and told me how guys only get them where they'll feel good during sex, so I was less nervous about them. Then he was so gentle the first time that I was able to pinpoint where they were rubbing. And once he finally upped the intensity, they definitely enhanced the experience. I literally passed out in what Dean called an 'orgasm coma' and slept for like ten straight hours."

"Holy shit!" Randi slapped a hand over her mouth as the door opened and a guest Allissa hadn't met entered the restroom. Once the lady stepped into a stall, Randi pulled Allissa from the room, whispering once they were relatively alone in the hall. "I'm definitely gonna hafta ask James about getting pierced, so I can have an orgasm coma."

Allissa dropped her wet paper towel in the first trashcan she saw, and they giggled like schoolgirls as they walked back to the ballroom. The emcee announced that it was time for the single ladies to step onto the dance floor for the bouquet toss just as they got back to their table. Allissa sat back down in her seat between Dean and Randi.

"Aren't you going to try to catch the bouquet?" Blair Avington looked at Allissa in confusion.

"No, not this time," Allissa smiled at the older woman.

"We had our turn catching the bouquet and garter at our boss's wedding a couple of months ago," Dean explained with a grin. "So, we're gonna give the rest of the single people in town the opportunity to have their turn."

"You're gonna let them be the next targets of the Matchmaking Mommas, you mean," James quipped, nodding at the newlyweds, who were stopped by Charlotte's mom as they were on their way out to the dance floor for the bouquet and garter toss. "The only reason we were able to avoid being instructed to toss them to ya'll at our wedding was because we set up the plan with Justin for his proposal to Amy before Ma could get to us."

"Wait, are you telling us the women of Heart's Destiny rig the bouquet and garter tosses at all the weddings in town?" Blair looked surprised. "And why haven't they brought me into the fold to match up my boys?"

"Oh, yeah," Randi corroborated James's story. "Kay and Anthony started it by tossing them to James and I. Then when Bobby and Brook got married, Hazel pushed them to toss theirs to Charlotte and Ian. And when Justin asked to rig ours, we looked good to all the Matchmaking Mommas because we planned it before they had to ask. And now that all ya'll are part of the Burleson family, I'm sure Hazel and Susan will be trying to fix up your sons just as soon as they get all their kids matched up."

"I wonder who influenced Rick and Fiona?" Allissa mused aloud as she turned in her seat to watch the bouquet toss.

"Obviously, Meemaw got to Fiona," Dean chuckled as they watched Charlotte turn her back to the young women on the dance floor.

"Just because I'm married and a momma now, doesn't mean I have to join the Matchmaking Mommas," Charlotte announced. "So, I'm going to make sure nobody can accuse me of targeting them by looking at my hubby instead of where I'm tossing the bouquet."

Charlotte pushed up on her tiptoes and pecked her lips on Ian's. Then, without warning, she took a step back from him, so she wouldn't hit him as she tossed the bouquet backwards over her head.

"Oh, isn't it fitting that Charlotte tossed the bouquet to her new sister-in-law?" Blair gushed. "Maybe Hazel has suggested one of our boys for her, so the Campbells can both marry into the family but not have a brother and sister marry another brother and sister."

"Yeah, I wouldn't bet on that," Dion chuckled. "They've been on me to bring my brother to town since I met them back in November, and I'm sure they'd have no objections to marrying us off to a pair of sisters."

"Dion's right on that one," Randi giggled as the ladies left the dance floor and the emcee asked the single gentlemen to join them for the garter toss. Dion and Liam stood to join the group as Randi continued. "Kay had to tell Hazel that James and I were already seeing each other when she first asked about me for one of Anthony's brothers."

"I suppose you want me to toss the garter the same way. Huh, Princess?" Ian arched an eyebrow at Charlotte, who nodded her head in agreement.

"Yeah, I've got a better idea." Ian grinned at her before turning and calling his son over to help him. The little boy ran over from the table where he was sitting with his new cousins, as Charlotte sat down in the chair that one of the staff carried out onto the dance floor. "Want to help me toss the garter?"

"Yeah!" Allissa couldn't stop her smile at how the child bounced with excitement, then slid across the dance floor in the slick-soled shoes he wore with his tuxedo to match his father.

"Okay, yeah, you do have a better idea." Charlotte grinned, as Ian went down on one knee in front of her and lifted the hem of her wedding gown up to just above her knees, so he could see to remove the garter.

"Oh, I like the way Ian does this," someone shouted from the group of guys gathering on the dance floor. "It's way better with a little leg showing."

"Hey, those are my sister's legs," Josh Burleson barked toward where the rowdiest of the group were congregated on the dance floor. "And you'd better not be looking at them."

"Dude, it's not a big deal." Allissa recognized the man who held up his hands in surrender toward Josh as one of the Walkers that she'd seen at several of the events she'd attended in town, but she couldn't remember which of them he was since there were several. "All the girls show off more leg than that every summer in their short shorts."

"Doesn't matter if a girl is wearing short shorts that show off her legs or not," Jake Burleson interjected, defending his sisters' rights to dress however they wanted without being ogled. "You don't get to look unless a lady asks you to, so avert your eyes."

"How about you hurry this up, hubby?" Charlotte suggested. "So we don't have a riot on our hands before you can toss the garter."

"As you wish, wifey." Ian winked at Charlotte as he removed the azure blue garter from just above her knee and lowered her dress back to the floor. He gave her a quick peck as he stood back up. Then turned and picked his son up, handing him the garter.

"How am I supposed to throw it and who am I throwing it to?"

"Shoot it like a rubber band," Ian suggested.

"No, you throw it like a baseball," Charlotte protested, jumping up out of the chair and stopping the boy from looping it around his finger. "I can't believe you taught him to shoot people with rubber bands." Charlotte shook her head and glared at Ian. "That's going to get him in trouble in school next year."

Allissa couldn't help but grin as she imagined having a similar discussion with Dean and their sons one day.

"No, Mom, we only shoot rubber bands at Aunt Cait when she doesn't put them back in the bathroom," the little boy announced.

"That'll still get you on Santa's naughty list," Charlotte warned her new son. "You should pick them up and put them away for her instead."

"Okay," the little boy shrugged, not seeming to care for the life lesson. Allissa giggled at the adorable child. "Who am I throwing the garter to?"

"Uncle Josh," Ian suggested, grinning at Charlotte.

"Just close your eyes and throw it," Charlotte countered. "That way, it'll be a surprise to see who catches it."

Ian turned his back to the group of guys gathered to catch the garter, apparently not realizing his position put his son facing the crowd of guys. The little cutie closed his eyes for a moment before opening them again and looking around.

"Oh, Brody's been listening to his Memmaw Hazel," Randi chuckled, as they watched the little boy search for the person he wanted to throw the garter toward. "He's absolutely aiming for whoever she wants to match Cait up with."

Finally, Brody seemed to make his decision and tossed the garter toward the crowd. Allissa couldn't see who caught it with so many tall men standing between her and the lucky man who would soon be posing for pictures with Cait Campbell.

"Who caught it?" Blair questioned.

"I don't know," Allissa replied at the same time Randi answered with "I can't see them to tell."

It only took a moment for the dance floor to start to clear for them to see a little boy holding the garter.

"Do you know that kid?" Dion looked at James and Dean before nodding toward the little boy holding the garter.

"No," Dean and James replied in unison, shaking their heads.

"Oh, aren't you a cutie," the photographer Allissa remembered as Philippe from him taking all the pictures at Randi and James's wedding, gushed as he approached the child who'd caught the garter. "Come on up here for the pictures and bring your dad to be in it with you."

"I'm, uh, here to meet my dad." The little boy, who looked to be about eight or nine years old, tentatively stepped forward, looking around like he wasn't sure where his parents were in the room.

"What's your name?" Ian knelt down, placing Brody on the floor beside him as he spoke to the little boy.

"His name's Josh," Brody answered for the kid. "We were playing before, while ya'll were taking pictures. You said to throw the garter to Josh, so I threw it to him."

"Isn't that adorable," Blair crooned, bringing a hand up to cover her heart.

"I said to throw it to Uncle Josh," Ian explained. "I didn't know you knew anyone else named Josh."

"Is your uncle's name Josh Burleson?" The kid's eyes widened as he looked at Brody expectantly.

"Yeah," Brody nodded, turning to point at Charlotte's brother, Josh. "He's right over there."

"Oh my goodness! He looks just like our Josh when he was a little boy." Hazel squealed and covered her mouth with her hand as the little boy turned and walked up to Josh Burleson.

"Holy shit, he does!" Dean whisper-shouted beside Allissa.

"I'm Joshua Jacob Jones." The child extended his hand to Josh Burleson as he introduced himself. "And I think you're my dad."

"Whoa!" James and Dean exclaimed in unison, but they weren't the only people in the room who gasped in surprise.

"It's nice to meet you, Joshua." Josh took Joshua's hand and shook it as he knelt down to eye level with the little boy. "Is your mom here, so we can all go somewhere to talk and get to know one another?"

Allissa saw the little boy shake his head before the Burlesons ushered them off the dance floor to go talk privately.

"Damn, I thought for sure if anyone I know might have a kid they didn't know about show up like that, it'd be one of the GWA guys," James hypothesized, looking shell-shocked.

"For real," Liam agreed, nodding somberly. "I'd expect a long-lost kid from Surfer Josh long before G.I. Josh."

"Don't let him hear you call him that," Byron chuckled, nodding at Liam. "G.I.'s are Army, and Josh is a Navy SEAL. And I don't think you want him to show you the difference."

"I meant no disrespect, sir." Liam held his hands up in surrender to Byron.

"I know, that's why I warned you," Byron grinned at Liam before his expression turned more serious. "Now, if you'll excuse us, I think we might need to go help track down that little boy's mother." Byron stood and extended his hand to his wife, who left the table with him.

Hating seeing how the mood at their table seemed to plummet and wanting Dean to relax back into his normal jovial self, Allissa decided to add her own joking comments to James and Liam's. "Quit looking so down, guys. And look at the bright side of Joshua showing up."

"I don't think they can see a bright side when they're too worried about how many ring rats might show up with their illegitimate kids," Randi chortled.

"Oh, but there is a bright side," Allissa asserted, not wanting to think about the possibility of a ring rat showing up with Dean's child someday. "At least now, I don't have to worry about my mom and Kandi being the most memorable wedding crashers this week."

"Very true, Darlin'," Dean chuckled, taking her hand, and giving it a squeeze. "Not only that, but if Joshua turns out to be Josh's son, Hazel won't have to do any matchmaking to get another grandkid. And we all know grandkids are the ultimate goals of all the Matchmakin' Mommas' schemes."

"Then your momma messed up by matching you with me," Allissa quipped. "Unless you're willing to adopt before I'm ready to take time off from the ring to have babies the old-fashioned way, 'cause it's gonna be at least a decade before that happens."

"Ditto," Randi grinned, raising her hand for a high-five with Allissa.

Leah Mae Wright

They all laughed, just as most of the Burleson family returned to the reception. Ian and Charlotte cut the cake before opening up the dance floor to continue the festivities.

Once they were on the dance floor where they could have a conversation with the relative semblance of privacy, Dean revisited the topic of children. "Just so you know, I'll be happy to have kids however you want to build a family with me, Darlin'," Dean vowed, smiling at Allissa as he spun her around the dance floor. "But even if all our children are adopted, I'm gonna enjoy practicin' baby makin' with you every night for the rest of our lives."

Allissa was speechless at his declaration, but she returned his smile. *Maybe I really can trust him with my heart for the rest of forever, like he's suggested.*

~~~

Sunday, September 8, 2019, Heart's Destiny, Texas

Sunday after church, while the ladies were either in the restroom freshening up or setting up the potluck dinner, Dean stepped off to the side of the room to talk to his boss, Rick Robertson, and the man in charge of the security company taking care of Allissa's stalker issues, Byron Avington. He wanted to get an update on the stalker situation, since Windy Walters hadn't been in Dead End, Nevada, to receive any packages from Allissa's stalker for over a week to be able to fill them in on what might have been sent.

"Hey, ya'll, I just wanted to see if there are any updates on Allissa's case."

"I think Windy not being home has thrown him off his game this week," Byron informed them.

"How so?" Dean arched an eyebrow inquisitively at the older man.

"He hasn't sent anything since ya'll left Amarillo for your Labor Day break," Byron explained. "Normally, there are at least five deliveries in Dead End when you're off for a holiday. Maddox hasn't seen anyone lurking around the house either, so we're not sure how the perp knows Windy isn't there to receive the packages for her daughter."
~~~

"Maybe it's someone who knows them? Or at least knows someone in their community who might know neither of them are in town?" Dean wondered aloud.

"Possibly," Byron nodded. "I've got Maddox looking closer at everyone going in and out of Windy's place of employment, as well as anyone either Windy or Kandi regularly interact with, who might have been informed they were going out of town this week."

"Do you think it would be safer for Windy to stay out of town for a while?" Dean knew from the short time he'd spent with Allissa's mom that Windy Walters would be hard to convince to stay away from her home and work for very long, but he had an idea that he thought might work to keep her in Heart's Destiny for a little while if Byron thought it would help him with breaking the case.

"Possibly," Byron shrugged. "It's not outside the realm of possibility that the stalker will want to punish Allissa for being inaccessible this week by targeting her mom when she returns home. But it's also possible that losing that link to Allissa during the GWA's holiday breaks could trigger him to be more aggressive in his pursuit of her, once you go back on tour and he knows where to find her again."

"Fuck," Dean cursed under his breath. He didn't like the thought of the stalker getting more aggressive.

"Relax, Dean." Rick put a hand on Dean's shoulder, trying to calm him down. "I was just asking Byron to send a team out with us tomorrow, just in case Windy being gone this week already triggered him."

"Okay." Dean took a deep breath, trying to calm the rage inside him at not being able to do anything to help catch the jackass obsessed with his girl. "Just FYI, Allissa and I will be going to a single room instead of a two-bedroom suite from now on, and I want that team to be in the room right next door to us, if possible. Hell, split them up and put one on either side of us if possible, so I know I have backup close by, in case this bastard tries anything. And tell me what I need to do to get a concealed carry permit that's good everywhere and not just in Texas, so I can be armed to protect her."

"Yeah, you don't have time to get all those permits," Byron chuckled. "But my guys all have them."

"What about when we go to Canada in a couple of weeks?" Rick questioned Byron, thinking of a situation Dean hadn't even considered.

"International gun laws are a little trickier," Byron sighed. "But everyone who works with Avington Security is well trained in other ways to protect our clients if they have issues getting their weapons through customs. Besides, since he didn't send anything when ya'll were in Calgary a couple of weeks ago, I don't think this perp is going to pull anything outside the US. He might be willing to hire couriers all over the country, but if he doesn't want to pay international postage, I doubt he'll want to deal with bribing government officials to smuggle anything through customs. So, even if he does escalate to finally show his face at one of your Canadian stops, he won't have a gun on him."

"Okay, I'm gonna keep trusting your guys to keep her safe," Dean decided, knowing it would be a struggle for him to keep standing by and not doing anything proactive to catch Allissa's stalker. "But I'm also gonna see what I can do to convince Windy to stay in Heart's Destiny for a few months. Maybe if neither one of them go back to Nevada for a while, it will throw him off his game even more and he'll make a mistake that will help you catch him."

"How are you going to convince the woman who lives to be the life of the party in Vegas to stay in Heart's Destiny?" Rick raised a curious eyebrow in Dean's direction. "You know she's bored out of her mind in this sleepy little town, right?"

"Yeah," Dean smirked at his boss. "But maybe she won't be so bored if she's planning our wedding while helping Ma start a winery at the B and B."

"You're not afraid she'll run an illegal brothel out of the bed and breakfast?" Rick quipped with a mischievous grin.

"Naw," Dean shook his head and smiled, deciding to see if he could shock his boss with a little of the family history he'd learned since Windy came to town. "Ma's doing too good a job marketing the place as a wedding and event center to let that happen. Besides, if she gets into any mischief, it'll most likely be convincing my grandparents to find some land nearby to open another nudist resort like they had back in the sixties."

"Wait, what?" Rick's jaw dropped open in surprise as Byron chuckled, obviously having heard some of the stories that had come to light in the last week. "Your grandparents used to have a nudist resort here in town?"

"Oh, yeah, and it was apparently pretty popular with the current octogenarians in town during the swingin' sixties," Dean confirmed with a grin, chuckling at Rick's stunned silence. "I've learned a lot about my family history this week with Meemaw and Grandma Joan trying to make sure Allissa, Windy, and Kandi feel welcomed. I also had a great-grandmother who provided for her children after losing her husband in World War II by being a prostitute. But she only had to do that for a few years before she married her wealthiest client. Oh, and the Hunter ancestor who moved here and built the Heritage House, apparently did that as an act of rebellion after his wealthy family back east disowned him for marrying a Native American woman. He also took her last name, so their name would die off along with their bigotry. That really made me proud to be a Hunter, even though the name was adopted by my Native American ancestors who tried to assimilate into a colony of English settlers before the Revolutionary War."

"Damn, I guess my family's not the only people around here who've really delved into the whole ancestry thing lately," Byron chuckled, just as Allissa walked up to them.

"Oh, no, the Burlesons just kicked off the ancestry fascination in town this year," Dean laughed.

"Not just in town," Rick corrected with a shake of his head. "They even got my parents to look into our ancestors and start spreading the bug to their friends in New York."

"And because Dean's family all did the DNA tests, and told my mom about how the Burlesons discovered relatives they knew and almost matched up with their kids, she wants us to send in our DNA, too," Allissa groaned, obviously not interested in spitting in a tube to satisfy her mother's curiosity.

"I take it you don't want to know about your ancestry?" Byron tilted his head curiously as he examined Allissa's reaction to his question.

"Let's see," Allissa started, tapping her finger on her chin as if she was thinking about whether or not she wanted to do a DNA ancestry test. "My mom's family disowned her because she dated a boy they didn't like. And I don't know who my biological father is because he was one of my mom's customers after she dumped the loser her parents hated. Nope, doesn't sound like there's anyone in my family tree that I want to know about."

"And I don't want her to take the test, so there's no chance we'll find out we're related and give her a reason to dump me," Dean joked as he laid his arm over her shoulders and pulled her into his side.

"I'd tell you the chances are slim that you'd be so closely related that you couldn't still be together, since we're not so closely related to the Burlesons that our kids couldn't legally marry one another," Byron hesitated as he looked back and forth between Dean and Allissa. "But after what you just told us about your family history, and how ya'll have the same color eyes, I'd be afraid Allissa's biological father could be the product of some of that sixties free love in your grandparents' pasts. So, ya'll might want to rethink checking to see if you're related if you plan on having kids together."

"We'll just adopt," Dean and Allissa declared in unison before breaking out in laughter at how they'd both had the same thought at the same time.

"Yeah, I'm going to go see if the food's ready." Rick raised his hands in surrender as he backed away from the conversation that had suddenly turned oddly uncomfortable.

"That sounds like a good idea," Byron agreed, walking away with Rick.

Once they were relatively alone, even though they were still standing at the edge of a room full of people, Allissa looked up at him with an obvious question in her eyes. "What is it, Darlin'?"

"Do you think I should do the test just to make sure we're not related?" Allissa bit her bottom lip nervously. "I know you said it could be submitted without putting any identifying information on the website, so I wouldn't have to worry about my bio-dad finding out my identity and suddenly wanting to be a part of my life now that I'm a semi-celebrity. But if we know each other's usernames on the site, then we could verify we're not in any kind of incestuous relationship."

After making love to her so many times over the past few days, Dean didn't want to take a chance on losing her if they were related and didn't know it. But he also didn't want her to worry about any possible repercussions for their children by not knowing if they shared any DNA.

Considering how many times he'd already come inside her, and knowing that no means of birth control was guaranteed to be one-hundred percent effective, Dean knew it was only a matter of time before he got her pregnant. Even though he was serious about wanting to adopt if that's how she chose to grow their family, he knew the chances were slim that they wouldn't have at least one biological child in the mix of however many she was willing to raise with him.

"I think it has to be your choice, Darlin'," Dean finally stated. "But I also think there's very little risk of adverse effects on our lives from taking a DNA test to set our minds at ease about potential health risks for our kids in the future. But either way you choose, I'll support your decision one-hundred percent."

Allissa sighed and stepped in to hug him. Dean brushed his lips over the top of her head as he held her for a moment, letting her think things through the way she seemed to think best while he enjoyed being the rock she clung to for support.

"Then I guess I'll take the test Mom gave me the other day," Allissa stated decisively as she pulled out of his arms and smiled up at him. "I just won't let her convince me to do a family tree when she sees me show up as her fifty-percent match on the site."

"We could always list you as male and with a username she won't recognize as you," Dean teasingly suggested with a grin. "Let her spend some time trying to figure out if you were switched at birth or have a fraternal twin that was stolen for a little bit before revealing the truth."

"Oh, my, gawd, Dean!" Allissa squealed, slapping a hand over her mouth before lowering it and whisper-shouting, "Your practical jokes are mean. And if you ever play a joke on me that cruel, you can consider this relationship over."

"Don't worry, Darlin', I'd never do something like that to you," Dean assured her. "But I might send in another sample with fake info to make my brother think we have a long-lost identical triplet."

"I can't even..." Allissa trailed off as she rolled her eyes and held her hand up with the palm facing him. She didn't finish her thought before she turned to walk over to where the line was forming for lunch, leaving him standing there chuckling.

Dean took advantage of their brief separation to wave Windy over to talk for a moment. It didn't take long for him to convince his future mother-in-law to stay in Heart's Destiny for the next three months to plan a Thanksgiving wedding.

If only it was that easy to convince Allissa to actually marry me.

Chapter Eighteen

Allissa couldn't believe she'd been so distracted by Dean's joking around the day before that she'd walked away from him long enough for him to convince her mom to stay in Heart's Destiny for the next three months. And possibly longer, if she stayed to manage the winery that they were now discussing adding to the bed and breakfast and convinced her best friend to move with her. Her mom had been inundating her with texts about wedding plans all day, as if Dean had actually proposed. Allissa was furious that his continued joke of teasing her about a Thanksgiving wedding was being taken so seriously by their families. And no amount of arguing with her mom that she wasn't planning a wedding until she actually had an engagement ring on her finger was stopping the crazy train Windy, Kandi, and Mandi were on, making plans for the next wedding in Heart's Destiny, Texas.

When Allissa had mentioned the texts to Dean, he'd shrugged it off at first, continuing to tease her with planning their wedding without actually proposing. But after a couple of minutes, he'd finally explained that he'd talked to Byron and Rick about how it would be safer for her mom to stay in town instead of going home, in case the stalker had been triggered to escalate his aggressive behavior after not being able to get any of the packages to her during their break.

Knowing Allissa had struggled with getting her mom to take some time off work to get out of her stalker's sights, Dean decided to help her out by giving her mom a reason or two to stay out of Dead End, Nevada, for the next few months. Allissa realized it was his way of trying to take care of her and her mom, and she appreciated how he was trying to be thoughtful and protective. But she wished he'd only dangled the job prospect under her mom's nose, and left the wedding planning off the table until they actually started talking about wanting to get married.

It wasn't that Allissa was opposed to marrying Dean on November thirtieth, as their mothers currently had it planned. Since they'd started making love multiple times a day, she'd started letting go of all her doubts about them lasting as a couple. But she felt like they were jumping over a few crucial steps to start planning a wedding, when they hadn't even uttered those three special words of "I love you" to one another yet. While she was sure she was in love with Dean, and thought she saw his love for her every time she looked into his eyes, she didn't want their first time saying those words to one another to be in their wedding vows.

She also didn't want to be the first one to say those three little words. Yeah, she was starting to believe they were meant to be together forever, but she still had a sliver of doubt that made her worry that telling him first would lead to him breaking things off. So, she continued to hold her feelings close to the vest, waiting for Dean to express his first. And she didn't think saying they were making love instead of fucking counted, no matter how many times he'd called it that in the past few days.

"You alright, Vic?" Emerald plopped down on the bench in the locker room beside Allissa, where they were gathering their things to leave the arena after the show. "You've been awfully quiet since we landed this morning. And that seems strange after everything you told us on the plane."

On the short flight between San Antonio and Austin that morning, Allissa had finally come clean to her girlfriends, who hadn't been in Heart's Destiny for the last week, about her mom's job, as well as filling them in on the events of the previous week with regard to her relationship with Dean. Then, as soon as they landed, and she turned her phone off of airplane mode, her mom had blown it up, causing her to slowly shut down to process her feelings for the rest of the day.

"Yeah, well, I wasn't feeling the effects of my period starting when we were on the plane this morning," Allissa scoffed, not wanting to explain that her mom's texts came at the wrong time of the month for her to be rational while dealing with them. "Now I'm feeling bloated and blah and just want to go take some Midol and sleep it off."

Allissa also didn't want to mention the latest update from Cage about her stalker sending creepy notes to the GWA headquarters when he couldn't find her, or torment her through her mom, during their Labor Day break. The stress of finding out the letters contained the implied threat that he might attempt to kidnap her was bad enough, but realizing she now had two bodyguards from Avington Security traveling with the GWA full-time and staying in the room next door to her and Dean's was exceptionally nerve-wracking.

Not that she didn't appreciate everything that was being done to keep her and her mom safe. She definitely appreciated every single member of the Avington family and all their employees, who were working around the clock to find her stalker. But having them so close and watching her every move made her uncomfortable.

Allissa especially felt bad for wanting to whine and complain about feeling like she was living under a microscope, when she knew the men were doing everything they could to keep her safe. Besides, she didn't want her friends to think of her as a whiny crybaby, so she kept those feelings bottled up as much as she could.

Hopefully, I'm just feeling like a sniveling ball sack because of my period and will be less emotional in a few days.

"Oh," Emerald nodded knowingly as she stood and picked up her bag. "Gotcha. Well, thankfully, you can go back to the hotel and let Dean take care of you for the rest of the night." As she turned to walk out of the locker room, Emerald turned back and winked. "And remember that orgasms work better than Midol for those cramps."

"Gross," Allissa cringed at the thought of trying to do anything sexual on the heaviest day of her period.

"Seriously, Vic, it's not too messy if you do it in the shower," Amethyst added with a chuckle as she shut her locker and shouldered her bag. "And it does ease the cramps."

Allissa just shook her head, knowing she'd never ask Dean to ease her period pain by making love to her. She finished putting her things in her bag and finally left the locker room a few seconds behind her friends.

Lincoln and Wright met her at the door, shadowing her as she walked over to catering to meet up with Dean for their trip back to the hotel. The other security change that had occurred since they left Heart's Destiny that morning was that the bodyguards now drove them around instead of just following them. Allissa was just glad they didn't follow her into the locker room, so she could have a few minutes of privacy sprinkled throughout the day.

I guess the drawback to sleeping with Dean and going down to one room while traveling is the loss of my alone time to unwind in my own space at the beginning and ending of each day.

"You alright, Darlin'?" Dean gave her a quizzical look as he took her bag from her shoulder. "It seemed like you took twice as long as you normally do to shower after your match. I was starting to get worried."

Allissa instantly felt guilty for worrying him, especially since she didn't really have a reason for sitting in the locker room doing absolutely nothing for so long after rinsing off the sweat from her match. "Sorry," she smiled sheepishly. "Needed a little extra time to deal with some feminine issues."

That's only a little fib, right? I mean, I did have to take some extra time to change my tampon, even though the time-consuming task of cleaning my panties when I started my period was technically this afternoon before my match.

"Oh," Dean nodded in understanding. "Is there anything we need to stop and get for that on the way back to the hotel?"

"No, I just need the Midol I have in my toiletry bag back at the hotel," Allissa informed him as they started walking toward the exit. "But don't you need your stuff from the locker room?"

"My bag is already in the car, Darlin'," Dean assured her, hugging her to his side as they strode out of the building with the bodyguards flanking them. "And I have an idea for how to help ease your pain when we get to the hotel."

"No, Dean," Allissa hissed, blushing at discussing sex while the bodyguards were clearly able to hear them. "I don't care what the Stones say about orgasms helping with cramps. We're not doing that until shark week is over."

"Then I guess it's a good thing I was talkin' about a hot bath followed by a massage," Dean chuckled before brushing his lips over her temple. "Though I wouldn't be opposed to following the Stones' suggestions if it would help you feel better."

"Stick with the massage, Aquaman," Allissa teased him, rolling her eyes as she pushed up on her toes to whisper close to his ear as they stopped at their car. "And maybe I'll be nice and reciprocate with a happy-ending massage before bed."

"Fuck, yeah, Darlin'," Dean grinned as they got in the back seat of the car. As she buckled her seatbelt, he leaned over to whisper in her ear, "Guess we'll continue foreplay lessons this week with hand jobs."

Guess I'll finally get a closer look at those piercings tonight, even though we can't make love in the traditional sense.

~ ~ ~

Monday, September 16, 2019, Saint Louis, Missouri

Dean felt extremely frustrated that Allissa's stalker hadn't been caught yet. None of the leads the Avington Security teams were following had panned out. The prepaid credit card he'd used to send Allissa flowers had been registered under an alias that left them with no clues to the bastard's real identity, and none of the return addresses on the various packages and letters appeared to be real in any way. So, the security company was left with making sure Allissa and her mom were safe while waiting on the psycho stalker to screw up, so they could finally track him down. While having Windy Walters staying away from home during their holiday break had succeeded in triggering him, it hadn't made him so angry that he actually made a mistake they could use to find him.

The jackass had upped his aggression with the letters that implied he planned to kidnap Allissa, which started coming in after their Labor Day break, but he still hadn't shown his face. And even though the letters mostly went through the GWA office in New York, they were coming in with postmarks from most of the same cities the GWA had been touring, with the exception of the ones sent from Dead End, Nevada, during their break.

Based on the dates, it appeared the stalker was following a schedule almost identical to the GWA's, only a day ahead of them. So, it appeared he was setting up the package deliveries to the arenas and hotels, and mailing a letter to the GWA office before leaving town just in time to keep from being caught.

At least, they all believed he left town just before the GWA arrived to keep from being caught. With his letters stating that he had almost finished setting up the home he planned to live in with Allissa, Dean was worried that he might decide to stick around to try to kidnap her once he'd completed the dungeon he planned to hold her in. Because of that, he wanted to talk to the security team about trying to catch the bastard before he managed to lie in wait for them in one of their hotels or arenas.

Dean waited until Allissa was in the women's locker room, changing after her match, to talk to Lincoln and Wright while they stood guard at the locker room door. It wasn't that he didn't want to include Allissa in the conversation, but more that he wanted to run his plan by the bodyguards before informing her about it, just in case they shot it down as a bad idea.

No point in worrying her more than she already is by sharing my fears before we have a plan in place to prevent them from happening.

"Hey, guys, I have a question for ya'll." When Lincoln nodded and Wright gave him a chin lift, Dean took their silence as his opening to continue. "The letters Allissa's been getting the past week all seem to be postmarked from the same cities we're touring, but a day before we arrive."

"Yeah, we noticed that," Lincoln agreed. "And we have the cyber team working on getting access to flight manifests from all the major airlines to see if we can find a name for whoever might be doing all that traveling."

"Damn, ya'll can get blanket warrants like that?" Being relatively certain that flight manifests weren't considered public records, Dean was surprised to hear that Avington Security was able to work through all that red tape so easily.

"No," Wright chuckled. "But since we're not trying to use the information in court, the boss can use his history of protecting the family members of some of the airline bigwigs to get our net nerds access to them without a warrant."

"Unfortunately, it's a lot of names to go through, though, so it may take them a while to cross-reference all of them," Lincoln warned

Dean, making sure he didn't get his hopes up that the stalker would be caught by the cyber team anytime soon.

"Yeah, well, maybe my plan might work faster than that," Dean mused aloud.

"What plan?" Wright arched a curious eyebrow.

"Since we already know his schedule to travel ahead of us, why don't we send a team out on the schedule we think he's following to search for him? Maybe get ahead of him and lie in wait for him, instead of letting him have the chance to lie in wait for Allissa."

"That's not a bad idea," Lincoln contemplated with a side-to-side bobble of his head. "But we don't know that he's actually going to the arenas or hotels, so it might be a waste of resources to stake those out."

"Possibly," Dean defended his reasoning. "But we know he has to be going through the airports a day ahead of us, so they might be able to figure out who he is if they see the same person day after day in different cities."

"True," Wright conceded, nodding as he thought about the likelihood of Dean's plan working. "All we can do is suggest it to Byron and see what he thinks."

They made a quick call to Byron Avington to get his thoughts on the idea for finding Allissa's stalker. After a brief discussion about whether they thought the perp was the one traveling the country, or if he'd hired a middleman to do his dirty work, they opted to assume it was the actual stalker based on the message that was written on the mirror in the bathroom of her hotel room in Birmingham. Besides, someone that obsessed wouldn't leave the tasks of picking out lingerie or writing personal letters to a subordinate.

Because they determined it had to be the stalker, Byron decided to pull the team who was watching Ron Langston to go as a pre-surveillance team to the major airports in each of the cities the GWA was scheduled to travel to, only a day ahead of the GWA schedule. Since Ron hadn't left a five-mile radius of his Los Angeles home in the entire time they'd been watching him, Byron didn't think he was still a valid person of interest in Allissa's case.

While Dean agreed with him, he also wished there was more that could be done to keep Ron from sexually harassing any other women in the future. *Hopefully, David will pass along the info I gave him when we were on set last month, so that bastard won't get the chance to torment any of the actresses on whatever projects he's been applying to write for since Rick canned his ass.*

Professional wrestlers might only be considered D-list celebrities compared to the Hollywood crowd, but Dean hoped the minor celebrity status of the GWA performers making the allegations against Langston would be enough to garner just enough attention to the matter. By just enough attention, he meant he didn't want it to become a major scandal that would embarrass Allissa or anyone else in the GWA, but would still be enough that the television and movie executives who might be considering working with Ron would think twice before hiring him.

Dean didn't get a chance to think much more about Ron Langston as Allissa walked out of the locker room, ready to go grab their version of an elevenses meal on the way back to the hotel. While they needed to eat like a hobbit to maintain the calorie intake needed to fuel all their exercise and their physical careers, being on the company plane most days at eleven in the morning meant they had to consider the meal they had at eleven at night after the show was over as their elevenses meal.

For their final meal of the night while in Saint Louis, they were hitting up a late-night diner for a Slinger, one of the famous foods he'd read about from the area. It consisted of a hamburger patty, eggs, and hashbrowns, topped with chili, cheese, and onions. Dean wasn't sure how much longer he'd be able to eat gut-busting meals like that without gastrointestinal consequences, but he was determined to keep up with his hot girlfriend's iron stomach for as long as possible.

Though to be totally honest, he was surprised that Allissa had agreed to go eat after the show with the two bodyguards driving them around and a few of the other wrestlers also planning to hit up the diner on the way back to the hotel. While he wanted to help push her to get over the traumatic events of her childhood and teenage years that caused her secretive eating habits, he also didn't want to push too far or too fast and make her uncomfortable. So Dean had to double-check with her before they walked into the diner. "Are you sure you're okay with eating here?"

"Yeah, I'm fine with it," Allissa assured him, wrapping her arm around his waist as she smiled up at him when they got out of the car. "With everyone being so cool with my mom now that they know her history, I'm sure they'll understand my past and won't ridicule me for eating like a pig now."

They walked into the restaurant and found seats with the GWA crew, who were planning to eat before hitting up a club. As usual, the conversations around the four large tables they took up were all about the show and everyone's plans for later that night, with several of their friends trying to convince Dean and Allissa to hit up the club with them.

"Sorry, guys," Allissa shook her head at Emerald and Amethyst, who were seated across the large, round corner booth from them. "I'm not going out partying the night before TV."

"But you're gonna eat a Slinger?" Emerald arched an eyebrow in surprise as she waved a hand at the dishes being placed in front of both Dean and Allissa. "I'd rather have a hangover on TV than be bloated and risk shitting myself in the middle of the ring from eating all that."

"Holy shit, Vic!" Amethyst's jaw dropped as she watched Allissa take her first bite of cheesy chili goodness. "You're the only one of us with the willpower to stick to a strict diet. Maybe dating Dean isn't such a good idea if he's got you going off the plan to eat the same crap he does."

"I have no say in Allissa's dietary choices." Dean held his hands up and shook his head at their friends, wanting to make his point perfectly clear while Allissa couldn't speak around the bite of food she was chewing. "But I support her in eating whatever she wants, whenever she wants, without anyone else making her feel bad for it."

Once she swallowed, she took over explaining to their friends. "I've actually been eating stuff like this all along," Allissa confessed. "But because of being picked on about my food choices for the last decade, I haven't let anyone see me eat anything they might consider unhealthy to keep from being ridiculed. Dean's actually helped me to see that I don't have to hide what I eat or how much I eat."

"Seriously? You've been hiding from us to eat unhealthy food?" Emerald looked appalled, putting Dean on edge about what she might say next. "I've been feeling like a pig because I can't eat as clean as you and all this time we could've been pigging out together?"

Allissa shrugged as she took her next bite. Dean just grinned as he dug into his own meal, enjoying how their friends were being supportive now that they knew about Allissa's eating issue.

"How'd Dean help you see that you don't have to hide it anymore?" Amethyst asked as she cut off a bite of her egg-white omelet.

"He convinced me to look at my eating issues, and a few other issues I have, in terms of mind over matter," Allissa replied with a smile once she'd swallowed her next bite.

"Mind over matter?" Emerald arched an eyebrow at Dean as she forked up some of the fruit cup she'd ordered.

Dean just smiled and continued chewing, feeling proud of Allissa as she gave him credit for talking her through dealing with some of her issues. In truth, all he'd done was be her sounding board as she talked through the advice she'd gotten from her therapist and reworded it from his perspective to make it more understandable. She'd done all the work in facing her fears.

"Yeah, the people who matter, won't mind," Allissa grinned. "And the people who mind, don't matter. It works for looking at a lot of things in life. We should all be able to live our lives the way we want, as long as we're not doing things to actively harm others. And nobody else's opinions about our decisions should have an impact on how we choose to live because the people who truly love us will love us regardless of whether or not they like our choices."

"So, kinda like 'haters gonna hate,' so ignore the trolls and eat whatever the fuck you want," Emerald clarified with a grin.

"Yeah, but when I was in school, my trolls weren't online," Allissa agreed. "So I'd tried to appease them and hid the real me. And once I got out of that toxic environment, I didn't know when it was safe to come out of hiding."

"Glad to see I was wrong in worrying Dean wasn't good for you if he showed you it's safe to trust us," Amethyst grinned before waving over their server and ordering another Slinger. "But seriously, you're gonna hafta help us stay in as good a shape as you now that we can eat more than this rubbery stuff when you're around and not feel guilty trying to eat as clean as you."

Dean had to chuckle at the way she poked her egg-white omelet with her fork when she said the words "rubbery stuff" before pushing her plate away.

"Yeah, I can't take credit for that," Allissa shook her head, as Crockett pulled Amethyst's plate over in front of him and finished off the rubbery food she no longer wanted. "You'll just have to get up and meet us in the hotel gym at six-thirty in the morning for one of Dean's killer workouts."

"Why are you guys up that early to work out?" Surfer Josh looked at them in confusion.

"So we can have our date time in the middle of the day when all ya'll are in the weight room," Dean informed him with a half-shrug.

"No wonder you quit coming out with us after the shows. You've gotta get back to the hotel as soon as possible after the shows to get any sleep in before getting up that fuckin' early." Crockett shook his head as he acknowledged their choice of sleep over partying.

"And I thought it was so they could do the horizontal mambo for an extra cardio session every night," Emerald quipped.

Dean just smiled and continued eating, knowing he'd only embarrass Allissa if he acknowledged the truth of Emerald's statement.

"Well, duh!" Allissa surprised them all by rolling her eyes and pointing her fork at Emerald. "But I'm not inviting any of you to join those workouts."

Dean wasn't sure if it was Allissa not seeming to be embarrassed about the sexual turn of the conversation, or a couple of the condoms Protection Detail passed out to the fans being tossed over their heads from one of the other tables and landing in the middle of their table, that made him choke on his food. Allissa turned and patted his back to help him as he coughed, trying to get the chili-covered hashbrowns back up before they made it to his lungs.

Unfortunately, his coworkers seemed to be having too much fun tossing condoms back and forth across the restaurant to notice that they almost killed him. *At least I have Allissa to keep me alive,* Dean thought as he finally swallowed the bite properly to be able to start breathing again. *But maybe we should get our food to go, so we can keep from getting caught up in the middle of whatever trouble these jokers cause tonight. I'd rather be back in our room where I can lick this chili off Allissa's tits, anyway.*

<center>~~~</center>

They were on day one of a four-day stint in Canada that Allissa hoped would prove the Avington's theory correct about her stalker not wanting to deal with the additional expense of taking his threats across international borders. While Cage and her bodyguards had intercepted most of his packages and correspondence before she had to see any of it, just knowing that they were having to deal with it almost daily was enough to be nerve-wracking for her. So she was hopeful for a four-day reprieve when they might all be able to relax a little bit.

Since she would be wrestling on their live weekly television show the next night, Allissa only had to put on her ring attire long enough to pre-record a promo, so she didn't risk screwing up her lines on live television. Once that was done, she was able to change back into her street clothes and watch the show that night on the backstage monitors alongside her boyfriend and their coworkers.

As she left the locker room after changing, she found Dean dressed in his gimmick wear for a run-in he and James would be doing during the main event. While she loved seeing him in his wrestling tights and shirtless when he wrestled and in the suits and button-downs he wore when out in public to meet the GWA's dress code for traveling, she really enjoyed seeing him in form-fitting jeans, a classic rock band t-shirt, and biker boots when he was supposed to be in character but not actually wrestling. While the leather jacket that he had draped over his chair didn't do anything for her, since she wasn't into the whole motorcycle culture, the rest of the look struck her as bad-boy rocker chic and looked smokin' hot on Dean.

"You should really ditch the biker gimmick and stick with this rock star vibe you've got goin' on," Allissa smirked as she approached him.

"Yeah, that was kinda what we used when we first got started," Dean chuckled as he took her hand and pulled her onto his lap. "But Anthony was still in the Navy, so we were missing the bass player in our band, and it was too much of a hassle to cart our instruments through airport security every day to make it seem more realistic."

Allissa didn't think it would be too hard for Dean to carry his guitar around the world with him. But after hearing about the band they'd played in as teenagers, she imagined James's drums would be a bit too cumbersome to take on tour without the roadies rock stars used to tote their equipment around. And she doubted the GWA ground crew would appreciate being treated like rock star roadies.

As she sat there watching the show on the monitors, Allissa started to wonder about the ground crews who traveled via eighteen-wheelers around the country to set up the ring, lighting, stage, and all the other equipment needed for each show. Since they were in the arena setting up while the performers were flying into each city and went to the company-provided hotels to sleep during the time the performers were rehearsing and putting on the shows, they could possibly be in town early enough to set up the package deliveries that had been sent to the hotels before Allissa arrived. They also knew the hotels the company used and could have easily found out her real name when they were on the European tour and some members of the ground crew had to join them on the flight from New York to Dublin.

Could my stalker be one of the guys on that crew? Hell, even if he isn't one of the guys who had to join us on the flight to kick off the European tour, we still could have crossed paths at some point for him to hear my real name.

Allissa started assessing all the interactions she'd had with every member of the ground crew since her first day on the job. She'd always tried to be polite to everyone, so she couldn't remember doing or saying anything to piss off one of the ground crew to make him want to start stalking her.

But didn't Byron say something about the stalker possibly thinking we had more of a connection than we really did? What if I was just being nice, and he took whatever I said or how I smiled as a sign of interest in him?

Allissa grew tenser and tenser as she realized the stalker could possibly be part of the ground crew that they couldn't catch because they were looking in the wrong place by sending out a security team to search for him in the airports the day before they were supposed to arrive in the area. *I need to call Byron and ask him if he's done background checks on everyone on the ground crew to make sure we've not missed him when he's right under our noses.*

"Hey, Darlin', you okay?" Dean whispered in her ear, his beard lightly tickling her cheek.

Leah Mae Wright

"Yeah, fine," Allissa answered as she scanned the room, looking for the two bodyguards that were assigned to her. "Just thought of something that I should probably run by Lincoln and Wright."

"Okay," Dean nodded, helping her stand from his lap. "Let's go talk to them and then see if we can sneak off somewhere private, so I can get you to relax a little."

Allissa was surprised by the way Dean grinned and winked at her as he stood, implying that he would do something sexual to relax her while they were in the arena in the middle of a show. She didn't get the chance to ask the meaning behind his nonverbal cues because he quickly directed her to the side of the room where Lincoln was standing.

"Where's Wright?" Dean looked around as if searching for the other bodyguard.

"Doing a perimeter sweep," Lincoln replied.

Since the bodyguards had been with them at several shows now, Allissa knew they took turns walking all around the backstage area whenever she was sitting and watching the show on the monitors. They'd already explained to her and Dean how they checked in with each of the building security guards, who were supposed to be manning the various access points to keep fans from being able to get backstage. It was an extra precaution they took in case her stalker was able to subdue one of the people provided by the arena, who might not be as well trained as the people who worked for Avington Security.

"Do we need to wait for him to get back?" Dean turned to Allissa, obviously thinking she might feel safer if both bodyguards were present when she posed her question.

"No, I'm sure Lincoln can tell me if Byron has checked out everyone on the ground crew," Allissa asserted, turning to look at the bodyguard. "I was thinking about how they go into town in the middle of the night before we get there and travel in eighteen-wheelers, so they'd bypass the airports the other team is checking out."

"If they work for the GWA, then they've been checked out," Lincoln assured her. "Back when this all started, Byron insisted on running background checks on everyone who works with the company, from the owners all the way down to the janitors who empty the trashcans in the office in New York. But if there's someone in particular that has made you feel suspicious of them, I'll call him with their name to check them out again."

"No," Allissa shook her head and waved off his offer. "I'm just letting my imagination run wild, trying to figure out who it could be. Dean mentioned something about traveling with instruments being an issue and I got to thinking about how rock stars do it. That led me to compare our ground crew to the roadies who lug around the instruments for concerts, and I realized their schedule could put them in place to set up the deliveries my stalker's been sending. But I haven't gotten any kind of vibes from the people on the ground crew I've met other than friendly."

"Even if it's not likely someone on the ground crew," Lincoln interjected, pulling out his phone. "I'm still gonna call into the office and see if they have any ideas for catching the perp if he's driving between cities. While we don't have the manpower to cover all the possible routes by car, our cyber team might be able to pull public records to see if any names pop up more than once on speeding tickets or other moving violations around the country."

"That's kind of a long shot, though, right?" Dean gave him a questioning look. "I mean, with as careful as he's being not to leave fingerprints or anything to identify him, I'd think he'd be careful not to speed between cities, too."

"Yeah, but I doubt he'll think about what resources we have to track his movements that way." Lincoln looked skeptical as he slightly shook his head at Dean. "So maybe we'll get lucky, and his lead foot will help us catch him. You know that's how they caught the Oklahoma City bomber."

"Seriously?" Allissa hadn't even been born when the Oklahoma City bombing happened, but she'd learned about it in school. She hadn't heard anything about the bomber being caught speeding, though.

"Yeah," Lincoln grinned. "They caught him speeding toward Kansas just a few hours after the bombing. Criminals can be really stupid about shit like speeding."

"Well, let's hope this one is just as stupid," Dean chuckled just as Wright walked up.

"What did I miss?"

"I'll let you guys fill him in while I go grab a bottle of water." Allissa nodded her head in the direction of the coolers set up on the other side of the catering area from where they were standing. "Any of you need one?"

After they all declined, Allissa walked over to get her drink while Dean and Lincoln filled Wright in on their conversation. It didn't take long before Dean joined her, taking her hand, and pulling her toward the rooms set up for the athletic trainer.

"Where are we going?" Allissa was surprised to see that the bodyguards weren't following them. But they also wouldn't be out of their line of sight unless they went into one of the training rooms, so she figured they were just giving them a little space.

"There's an empty room that Doc's not using tonight," Dean informed her as he ushered her to the door furthest from the room Doc was using, grinning as he reached for the door handle. "And since Wright just cleared it on his walk-through, he said it would be fine for us to go in there for a private talk."

"A private talk, huh?" Allissa had a feeling they wouldn't be doing much talking if they went in that room. *Holy shit! Was he serious earlier when he hinted about wanting to fool around here at the arena?*

"Yeah, Darlin'," Dean grinned, making her wonder if she'd voiced her thought out loud. He wagged his eyebrows at her as he ushered her inside. The lights came on as soon as their presence registered on the motion sensors controlling them, revealing a bare massage table set up in an otherwise empty room. Dean locked the door behind them, so nobody could walk in and interrupt them. "But since we're only about fifty yards from the rest of the guys, we'll have to use *body language* to stay quiet enough they don't know what we're discussin'."

"Oh my gawd, Dean," Allissa hissed in protest as he backed her up to the massage table, unsure if she could follow through with what he was suggesting. "We can't do anything in here. Everyone will know."

"So?" Dean shrugged and grinned. "Don't worry, Darlin', we're not the only couple in the GWA to sneak off for a quickie once in a while. Nobody's gonna be scandalized by it, unless you scream so loud the kids hear you when I make you come. Now turn around and bend over that table and let me help you relax."

"Dean!" Allissa whisper-shouted his name, not wanting to be loud enough to draw attention to them from anyone outside the room, as he caged her in with her ass hitting the end of the massage table.

"Sorry, Darlin', but if you didn't want me to fuck you from behind while massaging your back to relax you, you shouldn't have gotten so tense while wearing a skirt to give me easy access."

Remembering how his piercings rubbed differently inside her when Dean had her bent over a piece of furniture or gym equipment to make love, Allissa's brain quit protesting what her body clearly wanted. She didn't say another word as she turned around.

"That's my good girl," Dean whispered into her ear as he brushed her hair to one side and started massaging her shoulders before she could think clearly enough to bend over the end of the massage table. He gently pushed her upper body forward as he continued rubbing his big hands all over her back, neck, and shoulders, as if his goal really was to stroke the tension from her trapezius and surrounding muscles.

Allissa sighed in pleasure as she rested her upper body against the soft vinyl-covered table, while Dean kneaded her tight muscles for a few minutes. He continued massaging her with his left hand as he lifted his right hand from her body to push her skirt up around her waist. A moment later, she heard the sound of his zipper and the rustling of denim, as he lowered his pants while still rubbing her back.

"So fucking sexy," he growled in a low tone as he slid her thong to the side and ran his fingers through her folds. "Spread your legs a little wider, Darlin'."

Allissa did as he directed, loving the way he took charge and gave her what she needed, even when she hadn't realized how badly she needed it. She was already wet and ready for him, so he didn't have to spend much time fingering her to prepare her for his cock.

"You'd better hurry it up, Aquaman, if you want this to be a quickie," she teased, rocking her hips to rub her pussy on his fingers.

"Don'tcha worry, Darlin', we've got plenty of time for me to go at the speed I want." Dean lifted the hand massaging her back and lightly swatted her ass.

Allissa whimpered lightly, enjoying the minimal sting as it quickly morphed into a delicious desire for more of a spanking. Dean continued to tease her with his fingers, always more concerned with making sure she was aroused enough to accommodate his size than rushing to the finish line.

He finger-fucked her right to the brink before pulling his digits from her body before she could come. Then he lined up the head of his cock with her slit and coated himself with her cream. As always, he pushed into her slowly for the first stroke, but he didn't stop his forward movement until he was balls-deep.

"Fuck, you feel so good, Allissa," Dean groaned as he pulled back out.

"So do you, Dean," Allissa moaned, pushing back against him as he sank inside her once more.

Dean half-heartedly rubbed her back once more, not that she noticed with her whole focus on where their bodies were joined. She paid special attention to how it felt each time the balls of his piercing jewelry rubbed across her G-spot.

She'd quickly realized the first time they made love in this position how both piercings stroking over her G-spot stimulated her to orgasm faster than just the one through the head of his dick when they were face to face. And this time was no different. It might even be faster since she was also turned on by the semi-public nature of their copulation. She found herself right on the edge within seconds, unable to control the way she writhed beneath him as the pressure built in her core.

As his thrusts sped up, Dean quickly abandoned any pretense of giving her a massage, moving his hands from her back to grip her hips and control their coupling. He pounded into her in the perfect combination of pace and intensity to push her over the precipice.

"Fuck, yes, Dean," she whisper-shouted, trying to keep from screaming too loud as her orgasm washed over her.

It felt like her whole body convulsed as each wave hit her. Allissa gripped the edges of the massage table under her, arching her back to push her hips into Dean and opening her mouth for a silent scream. Her cries of pleasure were only suppressed because she held her breath as the orgasm peaked.

"Fuck, yes, milk my cock, Allissa," Dean commanded in a low tone as he pushed in as deep as he could go one last time and flooded her with his cum.

Allissa wasn't completely sure what he meant by the statement, but assumed it had something to do with how every time her inner walls spasmed he seemed to respond with a similar jerk of his body inside her.

They both collapsed forward onto the massage table as they basked in the afterglow of their simultaneous climaxes. Allissa loved the way Dean let her feel his strong body against her back while holding himself up on his forearms, so he didn't crush her small frame under his massively bigger body.

"We probably should have found a room that was at least stocked with some paper towels," Allissa giggled as she felt their combined bodily fluids sliding down her inner thighs as Dean's cock softened inside her and let them escape.

"Fuck, I didn't even think about that," Dean groaned as he pushed up and slowly pulled his dick from her body. "There are some cabinets over by the door. Maybe there's something stored there that we can use to clean up. Don't move while I go check."

"I hope so, 'cause my panties aren't gonna contain this mess." *Hell, they aren't made of enough material to even soak up my wetness, so there's no way they can wipe up Dean's, too. Guess that means I need to learn how to swallow, and we need to stick to oral when we get our freak on at work.*

"Ah, we're in luck," Dean declared as she heard him shut a cabinet behind her. He was back within seconds, kneeling behind her and wiping her off with the roughest paper towels she'd ever felt. "Though I should probably throw these away somewhere other than here, since the small trashcan under the counter doesn't even have a liner in it."

Allissa didn't have time to try to figure out how they could smuggle the cum soaked paper towels out to another trashcan because there was a knock at the door.

"Fifteen-minute warning, bro," James hollered through the door. "Main event just started, so you need to zip up and clean up in a hurry to do our run-in."

"Be right there," Dean yelled back at his brother, rushing through wiping her up, and repositioning her clothing.

Allissa knew she was as bright red as a firetruck as she pushed up from her bent-over position and double-checked that her clothing didn't contain any evidence of their activity. *If there's even the smallest drop of jizz on my skirt, the girls will notice it.*

Dean wiped off his dick and wrapped the cum covered towels in a few clean ones before pulling up his pants and putting away the half-used roll of paper towels. "Don't worry, Darlin'. Nobody's gonna say a word about what we were doin'."

With that, he pecked her lips and pushed her toward the door with his hand on the small of her back, carrying the ball of paper towels in the other. He moved his hand from her back long enough to unlock the door, so they could do the walk of shame to the locker room to clean up a little more.

Surprisingly, he was right. Nobody seemed to notice they'd been gone. Or if they did, none of them said a word about it.

Chapter Nineteen

Saturday, October 5, 2019, Atlantic City, New Jersey

Allissa stared at the numbers on her new GWA contract in shock. She couldn't believe that, in only a year on the roster, her salary was tripling to one-point-five-million dollars a year, plus bonuses based on her merchandise sales. Yeah, she was currently the women's division champion, but she thought for sure it would still be at least five years before she earned a salary in the million-dollar range.

"You alright, Darlin'?" Dean rubbed a hand up and down her back as he looked at her with concern from his seat beside her in Rick's office space at the arena.

"Yeah," Allissa nodded, still feeling speechless at seeing those numbers.

"I think I surprised her with her raise," Rick grinned, leaning back in his chair on the other side of the desk her contract was laying on.

"Are you sure these numbers are right?" Allissa finally tore her eyes from the contract to look up at her boss. "This isn't somebody else's contract you accidentally handed me?"

"Yes, Allissa, those numbers are correct," Rick chuckled. "Which is why I asked you to bring Dean to this meeting. I figured you might want to have him advise you on investment accounts to set up and decide on the best strategy for changing your direct deposit percentages and accounts. I need you to fill out a new direct deposit form in the next day or two, so the changes can all go into effect before the fifteenth."

"I've already helped her set up her investment accounts," Dean informed Rick. "So, she just needs to adjust the direct deposit percentages and add the accounts we set up a couple months ago.

Then she won't have to manually do the transfers every payday anymore."

"Perfect," Rick grinned, picking up his tablet to pull up the direct deposit form for Allissa to submit an update to human resources. "Then, as soon as you sign that contract, we'll amend this form and be done with the boring part of our business for another year."

Allissa quickly signed her name to the contract, afraid the numbers might magically change if she waited any longer to agree. She then listened to Dean's advice about what percentages of her income to put in each account.

They butted heads momentarily when he suggested dropping the percentage she deposited in her mother's account and setting up investment accounts for her, instead of almost tripling the monthly deposit into her checking account. After Allissa explained that she'd rather her mom set up her own investment accounts, Dean conceded and sent his dad a text message to have him help Windy with that, since she was still in Heart's Destiny.

Just as they were standing to leave the backstage area designated as Rick's office, Cage walked over with Lincoln and Wright. He was carrying a large manilla envelope in his gloved hand that Allissa just knew was more hate mail from her stalker.

"Boss, I think you might want to see this." Cage held up the envelope as Allissa sank back down into the chair she'd just vacated. He then laid the envelope on the desk that Rick had just cleared of her new contract.

When Cage pulled a stack of eight-by-ten photographs from the envelope and spread them out for everyone to be able to see them, Allissa gasped in shock. There were at least a dozen pictures of her and Dean together, either holding hands, or with his arm around her, as they walked into and out of hotels and arenas for the last few weeks, all of which had Dean's face crossed out with a black marker.

"Shit!" Dean cursed, pulling her up into his arms and cradling her head to his chest, so she could no longer see the images. He sat down in the chair with her on his lap as he reprimanded Cage. "She didn't need to see this shit."

As much as she wished she hadn't seen the latest round of unwanted mail from her stalker, she couldn't stop seeing the hateful words written across the pictures, even with her eyes closed and her face buried in Dean's navy blue button-down. Allissa sobbed as she tried to block out the realization that her stalker knew she was seeing Dean, and was now threatening both their lives because of it.

"Sorry, I didn't realize how bad they got." Allissa could hear the remorse in Cage's tone of voice. "I only saw the top one before I brought them over here to spread them out."

"I've already messaged the team who've been trying to find him by going a day ahead of us," Wright informed them as she heard someone shuffling the photos on the desk, as if putting them back in the envelope. "They're going to stay in Baltimore tonight and start traveling with us tomorrow to provide more security for both Allissa and Dean."

"And Byron's got a couple of the Burlesons doing pre-surveillance on our stops in Virginia on Monday and Tuesday until he can get another team out ahead of us," Lincoln filled them in on the outcome of his quick call into headquarters.

"Thank you," Allissa expressed her gratitude for their quick response to the escalation of the threats as she pulled back slightly from Dean's embrace and wiped away her tears. "I feel like I owe all of you so much more than I can ever convey with those two words. But I'm too flustered right now to figure out how to communicate how grateful I am for all your help in trying to stop this guy."

Before anyone could respond to her heartfelt appreciativeness, Chastity ran up clutching another envelope. "I'm so sorry, Boss," she cried as she waved the envelope toward Rick. "I don't know how this happened. I swear, I thought we just took pictures at the chapel in Vegas, not that any of us actually got married! But when I went through my mail while I was at my apartment to drop off my stuff, I found our certificate of marriage. I guess it takes a little while for them to mail it from Vegas."

"Fuck!" Rick swore as he took the envelope from Chastity and started to remove the contents. He then looked around at the rest of the people in his office space before looking at the new document in his hand. "I'm going to let you guys handle the security situation without me while I deal with whatever fallout we're about to have from our last trip to Vegas."

"We've got it covered, Boss," Cage assured Rick as he ushered everyone but Chastity out of Rick's office area.

"I wonder who she ended up marrying," Allissa mused aloud as they walked toward catering to finish discussing the newest round of changes to her security protocols.

"Who knows?" Dean chuckled and shrugged. "I'm just glad to know it's not one of us about to get their ass handed to 'em by Rick for that mess."

"Why are they getting reamed for getting married?" Wright looked confused as he looked back at Chastity and Rick, who were discussing the information on the marriage certificate.

"It's not because they got married," Dean explained. "It's because Protection Detail, the Precious Stones, and a few of the other guys got so wasted they went to a chapel in Vegas and took a bunch of pictures without making it clear which couples they were implying got married. Then they posted them all over social media and fucked with the angles he had planned for them."

As they took a seat at one of the tables in catering, Allissa kept looking back over at Chastity and Rick. While she knew she should be paying attention to what was being said about how they were going to change her security, she was too intrigued with the situation her friends were in to focus on her own worries at that moment.

I wonder if Chastity and her new hubby are the only ones who got married that night? And what are they going to have to do to get out of the marriages, since none of the people who went to the chapel that night are coupled up?

Based on the look on Chastity's face, Allissa wasn't sure if her friend was really as upset about the surprise marriage as she'd sounded when she first approached Rick. *Huh? Does she have a little crush on her new hubby?*

Allissa watched as Rick pulled his cell phone out and sent off a text message, wondering whom he was texting. *Just the person Chastity married? Or everyone who was in those pictures to make sure they were the only ones to get hitched?* Allissa wasn't sure which she hoped it was. If it was just the person Chastity married, then she'd probably figure it out pretty easily if he was the only one who showed up in Rick's office space in the next few minutes. But if he texted all of them, then she'd have to wait until she could talk to Chastity to find out.

When the other two members of Protection Detail soon joined Rick and Chastity, followed shortly after by the Precious Stones, Red, Crockett, Surfer Josh, and Blade, Allissa knew she wouldn't get any answers to her nosy questions anytime soon. Especially when Sawyer, Killer Kade, and the Bennington brothers joined them.

As soon as they're done talking to Rick, I'll try to get a little time alone with Chastity, or maybe the Stones, to find out what's going on. Preferably Chastity, since I know she got married by mistake and probably needs someone to talk to about it. I don't know that I can be much help in fixing the situation she's in, but I can definitely be there for her to talk to when she needs a friend.

Emerald and Amethyst are probably just there because they were in some of the pictures. I doubt either one of them actually went through with getting married. They like playing the field too much for that. Well, Em does anyway. Amethyst doesn't really flirt with the guys as much as Emerald. Then again, Emerald doesn't do much more than flirt either. So, I guess it's possible that they're both crushing on a couple of the other wrestlers and might have gotten married, too? And if so, I'll be there for them to talk to if they need me as well.

And who knows? If any of the three of them have the hots for their husbands, then maybe I can get Kay to join us and work some of that Heart's Destiny matchmaking magic for them the way they did with me and Dean to help them win over their men.

~~~

Sunday, October 13, 2019, Savannah, Georgia

After a week with double the amount of security they'd previously had, Dean was starting to get pissed that they still hadn't managed to trip up Allissa's stalker enough to catch him. He was also mad as hell that the pre-surveillance of the airports, hotels, and arenas had turned out to be a bust. He didn't understand how the Avington teams hadn't been able to find someone traveling to all the same cities they were, when they were looking both physically and electronically. Yeah, the possibility of the stalker driving instead of flying could make things harder to track, but surely someone should have been able to see him
~~~

at the hotels or arenas to set up the deliveries, even if he never went near the airports.

We're just gonna hafta do something to really piss him off to lure him out of hiding, Dean decided while sitting backstage, watching the show on the monitors while waiting for his turn in the ring. *Not having access to Allissa through Windy in Dead End was enough to get him to start writing letters. And seeing that Allissa and I are a couple was enough to get him to start making actual threats instead of just implying them. So, what's it gonna take to set him off enough to show his face?*

As Dean started brainstorming ideas, he flashed back to the photos that had started showing up over the last week. The more he thought about the pictures, the more the pieces started to click in his mind. *Those weren't all taken by the same person,* he realized, wondering if anyone around him could see the lightbulb turning on in his head. *Those were paparazzi pictures, probably taken by the same people who keep speculating in the dirt sheets about who got married in Vegas.*

Fuck! That bastard probably wouldn't have known about me and Allissa if he hadn't read whatever was posted on the gossip sites with those pictures. And that's how we're gonna catch the asshole!

"Linc! Wright!" Dean called out as he jumped up from his seat, startling Allissa beside him. He spun to find the bodyguards suddenly on alert with the two new guys, Bishop and Thor, flanking them.

Thor was actually short for Thoreson, which was the bodyguard's last name. When they'd been introduced the previous week, they'd explained how it was also his call sign when he was a SEAL. With more of the Avington team also shortening Lincoln's name down to just Linc, everyone in the GWA had started doing the same.

"I know how we can catch this bastard," Dean informed them, taking Allissa's hand and pulling her from her seat to step away from the rest of the GWA crew watching the monitors, so they could talk with the bodyguards without interrupting the show for their coworkers.

"How?" Wright looked at him skeptically.

"Those pictures he's been sending are all paparazzi shots he's been pulling from the dirt sheets," Dean explained. "He's not sticking around to take them himself. So I figured we've gotta piss him off enough to get him to stick around, so ya'll can catch him. And since we know he's reading the gossip sites, what better way to piss him off than to leak something happening at the next pay-per-view to the dirt sheets?"

"Issuing a statement about everyone being in Heart's Destiny for your boss's wedding didn't get his attention," Linc pointed out. "So, why do you think another press release will do it?"

"Because we're not gonna issue a press release and send it to the legit news outlets like they did for the wedding," Dean explained. "We're gonna leak it to the lowlife tabloids and wrestling gossip sites."

"Something like a special autograph signing where he might get a chance to nab Allissa?" Thor suggested, nodding his head in agreement with Dean's plan.

"No, that won't work because he knows we do autograph signings at every fan expo," Allissa argued, shaking her head.

"Not only that, Darlin', but you signing autographs isn't something that'll piss him off enough to slip up," Dean grinned at her. "But rumors about me planning to propose at the **Halloween Horror** show the same way James did at the **Saint Valentine's Day Massacre** show might."

"Like all your joking around about a Thanksgiving wedding isn't bad enough," Allissa rolled her eyes at him.

"I'm not really jokin' around about that, Darlin'," Dean informed her with a smile. "But the only people who know about those plans are our close friends and family, so I doubt your stalker is in the know enough to show up in Heart's Destiny during our Thanksgiving break."

"Seeing you guys as a couple was definitely the trigger that got him to escalate the threats," Linc acknowledged, nodding like he was starting to agree with the idea. "So leaking your proposal plans might be just what it takes to get him to make a move to stop it from happening."

"But we're really going to have to up the amount of security on you two from the moment it's leaked, not just that weekend in New Orleans like we currently have planned," Wright advised them.

"We should probably run this plan by Rick, Cage, and Byron, too," Allissa suggested, still looking unsure of the idea. "But in the middle of a show is not the time to discuss any of it with Rick."

Leah Mae Wright

Dean wasn't sure why Allissa was showing such trepidation at the thought of using a public proposal to lure out her stalker.

Is she afraid it might work, and she thinks it's too risky to lure him out?

Or is she upset by the thought of sharing a part of our lives that she wants to keep private with the rest of the world?

Fuck! I hope she's not having second thoughts about us as a couple and doesn't want me to propose at all.

He took a second to think of how to talk Allissa through her fears before addressing what she'd just said. *I'll leave that until we're alone in our room later.* "It's a house show, Darlin'. Since it's not televised and there aren't any try-out matches he has to watch tonight, Rick won't mind if we talk to him now."

Allissa glared at him for a moment before she finally sighed. "Okay." She then turned away from him to lead them over to where Rick was sitting with his wife and daughter in the classroom area they had set up backstage.

When the boss noticed the six of them walking toward him, he stood and motioned for Cage to join them. They all ended up moving over to an empty table in catering, sitting down where they were far enough away from everyone else in the company to have a private conversation.

"What's going on?" Rick directed his question to Allissa first, then turned to Dean when Allissa nodded in his direction.

"I have a plan to draw out the stalker," Dean explained, cringing as he realized he was going to have to be the one to suggest something that might endanger everyone in the company. *Fuck! Rick's gonna hate this idea when he realizes I'm planning on drawing the stalker to one of our shows, where his wife and daughter could be caught in the crossfire when the asshole comes after me to stop me from proposing.*

"Okay." Rick gave him a look that clearly told Dean he didn't want to wait to hear it. "What's the plan?"

"I wanna leak spoilers to the dirt sheets that I'm gonna propose to Allissa at the end of **Halloween Horror** the way James did back at **Massacre**." Dean could see the objection on Rick's face, so he cut his boss off before he could vocalize it. "Hear me out, Boss. Unlike when you issued a press release about your wedding, this'll just go to the gossip sites that he's been pulling pictures from, so we know he'll see it. And it will piss him off and get him to focus on me, so Allissa will be safe while we're taking him down."

"It'll definitely piss him off," Cage agreed. "But I don't know if it'll get him to focus on you. It might just make him rush his timeline for abducting Allissa."

"Yeah, but to get to her, he'll have to go through me and all these security guys." Dean bobbed his head in the direction of the Avington team on the other side of Allissa to his right while pointing with his thumb at the Avington team on his left. "And if he thinks he has to take me out before he can take her, then splitting his focus between the two of us will give these guys a better chance of catching him."

"What do you guys think of this plan?" Rick surveyed the bodyguards.

"It's definitely a valid idea to trigger him to escalate," Wright stated. "But I think we need to tighten up the security plan before implementing it."

"I'd feel better about it if you didn't have all the kids traveling with you for the next couple of weeks," Linc added. "But if we bring in a few more of our teams to cover the rest of your crew and your families and limit the time Allissa and Dean spend with everyone else in the company to just when they have to be in the arenas together, I think we can keep everyone safe. And we should be able to catch this guy when he goes after them."

Rick turned to look at Bishop and Thor, obviously wanting their opinions as well.

"I hate to say it, but the only way we're gonna catch this perp is by baiting him," Thor shrugged. "If we keep waiting for him to slip up without purposely triggering him, he could revert back to one of his earlier behaviors and harass her for years without ever giving us any clue who he is."

"It could turn into another long assignment like that actress we got stuck with for like three years," Bishop agreed with his partner, Thor, who groaned at the mention of a previous assignment they'd apparently been on together. "And while ya'll are a lot more fun to hang around than she was, I don't want to see you tormented by this any longer than you have to. And if you're brave enough to do what has to be done to stop it, I'm down for backing this play."

"And what does Byron think of this plan?" Rick looked back over at Dean and Allissa, who still sat silently looking down at the table, like she wanted to be anywhere but there at the moment.

"I wanted to run it by you first, Boss," Dean explained, running his hand up and down Allissa's back to try to calm her nerves. "I figured you've gotta sign off on us possibly pissing him off enough to attack, when your family and company could be caught in the crossfire, before we need to ask Byron to send more security and figure out how to leak the info to piss off the psycho."

"My family and company are already in the crossfire, whether you piss him off more or not." Rick shook his head. "But I appreciate you considering my opinion before taking action. If only all my employees showed me the same respect…"

Dean was pretty sure Rick's last comment was because of the stress he was under due to the Vegas wedding fiasco. He wished he knew what to say to help Rick out with that situation, but he was totally at a loss on that one, so he kept his mouth shut.

"But yes, I think you're right about this being the best course of action to try to trip up the stalker," Rick continued, jumping over whatever he'd stopped himself from saying about the other people he employed. "So, let's give Byron a call and set it up."

Unfortunately, Dean was called to the ring before they had the chance to make that call. *I should probably talk to Allissa a little more about this before we get the ball rolling, anyway. Maybe I can discuss it all with her tonight and call Byron tomorrow?*

~~~

Allissa felt bad for suggesting they wait until the next morning to call Byron after Dean had to step away from their impromptu meeting backstage to wrestle on the show. Yes, she thought they should wait to talk to him because he didn't need to be disturbed on a Sunday night for what was basically a strategy session. But the reason she gave Rick and the security team for delaying the call wasn't the real reason she wanted to wait to implement Dean's plan. Her biggest reason was that she was afraid of what the stalker might do to Dean if he thought they were really serious about one another.
~~~

Dean had obviously picked up on her fear, trying to soothe her through the talk with Rick by rubbing her back. But they hadn't had the chance to privately discuss his plan, or her anxiety about the fallout it could cause, because of the show going on that night and being surrounded by people until they got back to their hotel afterwards. Now that they were alone in their room, sitting on their bed with their late-night meal ordered from room service, Allissa knew she had to try to talk Dean out of poking the bear that was her stalker by taunting him.

He'd picked up the remote and started flipping channels on the television while they waited for their food to be delivered, but Allissa didn't have the patience to wait for him to find something for background noise before they talked. "Can you just turn the TV off while we talk?"

"Sure, Darlin', if that's what you want," Dean agreed, pushing the power button, and tossing the remote on the bedside table before turning to give her his undivided attention. "I figured we need to talk about why you tensed up when I mentioned my plan earlier, too."

"I know everyone seems to think pissing him off will give us the best chance of catching him," Allissa started, fighting back the tears that threatened to escape at the thought of what could happen to Dean if they went through with his asinine plan. "But I don't think I can do it."

"That's just it, Darlin', you don't have to do anything different from what you're already doin'. We're just setting a trap for him to walk into and planning for how to respond when he finally shows up."

"But what if you're right about this bringing his focus on you?" Allissa fretted, wrapping her arms around her middle to try to hold herself together. "What if he's able to set up somewhere and shoot you as we're walking into a hotel or arena without getting close enough for any of the bodyguards to catch him?"

"Darlin', considering the threats on those pictures, that's a possibility now, even if we don't do anything to try to get him to make a move." Dean reached over and pulled her onto his lap, wrapping her in his strong arms, as she started to cry at the thought of losing him like that. "That's why the bodyguards are always surrounding us when we're out in the open and looking up to check for any signs of a sniper.

Besides, I doubt he's capable of sniping me, when he's not even sticking around to take pictures of us."

Allissa continued to sob, clinging to Dean as she let her fear out through her tears.

"It's okay, Darlin'," Dean cooed, trying to soothe her. "From what he's said in his threats, we're ninety-nine-point-nine percent sure his big move will be trying to get close enough to kidnap you. And there's a chance this plan will convince him to back off, since he won't be able to get close to you without going through me."

"But what if he doesn't back off, though?" Allissa whimpered, still worried. "I don't want to risk you getting hurt if he shows up armed to kill you before kidnapping me."

"Then I'll show him the skills that earned me the all-state wrestling championship and 4H sharpshooter awards multiple years in a row by disarming him and shooting him with his own gun," Dean boasted as she lifted her head from his chest to look in his eyes. From his expression, she could see that he really had won those titles and wasn't just being cocky to try and joke his way past her fears. "And at least this way, I feel like I'm doing something to protect you, instead of just twiddling my thumbs while waiting for him to come try to take you from me."

"He's not going to take me from you," Allissa assured him, even though she wasn't completely confident in her own ability to escape should someone try to grab her.

"Damn straight he's not," Dean grinned, wiping her tears from her cheeks. "I may not have convinced you to marry me yet, but I'm not gonna give up. Or let some pipsqueak stalker steal you away from me. We're gonna be together forever."

"I'm not saying yes to a fake proposal, either," Allissa asserted, hating the thought of this stalker interfering with their current angles by waiting to see if Dean followed through with the proposal he wanted to leak to the dirt sheets. "So if he doesn't make a move before *Halloween Horror*, don't you dare propose after my title defense."

"Darlin', when I propose, it won't be fake. It'll be one-hundred percent real and not in the middle of the ring with all the fans watching. Backstage with our family and friends watching, maybe." Dean bobbed his head from side to side and grinned at her before straightening his expression to something much more serious. "But I won't break kayfabe in the middle of a show. I know how important your career is to you, and I love you too much to risk screwing up your current angle like that."

Did he just say he loves me? Allissa floundered for a moment, letting his words sink in as Dean continued to elaborate on how his plan to piss off her stalker was just to leak a rumor to try to trigger him to make a move, not his actual plan to propose to her. He went on with his reasoning, showing her that he really believed they were safe with the Avington Security teams protecting them, and leaking something to piss off the stalker would only speed up the timeline, so they could get it over with sooner rather than later.

When he finally paused in his diatribe to take a breath, Allissa smiled at him and returned the three little words that meant the most to her in his long-winded speech. "I love you, too, Dean."

"Damn, Darlin', that wasn't how I meant to tell you that for the first time," Dean groaned as he leaned over and brushed his lips over hers briefly. "I planned to tell you over a romantic dinner the next time we have a night off to go on a real date. But, fuck, I'm glad I let it slip out now, 'cause I really needed to hear you say it, too. I love you, Allissa. And now that I know you love me too, I'm gonna start planning that proposal, so maybe we can make that Thanksgiving wedding."

Allissa was starting to believe he wasn't joking about marrying her the way she'd believed for the last three months. And truth be told, she'd realized in that same time frame that life was too short and unpredictable to waste time by planning a long engagement, especially when she wanted the fairy-tale ending with him.

"As long as it's a hundred-percent real proposal," Allissa quipped with a grin at him as she wrapped her arms around his neck and leaned in for another kiss. "I just might say yes."

As soon as Allissa told him she might say yes to his proposal, Dean wanted to get down on one knee and ask her to marry him. If he'd have brought his great-grandmother's ring, which Meemaw had promised to give him for Allissa after she had it cleaned, with him when they left after their Labor Day break, he would have right then and there. Since his proposal would have been interrupted by their late-night meal being delivered, Dean was almost glad Meemaw hadn't had time to get it back from the jewelers before the last time he and Allissa left town to go on tour with the GWA.

As they ate and talked about what she wanted to do for her birthday, which was only ten days away, Dean started putting together his plan for how to pop the question. He knew he needed to do it soon if he wanted to pull off a Thanksgiving wedding, so she'd have time to pick out a dress from all the pictures their mothers had been sending her for the last month.

I should probably call everyone back home first thing in the morning to see when they can fly out to witness the proposal, he thought as they were brushing their teeth to get ready for bed. *I know she doesn't want me to propose during a show, but with as much as wrestling means to both of us and how close we are to our GWA family, I wanna do it backstage when they can all witness it, too.*

Should I get the family all here in time for me to propose on her birthday? No, even though I know our families are both open-minded when it comes to sex, I don't want to give her sex toys for her birthday when they'd probably insist on celebrating together. Not that I plan on giving her those things at the party backstage that night, but if they're in town, they'll keep us from goin' shopping for them that afternoon.

Maybe I can ask her at the fan expo for **Halloween Horror**? *That would give our families a couple of days to hang out with us and finalize the wedding plans, so they can set it all up when they get back home, too. Yeah, that's the ticket. Backstage at the fan expo. And maybe her mom won't grab my ass at this one.*

I'll have to ask Mom and Dad if they can get the grandparents to all sneak away that weekend and bring Allissa's mom with them. Hell, it'll probably be better if I call and ask each of them individually. And when I make those calls, I'd better remind Meemaw to bring me the ring. I don't want to screw up the perfect proposal by not having it.

With his proposal mostly planned out in his head, Dean relaxed and finally focused on his favorite daily activity — showing Allissa how much he loved her. As soon as they finished rinsing their teeth, Dean scooped Allissa up in his arms and carried her from the ensuite bathroom before they could strip down for a communal shower before bed.

"What are you doing?" Allissa squealed, wrapping her arms around his neck.

"Carryin' my future bride to bed for a little honeymoon practice." Dean wagged his eyebrows suggestively as he grinned at her.

"You can't call me your future bride until you actually propose," Allissa laughed as he dropped her on the king-sized bed.

"Don't worry, Darlin', I'll be proposin' soon enough to go ahead and start callin' you my future bride. I just won't call you my fiancée until I put that ring on your finger."

"And quit being a neanderthal," Allissa admonished, playfully pouting up at him.

"Ah, but I thought you liked it when I'm a neanderthal, Darlin'." Dean pounced on the bed, landing with his hands and knees straddling her and the bulk of his body over the top of her. "You know, since my inner caveman is the one who keeps coming up with the creative and adventurous ways to make love to you."

"It's your inner caveman that came up with all those positions in your home gym?" Allissa arched an eyebrow at him as her palms brushed over his biceps. "And keeps finding empty rooms at the arenas?"

"Oh, yeah, Darlin'." Dean slowly lowered his upper body, eager to taste her.

"And here all this time, I thought those were all times when you were thinking with your dick brain," Allissa quipped with a grin as she pushed him back and kept him from kissing her just yet. "Caveman thinking would be more of the toss-me-over-your-shoulder-and-carry-me-off-to-have-your-way-with-me type of thoughts, like dropping me on the bed just now. Not trying new positions and places to see which makes me come the most."

"Damn, Darlin', you might be right," Dean admitted with a smile. "All this time, I've been thinking I had this inner caveman that just wanted to claim you, when it's been my dick brain doin' the thinkin' all along. But now that you've enlightened me, I think we should let him have what he wants."

"Him? Your dick is a separate entity from you?"

"Well, he does have his own brain," Dean shrugged. Or rather half-shrugged, since he was supporting his bodyweight on his hands, so he didn't squish her since he weighed more than double her bodyweight. "So, he should have his own identity."

"Oh, yeah, I guess I can concede that point. And what does Aquaman want?" Allissa giggled as she gave his dick the nickname she'd jokingly called him a couple of times.

Unable to hold back the reference to a water activity after she'd chosen the Aquaman moniker for his cock, Dean chuckled as he told her, "to go muff diving in you, Darlin'."

"I thought that term meant oral," Allissa laughed as she ran her hand down his torso until she cupped his cock. "Aquaman can't really do that, can he?"

"Oh, I plan on eating your pussy, too, Darlin'," Dean replied as he rocked his hips to hump her hand, wishing he'd thought to wait until they were undressed before bringing her back to the bedroom. "But if you're gonna call my cock Aquaman, then we're gonna hafta change the meaning of any kind of diving to be something he can do. So from now on, muff diving and cave diving are both references to my dick in your pussy."

Since she'd told him about the way she and her mom changed the meaning of pussy and balls to be more reflective of the actual toughness of women's vaginas and the delicate nature of men's balls, he was pretty sure she'd be open to having their own meanings for all kinds of sexual terms. But he still relaxed a little when she finally agreed and pulled him down for a kiss to seal the deal.

"Finally," he growled just before plunging his tongue into her mouth to tangle with hers. They kissed for several long minutes before he reluctantly broke away to confess his lack of forethought. "I screwed up and didn't think to wait until we were naked…"

He let his sentence trail off as Allissa laughed and pushed him off of her. "Then we'd better get up and fix that botched move."

Dean flopped over on the bed as Allissa kipped-up to stand beside it. She impressed him with how she pulled off the move, since he needed a much harder surface to push off of than the bed to be able to do the same maneuver. "Fuck, I love how athletic you are, Darlin'."

"I thought you loved my flexibility," Allissa teased as she pulled off her top.

"That, too," Dean agreed as he pushed himself up to a seated position on the side of the bed to start removing his own clothes.

It didn't take them long before they were both undressed, and Dean was ready to toss Allissa back on the bed.

"Wait!" Allissa stopped him just as he reached for her waist to pick her up, looking up at him with a nervous expression as she pulled his hands from her body and pushed him back onto the bed. "I, um, have something else I want to try tonight."

"Okay," Dean drawled, imagining she wanted to try one of the positions with her on top that they hadn't done as often. "How do I need to lay for you to be able to try…whatever it is you want to try?"

"You don't need to lay down at all." Allissa shook her head as she bit her bottom lip. "Just sit there on the side of the bed and spread your legs."

"Alright, Darlin'," Dean grinned at her as he got into the position she requested, imagining her straddling him and riding him in the seated position.

Allissa surprised him by dropping to her knees between his feet and running her hands up his thighs as she dipped her head toward his cock.

"Whoa, Darlin'. You don't have to do that. I know it's a trigger for you," Dean protested, running his hands through her hair, and lightly tugging it to stop her forward momentum, even though Aquaman was eager to feel the wetness of her mouth.

"I know I don't have to, Dean." Allissa looked up at him with nothing but love shining in her blue-gray eyes, as she cupped his balls with one hand and started stroking his shaft with the other. "I want to. I want to wipe away those memories of being teased for sucking a banana with much better ones of giving you pleasure by sucking your cock. I trust you not to make me feel bad, even if I'm really bad at this and you have to teach me how to do it better."

"Fuck, Darlin', I can't say no to you ever, but especially when you have such a wonderful reason for what you want to do. And I guarantee I won't think you're bad at it, no matter what you do. Hell, I'll love it, even if you only take one lick and decide you never want to do it again."

"You want me to lick it like a lollipop?" Allissa grinned up at him.

"I want you to do whatever the fuck you want, Darlin'," Dean assured her as he released her hair, placing his hands behind him on the bed, so she had total control. "You have complete control of this, but you have to promise me you'll stop immediately if it feels like too much."

"I will, Dean," Allissa promised with a smile. "But I don't think it will be too much, even though you're a lot bigger than a banana." With that, she stopped talking and closed her lips over his crown, slowly sucking him to the back of her mouth while continuing to stroke the half of his shaft that couldn't fit in her mouth with her hand.

"Fuck, Allissa, your mouth feels like heaven," Dean groaned as his dick twitched from the way she ran her tongue over his frenum piercing as she pulled back to only hold the head in her mouth.

They maintained eye contact as she gave him the most sensual blow job of his life. Dean wanted to maintain that visual connection, so he would know if she was truly enjoying the experience, or just doing it because she thought he wanted it. When he saw nothing but arousal in her gaze as she moved up and down his length, Dean knew she was enjoying it almost as much as he was.

"Touch yourself, Darlin'," he commanded, wanting her to feel as much physical pleasure as he was at that moment. "Play with your clit while you suck my cock. Get yourself wet and ready to ride me, 'cause I'm not gonna last much longer before I need to be in your tight little pussy."

Allissa's red lips wrapped around his cock as she leisurely sucked him, while twirling her tongue around his piercings, was the most erotic sight he'd ever envisioned up to that point. But when she followed his instructions and started fingering her creamy cunt at the same time, she surpassed even his wildest dirty dreams.

"Fuck, Darlin'," Dean moaned as his balls started to tingle at the sight of her juices running down her thighs. "Are you wet for me? Are you turned on so much you're dripping from suckin' my dick?"

Allissa nodded at the same time she sucked him in, allowing his head to push into the tight passage of her throat slightly.

"Fuck, Darlin'," Dean groaned. Worried the barbell in his apadravya piercing was too long to go that far back safely, he gently gripped her head and pulled her back. "You've gotta stop, or I'm gonna come, and I don't wanna come until I'm in your pussy."

Allissa didn't have to be told twice, smacking her lips as she pulled off his dick and pulled her hand from her pussy. She quickly stood, gripped his shoulders for balance, and started to straddle him.

Dean didn't waste any time lining his cock up with her slit, so she could slide down his length as they fused their mouths together in a passionate kiss. He could taste his precum on her tongue and wished he'd had the chance to eat her pussy earlier, so their flavors could meld in their mouths.

Thrusting up into Allissa in this position felt more like bouncing on the bed while doing pulsing squats than his normal controlled movements when they made love. But somehow, they managed to sync up his bouncing thrusts with her rocking hips as she rode him to bring them both to the brink within seconds.

Dean considered how they were always so in tune with one another in bed, or wherever they made love, as just more evidence that they were made for one another. Even though their size difference and the circumstances of their upbringing made them appear to be a mismatched pair, whenever they were together, he always felt like they fit together perfectly.

And he didn't just think that when they were putting tab A in slot B and connecting their bodies like two perfectly matched puzzle pieces. They also felt like two peas in a pod when they were fully dressed and talking about wrestling, training for wrestling, exploring the places they traveled, trying new foods, and even discussing their beliefs, morals, and ethics.

Allissa was the piece of his soul that he hadn't realized he'd been missing until he met her. And Dean was determined to show her how much he loved her every day for the rest of his life.

Starting with making sure she was fully satisfied sexually, multiple times, before he found his release. Needing to see her fly, Dean gripped her hips to take control of their mating. He modified his bouncing thrusts to grind his pubic bone over her clit just after his piercing brushed her G-spot, knowing the dual stimulation would send her soaring faster than either one alone.

Allissa's nails dug into his shoulders as she arched her back, breaking their kiss as she started to come. Dean loved the feel of her scratching him, knowing she was leaving marks that would be visible to the world when he wrestled on the live televised show in a couple of days.

"Oh, gawd, Dean!" Allissa cried out as her inner walls spasmed around his cock.

"That's it, Darlin'. Come on my cock." Dean continued bouncing, using his hold on her hips to lift her up and slide her back down on his dick when she lost control of her bodily movements as her whole body convulsed in orgasm.

The look of bliss on her face as she came was the most beautiful thing Dean had ever witnessed. It took all his willpower not to come with her, the tight clutch of her cunt desperately close to milking him of his release. She continued chanting his name until she collapsed, resting her head on his shoulder as she caught her breath.

"Fuck, Darlin', ya can't go into that orgasm coma yet," Dean chuckled as he continued to fuck her through her recovery period. "I need to watch ya come a couple more times first."

"You really have a thing for watching, don't you?" Allissa lifted her head and smiled at him as they locked eyes once more. "What else do you like to watch besides me coming and your cum dripping out of my pussy?"

"I like to watch your tits bounce when you ride me," Dean confessed with a grin as he slowed down their rhythm to make sure she was completely recovered before pushing her to another climax. "And the way your pussy stretches to take my cock. And of course, I love watchin' every part of you, no matter what you're doin', even when we're not makin' love. But my absolute favorite thing to watch is the way your eyes light up whenever you get excited about somethin'."

"Are you tryin' to sweet talk me, Dean Hunter?" Allissa feigned a Southern accent as she ran her fingers through his hair. "'Cause that's not really necessary to get in my panties, seein' as how you're already there."

"No, Darlin'," Dean chuckled as he added a little bit of a swirl to his hip movement to tease her G-spot in a different way with his dick jewelry. "It's not considered sweet talkin' when it's a true statement. Besides, I learned the first day we met that sweet talkin' wouldn't work on you."

"Oh, Dean," Allissa moaned in response to the new stimulation, not responding to his last statement. "I don't know what you're doing differently, but keep doing it."

"Just makin' sure I'm takin' care of you, Darlin'," Dean assured her as he repeated the swirling movement with a little faster pace.

It didn't take long for Allissa to figure out how to writhe on him to enhance the feel, quickly hitting her second peak. "Oh, Dean, yes, Dean!"

"Fuck, Allissa, I can't hold back this time," Dean groaned, losing control of his orgasm as her inner walls pulsed around his cock.

"Don't hold back," Allissa demanded. "Come with me."

"Fuck, yes, Allissa!" Dean thrust up into her one last time, burying himself balls-deep as he shot his load inside her.

He was pretty sure he felt her cervix at the tip of his cock and knew that he would have just gotten her pregnant, if he hadn't seen her take her pill that morning. He felt the slightest bit of disappointment at the realization that he wouldn't get to see her round with his child anytime soon. But he quickly shut it down, knowing it would eventually happen, just not before she achieved all her career dreams.

"I love you, Allissa," he shouted as the final jet of his jizz left his body.

"I love you, too, Dean." Allissa pressed her lips to his. They kissed for several long moments as they recovered. When they finally had to break the lip lock to breathe, Allissa gave him an ornery grin. "Now carry me to the shower for round two before we clean up for bed."

"You got it, Darlin'," Dean agreed as he wrapped his arms around her, lifting her as he stood from the bed. He carried her back to the bathroom, leaving his still-hard cock inside her as a plug until they were in the shower, so he wouldn't miss seeing a single drop of their combined bodily fluids dripping from her pussy.

Chapter Twenty

Allissa couldn't believe they'd made it all the way to the fan expo leading into the **Halloween Horror** show without her stalker making a move in response to Dean's proposal speculation hitting the dirt sheets. She was beginning to think she'd been nervous about the risk associated with pissing him off for absolutely no reason. She hadn't received any new packages or letters from the stalker since the day after the story broke a week before, so she was wondering if the whole nightmare was finally over. *Could we have really gotten so lucky that the story made him realize he needs to back off?*

Allissa wasn't sure if she was happy with that possible outcome or not. On the one hand, she'd be glad if it was finally over. But on the other hand, she worried that he would just move on to terrorize another woman because he hadn't been reprimanded for the bad behavior with her. With everyone still being on high alert around her, though, Allissa felt like her anxiety was only amplified as she struggled with her conflicting emotions about the potential end to her stalking situation, which was why she was jumpy as she walked backstage with Dean after doing the first round of autograph signings at the fan expo.

The way Dean had suspiciously disappeared from their room early that morning hadn't helped, either. He never left her alone in their room like that unless he had to go to the lobby of the hotel to meet a food delivery driver. But they had ordered room service for breakfast that morning, so she was at a loss as to where he might have gone without her.

Hell, he even took me with him to pick out my birthday presents the other day, so him taking off like that doesn't make any sense.

The memory of her first foray into an adult toy store to pick out a few things for them to try out together brought a smile to her face, momentarily overriding her curiosity about Dean's mysterious errand that morning. They hadn't gotten too crazy with their choices, just a few things they could each put in or on under their clothes to tease each other on their daily flights and a couple of things to try that would increase both of their stimulation when they were joined during lovemaking. So far, Allissa had loved trying out every single one of her birthday presents from Dean.

If only he'd stayed in bed to try out that vibrating cock ring with the clit stimulator this morning, instead of sneaking off on his "errand" that he won't tell me about.

Allissa sighed as she realized she was becoming a clingy girlfriend. She hated the feeling of needing to know where he was twenty-four-seven. *What the hell happened to the independent woman I used to be, who loved spending most of my time off on my own? Oh yeah, I got a stalker and turned into a sniveling coward, who can't stand to be without Dean glued to my side to make me feel safe.*

I wonder how long it will be before I feel more like my old self? If this stalker has really backed off the way I think he has, then surely it won't take me too long to get over the fear. Right? Not that I want to go back to avoiding Dean or anything like that. But I'm sure his disappearing act this morning was partially because I'm smothering him with needing to be with him constantly. So I should probably start trying to work through my issues to back off a little and give him the space he needs.

Hell, I'm going to have to learn how to live again with the space I used to need. Maybe I should book some extra therapy sessions in the next couple of weeks, instead of waiting until my appointment next month?

She was so lost in her thoughts that, when they got to catering to grab a mid-morning snack between sessions at the fan expo, Allissa was surprised by seeing the area packed with practically everyone who worked for the GWA, and a good portion of the extra security there for the weekend. *What on earth? Shouldn't some of these people be out taking their turn at the expo?*

And why are Kay, Anthony, and their kids here? The flight crew has the day off, since we're here until Monday morning, and they haven't come to one of these since Randi's first weekend as the Dangerous Twins manager last year.

She started to ask Dean what was going on, but she didn't get the chance. Just as they got to the middle of the crowded space, Dean pulled her to a stop, taking both of her hands in his as he dropped to one knee.

Oh, shit! He was serious about proposing soon! I thought he was just joking around like he's been doing for the past few months.

Allissa's fears about being a clingy girlfriend immediately came to mind. *How am I going to get over that if we're planning a wedding? I can't very well distance myself from him a little and say yes to his proposal. Can I?*

Won't marrying him just make me even more clingy and dependent on him?

"Allissa, Darlin'," Dean started, as Allissa's eyes welled up with tears. "I fell head over heels in love with you the first time I saw you. And over the last year of getting to know you, I've just fallen deeper in love with you each and every day. That very first day, I was worried about seeing you wrestle because I couldn't protect you from getting hurt in the ring. Then I saw you steal the show during your try-out match and felt like the biggest asshole on the planet for doubting your talent and thinking you'd ever need me to protect you. You've continued to show me, day after day, that you are the strongest woman I've ever met and don't really need me for anything."

Allissa didn't agree with that statement, feeling like she'd proven the exact opposite with the whole stalker situation. But Dean didn't even give her a moment to open her mouth and object, continuing with his obviously heartfelt sentiments.

"You've shown determination and resilience both professionally and personally that far exceeds anything I've ever witnessed. You've overcome obstacles that would have prevented anyone else from achieving their dreams the way you have, and you've done it with the utmost grace."

Allissa looked around and noticed it wasn't just their GWA family watching them. She saw her mom and Kandi standing with Dean's family, and realized that his errand that morning had to have something to do with getting them all there to witness his proposal.

Oh, Dean! You're totally not playing fair with bringing them all here now, knowing I'd want them all to be a part of our special moment.

"For the last five months, you've given me the great honor of being the man you lean on when you need to gather your strength to continue kickin' ass and achieving your dreams. I know you don't really need me for that or anything else, but I'd still like to be there for you every day for the rest of our lives. I feel like I've finally found my place in the world when we're together, and like a piece of me is missing when I'm not right by your side. I don't want either of us to ever feel like we're missing pieces again, Darlin', so I wanna fuse us together forever. Will you, Allissa Victoria Walters, allow me the honor of standing by your side for the rest of our lives, cheering you on as you conquer all your dreams, holding you in my arms when you need to recharge your strength, and being your tag-team partner in all aspects of life? Will you marry me?"

Allissa couldn't contain the tears that started pouring down her face. She knew some people would say they were moving too fast and couldn't really build a relationship that would last the test of time when they started out in the midst of dealing with a stalker. She knew some people would consider her weak for feeling like she needed to lean on Dean to get through life.

But like Dean had taught her, living her life was a case of mind over matter. The people who minded how she lived her life didn't matter. Those people would never know the truth behind the words Dean had just spoken. They wouldn't realize how right he was in describing how a hug from him felt like it recharged her ability to face the harder aspects of life. And they wouldn't know how she'd never felt more at home than she'd felt in his arms, no matter where they were in the world at the time.

Screw giving us both back our space! I want to spend my life interlocked with him, the other half of my heart, so we can lean on each other to get through the toughest times of life and love each other through to the other side.

"Yes, Dean," Allissa sobbed, pulling her hands from his to throw her arms around his neck. "I can't wait to be your wife for life!"

Dean wrapped her in his big, strong arms as he stood, picking her up as their mouths collided in an explosive kiss. Allissa instinctively wrapped her legs around his waist as they sealed their engagement.

They didn't realize how inappropriate their kissing was becoming until they were interrupted by the catcalls of their friends and family.

"Ya'll need to save that for the honeymoon," Anthony called out. "When you don't have an audience full of kids."

"Yeah, go to your room, Uncle Dean," Maria added, causing a roar of laughter from the rest of the people around them. "You're still too young for canoodling and you don't get a waiver of the age requirement until after you get married."

Allissa couldn't help but laugh as Dean released her and placed her down on her feet.

"We already gave them a waiver," Mandi informed the little girl. "So they can start working on making ya'll some more cousins."

"They should probably still wait until they don't have an audience, though," her husband, David, corrected her.

"Please don't hold my crazy family against me and try to back out of sayin' yes," Dean chuckled.

"We're gonna need to swipe Lissie's pills while we're here if you want them to start giving us grandbabies already," Windy announced.

"You say that like my mom isn't the craziest among our family members," Allissa chortled before turning in the direction of their families. "And no, Mom, you're not stealing my pills. We're adopting if we want kids before I'm finished with my wrestling career."

"Enough with the talk about grandbabies for now," Joan interjected, hugging the two of them as the crowd started coming in closer to offer their best wishes. "Congratulations. Now you don't have an excuse to put us off on the wedding plans any longer. So, we need to know which dress you like best before we head home Monday morning."

"Oh, um, okay," Allissa sputtered, returning the hug from Dean's grandmother.

"Oh, goodness, Dean," Meemaw exclaimed as she approached them to offer her congratulations. "You didn't even give her the ring!"

"Boy, you made us get up and fly out here at the ass crack of dawn, so you could get that ring before she woke up. And you didn't even show it to her when you popped the question?" PopPop shook his head at Dean. "I thought I taught you better than that."

"Yeah, I kinda needed both hands to hold her here when she looked like she was about to bolt," Dean explained as he reached into his pocket and pulled out a vintage diamond ring in a gold setting. "Then I got on a roll and forgot to pull it outta my pocket."

Dean held the ring out to Allissa as he reached for her left hand. "This was my great-grandmother's ring."

"From her second husband," Meemaw interjected, as Dean slid it on her finger. "My daddy was a poor soldier and couldn't afford an engagement ring. But I thought you might like to have something of hers since you understand her story so well."

"It's perfect," Allissa agreed, smiling at Meemaw before holding her hand out to examine the ring resting on her finger. "And a perfect fit. How'd you do that?"

"I helped with that," Windy informed her as she squeezed in beside Allissa and put her arm around her shoulders.

"How did you know my ring size?" Allissa was shocked that her mother knew her ring size when she didn't even know it.

"Because you're my daughter," Windy shrugged. "I know all your sizes because I was the same size as you before you were born. Which is why I'm glad to hear you're adopting, so the hormones won't mess with your weight and shorten your career."

Thankfully, their friends crowding in to offer their best wishes prevented them from getting into a long discussion about children and pregnancy and their impact on the careers of women wrestlers. Allissa had a feeling Shauna and Holland would both prove her mom wrong about pregnancy weight gain possibly being an issue in her career, since both women had joined the GWA roster after having their children.

It was actually because of talking to her coworkers that Allissa wanted to wait to go through pregnancy and birth. They had both trained with their husbands and been well on their way to establishing themselves as wrestlers when they ended up having to take time off from the independent promotions they worked with during their first pregnancies.

Holly had gone back to training as soon as the doctor cleared her after having her daughter Addison, but said she felt like she was starting over from scratch trying to work her way up in the business. So when her husband got his break to start with the GWA, Holly decided to try for the second baby they wanted before pursuing her own career.

Shauna was actually pregnant with her daughter, Baylee, when Vaughn signed on with the GWA. Seeing the family atmosphere of the company firsthand, they decided to start trying for their second child as soon as the doctor cleared her, so she didn't have to take time off from her career twice.

Weight gain after having babies hadn't been a problem for either of them restarting their careers with the GWA. The high activity level of training for professional wrestling clearly helped combat the hormonal changes in a woman's body from pregnancy that made it seem harder to lose weight after having kids. So Allissa wasn't worried about gaining weight causing issues with her career.

She was more concerned with being forced to take nine months off from wrestling when she was just starting out on the most financially lucrative time of her life. She wanted to be well-established and have substantial savings to be able to provide for her family before she had to take time off. She also wanted to be recognized as one of the company's main eventers before taking that break from performing, so she wouldn't have to start over from scratch, like the other women she knew. But right after getting engaged wasn't the time to explain that to her mom.

"Alright, guys, I hate to break this celebration up, but we do need to get on with the next session of the fan expo," Rick announced, slapping Dean on the back after offering his congratulations.

Several of their coworkers headed out of the backstage area, while Allissa, Dean, and the rest of the group that had been out on the arena floor with them for the last hour grabbed a bite to eat with their families.

<div style="text-align:center">~~~</div>

Dean had just convinced their families to meet them back at the hotel after the fan expo to continue going over wedding plans, when Allissa insisted on going to freshen up in the locker room before going out for their next session. Thinking he'd take the few minutes when he couldn't stay glued to her side to empty his bladder, Dean headed into the men's locker room at the same time, knowing the four bodyguards assigned to them would stand right outside the locker room doors to keep her safe while the extra guards there for the weekend maintained the perimeter and watched over the rest of their GWA family.

He'd been surprised that the stalker had stopped sending Allissa threats right after the story of his planned proposal the next day had hit the internet. But he didn't think the bastard was truly gone from their lives the way Allissa wanted to believe. Deep in his gut, he knew the psycho had one final play to make, and he expected it to happen the next day at the **Halloween Horror** show.

There's no way he's going to walk away and give me the opportunity to publicly claim her at the end of the show tomorrow night. So I'm sure he'll try to take me out either before the show or while I'm in the ring. Or maybe he'll try to grab her then. Fuck! Maybe I shouldn't have suggested pissing him off. Now I've put the fans in danger of what this jackass might try, as well as Allissa and everyone else in the GWA.

"Whaddya know, he can take a piss without the Avengers babysittin' him," Liam quipped as he and Dion joined him at the urinals.

"The Avengers?" Dean chuckled as he finished and zipped his fly, wondering what Red was gonna pop off with next.

"Yeah, I've decided your bodyguard team is the new secret identity of the Avengers," Liam explained, as Dean walked over to the row of sinks to wash his hands. "Since your brother is named after Iron Man, and the two new guys are Thor and Hulk, it was easy to see through their cover."

"It's Thor and Bishop, not Thor and Hulk," Dean chuckled as he soaped up his hands. "Though I suppose he is big enough to play the Hulk without much CGI work needed."

Before either Liam or Dion could reply, they heard a blood-curdling scream coming from the direction of the women's locker room. "Fuck!" Dean turned to go check on Allissa without even thinking about needing to rinse his hands.

"Wait!" Dion stopped him, having just walked over to the sink beside Dean.

"That bastard is making his move to kidnap Allissa. I'm not gonna wait to go rescue her!" Dean tried to push past Dion, only to be stopped by both members of Red Velvet holding him back.

"I'm not tellin' you not to go rescue her," Dion argued, nodding his head toward the back of the locker room, where the training rooms were located in this arena. "I'm just tryin' to get you to go in the other way. The bodyguards will all be going in through the main doors from backstage. But if we go in through the training rooms, we can surround him."

"And unless you plan on blinding him by gouging his eyes out with soapy hands, you might want to rinse off, so you can get a good grip on him," Liam added.

Dean did a cursory swipe of his hands under the faucet before brushing his hands over his pants to half-ass dry them, as the three of them ran out the back door of the locker room. Since there wasn't an athletic event going on at the time, the training rooms were all empty as they ran through them to get to the door leading into the women's locker room.

They slowed their movements then, hoping to sneak up behind the stalker and assess the situation before taking action. Not that three six-foot-plus professional wrestlers could really sneak anywhere.

"Please, you don't have to do this." Dean heard Allissa pleading, as they made their way past the showers at the back of the locker room.

"Lower the weapon and turn yourself in, man," Linc commanded, trying to settle the situation peacefully.

"No, you lower your weapons, so Allissa and I can leave," the psycho countered as Dean, Liam, and Dion came around a bank of lockers to see the situation unfolding near the bathroom stalls.

Dean could see the top of Allissa's head over the shoulder of a balding man with salt and pepper hair around the sides and back of his head, who looked to be an inch or two under six feet tall. From the back, he couldn't be sure he didn't recognize him. But he was certain that it wasn't Ron Langston, since the hair color and build of their bodies didn't match. This guy was short and portly, while Ron was a couple of inches taller, way thinner, and had a full head of lighter brown hair.

He was waving a gun around and apparently holding Allissa in front of him like a human shield to keep the bodyguards from shooting him, since all of them also had their weapons drawn. The bodyguards were all standing in the area just past the toilet stalls, where Dean assumed the sinks and mirrors were since the rest of the layout seemed to be exactly like the men's locker room, with the exception of having two rows of toilet stalls instead of one, since a row of urinals took the place of the second row of toilets in the men's locker room.

"We're not going to let you leave here with Allissa," Wright argued with the stalker. "So, if you want to walk out of here at all, you need to lower your weapon and let her go."

Instead of following the directions of the bodyguards, the bastard started ranting about how he'd known he'd met *The One* when he first met his lady love over twenty-five years ago, and no matter how many times she tried to hide by changing her name, he wasn't going to let anyone keep them apart. Dean used the time the stalker was ranting to his advantage as he started moving slowly toward the stalker's back. If he could get close enough to grab the gun with his right hand and get his left arm around the guy's neck, he knew he could end the standoff without anyone firing a shot.

The Avington team continued to try to talk the bastard down as Dean motioned for Dion and Liam to flank him, hoping one of them could get Allissa out of harm's way while the other helped him subdue the gun-wielding asshole. Unfortunately, when Dean tried to use the signals that they sometimes used in the ring when they had to change up a sequence of moves to direct Dion and Liam, the bodyguards didn't understand them. At least, that was why Dean assumed they tried to wave him off and gave away his position to the psycho still brandishing a gun too close to Allissa.

"Who's back there?" The stalker spun around as he screeched out the question, bringing Allissa with him.

Allissa's eyes widened in fear when she realized the stalker now had his gun aimed directly at Dean. "No, don't shoot him. I'll do whatever you want. Just don't hurt Dean."

"Like hell you will, Darlin'," Dean growled as he gave the go signal for Liam and Dion and lunged for the weapon, planning to twist it out of the stalker's hand.

When he lunged, Allissa elbowed the asshole in the gut and twisted out of his hold around her waist. Her unexpected movement caused him to spin with her and flail his arm out to the side in the opposite direction of where Dean was reaching, just as he pulled the trigger. With the change in position of the gun in the stalker's hand, Dean grasped at empty space, just before Liam tackled him to the ground.

Dean heard four more loud bangs of obvious gunfire as he and Liam crashed into the door of one of the toilet stalls. He got lucky that the door wasn't locked and gave way for him to take the back bump on the floor without injury, other than having the wind knocked out of him by Liam landing on top of him.

When he looked across the room at Allissa and Dion where they crashed into the other row of stalls, however, he realized they hadn't all gotten so lucky. Between them, the stalker laid there bleeding out from the four gunshot wounds inflicted by the Avington Security team. And Allissa was trapped under Dion, who was out cold and bleeding from his head.

"Fuck!" Dean screamed as he pushed Liam off of him to scramble over to Allissa and Dion. "Allissa, Darlin'!"

Thor and Bishop secured the stalker and his gun while Wright called for assistance from the police and an ambulance. Linc helped Dean and Liam as they carefully rolled Dion off of Allissa to assess their injuries, hoping they didn't exacerbate any they already had from the shot the stalker got off and their impact with the ground.

"I'm not hurt," Allissa assured him as Dean ran his hands over her, trying to feel for any injuries. "But Dion hit his head really hard on that door frame."

"Yeah, that blood's not coming from where he hit his head," Linc informed them as he applied pressure to the other side of Dion's head from where Allissa was pointing. "He was also grazed by the bullet the perp got off when you all went rogue instead of letting us keep trying to negotiate."

It didn't take long before the space was full of police officers and paramedics, who quickly took over assessing injuries. Once they got Dion loaded up and on his way to the hospital, Dean insisted they check Allissa out while he held her on his lap, not wanting to let go of her for a second if he didn't have to.

"I'm so sorry, Darlin'," Dean choked out, feeling guilty as fuck for the way the confrontation with her stalker ended up happening. "If I'd have known it'd go down like this, I never would have suggested tryin' to piss him off to get him to make a move."

"This is not your fault, Dean." Allissa twisted around in his arms to cup his face in both her small hands. "Kidnapping me was always his plan, so it could have happened just like this, whether you tried to piss him off or not. So don't you dare take an ounce of blame for how it happened. You, Dion, and Liam are my heroes for jumping in to save me when you weren't even armed. And you damn well better not feel guilty for saving me from that psycho."

Dean wasn't sure he could let it go quite that quickly. But he looked into her eyes then and uttered the words his dad and PopPop had told him to be prepared to say often to maintain a happy marriage. "You're absolutely right, Darlin'."

Then he kissed her like they were the only two people in the world, needing to feel their connection and know that they were both going to be able to put this horrific event behind them. He didn't care if it was completely inappropriate to make out with his fiancée in the middle of a crime scene. He also didn't care how many first responders were there to witness their public display of affection.

~~~

The day felt like the longest of Allissa's life. And the one when she fluctuated between the most emotional highs and lows that she'd ever experienced. Unfortunately, it didn't look like she'd be getting off the dysfunctional-feelings roller coaster any time soon.

After starting the day worried about her relationship with Dean being smothering, she'd soared to the height of excitement at his proposal, realizing that they weren't smothering because they both needed one another to feel at peace. She'd leveled out at happiness during the time she spent with their family and friends looking at dresses and tuxedos to decide what they wanted for their wedding in just over a month. Then she plunged down to the depths of fear when she went to the restroom and was grabbed by her stalker just as she came out of the toilet stall.

She'd instinctively screamed when the man she hadn't recognized first grabbed her, knowing it would bring Dean and her bodyguards to rescue her. Unfortunately, the man had clearly lost his mind and refused to surrender, even when he had four guns trained on him. Instead, he'd ranted and raved a bunch of nonsense about meeting her in 1993, two years before she was even born, and watching over her ever since. He went on and on about how she'd changed her name and
~~~

appearance slightly over the years, trying to hide from him, but he wasn't fooled and always found her again. He reiterated the plans he had in place for them to finally live together that he'd mentioned in his letters, and didn't listen to the bodyguards as they tried to talk him into letting her go.

When she realized Dean was there to step in and save her, she had a flicker of hope that they could end the situation without any injuries. She was momentarily confused by the hand signals he tried to discreetly use to alert her to what he was doing. But when Dion and Liam responded in kind, she figured out it was part of the code they all often used in the ring and recognized his plan pretty quickly. When she realized Dean was lunging for the man's gun, she tried to do her part to help him by fighting her attacker at the same time, so he'd be distracted and unable to shoot Dean before he got the gun away from the stalker.

Then, when the gun went off, and Dion and Liam tackled them out of the line of fire, she fell to the depths again. This time with fear for Dion, who didn't wake up after being knocked out when he hit his head. At least, she thought that hitting his head on the door frame of the toilet stall was what knocked Dion out. Linc said he was just grazed with the bullet from the stalker's gun, so she hoped it wasn't a deep enough injury to cause any lasting damage.

But there was so much blood! Allissa fretted over Dion's condition as she sat in the waiting room of the hospital, holding Dean's hand, and waiting to hear how their friend was doing. *But even a little cut to the head bleeds a lot, so maybe he's not as badly injured as he looked.*

At least, that's what everyone kept saying, including the paramedics and police officers they'd had to spend the afternoon talking to before they could go to the hospital. The police officers hadn't liked the fact that Dean refused to leave her side to be questioned separately. But when she'd freaked out and clung to him as she cried over the traumatic events of the day, they'd soon realized that they wouldn't get much out of her, if they didn't let her lean on Dean while she gave her statement.

As always seemed to be the case, Allissa found her strength in Dean's arms as he held her and let her cry it out. It wasn't the way she'd envisioned herself being a strong, independent woman, the way she'd always heard described as the goal for the women of her generation, but she was through worrying about meeting someone else's goals.

She was perfectly fine with leaning on her partner in life to shore up the strength inside her to be able to face her demons. And as always seemed to happen when she cried in Dean's arms for a few minutes, she was able to let all the negative emotions out so she could deal with what needed to be done. Dean still held her hand as she gave her statement, but she'd done it calmly and rationally, relaying the details of what happened in the seconds she was alone with the stalker before the bodyguards and her fellow wrestlers came to her rescue.

Even with her, Dean, and Liam giving their statements to explain how the bodyguards were defending them from the gunman, Linc, Wright, Bishop, and Thor had to stay behind, instead of accompanying them to the hospital when the police finally let them leave the crime scene. She was pretty sure they'd have to surrender their weapons, too, since they'd killed the stalker.

Even with the stalker dead, Rick and Byron had insisted on Barrett, Blaine, and Brady watching over Allissa and Dean for the rest of the day, while the rest of the men they'd brought in for the weekend protected their GWA family. Though at this point, all the security personnel were doing was preventing the reporters from getting into the hospital to try to interview them about the events of the day. The vultures were swarming so badly that Rick had asked Byron to keep his men posted with the GWA until the news of the shooting died down.

Unfortunately, they hadn't dealt with the reporters in time to keep their families from hearing on the news that there had been a shooting at the arena. Both their phones had blown up while they were talking to the police, and they hadn't been able to answer them until after they'd given their statements.

With having to turn their blood-stained clothing over to the authorities, they were actually delayed long enough at the arena for their family members to beat them to the hospital. And they'd apparently caused quite the scene, trying to find out if Allissa or Dean were among the injured.

Rick had dealt with a lot that afternoon, but thankfully, he'd still been at the arena when Allissa and Dean arrived at the hospital to quell their families' freak out. So that was one situation he hadn't had to manage for them.

The last half of the fan expo had to be canceled, even though the police didn't let anyone leave the arena until they'd spoken with them to verify they hadn't helped the gunman gain entry to the locker room. In addition to coordinating refunds for the fans whose interaction with the GWA superstars was interrupted by the police lockdown, Rick had also had to coordinate with the authorities about whether or not the crime scene would be released in time for the **Halloween Horror** show that was scheduled for the next day, contact Dion's brother to meet them at the hospital, and make the decisions about how this altercation would impact the show. Specifically, he had to figure out how the company would deal with the fact that four of the top performers on the roster might not be physically or psychologically ready to wrestle the next day. Not that that would be a big deal if the authorities weren't able to release the arena in time for the show.

As shaken up as she felt after the incident, Allissa wasn't sure she'd be ready to walk into that locker room again, even if she did want to go out and wrestle. *Maybe we can somehow share the men's locker room for the day? Or they can find an empty office or training room I can use to change in?*

Who am I kidding? We're probably going to have to cancel the show. The police are going to need to keep the crime scene locked down while they investigate. And they won't care that Dion would want us to honor his bravery by entertaining his hometown crowd. They also won't care that we need our routine, our time in the ring, to suspend reality for a little bit and feel like everything is still right with the world after living through this nightmare.

"Any updates on Dion's condition?" Allissa was brought out of her head by Rick's booming voice as he addressed the waiting room full of GWA personnel as soon as he and Byron walked in.

"Not yet, Boss," Dean answered for the group. "Last we heard, he was stable and going for tests. But Darius is the only one who's been allowed to go back to see him, since the hospital doesn't consider any of us family."

Rick nodded in acknowledgment of Dean's words before walking over to the desk to see if he could get an update on Dion. As he walked away, Byron walked over and sat on the coffee table in front of

Allissa and Dean. Dean started to get up and offer the older man his chair, but Byron declined, motioning for Dean to stay where he was to keep comforting Allissa. She smiled at him gratefully, needing to maintain that physical contact with Dean to feel safe.

"How are you holding up?" Byron looked at her with concern as he leaned over and rested his elbows on his knees.

"I'm okay," Allissa tried to assure him, though she wasn't sure her voice sounded strong enough to convince him. "And I'll be better once I know Dion is gonna be okay."

"The officers said you declined to speak with a crisis counselor…" Byron's words trailed off as he examined her. It almost felt like he was assessing her mental state to determine how much he was willing to tell her about what he'd learned so far in the investigation.

"That's because I already have a therapist I plan to call first thing Monday morning when her office reopens," Allissa explained, wanting him to know she was already being proactive about her mental health. "And I'll be setting the first available appointment she has for me and Dean to speak to her together."

"Good," Byron nodded. "Do you feel up to hearing the details we've learned now? Or do you want to wait until after you've talked to your therapist to feel better prepared to handle them?"

"I want to know now," Allissa asserted, and Dean nodded in agreement. She wanted all the facts she could get, so she could relate the whole picture to Kelly on Monday to be able to work through the trauma.

"Very well," Byron nodded just as Rick rejoined them. "Your stalker's name is Marcus Gardner. I know you told the police you didn't recognize him, but does his name sound familiar?"

"No, I don't know who he is." Allissa shook her head just as her mom grabbed her hand from her seat on the opposite side of Allissa from Dean.

"But I might," Windy interjected. "Do you have a picture of him I could look at? Like, preferably, one from before today. I don't think I can stomach looking at a picture of him after he died."

"Luckily for you, the police are the only ones with access to the crime scene photos," Byron assured them as he pulled out his cell phone and swiped across the screen. "But my cyber team included his social media profile in the information they gathered about him once he was identified."

When Byron turned his phone around for Windy to look at the pictures on Marcus Gardner's social media, Allissa caught enough of a glimpse to know it was indeed the man who'd tried to kidnap her earlier in the day. She turned to Dean, burying her face in his chest to keep from seeing her tormentor's face again. Dean wrapped his arms around her as her mother confirmed she'd known the man.

"Yeah, he was one of my regular customers back before Allissa was born. He got pissed when I had to take time off to have her and was banned from coming back for a while. But when one of his friends bought into the business, the ban was dropped and he started coming back about five years later. I think they might have told him he had to avoid me to be allowed to come in there, though, 'cause he never comes near the bar since I started working in that part of the club."

"Well, that explains why he was ranting about meeting me before I was born," Allissa scoffed, barely lifting her face from Dean's chest to be heard. "He was mistaking me for you when you were my age."

Realizing the timing of when her mom said she knew the man, Allissa whipped her head around, pulling from Dean's embrace to gape at her mom. "Please tell me there's no chance he's my sperm donor."

"Oh fuck," Dean cursed under his breath, but as close as they were seated, Allissa still heard him and agreed wholeheartedly with the sentiment.

Windy's face paled as she opened and closed her mouth like a fish out of water without saying a word.

Oh, shit! Maybe I should have looked closer at the list of people who matched DNA with me on that site, instead of just verifying Dean wasn't on it.

"I'll see what I can do about getting a sample of his DNA to make sure that's not a factor in the case," Byron barked, taking his phone back from Windy to start firing off text messages to his team.

"I'm so sorry, Lissie," Windy apologized to her daughter as her eyes filled with unshed tears. "I should have tried to figure out who your father was back when you were a baby, but I really didn't like any of my regulars enough to want to be stuck with one of them in our lives."

For some reason, her mother's words struck Allissa right in the funny bone. She started giggling and couldn't make it stop.

"Allissa, Darlin', are you okay?" Even Dean's worried tone couldn't suppress Allissa's hysterics.

"No," Allissa chuckled, shaking her head as everyone stared at her with concerned looks. She was literally laughing so hard she was crying and had to take a second to wipe away the tears before she elaborated. "I grew up without a dad because my mom didn't like any of her regulars enough to want to find out who he was, so we didn't get stuck with any of the losers in our lives. And because she wasn't very discriminating in choosing her partners, my biological father may very well be the psycho who's been stalking me and just tried to kidnap me at gunpoint with plans to take me back to his house and rape me. My life is like a cheesy soap opera that's too outlandish to even sound believable. So, I'm gonna follow Randi's advice and laugh my ass off to keep from crying."

"Do we need to put her in the bed next to my brother for a psych eval?" Darius's sudden appearance beside Rick surprised her enough that she was able to stop laughing.

"Oh, Darius, is Dion okay?" Allissa jumped up from her seat, wanting to hug Dion's brother since she wasn't allowed to go back and properly thank the man who'd jumped in front of a bullet for her.

"Yeah," Darius informed them as he returned Allissa's brief embrace. "He can't remember shit, but he's awake and gonna be fine."

"What can't he remember?"

"When can we see him?"

"How soon will he recover?"

It seemed like the whole room crowded around them, shouting out questions for Darius, since he was Dion's only blood relative, and therefore, the only one allowed to go back and see him in the emergency room.

"I'm not sure about all that." Darius held up his hands to get the questions to stop. "The doctor said he has retrograde amnesia and a pretty bad concussion, but he didn't give me any idea about his recovery time or if he'd get his memory back to be able to give the cops his statement about what happened today or not. They're gonna keep him in the ICU for a couple of days. I guess they have to do some more tests and watch him to make sure he doesn't have a brain bleed or something more serious pop up. And it's only family allowed to visit him in the ICU, just like in the ER. But I've got his phone 'cause he's not allowed to use it right now with the concussion, so I'll keep ya'll informed via text."

"Is there anything we can do for you? Like, go grab you some food or something?" Allissa wanted to do something to help take care of Dion and his brother. She knew it wasn't nearly enough to thank Dion for saving her life, but she felt like she needed to do something to show her gratitude, especially since they were only in this situation because of her stalker.

"You don't have to do anything like that," Darius smiled at her. "I'm actually on my way to the cafeteria right now to grab a bite to eat while they're transferring Dion up to the ICU. But ya'll can come with and finish filling me in on what happened, if ya want."

Since she and Dean had just arrived at the hospital and barely started to tell Darius how his brother was injured when he was taken back to sit with Dion, they went with him to grab a bite to eat and fill him in on all the details. Rick and Byron joined them, but sent everyone else back to the hotel with plans to meet up in the morning once they knew if they could use the arena the next day or not.

Once the five of them were mostly sequestered to be able to talk freely with Byron's sons blockading them from the other patrons of the cafeteria, Allissa and Dean filled them in on their version of events. Byron then gave them more details about the stalker, filling them in on how Marcus Gardner had been able to track her because of his job traveling the country to oversee the upgrades at stadiums and arenas, including several of the ones that hosted GWA events. He'd apparently been able to get past security at the fan expo because of having a badge from the arena from his time upgrading the locker rooms and training facilities the previous year.

When Darius went back to sit with his brother, the rest of the GWA crew finally left the hospital to spend the evening with their families. As much as Allissa wanted to take that time alone in the hotel room with Dean to reaffirm their connection and celebrate their engagement, she also knew their family members needed that time with them to have the reassurance that they were alive and well. So, they spent the rest of the evening with their families, thanking their lucky stars that they all came out of the ordeal earlier in the day mostly unscathed.

She and Dean had all night to reconnect and physically express their love for one another, so Allissa was happy to spend a few more hours with their families. *Not just all night,* she mentally corrected herself. *We have the rest of our lives to make love and reaffirm our soul-deep connection to one another.*

Chapter Twenty-One

Surprisingly, the local authorities had worked quickly to release the arena, so the GWA's **Halloween Horror** show could go on as planned. Well, mostly as planned. The tag-team title match between Red Velvet and Protection Detail had to be scrapped, which meant another derailment of the angle they'd salvaged out of the Vegas wedding of Red and Chastity. They also all had to use the men's locker room to shower because the crime scene clean-up crew didn't have time to prepare the women's locker room for use in such a short timeframe. Which meant they were all changing in the other bathrooms on the main floor of the arena, and adjusting the timing of their showers to rinse off after their matches to maintain some semblance of modesty.

While it was pretty well accepted that the couples, and throuple, on the roster would have been fine showering together, there was a general consensus among them that none of the people who were in relationships wanted anyone else to see their partners in the shower. Though Allissa had giggled at Dean when he acted like a caveman, grunting out that nobody but him could see his woman naked, she had to agree that she didn't like the idea of her female friends seeing Dean in the buff either, even if they were all technically married women now.

Luckily, in this arena, they were able to cordon off the entire lower level around the arena floor to use as a backstage area. The fans with floor seats had to go up a level for their bathroom and concession needs during the show, but the GWA crew had the use of more space, which meant more restrooms. So the kids and anyone else who wanted to avoid the locker rooms completely were able to take care of their bodily functions without any risk of further trauma from the events of the day before. If one of those extra restrooms had only had a shower in it, Allissa would have gladly avoided the locker rooms completely.

As the showers in the men's locker room were her only option, however, she wasn't looking forward to the time she had to venture in there after her match. Her trepidation had her distracted as Rick finished going over the changes in the plans for the show while they were all gathered in catering. So she was caught by surprise when Dean nudged her to reply to whatever Rick had just mentioned.

"Sorry, Boss," Allissa apologized sheepishly. "I was still stuck on having to go in the men's locker room to shower after my match and missed what you just said."

"I was just saying that we want to issue a statement at the beginning of the show, dedicating it to Dion and informing the fans that he's going to be out on medical leave for a while. Do you want to be the one to address the crowd? Or do you want me to do it?"

"I'd rather you do it, please," Allissa stated, with more strength than she felt. "I'm not sure I can talk about, um, everything so publicly yet. Not and be able to compartmentalize everything to be able to wrestle afterward."

"I understand," Rick reassured her with a sympathetic smile. "I want to give him a twenty-one bell salute to kick off the show and will mention that he was injured while rescuing a fellow wrestler from a stalker, but I won't mention your name, so hopefully the press coverage will drop off and they'll leave you alone."

Allissa nodded in agreement as Rick continued laying out his plans for the show.

"I also think we should drop kayfabe for the salute and have the whole roster on stage to dedicate the show to Dion. He won't be able to see it while he's still in the hospital, but I'll make sure Darius gets a digital copy of the card to show him whenever the doctor allows him screen time again. So he'll know we're all thinking of him and wishing him a speedy recovery."

Rick continued their meeting by running down the new card for the event that night and gave them a new schedule for their promo tapings, since they had to be skipped the day before due to the lockdown of the arena. He also gave them the latest update on Dion's condition, which hadn't changed any since they left the hospital the night before, and informed them that Dion would be in the hospital for a few more days. Unfortunately, that meant none of them would be able to see him because of having to fly out of town the next morning to stick to their schedule.

Allissa was most distraught about not being able to go and personally thank Dion for saving her life. But as their meeting broke up for them to eat and go through their final rehearsals for the show, Dean assured her that Dion already knew how grateful they both were and would want them to go on with the show and keep the ring warm for when he returned.

She wasn't sure how Dean could read her thoughts without her even saying a word, but she loved that their connection was so strong that he was able to calm her inner turmoil, even when she didn't realize she needed it. Allissa hoped she was able to be that same soothing presence in Dean's life that he was in hers.

His sentiments were reinforced by Emerald and Surfer Josh as they lined up behind them to fill their plates, making her feel even better about her decision to push through and wrestle that night.

Soon, they were joined by their families once more and the conversation around them turned to their wedding plans.

"We need to know who all is going to be in the wedding party, so we can get their measurements while we're here to order their dresses and tuxedos in plenty of time." Mandi put them on the spot for selecting their bridal party while the majority of the people they'd pick were present backstage.

"I was thinking James, Anthony, Liam, and Dion as my groomsmen," Dean replied to his mother.

"I was thinking Randi, Kay, Emerald, Amethyst, and Chastity as my bridesmaids," Allissa added before turning to look at Dean with a mischievous grin, thinking their wedding would be a good time to do a little matchmaking with their mistakenly married coworkers. "And after yesterday, I wanted to ask Dion to walk me down the aisle, so you'll need to pick a couple more groomsmen."

"Oh, Darlin', I see what you're doin'," Dean grinned.

"Trust me, son, go along with her plans." David slapped a hand on his son's back and grinned at Allissa as he walked by, carrying a plate of food.

"Happy wife, happy life," PopPop reiterated with a wink at Allissa from his seat across the table.

"Fine, Darlin'," Dean chuckled. "But you're gonna hafta convince Red, Crockett, and Surfer Josh to walk their wives down the aisle."

Allissa just grinned as she looked around the table at her mom, Kandi, and the women in Dean's family. "Yeah, I don't think I'll have to do anything to convince them. Between our moms, your grandmas, and their matchmaking friends, those boys won't stand a chance at saying no to whatever we want 'em to do in our wedding."

Meemaw Patty and Grandma Joan nodded in agreement before getting up and going to start getting the groomsmen's measurements. Mandi, Windy, and Kandi soon joined them, only targeting the bridesmaids.

"We should probably check with Dion to make sure he'll be recovered enough for us to have the wedding next month," Dean pointed out once the older generations of women were out of earshot.

"Yeah, I'll let you break the news to our wedding planning committee if we have to postpone it," Allissa smirked, enjoying feeling like they were well on their way back to their typical teasing selves after the scary seriousness of the previous day. And looking forward to a long life filled with more laughter and love than she'd ever dreamed possible.

"Guess I'd better call Darius to see what we can do to speed up Dion's recovery," Dean chortled.

Dean couldn't believe he'd convinced Allissa to sneak into the hospital with him to see Dion. While he understood the hospital rules about only family members being allowed in the ICU, he couldn't get on the company plane the next morning without seeing his friend to personally thank him for helping to save Allissa from her stalker. He knew Allissa felt the same conviction he did about needing to see Dion before they left town, but he really hadn't thought she'd be willing to risk getting in trouble with him to try sneaking in after visiting hours.

I'm gonna hafta watch that I don't let her blind trust in me go to my head and get us both in more trouble than we can easily get out of in the future. Dean loved that she trusted him so much that she'd follow his lead. He just hoped he was worthy of her trust and had outgrown some of the stupid stunts he'd pulled James and Anthony into when they were younger, so he wouldn't ever risk her losing that trust in him.

"Are you sure this is gonna work?" Allissa gave him a nervous glance as they walked into the hospital.

"Yeah, Darlin'." Dean brought her hand up to his lips and kissed the back of it. "The staff in the ICU is different from the staff in the ER yesterday, so they won't recognize us. And I doubt they'll ask us to show the adoption papers to prove he's our brother."

"But what if Darius is in there? You don't think he'll contradict our story?"

"That's why we're goin' so late. Darius has to go home to sleep, even if he's not goin' to work at the club, so I'm sure he's not here now." Dean grinned at her reassuringly as they got on the elevator. Not that Dean was worried about Dion's brother contradicting their story. From the few times he'd met Darius whenever they were in New Orleans, Dean knew that he would play along with whatever they told the hospital staff. "Besides, Dare might tease us about it later, but he'll be cool if he's still here."

Allissa still fidgeted nervously, even though they were alone as they rode up in the elevator.

"Relax, Darlin', or your jitters will give us away." Dean pulled her in for a quick hug, knowing that was the secret to getting his girl to calm down. There was just something about hugging one another that seemed to settle both of them. No matter what else was going on around them, or what they were having to deal with at the time, when they took a brief pause to hold each other, they both felt stronger and more capable of dealing with the stressful situations in life once they stepped out of the embrace.

He released her when the elevator doors opened, putting his hand on the small of her back to lead her out into the hallway. They followed the signs for the ICU before coming up on a set of locked doors with a nurse acting as a guard in the window beside them.

"How can I help you?" The woman, who looked to be about the same age as his mother, greeted them with a blank expression.

"We just got into town after hearing our adoptive brother was admitted here yesterday." Dean gave the woman his best smile, hoping to sound convincing. "I know it's after visiting hours, but I'm hoping you can let us see him for a few minutes to ease our worry about him before we go try to find a hotel for the night."

"Nice try, Mr. Dangerous," the nurse laughed. "But I know you work with the GWA and have been in town all weekend."

Fuck! Dean inwardly cursed, momentarily hating his semi-celebrity status as a professional wrestler.

"Please, ma'am," Allissa pleaded, giving the nurse the puppy-dog eyes he could never turn down. "I know the ICU is supposed to be restricted to family members only. But Dion saved my life yesterday, and I can't leave town tomorrow without personally thanking him. We won't stay long or disturb anyone, I promise."

The nurse turned to look at the monitor on her desk before turning back to them. "Since he's awake, I'll let you back. But if anyone else asks, I fell for your story about being his adoptive siblings."

"Thank you," Dean and Allissa gushed at the same time.

The nurse pushed a button, and there was a buzz alerting them that the doors were opening.

"He's in room three," the nurse informed them as they walked through the doors to see her behind the desk to their left.

Now that the wall wasn't blocking his view, Dean could see her hospital badge clipped to her scrub top to read her name as "Lisa Newman, RN." He pulled Allissa back over to the desk where the nurse was seated before whispering, "Nurse Newman," to get her attention.

When she looked up at him from across the desk, he continued whispering, "We don't have anything with us for autographs right now, but if you have a card or something with your email address on it, we'll schedule tickets to our next show in town with a private meet and greet for you and your family to show our appreciation."

"I'm really not supposed to accept stuff like that," Lisa protested as she opened a drawer and pulled out a business card. She flipped it over and wrote down an email address before smiling up at him and handing it over. "But my husband will be mad as a hornet if I don't this time."

"Your secret is safe with us," Allissa grinned before pretending to lock her lips.

Dean pocketed the card and promised nobody else would know they were there that night. They quickly walked in the direction the nurse pointed them, easily finding Dion's room. When they walked in, they found him reclining in the mostly dark room with a faraway look in his eyes.

"Jewel?" Dion sat up just in time to catch Allissa, who threw her arms around him with a sob of relief to see him alert. "You're not Jewel."

Who's Jewel? Dean wondered as he watched his friend try to comfort his fiancée.

"Oh, Dion, I'm so glad you're gonna be okay," Allissa wept into Dion's shoulder.

"Yeah, sweetheart, I'm fine." Dion awkwardly patted Allissa's back before looking up at Dean and mouthing, "Who is this?"

Fuck! How far back does his amnesia go if he doesn't remember Allissa after she's been with the GWA for over a year?

"Allissa, Darlin', why don't you give Dion a little breathing room?" Dean pulled a chair over for Allissa to sit beside Dion's bed. Once she was settled, he wiped her tears from her cheeks before turning to Dion. "The doc said you have amnesia after yesterday. What's the last thing you remember?"

Dion reached up to touch the stark white bandage around his head with the hand that wasn't attached to his I-V. Dean wasn't sure if he was touching the spot where the bullet grazed him or the place he busted open when he hit the doorframe on the way to the floor, but either way, it was probably the spot he associated with his memory loss.

"Talking to Rick about teaming up with Red because we lost another tag team to retirement, but I can't tell you who retired."

"Wow, that was like two years ago," Dean pointed out, shaking his head. "So that's why you don't remember Allissa joining the roster last year."

Allissa gasped, covering her mouth in surprise at the realization that Dion didn't remember her. "I thought the doctor just meant that you don't remember what happened yesterday. How am I supposed to thank you for saving my life, when you don't even remember who I am?"

Dean rubbed a hand over Allissa's back to comfort her, as Dion reached out with his free hand to take her hand to do the same.

"I don't have to remember you or what happened to appreciate you coming up here to see me. And the doctor seems to think my memory might come back once the headaches ease up and I'm cleared to wrestle again."

"Yeah? How long does he think that'll take?" Dean wondered if Dion would be fully recovered in time to be in their wedding if they had it over their Thanksgiving break, as they currently had it planned. He was worried that if the amnesia was that bad, his friend might not be able to come back to the GWA, much less be in their wedding party.

"He wants me to rest for a little while, with no screen time or strenuous activity, for at least a couple of weeks. I'm not really injured enough to need to be in the ICU. They just kept me here to keep the press out of my room while I have to stay for observation for a couple of days." Dion smirked before continuing. "With the GWA having to fly out on Monday, and Darius having to work, the doc didn't trust the ring rats who tried to sneak in earlier to follow the concussion protocol."

"Yeah, I imagine not," Dean chuckled, assuming there'd been more than one ring rat attempting to sneak in to see Dion. "Any chance you'll feel up to being in our wedding next month? Or should we plan it farther out to make sure you're all healed up?"

Dion arched an eyebrow at Dean when he mentioned the wedding. He looked back and forth between Dean and Allissa, as if trying to figure out what all he'd forgotten over the last year. Finally, he noticed the ring on Allissa's hand and smirked up at Dean. He knew his buddy wanted to rib him about his status as a reformed player, but he wouldn't do it in front of his fiancée.

"I'll definitely be healed up enough to make it to your wedding in a month," Dion assured them. "I might need you to come pick me up and drive me there if the doctor doesn't clear me to fly by then. But hopefully, the headaches and dizzy spells will have cleared up enough by then that I can stand up with you for the service."

"I was actually hoping you'd walk me down the aisle," Allissa informed him, garnering a look of surprise from Dion. "I know you're way too young to step into the father-of-the-bride role, but since you stepped up and protected me from the man who might be my biological father, it seemed kinda fitting. And you can sit down as soon as we get to the altar, so it won't be too much if you're still having concussion symptoms."

"I would be honored to walk you down the aisle," Dion smiled at Allissa. "And it might be a good idea to be able to sit down through the service, in case the doc's wrong about me being back to normal in a month or so."

"That's how long he said it would take you to heal?"

"Yeah, two weeks of dark rooms and rest, and then two weeks of starting to get up and around with light activity," Dion confirmed. "Then I'll have to see him to be cleared to fly and increase my activity level."

"Since you remember all that, I'm guessing you remember what's happened since you woke up." Dion tucked his chin in a half-nod that Dean took as an affirmative. "What about your older memories? Have any of them started coming back?"

"Some. Everything's coming in flashes, not like normal memories," Dion explained, looking from Allissa up to Dean. "Darius has been helping me figure out when things really happened, but he can only help with the stuff from before I started with the GWA. Maybe you can help me with the stuff he doesn't know about?"

"Of course," Dean agreed, nodding at Dion. "I'm happy to help as much as I can. What's the first thing you wanna know?"

"There's a woman." Dion looked at Allissa and gave her a slight smile before shaking his head, obviously recognizing Allissa wasn't the woman he was remembering. "She's about the same size as you, but maybe a little thicker. She's got blonde hair and the brightest blue eyes. Looking into her eyes is like looking at the water in the Caribbean."

"Okay…" Dean drawled out the word, trying to think of who Dion might be remembering. "Jen and Julie Burleson both have blonde hair and blue eyes. Do you remember one of them?"

"No, the only Burleson I know is your friend, the pilot." Dion shook his head before clutching it, as if the movement caused him pain.

"Yeah, he got married last year, and you came to the wedding," Dean reminded Dion. "You met Jen and Julie and the rest of the Burlesons then. And every time you're in town for a wedding or holiday, the Matchmaking Mommas in town seat you with them. Is that possibly where you remember her from?"

"No, her name is Jewel, not Julie," Dion disagreed, his face contorting in a frustrated expression. "And the memories aren't from weddings or holiday celebrations. They're in different hotel rooms. It's like she's visited me on tour or something, but I can't figure out when or where. I just know she's my girl, and I have to let her know what happened, so she can come here while I'm recovering."

"Dude, I haven't seen you meeting up with anyone at our hotels, not even ring rats in the last year or so." Dean looked to Allissa to see if she'd seen Dion with anyone. She shook her head to indicate that she hadn't seen Dion hook up with anyone, either. "But I'll ask the guys tomorrow if they remember your girl."

"Yeah, thanks. Darius says I haven't mentioned her to him, either. Which makes me wonder why we're keeping our relationship a secret." Dion closed his eyes and let his head fall forward for a moment before looking back up at Dean and Allissa. "Hell, it makes me wonder if she's even real. Or if I'm more brain-damaged than the doc thinks, and have completely made her up in my head?"

"I'm sure she's real," Dean tried to assure his friend. "But maybe you're doin' like Anthony did before he met Kay, and dreamin' about your soulmate before you meet her."

"Fuck, if that's the case, then I hope my dreams about her come true just as soon as I get outta here," Dion groaned and leaned back on the bed.

Dean didn't get the chance to respond before the nurse peeked her head in the door and informed them their time was up. They each hugged Dion and promised to text Darius for updates on his condition and keep him in the loop on the wedding plans before they left for the night.

As he drove them back to the hotel, Dean finally started to relax and put the bad parts of the day before behind him. He'd managed to be stoic since the confrontation with the stalker, and reassure his family and friends that he'd come through the ordeal the day before without any injuries. But in reality, he'd been struggling mentally with his guilt for Dion getting injured.

He knew he wasn't responsible for what had happened, but he'd still needed to see his friend to be reassured that he would fully recover before he could start the process of letting go of the guilt. Now that he'd seen that Dion would eventually be back to his normal self, Dean was resolved to talk to Allissa's therapist to help him get over the rest of the trauma they'd all suffered through the day before.

My mental health is gonna hafta be as much of a priority as my physical health, so I can be the best man I can be for Allissa.

Fuck, now I get what everyone meant when they said the right woman will make me want to be a better man. I wanna do everything I can to be better for her, so I can be a true partner she can count on for the rest of our lives.

<div align="center">~~~</div>

Allissa was doing better than she expected, as she got back into her normal routine. She'd had a couple of nightmares after the ordeal, but luckily, Dean was there to console her with cuddles, and wipe the incident from her mind with multiple orgasms in the middle of the night when they happened. After dealing with the nightmares, she'd been slightly afraid that she'd need Dean to accompany her into the locker room that night, the same way she had when she needed to shower after her match at the ***Halloween Horror*** show in New Orleans. But after they'd talked through the trauma with Kelly that afternoon, she and Dean had both felt so much better that they were able to separate for longer than just the time they were each in the ring.

Allissa still hadn't been able to go in the locker room alone, but she was fine with her fellow female wrestlers surrounding her each time she had to go change, use the restroom, or shower, instead of having to have Dean accompany her the way she had in New Orleans on Sunday. She knew that part of that was because it was a different arena and a totally different locker room layout. But she was convinced that with continued therapy sessions, she'd be able to go into the women's locker room at the New Orleans arena again when they returned to the city in six months, without the need for Dean or anyone else to accompany her.

In addition to scheduling their additional therapy sessions on Monday, Allissa and Dean had also informed their families that the wedding was a go for their Thanksgiving break, and put them in touch with Darius to get Dion's tux measurements. Mandi had promised to make all the arrangements with him for both Dion and Darius to travel to Heart's Destiny in time for all the wedding events.

Allissa was pretty sure Mandi, and the rest of the Matchmaking Mommas of Heart's Destiny, would spend that week trying to convince Darius to move to town and settle down. They'd want to match him up with one of the local women, even if Dion was too focused on finding his Jewel to consider going along with their plans any longer.

I really hope Dion gets his memory back soon, so he can remember where he met her and how to contact her before she hears about his injury on the news. Then again, if she is real and not a figment of his imagination, maybe she'll see the news and call him, so Darius can give her the information she needs to go nurse Dion back to health.

Allissa was surprising herself with how much she wanted to play matchmaker for all her friends, now that she was confident in her relationship with Dean. It was almost like his dropping to one knee to propose flipped a switch inside her to suddenly want to help all her friends find the same happiness they had with one another.

With three of her best friends having recently found out they'd married three of Dean's best friends in Vegas a couple of months ago, and none of them having time off to find lawyers to talk about divorces or annulments until their Thanksgiving break, when they'd all be in Heart's Destiny and paired up with their new spouses for her and Dean's wedding, Allissa felt like she was well on her way to being inducted into the matchmakers club. *Now I just have to make sure our moms know to plan so many activities for us that week that they can't skip off to speak to any attorneys about separating from their spouses. And maybe they'll all finally realize just how perfect they are together.*

"What are you plotting over there, Darlin'?" Dean's question brought her out of her matchmaking thoughts, as they sat across from one another at the small table in their hotel room, eating their late-night meal.

"Just thinking about what activities we can plan for our wedding week," Allissa partially confessed with a grin at her fiancé.

"Yeah?" Dean arched a skeptical eyebrow at her. "Alone time for you and me? Or kinda like all the stuff I planned to spend extra time with you when we were back home without wedding events to attend, so you can play matchmaker for our friends?"

"Maybe a little of both," Allissa admitted before stuffing the last of her pizza in her mouth. Now that Dean had put the alone time ideas into her head, she found she was rather looking forward to what they'd do that night after they finished eating. She quickly chewed and swallowed, eager to get to naked, naughty time with Dean. "But now I'm thinking about things to do tonight during our alone time."

"Oh, and what kinda dirty ideas are running through your head, Darlin'?" Dean's sexy grin made it obvious that he could practically read her mind.

"Well, since I failed so miserably when I tried to take charge during our dirty talk Skype lessons, I've been studying some of the dialogue during the sexy scenes in the books I've read," Allissa started explaining how she'd prepared herself to try to take the lead in their lovemaking, even though she wasn't sure either one of them would like the role reversal as more than a one-time thing.

"When have you had time to read?" Dean shook his head, knowing she hadn't touched her Kindle at bedtime since they started sleeping together every night.

"I downloaded the Audible app to my phone and listen to audiobooks while I'm on the treadmill," Allissa shrugged, playing it off as no big deal. She wasn't about to admit that the majority of the moisture between her legs during a workout wasn't from sweat. Between listening to erotic romance audiobooks on the treadmill and watching her hot hubby-to-be while he was working out, she could barely concentrate to exercise with how aroused she got during their workouts each morning.

"Okay," Dean drawled out the word like he was skeptical of what she thought she'd learned. "And you think all that studying has prepared you to do what, exactly?"

"I thought I could try on the Domme role for the night, so you can relax and just enjoy the pleasure I give you." Allissa reached across the table and ran her hand up Dean's forearm, trying to be seductive. She was really hoping for another opportunity to suck his cock, since he hadn't let her spend enough time doing that to make him come yet. "I want you to experience the wonderful way you make me feel every time we make love."

"Oh, Darlin'," Dean sighed, giving her the slightest smile. "If you wanna take charge tonight, I'll let you. But I'm not gonna relax while you're touching and teasing me. I'm just not wired that way, so you'll just be taunting the beast inside me until I can't control it and take you like a wild animal. So you might wanna think about whether or not you can handle that before you bite off more than you can chew tonight. 'Cause I don't wanna do anything that might trigger you by reminding you of the things in those letters. I only want our lovemaking to give you pleasure, never pain or fear."

Allissa's core clenched and flooded when Dean mentioned taking her like a wild animal, temporarily blocking her from hearing his reference to the letters sent to her by the stalker. He was always so careful with her that, even when he unleashed a little of his intensity when he was close to climax, she could tell he was still holding back to keep from even slightly risking hurting her.

While she wasn't completely sure she really wanted to be in the driver's seat of their lovemaking, she was willing to risk failing at it again if it meant he might unleash a little more of that inner beast. But before she could convince Dean of that, the rest of his statements finally registered in her brain, and she realized she had to make it clear that he could never do anything that would remind her of her stalker first.

"You won't trigger me, Dean," Allissa assured him as she stroked his arm with her thumb. "There's a big difference between the rape scenes in those letters and me pushing you to lose control and get a little rougher."

"Yeah, what's that?" Dean shook his head like he didn't believe her.

"Love," Allissa stated matter-of-factly. "Even if you were to act out a rape fantasy, the difference is that I love you. *We're always making love.* Remember, you made me promise that our first time. So you can quit holding back and get as rough as you need to really enjoy it."

"I really enjoy it now, Darlin'," Dean argued, shaking his head at her. "I don't need to let my inner beast out to get rougher than you can handle to enjoy it."

"Oh, I'm sure I can handle whatever your inner beast can dish out," Allissa taunted Dean with a saucy smile. "I'm not nearly as fragile as I look. And I really wanna know what primal, carnal fucking feels like, Dean, 'cause I know it's more than what we've been doing."

"Well, fuck, Darlin'," Dean growled, standing from the table, and lifting Allissa from her seat. "You don't hafta tease me with tryin' to take control to get that. All ya gotta do is tell me when I'm not going hard enough for you."

He carried her with one hand on her ass and the other in her hair at the back of her head as he took her mouth in a claiming kiss. Allissa wrapped her arms around his neck and her legs around his waist, returning the carnal kiss as she clung to him.

She was surprised when he took her into the bathroom instead of to the bed. But instead of voicing her confusion, she waited, slightly impatiently, for him to clue her in on his plan for them. She didn't have to wait long before he broke their kiss to place her on her feet.

"Strip," Dean commanded in that gravelly tone that brooked no argument from her. "Unless you want me to rip your clothes off before I fuck you, Darlin'."

While she thought the idea of him ripping her clothes off was hot, Allissa didn't want to go through the hassle of replacing them, so she quickly removed her garments. As she was undressing, Dean was doing the same while watching her with an expression of intense longing. She enjoyed the show as Dean's muscular body was revealed to her, knowing he could see how much she wanted him in her eyes the same way she could see his desire for her in his navy-blue orbs.

She couldn't stop herself from licking her lips as he pushed his pants down his thighs and his long, thick erection stood proudly between them. The bulbous, purple head was already glistening with precum, with a drop balancing precariously on the ball of his apadravya piercing that she could see facing out at her.

I wonder if the ball on the other side of that piercing causes his precum to end up in his belly button, since it's positioned right over it when he's hard?

"Turn around, lean over, and grip the counter," Dean demanded as soon as they were both fully nude. "I want you to watch in the mirror while I fuck you, Darlin'. So don't bend so far that you can't see your pussy in the mirror."

"Yes, Sir," Allissa eagerly chirped the words she'd read often in the BDSM romance novels she loved, as she spun around and quickly followed his other commands.

"No, I'm not some random sir," Dean reprimanded, swatting her ass. "You say my name when you address me, Allissa. I wanna know you know who's fuckin' you."

"Aquaman?" Allissa arched an eyebrow at Dean in the mirror, loving the way they teased each other.

"No, Aquaman is my dick." Dean swatted her ass again, the slight sting quickly transforming into pure pleasure as Dean rubbed his large hand over the area he'd just slapped. "If you want my cock, you need to call me by name when you beg for it."

"Please, Dean," Allissa begged, unable to wait a moment longer to feel him inside her. "Please, fuck me with your big, thick dick, Dean."

Dean squatted down slightly as he took his glorious dick in hand to line it up with her slit. He rubbed the head through the soaking wet folds of her pussy while sliding his hand up and down his shaft, coating his whole cock in a mix of her juices and his precum.

"Fuck, Darlin', just thinkin' 'bout watching me fuck you hard, has you so fuckin' wet," Dean growled as he finally lined up with her opening. "You love it when I tell you what to do, don't you?"

"Yes, Dean," Allissa moaned, loving the feel of the way he was teasing her with the head of his cock rubbing against her pussy to stroke the balls of his apadravya piercing over her clit.

"Guess that means I get to be in charge every time we fuck. And I don't have to start off quite so gentle this time."

"No, Dean, don't be gentle. Please just fuck me," Allissa begged, wiggling her hips to try to coax him in when he held still with just his tip touching her.

Dean slapped her ass once more as he urged her to "hold still." Then he gripped her hips to hold her in place as he thrust into her, impaling her on every inch of his cock in one stroke.

"Oh, fuck, Dean," Allissa cried out, shocked by the sudden invasion, though it wasn't painful in the slightest.

"I think you missed a word there, Darlin'," Dean chuckled as she grinned at him in the mirror. "It's 'fuck *me*, Dean', not 'fuck Dean'."

"Fuck me, Dean," Allissa chanted repeatedly as Dean pulled out before slamming back in. He set a brutal pace, with each plunge of his cock into her pussy feeling more powerful than the last. She wasn't sure if it was the increased intensity, his dirty dominance, or the visual stimulation of watching where their bodies were joined in the mirror that sent her soaring in mere seconds.

"Fuck, you feel so good, Darlin'." Dean fucked her through the orgasm, reaching around her body to tweak her nipples and send her back over the edge a second time, just as she was starting to come down from the first. "So tight and wet. Your pussy's the perfect fit for my big dick."

Dean demonstrated his stamina by holding back his release as he took her breath away at least half a dozen times. He interspersed words of love and affection with his dirty talk, but it no longer felt like he was holding back his inner beast, as he continuously pounded into her hard and fast, through each and every orgasm.

Or if he is still holding back some, it's only because he's recognized the limit of how much I can handle, Allissa realized as she floated in the heavenly space where only Dean could take her.

As she drifted back to Earth, Allissa started to wonder if she was going to have to tap out on the counter to get Dean to come before she collapsed into a comatose state until morning. Not wanting to admit to not being able to keep up with him all night long, she opted to start begging for him to come instead of tapping.

"Oh, Dean, please," she pleaded, even as she pushed back with her hands on the counter to add more impact to their thrusts. "Come with me this time, please. I need to feel you filling me up with your cum."

"Oh, yeah, Darlin'," Dean groaned as her core tightened around his shaft with the first waves of her next climax. "I'm gonna fill you up with so much cum, your pussy will be overflowing before I even pull out."

"Oh, yes, Dean," Allissa cried out as yet another orgasm overtook her.

Dean speared into her a few more times before he finally delved as deep as possible, holding still inside her when he joined her in orgastic bliss. "Oh. Allissa. Fuck. Darlin'." Allissa reveled in the feel of his cock pulsing inside her to punctuate each word with a spurt of his cum, as she watched his expression of pure nirvana in the mirror.

"I love you, Darlin'," Dean declared, as they locked eyes in the mirror.

"I love you, too, Dean." Allissa returned the words of affection, reveling in the elation they felt as they physically expressed their love.

They stayed in that position, connected mind, body, and soul, until the aftershocks subsided. Then Dean pulled her back up to standing, holding her with his left arm banded around her middle and her back to his front. With his free hand, he lifted her right leg to open her up, so they could both watch as he slowly pulled his softening cock from between her folds.

Seeing his semen flowing out of her body for the first time thanks to the mirror, Allissa finally understood his fascination with what she'd previously considered his strangest fetish. She propped her right foot on the counter and hopped to the side on her left foot, so she could see his cock glistening with the mix of their cum once he'd stood back up to his full height.

"What are you doin', Darlin'?"

"I want to see you marked by me, too," Allissa explained without taking her eyes off his semi-soft dick in the mirror.

"Damn, Darlin', if you keep looking at my cock like that, we're not gonna get any sleep tonight," Dean smirked, as the cock in question started hardening again.

"Fine by me," Allissa grinned back. "But we might have to go back to gentle for the rest of the night, or I won't be able to walk onto the plane in the morning. Or wrestle for TV tomorrow night."

"Gentle it is, Darlin'," Dean promised with a wiggle of his eyebrows as he pulled her back into his arms, ready to start round two of what Allissa knew would be millions over the course of their life together.

Epilogue

Dion Davis wasn't sure if he was up to the party atmosphere of a bachelor party for his friend, Dean Hunter, or not. He was still suffering from concussion symptoms almost a month after being shot and hitting his head while pushing Dean's fiancée, Allissa, out of the line of fire of her stalker. While he still didn't remember the events surrounding his injuries, or pretty much anything from the last two years of his life, his brother, Darius, had filled him in on the details of the incident that caused his injury after talking to his coworkers the day it had happened. Dion was grateful for his little brother stepping up to help him handle life after a traumatic brain injury. But as his head started pounding while they drove from their hometown of New Orleans to the small Texas town where Dean was from for all the wedding festivities, he started to wonder if Darius was being too optimistic by assuring the Hunters that Dion was up for all the wedding events they had planned that week.

If it was just the headache he had to worry about, he wouldn't be so worried about going to the party that they were barely going to make it to town in time to attend. He could simply take a couple of the pain pills the doctor had prescribed for the headaches and try to enjoy the party until they wore off. Well, as much as he could enjoy a party without having any alcohol, since he couldn't drink while recovering from the concussion.

But, unfortunately, it wasn't just the headaches he was dealing with after the incident. In addition to the concussion and retrograde amnesia the doctors diagnosed on day one, he was also having problems with vertigo, aphasia, and spells where he would pass out whenever he got too anxious. Needless to say, he was worried the party they were going to after checking in at the bed and breakfast in Heart's Destiny would amp up his anxiety to the point that he'd pass out in the middle of the bar.

Thankfully, Dion was quickly learning how to recognize when those spells were about to happen, so he could lay down in time to keep from risking falling down and hitting his head again when he blacked out. But since he knew the middle of a rowdy bar crowd wasn't a place he'd want to lay down, he was already feeling anxious about how he would deal with a spell if he felt one coming on in the middle of the party, which might be what triggered his current headache.

The doctors classified those spells as an unusual symptom of post-concussion syndrome, but they hadn't figured out exactly what they were or how to stop them yet. They'd tried a few different medications so far, some in the hospital and some after sending him home, including an anti-seizure medication that didn't do anything but knock him out cold for thirty-six hours. That had totally freaked Darius out because he couldn't get Dion to wake up during that time, no matter what he tried. Needless to say, Dion didn't take that medication but the one time after being taken by ambulance back to the hospital.

The doctors also tried a couple of different anti-anxiety medications, but not until after Dion pointed out that the spells only happened when he got overwhelmed by not being able to process everything going on around him, or struggled with the aphasia that caused him to have difficulty remembering the right words for things, or couldn't comprehend anything people tried to communicate to him, no matter if it was written down or said during a typical conversation. Those medicines hadn't seemed to do much, if anything, so he'd only been on them a couple of weeks before he gave up taking them.

The only medication the doctors had given him that actually seemed to help prevent any of his symptoms was the one to help with vertigo. He had to take it three times a day, and go slow when he was transitioning from laying down to sitting up, or sitting up to standing. But at least the room spinning feelings were only if he moved too fast now, and didn't make him feel like he was gonna barf every time he turned his head anymore. He doubted he'd have been able to ride so long in the car with Darius driving to be able to make this trip if the vertigo was still at its worst, so he was really glad those pills at least worked.

He didn't really consider the pain pills for the headaches as effective because they didn't completely get rid of the pain. Besides only partially taking away the discomfort, the headaches always felt twice as bad when the pain pills started to wear off. So, Dion avoided taking them if at all possible, which was why he closed his eyes and slept through most of the drive instead of taking them.

Since he hadn't taken anything but the vertigo medication, Dion easily woke up when Darius turned off the car. He looked around to see if he recognized anything as they got out of the vehicle at the bed and breakfast Dean's family owned. Since he'd been told that he'd stayed there during every break he had from wrestling for the last year, Dion hoped seeing the place again would trigger a memory.

Even if it was just a brief sense of familiarity at first, his doctors had told him that being someplace where he'd spent so much time might help his memories return faster. Since they wouldn't release him to fly while he was still suffering from post-concussion symptoms, he couldn't rejoin the GWA crew on the company plane to go to the hotels and arenas, where he'd spent the majority of his time for the last several years. So, being driven to Dean's hometown by his brother was his only option for trying to regain his memories by being someplace where he'd spent a lot of time recently.

It was with the hope that it would help Dion heal faster that Darius and Mama Marcel had both decided to take some time off work, so they could spend the rest of the year in Heart's Destiny, Texas, even though Mama Marcel wouldn't be joining them until after her cruise over the Thanksgiving holiday. Apparently, in all their talks with Dean's family over the last month, Dare and Mama Marcel heard enough stories about Dion's time in town for the last year to think it might be a more healing environment for him than the building where they each had a condo in the French Quarter.

While he wasn't sure if he recognized the buildings from the outside, he did recognize Dean's mom when they walked into the lobby to check-in. Since he'd met her along with the rest of Dean's family several years ago, when they came to see Dean and his brother James win their first GWA tag-team titles, though, Dion wasn't sure if he really was remembering her from the times he'd stayed at her bed and breakfast over the last year or not.

They had a pleasant conversation as they got checked in and got their room keys. But since they were so late getting to town, they didn't bother carrying their bags over to the other building and up to their rooms. Mandi gave Darius directions to Tully's Roadhouse, where the joint bachelor and bachelorette party was just getting started, before ushering them back out to the car, so they wouldn't miss too much of the festivities.

Dion continued to examine his surroundings as Darius drove through town to get to the bar. Unfortunately, he didn't have even a flicker or recognition of any of the businesses or other buildings they passed. At least, he didn't at first.

"Wow, this place is like going back in time to the Old West," Darius commented, as they drove by block after block of rustic wooden architecture, complete with wood plank sidewalks and posts for hitching up a horse.

"Yeah, but without the segregation and bigotry," Dion chuckled, vaguely getting a flash of a memory of fireworks as they passed the town square. He thought he remembered a gathering where everyone was welcome to join the festivities and accepted regardless of race, color, gender identity, or sexual orientation.

"You remember something?" Darius glanced over at Dion before turning his eyes back to the road.

"Yeah, I think I went to a cookout or something on the town square. There were fireworks and everyone was welcome and treated like family." Dion turned in his seat to look back at the City Hall building, trying to bring back the image in his head as the fuzzy memory of sitting on a blanket with a blonde woman faded before he could clearly see her face. "I wonder who I was there with?"

Was that Jewel? No, Dean doesn't know anyone named Jewel, so it couldn't have been her. It must have been one of the Burlesons he said their moms are always trying to fix me up with whenever I'm in town.

"Don't ask me, D. I wasn't there to know," Darius chuckled as he made a right turn once they reached the street the bar was located on.

They arrived a couple of minutes later, not giving Dion enough time for his damaged brain to switch gears from thinking about Jewel to worrying about the party once again.

As soon as they walked into the bar, Dion was hit with another flash of memories. It was like a slideshow flipping through his brain, showing him image after image of his dream girl. He saw Jewel dancing on the same dance floor he saw to his left. He pictured Jewel playing pool at the tables he could see through the archway into the back room. And most vividly, he remembered Jewel pressed against a door that seemed to fit into the décor of the bar, possibly leading to a bathroom or storage room, as he plowed his hard cock into her tight, wet pussy.

The flashes of memory hit him so hard, he thought he had to be hallucinating when he thought he saw her sitting at a table on the other side of the bar. But even if she was a figment of his imagination, he couldn't stop himself from calling out to her as he walked across the room to get to her side. "Jewel!"

Her head popped up and their gazes locked on one another for the first time since before his injury. But instead of the love Dion saw shining in her bright blue eyes every night in his dreams, he only saw anger as she glared at him.

"No!" Jewel held up a hand as if to block him from even looking at her. "Don't you dare call me that after ghosting me for the last month!"

"I didn't ghost you, Jewel," Dion asserted, wanting nothing more than to pull her up out of her seat and into his arms. "At least, not on purpose. I was injured and can't remember how to contact you."

"Oh, I heard all about your injury," Jewel argued, shaking her head at him. "From my cousin! When he got home four days later! But he was too late for me to be interested in hearing what happened, since I saw the news reports the day it happened and tried calling you. Do you know what I found out when I called you, Dion?"

Dion shook his head, unable to say a word in response to her anger.

"I was told never to contact you again," Jewel seethed. "That you didn't need to be bothered by a *ring rat* trying to take advantage of your injury to con you out of your money. Well, newsflash, *Dark Chocolate*, I'm a Burleson. I don't *need* your fuckin' money. And after being treated like shit when I called, concerned about you possibly being shot, I don't *want* you in my life. Or my babies' lives." Jewel placed a hand over the baby bump that Dion could clearly see now that he looked closely at her. "So go hang out with your boys in the back, and stay the hell away from me while you're in town this week."

Dion was at a loss for words, struggling to comprehend everything Jewel had just screamed at him. The whole situation was completely overwhelming his system, causing him to start feeling the tingling and weakness in his body that he recognized as the signal to lay down before he passed out.

"Dare, I need to lie down." Dion reached out to his brother as the room started fading into darkness.

"I'm sorry, D. I think I screwed up…" Dion registered that his brother was speaking as he helped him back out to the car. But he couldn't comprehend what he was saying as it took all his focus to make it to the vehicle where he could lay down before everything faded to black.

Hopefully, I'll still remember the last couple of hours when I wake up, so I can ask him to help me figure out what just happened with Jewel.

Not that he had much hope, since he hadn't remembered what triggered any of his other blackouts so far.

<div align="center">~~~</div>

Saturday, November 30, 2019, Heart's Destiny, Texas

Dean couldn't believe how great he felt at being able to finally call Allissa his wife. No matter what she wore, he always thought she was gorgeous. But seeing her in her long, white dress as she walked down the aisle to marry him, she absolutely blew him away with her unrivaled beauty. He knew he was strutting around with a shit-eating grin all through the reception and probably annoying everyone around them as he kept calling her Mrs. Hunter. But he couldn't stop himself from showing off the magnificent woman, who now wore his ring and shared his last name.

When they had talked about whether or not she wanted to change her last name when they got married, she'd told him about how her maternal grandparents had disowned her mom after she ran off with a boy they didn't approve of. Since Walters was also her mom's maiden name because she'd never been married, Allissa held no real attachment to her maiden name and was happy to change her last name. But the conversation sparked more discussion about her biological father, and if she'd ever thought of looking him up or using his last name.

Since Allissa had sent her DNA to the same ancestry site that Dean and half the town of Heart's Destiny had used, Dean had seen her biological father show up on her match list when they checked it to make sure they weren't related. But he didn't push her to look at the match until she brought up the fear that her stalker could have been her sperm donor.

Thanks to that site, they hadn't had to get a sample of Marcus Gardner's DNA to figure out her stalker wasn't her biological father. While that didn't stop the Avingtons from getting the sample to make sure the man wasn't even slightly related to her, it did allow her the opportunity to find out more information about her biological family to make sure there weren't any genetic health issues she'd need to watch out for in the future. When Dean pointed that out, Allissa had actually contacted the man she shared fifty percent of her DNA with through the site.

It turned out her biological father hadn't been one of Windy Walters' regulars back in the day, after all. Grant Cohen had been a kid going into the Marines at eighteen, whose friends had taken him to the brothel the night before he left for boot camp, so he didn't go off and risk dying a virgin.

Allissa and Grant started talking regularly and getting to know one another, but Dean wasn't sure how close Allissa would end up being with her dad. Since he hadn't ever married or had any children that he knew of, Grant seemed to be struggling with figuring out how to interact with a grown daughter he hadn't ever expected to meet. Because their conversations were so stilted when they talked on the phone, Dean suggested they Skype, so they could see each other, and possibly meet in person, so he could be a buffer and make them both feel more comfortable building a relationship.

Surprisingly, that had worked wonders and set them up to have a stronger relationship in the future. Allissa was so excited about finally having her father in her life that she'd invited him to the wedding. There'd been a moment of awkwardness when she'd explained that Dion would be walking her down the aisle. But once she told Grant about Dion taking a bullet for them, he'd agreed that the honor of walking Allissa down the aisle should go to Dion.

When they'd all Skyped to discuss the particulars of Grant coming to town for Dean and Allissa's wedding, Windy had recognized him immediately. She'd joked about how the Marines should change their motto to "The few, the proud, the virile enough to get their sperm behind enemy lines through two forms of birth control."

Dean wasn't certain if things would work out between them or not, but if the way his new mother-in-law had been flirting with her baby daddy all week while he was in town for the wedding was any indication, Windy and Grant might be joining the long line of couples he knew getting together recently. At least, if Grant continued to return the flirtation, anyway.

Dean had to smile at how his new bride had tried to push things along for several of their friends, who were fighting what she called the "Love Bug" going through his hometown and the GWA in recent months. In addition to pairing up the GWA couples who'd gotten hitched in Vegas for their wedding party, and pushing Windy and Grant to spend time together since they were both still single, Allissa had assisted the Matchmaking Mommas of Heart's Destiny by having them put together the seating charts for each wedding event, so they could pair up their kids with the people they had chosen for them. She'd also tried to help Dion get a little more time with Julie for the last week after witnessing his realization that she was his Jewel at the bachelor and bachelorette party.

Dean still couldn't believe he'd been right when he asked if Dion was referring to Julie when he was in the hospital. Apparently, in trying to keep their relationship on the down-low, Dion had given her the Jewel nickname. Then he couldn't remember it wasn't her real name because of the amnesia.

He also hadn't told Darius about her before she called him on the day of the incident because of the rift between the Davis brothers for the last year. Since he'd already dealt with a couple of calls from reporters and had ring rats trying to get to Dion in the hospital, Dare had told Julie off when she called, blocking and deleting her from Dion's phone without looking at the name on the contact.

Dion's brother felt like shit for being the reason Julie refused to even talk to Dion. So he was doing everything he could to convince her sister and cousin, who were effectively blocking everyone from talking to Julie about the situation, to give him a chance to explain to Julie what happened. *Hopefully, he'll get through to those stubborn Burleson girls soon, so Dion and Julie can work things out.*

As he spun his beautiful bride around the dance floor for their first dance as husband and wife, Dean had to wonder which of the lucky couples Allissa wanted to target when they tossed the bouquet and garter. He knew she'd been given a list of options when Meemaw had pulled her out of the receiving line to talk before they left the church.

"So, Mrs. Hunter, who have you decided to toss your bouquet to when we get done with all these special dances?"

"I'm still not sure," Allissa sighed as she looked up at him. "Who knew the most pressure I'd feel on our wedding day would be picking who needs the biggest push to be with their soulmate?"

"I'm surprised the Matchmaking Mommas didn't pick one couple for us," Dean chuckled and grinned at her.

"Oh, no, they gave me a list of about ten," Allissa chortled. "Most of whom I don't know well enough to know if they should be matched up or not."

"Okay, so that narrows it down to someone who works with the GWA, so we've seen them together enough to have an idea that it might work out for them as well as it has for us." Dean pointed out the obvious to try to make the decision easier for them. Not that he had any idea which of the three newlywed GWA couples might actually be ready to give up their player statuses to stay married. Well, other than Surfer Josh and Emerald, since they'd been pretty much banging like bunnies since they first found out they were married.

"Yeah, I was thinking the same thing," Allissa agreed, but then shook her head in the negative. "But since they're already married, it feels wrong to toss 'em to Chastity and Red, Emerald and Surfer Josh, or Amethyst and Crockett. I mean, they can't really be the next to get married when they're already married, so I doubt any of them will even go out there to try to catch the bouquet or garter."

"Okay, what about your mom and dad? They've both been flirting a lot this week…" Dean didn't get to finish his thought before Allissa adamantly shook her head to veto that suggestion.

"No way. Yeah, they seem to be leaning toward wanting to date. But I'm not gonna be that daughter — the one who finds her bio-dad and tries to push her parents together to form a happy little family. I'm trying to be more respectable now that I'm an old married woman, so I'm not about to do anything that resembles a bad soap opera storyline like that."

"Sorry, Darlin'," Dean chuckled at his overdramatic wife. "Forget I suggested it."

"Already forgotten, husband," Allissa beamed up at him. "And thank you for talking it through with me. Like always, you've helped clear up my thoughts, so I know who we need to toss the bouquet and garter to now."

"And who would that be?"

"Julie and Dion," Allissa decided, giving him a beatific smile. "She's the only person he remembers from the last couple of years since his amnesia, so obviously she's his soulmate. Yeah, I know she's pissed about being lumped in with all the ring rats when he was in the hospital, but when she finally calms down and talks to him to find out the whole story, I'm sure she'll get over that. Besides, they're expecting twins, so they need that push to work things out. Even if they don't end up being a couple in the long run, those babies need to know both of their parents from day one."

"Then, by all means, Darlin', let's give them a little push." Dean bent down to give his wife a peck of a kiss, smiling at the love of his life as the song ended. "Who knows? Maybe this is exactly what they need for Dion to get his dream girl the same way I have mine."

Next in Heart's Destiny

Joshin' Around

Heart's Destiny Book 6

Lt. Josh Burleson was known as the jokester of his family due to his penchant for finding the humor in life to help him deal with the darker aspects he saw in his job. Raised on the family ranch, he'd been taught to work hard and play harder. And his playtime wasn't limited to just joshin' around with his family and friends.

As a Navy SEAL, he wasn't lacking when it came to available women to spend his nights with when he wasn't off on a mission. With him also being one of the Burleson bachelors, it wasn't just the frog hogs who chased after him. As a single guy, he'd had more than his fair share of one-night stands, starting with the buckle bunnies who offered themselves up back when he was a teenager, competing in the team roping competitions of the rodeo with his twin, and ending when he met the woman that he fell in instalove with at Christmas.

As soon as Josh saw Cait walk into his childhood home for a late Christmas celebration, he fell head over heels for her. But after seeing the toll of military life paid by the relationships of his fellow SEALs, Josh knew he couldn't pursue anything with her until after his minimum service requirement was over. So Josh did the only thing he could do — he started a long-distance and leave-time friendship with Cait while making plans to get out of the Navy to move home and marry her.

While home during one of his leave times, Josh sent in a DNA sample to an online family tree site like the rest of his family. When the results came in, he saw an extra person listed as sharing fifty percent of his DNA in the Parent-Child section of his DNA match list on the site. Floored by the realization that he was a father, Josh had to put his plans to build a relationship with Cait on hold. He needed to settle the situation with his child, and his child's mother, before he could commit to moving home to pursue the lovely Cait.

Cait Campbell wasn't sure she'd ever feel comfortable going out and dating again after the trauma her family had endured over the past few years. Not only had her brother lost his first wife, but both he and Cait had been injured in the drive-by shooting that ended Mari's life. While her physical scars had long since healed, Cait wasn't so sure the internal ones that kept her trapped in her brother's house ever would.

When her brother had the idea of moving their family from San Diego to Texas, she developed high hopes of moving on with her life. Getting away from the cartel hub of the city and learning about life in a rural area seemed like just what she needed to move past her agoraphobia and start feeling social again. She even felt an instant attraction to one of the men she met during her first week in Heart's Destiny, Texas.

Then she found out their move was her brother's way of hunting down the head of the cartel, who had targeted them back in San Diego, and her fear of leaving the house came back tenfold. And even though the one man she'd been attracted to in the last two-and-a-half years was the same man who ultimately killed the leader of the cartel to set her free of her fear of another attack on her family, she still didn't think she could have more than a little light flirtation with Josh because of his dangerous career as a Navy SEAL.

When Josh's son showed up at the wedding reception for his sister and Cait's brother, they faced even more barriers to the relationship they both secretly craved. Could they come together to form an unconventional family? Or would all that joshin' around just lead to trouble and more heartbreak for Cait?

DISCLAIMER: This surprise Navy SEAL dad, friend's sister, instalove, alpha male, scared woman, cowboy romance book contains references to past gun violence, profanity, and graphic sex scenes, as well as multiple scenes with the hero rescuing kidnapping and rape victims alongside his fellow SEALs and family members. It is intended for adult readers (18+) who are not easily offended.

Also in Heart's Destiny

Dion's Dream Girl

Heart's Destiny Book 7

Dion Davis didn't remember the most important events of his life after helping to rescue one of his fellow wrestlers from a deranged stalker. Truth be told, he didn't remember meeting Allissa, much less helping to rescue her. But he did remember his good friend, Dean Hunter, who just so happened to be Allissa's fiancé, so he couldn't say no when they asked him to be in their wedding.

From what he'd been told after waking up in the hospital with amnesia, he spent a lot of time in Dean's hometown over the last year. So, he hoped his trip to Heart's Destiny for their wedding would bring back a few of the memories he lost. Especially if those memories revealed the identity of the woman he dreamed about nightly since he woke up in the hospital after the altercation with Allissa's stalker. *Jewel. My Dream Girl. My Jewel. She has to be real. Making love to her in all those different hotel rooms has to be my memories trying to come back to me, not just dreams, like the, uh,…guy in the white lab coat thinks they are.*

After almost a year of sneaking around to see Dion without letting on to her matchmaking mother that she'd met *The One*, Julie Burleson was almost ready to announce to the world that they were in love, and possibly starting a family. Then, two days before she was scheduled to see her doctor to verify her suspicion that she was pregnant, Dion was injured while helping to rescue one of their friends from a stalker. After frantically trying to call him in between bouts of nausea at hearing the news, Julie finally got through, only to be told not to call him again because he was blocking her number.

Devastated by the sudden rejection of the man she thought was her soulmate, Julie struggled with her emotions as she tried to move on with her life. Hurt and angry, she didn't want anything to do with him when he returned to Heart's Destiny for Dean and Allissa's wedding, no matter how much her heart and her libido contradicted the thoughts in her head.

But Dion was nothing if not determined. Determined to heal, not only his injuries, but also his relationship with his Jewel. Could this former professional wrestler win the biggest battle of his life — the emotional wrestling match for Jewel's heart? He might not ever be able to step into the squared circle as a pro grappler again, but he planned to spend the rest of his life fighting for his family. Dion knew the most important victory of his life would be winning the heart of his dream girl.

DISCLAIMER: This small-town, second chance, multicultural, surprise pregnancy, amnesia romance contains scenes depicting the physical and mental symptoms experienced after a traumatic brain injury, profanity, and graphic sex scenes. It is intended for adult readers (18+) who are not easily offended.

Next in the GWA

Mistakenly Married?

Galactic Wrestling Association Book 3

What happens when the Galactic Wrestling Association celebrates a little too hard after a successful show in Las Vegas? Too much drinking that leads to a night several of the wrestlers have completely forgotten. Especially when one of their meddling, matchmaking mommas instigates an excursion to take pictures at a local wedding chapel.

The photographic evidence on social media of thirteen inebriated performers stopping at a wedding chapel caused quite an uproar, making them wonder if some of their angles needed to be rebooked. But with all of them waking up in their own rooms at the hotel the next morning, with only vague memories of what had happened, they all believed they'd stayed outside the chapel, as the pictures indicated.

Until a few weeks later, when Rylie Long checked her mail while the GWA was in her hometown for a show, and learned that what happens in Vegas doesn't always stay there. Finding out she'd actually married Liam Connery that night in Vegas was a shock. She hadn't wanted to let on to anyone in the company that she had a little crush on the older wrestler. Now she had to figure out if she wanted to take advantage of their situation to see if her little crush could turn into more.

Leah Mae Wright

When Rylie took her marriage license to the arena to inform her boss, several of her coworkers suddenly scrambled to check their mail to find out their marital statuses as well. Apparently, Rylie and Liam weren't the only GWA wrestlers who got mistakenly married.

Teagan Shields and Josh Parker also got married while drunk that night, as did Aiken Pearson and Brent Crockett. Now they all had to figure out how they wanted to handle the legalities of their situation, while the GWA bookers reworked their angles to try to control the celebrity gossip. Would any of them stay married? Or would they get divorced? Or have their marriages annulled? And how did the fact that none of them had their legal residences listed in the same state as their spouses, or the state where they got married, factor into their options?

Taking the time to meet with attorneys and determine the requirements for each of their situations was difficult with them traveling with the GWA. Especially when their coworkers conspired to keep them together by pairing the three couples in the bridal party for Dean and Allissa's wedding, so they couldn't go home for their Thanksgiving break.

DISCLAIMER: This multicultural, age gap, forced proximity, friends-to-lovers, drunk Vegas marriage, sports romance contains profanity, graphic sex scenes, and references to infertility issues. It is intended for adult readers (18+) who are not easily offended.

Books by Leah Mae Wright

Heart's Destiny Series

A Brief History of the Founding Families of the Fictional Small Town of Heart's Destiny, Texas — Free on Book Funnel
Courting Kay — Anthony Burleson and Kay Lee
Courting Kay Bonus Scenes
Wrestling with Randi — James Hunter and Randi Lee
Bobby's Bride — Bobby Burleson and Brooklyn Barns
Adoring Amy — Justin Burleson and Amy Lawton
Charlotte's Wedding — Ian Campbell and Charlotte Burleson
Joshin' Around — Josh Burleson and Cait Campbell
Dion's Dream Girl — Dion Davis and Julie Burleson
Destined for Deanna — JJ Burleson and Deanna Wolfe (Coming Soon)
Lights, Camera, Ashlyn — Darius Davis, Ashlyn Lawton, and Cade Starling (Coming Soon)

Galactic Wrestling Association Series

About The Author

Leah Mae Wright lives in Florida with her husband and fur babies. Her head has been filled with romantic stories for as long as she can remember, beginning with fairy tales as a small child growing up in Oklahoma and carrying through to countless ideas of her own throughout the years, as she has moved around to live in several different states. Now that her children are grown and life has slowed down, she's letting them out of her head, so they can join the libraries of her fellow fans of romance. Leah's literary world is a wonderful place that has no Covid, no real politicians, and a few unreal towns. Her favorite part about her characters living in her literary world is knowing that they are guaranteed a happily ever after.

You can keep up to date with Leah's future book plans at:
www.leahmaewright.com – Be sure to sign up for the Newsletter to receive emails about new releases, sales, and freebies.
www.facebook.com/LeahWrightAuthor
www.amazon.com/author/leah_wright
https://www.instagram.com/leahmaewrightauthor/

Leah Mae Wright
https://www.pinterest.com/LeahMaeWrightAuthor/

Provide your feedback to the author at:
Leah's Literary World Facebook Group
LeahWrightAuthor@gmail.com
Leah@LeahMaeWright.com

You can also review Leah's books on Amazon, Goodreads, Bookbub,
and Fictiondb.

www.ingramcontent.com/pod-product-compliance
Lightning Source LLC
Chambersburg PA
CBHW010556310726
48969CB00009B/2447